Fudge Shop My
Holly Jolly Fudge Folly

By Christine DeSmet

Writers Exchange E-Publishing
http://www.writers-exchange.com

Fudge Shop Mystery Series: Holly Jolly Fudge Folly
Copyright 2023 Christine DeSmet
Writers Exchange E-Publishing
PO Box 372
ATHERTON QLD 4883

Cover Art by: Aprampar

Published by Writers Exchange E-Publishing
http://www.writers-exchange.com

Dedication

For grandfathers everywhere, most especially mine--Delmar and Henry

Acknowledgements

My books come about because of many kind professionals, special places, friends, and family members.

First, thank you to Bob, who is always happy to hear about Ava and Grandpa in Fishers' Harbor. Thanks for dragging me away from the computer now and then.

Next, thank you to my writer-author support friends. You are special to me because you listen to my pitches and problems--and joys--about story and character, and you understand how hard it is to write a novel. You cheer, thank goodness! There are too many names to list here; you know who you are. Thank you!

Thank you to the team at Writers Exchange E-Publishing, including the artists and editor Sandy Cummins. Your engagement with your authors is wonderful. You're always working to make things better for readers and I appreciate that.

Where would an author be without a beta reader with a red pen willing to circle things that need attention? Thank you, Mary Clay, for your time and expertise in looking over my manuscript.

Thank you to the generous support I have from bookstores, especially Mystery to Me in Madison, Wis., and Kismet Books in Verona, Wis. You owners and managers rock this world. And they take book orders from anywhere!

Good stories depend on good locations for mystery and fun. Door County, Wisconsin, is known as the Cape Cod of the Midwest. Its many beautiful locations, businesses, residents, and visitors create the basis for the fun adventures in the Fudge Shop Mystery Series. Thank you to the Belgian Heritage Center in Namur and many who have all the answers to my questions about Belgian food and customs.

Finally, thank you to you--wonderful readers and fans on Facebook and everywhere who enjoy quirky Grandpa and Ava and all the characters that are so real to me. Your engagement and support for this series mean so much. A virtual hug or shake of the hand from me, dear readers!

Chapter 1

Snow-covered Secrets

Who was leaving the small gifts at my doors during the night? The items--trinkets and jewelry crafted from natural materials--had been surprising me every morning since the unofficial start of the Christmas season. That's the day after Thanksgiving here in Door County, Wisconsin. Shoppers had streamed in and out of Oosterlings' Live Bait, Bobbers, Belgian Fudge and Beer. By now, a week later on Thursday, December first, I'd totaled six mystery gifts.

Was somebody trying to spook me? Signal something? Say something?

I couldn't afford to lose sleep over this mystery. Ava Oosterling--me!--had fudge and candies to make and then sell and ship.

My apartment is on the first floor and at the back of the Blue Heron Inn. I was glad I didn't have guests. I kept popping awake to run to my window overlooking the back yard and concrete steps to the kitchen. At night I'd also taken to creeping through the dark first floor, stubbing a toe now and then on a table leg, in order to peek out the front windows.

Even mounting cameras outside didn't work. Mysteriously, blank spots appeared in the recordings. The computer screen showed only each gift box nestled at either door.

My first guess was Grandpa. A scoundrel of the highest form, Grandpa Gil Oosterling loved to play tricks. Especially on his only grandchild. Even if she were in her early thirties and no longer five or ten years old.

Grandpa guffawed at my guess. "Ava, the Christmas elves are doing it. Though maybe the Belgian skritek are helping. Those gnomes are tricksters when in a jolly holly mood. It's the snow, you know. Mischief comes when there's early snow. Elves and skritek gnomes like to help people smile once the days grow darker and snow falls."

Deep snow--a good foot--had blanketed Fishers' Harbor last night. Our village nestled north of the canal zone in our peninsular county that jutted into Lake Michigan like a thumb of a mitten. We were officially "Up North".

After fitful sleep, I woke at four-thirty to a pleasant hush and frosty, filigreed patterns in the window glass. I flicked on a light and flung up the window sash. Icy air whooshed about my nightshirt, causing a shiver. A story below, and sheltered by the roof overhang, a green box with a red ribbon sat snug against the kitchen door and only inches from a snowdrift. Snowflakes eddied about, sparkling in the glow from the bedroom's light.

I shut the window and got dressed.

The gifts weren't from guests. The 1800s blue-and-cream, two-story inn perched atop the steep hill at the south end of Main Street was empty at the moment. My next guests would arrive for the upcoming weekend Saint Nicholas festival. More would then arrive for my best friend Pauline's wedding the following Saturday. The inn would be the setting for her Victorian-style wedding luncheon following the traditional Belgian matrimonial parade in a carriage drawn by horses down Main Street. If we could find horses. That was another problem. Wineries and other businesses offered sleigh rides and hayrides in winter, so there wasn't a dobbin for rent anywhere it seemed.

I'd adorned the six upstairs rooms in the past week with extra Christmas trimmings and Victorian-inspired bedspreads for guests staying for the wedding. Pauline loved satin and tassels. Another friend of ours created holiday soaps made from the goats' milk on her farm. Each bar of soap was folded within a souvenir handkerchief embroidered in one corner with tiny green holly and red berries and "P and J" for Pauline and John. Pauline's mother had made the kerchiefs.

Three guest rooms overlooked the harbor to the north and the neighborhood below a cliff where my grandparents lived on Duck Marsh Street. The other rooms upstairs faced the woodland south of the inn. My first-floor apartment window framed the quiet southwest view of the inn's backyard with its gazebo and woodland beyond.

Grandpa said that gnomes and elves lived in the trunks of the maples and oaks. Of course, when the snow got this deep, the elves were known to come inside houses and gnomes favored sheds and barns to look after animals.

Shaking my head, I donned a red sweatshirt over the white blouse worn while making fudge. With holly-themed slippers of red and green on my feet, I set off through the parlor with its blue loveseats, the foyer with its grand chandelier, the dining room with its long table and Belgian lace cloth, and then I finally headed through the swinging door into the kitchen.

After bringing the most recent gift box inside, I sat at the kitchen's white marble island. A small batch of an unnamed holiday fruitcake-inspired fudge waited for cutting and taste-testing. I ripped off the gift box's red ribbon, my heart fluttering.

I had eliminated several suspects: grandparents, my best friends Pauline and Laura, my soap-making friend Fontana, and my fiancé.

Elves? Grandpa had said days ago at our shop, "Leave milk and sugar out at night for those faery folk as a way to contact them."

"Why would I want to contact an elf or a gnome?"

"To appease them, to avoid tricks being played on you. It's that time of year when a mouse might actually be an elf, and what you think is a raccoon scurrying through the back yard is really just a gnome in a fur coat."

And so I had dutifully set out milk and fudge each night at the back door. For Grandpa's sake I did the same at the shop. The libations disappeared each time. Not a surprise, what with our wildlife in our rural county. We had a total population of twenty-eight thousand people. That left plenty of room for fox, coyotes, rabbits, squirrels, owls--anything coveting milk and fudge.

To my shock, this morning's gift appeared to be a hand-pounded gold birch leaf.

It made me sit back. All of the gifts thus far had been trinkets of nature, braided straw bracelets, polished agates and such. This was precious metal. Expensive-looking. About the size of a quarter, it was affixed with a loop for stringing onto a necklace or an earring post. White-barked birch trees peppered our county, their leaves turning vibrant gold in autumn.

I took the gold leaf and box to the dining room where I set it on a shelf among the other items I'd received. Hoping some visitor might be guilted into confessing, I had moved my grandmother's collection of yellow rose-patterned antique porcelain dessert plates and Belgian chocolate sipping cups to the kitchen.

The inn creaked in the wind, protesting the cold leaking into its old wooden bones. Immigrants--lumberjacks and fishermen--from Scandinavian countries and Belgium had built the inn as well as the shop on the harbor in the mid-1800s.

Before I could head down the steep hill to my shop, I had to shovel myself out. Well after five in the morning now, it remained black outdoors save for the pool of light shed by the lamp above the back door. The fluffy snow flew like feathers off the shovel.

Soon, I tackled the front verandah and its steps.

A lone street lamp below my hill split apart Main Street's wintery darkness. The street appeared to have zigzagging, serpentine paths amid the snow, as if our snowplow driver had been nipping at a bottle of brandy. I thought I heard the plow grinding in the distance.

By the time I finished shoveling, it was after six o'clock--an hour after the time my grandfather usually made his way to Oosterlings' Live Bait, Bobbers, Belgian Fudge & Beer. Grandpa likes to say to every customer coming in, "Everything goes better with beer. Even fudge." Customers usually laughed.

Lately, Grandpa hadn't always been in the shop at his usual five o'clock, or "Smelt" on his handcrafted fish clock. When he came in later, he seemed obsessed about the newspaper. A pencil in his hand scratched notations he wouldn't let me see. If only his skriteks would tell me what he was up to, they would set my mind at ease. Grandpa and I loved sharing secrets, but not this time. That worried me.

As I set the snow shovel aside in the inn's front entry hall and removed my coat, my phone buzzed. The number belonged to my best friend, Pauline Mertens.

"Pauline, it's early. What's wrong?"

She was breathing hard. "Just finished shoveling. Nothing's wrong, Ava. In fact, this is a perfect day to work on your dress for my wedding."

The last thing I wanted to think about on a cold, blizzard-like winter's morning was that ridiculous dress. "Don't you go into virtual teaching mode today? Aren't snow days a thing of the past?"

Pauline taught kindergarten. She had ten students this year, a smaller group than usual. They were going to be in the wedding, too--all dressed like either Victorian Christmas angels or elves tossing flower petals on the church aisle.

Pauline said, "A communication tower is iced up and power lines are down somewhere, too, so no Internet for a lot of kids today. And did you forget I'm officially not teaching as of today?"

"I forgot."

"Brecht and Bethany are great subs."

"Neither has a teaching license. I still don't understand how they got hired." I wanted to keep her talking so she'd forget about the dress.

Her subs were Brecht Rousseau--our friend Laura's husband who'd left the Army with PTSD, and Bethany Bjorklund, the on-and-off girlfriend of my shop helper, Cody Fjelstad.

"Ava, listen to the newscasts. Our state is short of teachers. The school district got an okay for each. Anyway, instead of waiting until Sunday to work on your maid-of-honor dress I thought I could come over to your grandmother's house this morning. A snowy morning is perfect to work on a dress."

"How are you going to get over here? This snow is deep and Main Street is a mess."

Pauline lived with her mother several blocks away in our village of a few hundred residents. Backstreets were the last plowed, sometimes taking until the next day--after the crew cleared Highways 42 and 57--the only arteries in and out of the county.

Pauline said, "I've got tall boots and snow pants like everybody else. I'll trek over. I'm dying to see how this lace I bought looks on your dress."

Ugh. I had lost this battle because I loved my friend. Lace was winning. Pauline's wedding was a week from this coming Saturday. For her Victorian-themed wedding I was supposed to wear an elaborate cherry-red velveteen gown with puffy sleeves and a low-cut bodice and a skirt the size of which would hide a bear.

"Pauline, I'm really in a hurry to make--"

"Fudge. Yeah, yeah. You sound cranky. I bet you still haven't come up with your new Christmastime fairy tale fudge flavor or its name, have you? You're behind on everything as usual."

She knew me too well. A new recipe sat on my kitchen counter without a name. My mind was on the mysterious boxes.

Pauline said, "I bought the extra lace yesterday down in Sturgeon Bay for the trim on your bonnet, too. I'm dying to show you."

"What bonnet? I agreed to the dress, but not a bonnet." Chills overwhelmed me as I stepped again outside the front door.

"Women in Victorian times wore bonnets and hats. It'll have white lace trim that will match the white lace on your muffler and reticule. With your dark auburn hair, you'll be stunning."

"I assume by a muffler you're not talking about a car."

"Certainly not."

"And I'm not about to carry a reticule and be ridiculed."

Pauline had shown me endless pictures of Victorian gear for women, including the reticule--a dainty drawstring purse. I disliked purses. The muffler was a thick scarf for my neck. I did like mufflers--noisy ones on fast cars.

She laughed. "The lace on the bonnet and muffler will match the lace trim atop your button-up slippers."

"Can't I just wear my work shoes under that skirt? Or boots? Who's going to know?"

"Ava Mathilde Oosterling! You are going to lose your status as my best friend if you continue in this vein. What time is good for me to meet you at your grandparent's house?"

Grandma considered Pauline a grandchild, too. Grandma had leaped at the chance to be the seamstress for this Victorian Christmastime wedding.

"I'll have to call Grandma and get back to you."

Pauline hissed. She did that a lot but I always ignored it, which made her hiss more. "Why don't I help at the shop so we can head over to your grandmother's house by mid-morning?"

I agreed. She'd be at the shop by seven. If I hurried, that would give me a few minutes yet to talk to Grandpa and get more fudge made and packaged for mailing.

At the bottom of my hill I turned left as usual onto Duck Marsh Street where my grandparents and my fiancé Dillon Rivers lived. After only a couple of steps in the deep snow I halted to stare at a big mess.

Chapter 2

Snowplow Mischief

The plow had left a zigzag trail down the middle of Duck Marsh Street. Thigh-high snow piles blocked driveways.

The driver had to be drunk. Or were they ill? Concern swept over me. The plow drivers in our village--Al Kvalheim or Mercy Fogg-- were in their sixties or so, prime age for a heart attack statistics showed. I monitored such things because Grandpa was in his seventies and always teasing death with his misadventures.

In the chilly stillness came the echoes of shovels scraping somewhere across the village.

The plow driver had snapped off my grandparents' mailbox. Again. Grandpa growled about fixing it because usually his arch-enemy--Mercy-- drove the plow when that happened.

Across the street from my grandparents' cottage sat the cabin belonging to my fiancé and the curly brown hunting dog that shared us-- an American Water Spaniel--called Lucky Harbor.

I still wasn't used to "fiancé". Or "beau" or "intended" and "engaged" and other terms people used for Dillon Rivers. The trouble was, he and I had been married once before long-ago but never engaged. We'd eloped. Then divorced. A long story. Now we were engaged. After a trip to Belgium last fall. Another long story.

Light glowed from inside the cabin but I had no time to slow down. Pauline would be on her way.

Snow coming off tree limbs spattered my face as I forged ahead. The choppy water of the nearby harbor slapped in the near distance against the harbor's concrete wall on the other side of the fudge shop. The harbor and bay wouldn't freeze over until sometime in January. Our shop would get busy again selling ice-fishing equipment.

As I pushed through the deep snow, my head turned to worries. Pauline's long-missing and younger sister had not shown up yet in our attempts at finding her. Lucie was doing social work, we thought, in a foreign country. Lucie traveled at will, not always staying in touch. On purpose. She'd given up mostly on the Mertens family because of the miscreant, abusive, drunken father. He had abandoned them long ago but Pauline feared he might hear about the wedding and attend, causing chaos and heartache. We thought Lucie might be avoiding the whole event. I wasn't ashamed to hope the man was still in prison. What if he'd contacted Lucie? Was that why we hadn't heard from her?

The chill coming over me hurried me through the snow topping my boots.

Humid air caressed my cheeks as I burst through the shop's back door. I flipped on the lights. Savory perfumes of yesterday's cooking with chocolate and vanilla and peanut butter and cherries and sugar assailed me.

"Grandpa?"

No response. I didn't smell his coffee. Grandpa couldn't work without strong coffee laced with real bits of imported Belgian chocolate.

After hanging up my coat, stocking cap, and gloves in the hallway, I peeked in the storage room to the right and kitchen to the left. No grandfather.

In the front shop, the wood floor creaked under me.

The fish clock above the front door indicated almost seven o'clock-- Muskellunge or "Muskie" time, well past Grandpa's usual arrival time. A strip of pink showed in the sky to the east.

I turned on the switch that lit the bulbs on six Christmas trees Dillon and I had set up along the harbor docks at the posts. The evergreen branches sagged under dollops of snow, but pleasant orbs of red, blue, green, and yellow glowed.

The parking lot had one trail plowed through it but would need a lot more work.

The weekend's snow sculptors would welcome the snow. The Main Street businesses--the backs of which were across the harbor from me-- had put out several trash barrels for collecting snow. The snow artists would pack down the snow within the barrels, then dump the barrels upside down along Main Street and start carving as early as tomorrow.

The sweet aroma in the shop from the candies in the glass cases created the proverbial sugarplums dancing in my head. Making Christmas Elf Fudge today was in order.

Elves. I was still thinking about the gold they'd brought to my back door. Grandpa said that elves or nisse could spin gold from wheat.

We had a significant Scandinavian population in Door County. Stories about the Christmas nisse abounded in the storybooks I sold on my shelves. Sharing a storybook while eating fudge or chocolate treats was a perfect way for an adult and child to spend Saint Nicholas Day (coming up Tuesday!) or Christmas. I encouraged the Christmas Eve tradition of gifting every child in the family with a book and letting them open it so it could be read before bedtime. Of course, a gift of fudge with that book made sugarplums dance in a child's head even more.

I called my grandfather's number but got no answer, so I called Grandma.

"Ava, he left the house by five o'clock. Didn't even wait for my first batch of snickerdoodles to come out of the oven. He was supposed to take those to your shop."

"The mailbox is broken again, but I didn't see him around. You don't think he's hunting down the driver?"

"I hope not. Maybe he took the dog out for Dillon. He might have lost his phone again and that's why you're not getting an answer."

Losing phones often happened to Grandpa and me. It seemed hereditary. I'd seen the lights on at Dillon's cabin, so I felt better knowing Grandpa was likely fine.

Within a short time I had made a fresh batch of peanut butter fudge and set it in a big pan on my register counter to cool. I also whipped up Belgian cookies called speculoos. The kitchen air swirled with cozy warmth and mouth-watering scents of cinnamon and almonds.

As I removed the last tray of speculoos from the oven the cowbell on the front door clanked several times. Yelling and choice words erupted. To mimic the familiar Christmas poem, there arose such a clatter that I ran out into the shop to see what was the matter.

There stood Grandpa in his coat, snow pants, and stocking cap--with the sheriff next to him with a hand clutching Grandpa's coat sleeve. The sheriff's face was red, as if extremely cold or this situation had caused him to steam.

"Grandpa? Jordy? What's going on?"

With twinkling eyes, Grandpa hesitated, never a good sign.

Sheriff Jordy Tollefson, a man only a couple of years older than my thirty-two years, let go of Grandpa with his fist but his steely gaze remained. "This man related to you stole the village's snowplow."

"Nothin' doin'." Grandpa snorted, snapping off the stocking cap. His thick, shaggy silver hair stuck up in all directions by about three inches with static electricity. "I was merely helping out."

Now I understood why I'd seen the crazy plowing patterns in the streets. "Why would you steal the snowplow?"

"Because darn Mercy Fogg doesn't know how to plow out my street. I need to teach her a thing or two."

I took Grandpa's stocking cap and coat. "Old grudges aren't attractive on you, Grandpa."

When Mercy was village president she had tried to gain support for razing our shop and the homes on Duck Marsh Street in order to put up expensive condos. They would reap more tax money for the village than 1800s sheds and cabins turned into cottages like the ones in which Grandpa and Grandma and Dillon lived.

I laid Grandpa's things across his register counter a few feet away from mine and on his fishing-tackle side of the shop.

Sheriff Tollefson pulled out a ticket folder from a back pocket.

"Hold on, Jordy," I said. "You can't write a ticket for, uh, what? Is the snowplow in one piece?"

Jordy grimaced. "It's in one piece but Main Street is not. He drove erratically, leaving piles of snow across sidewalks and little access for cars to get through."

"But your squad must have made it. I see it parked outside." I raised my eyebrows.

Jordy's face grew redder, about to blow. "My vehicle barely navigated the winding trail. And there's a car buried on Main Street because of Gilsen."

Grandpa Gil darted to his side of the shop where he kept his beloved coffeemaker on a wall shelf. "You'll feel better, Sheriff, after some of my coffee." He grabbed the glass carafe and took off for the kitchen in back.

"Bribes won't work!" Jordy yelled. "And if you go out the back door, Gil, the next door you'll go through will be a jail cell door."

Jordy wrote the ticket as grumbling Grandpa returned with the water for the coffeemaker.

While Grandpa created his special chocolate-laced strong coffee I pleaded with Jordy. "No need for a ticket. Everything is fine, you said. He didn't crash the plow."

Grandpa turned to us. "It's not fine, Ava honey. That Mercy only takes one swipe down our street instead of two. She expects us to shovel out mounds of snow. What's more, she always plows over my mailbox."

I offered, "In reality, Mercy does her best with that narrow street and Dillon has dug out your walkway and mailbox every snowfall with his big snow blower."

"That's because you and Dillon think I'm not capable of anything. You think I'm old!"

Jordy blinked at the outburst. So did I.

I went over to Grandpa, laying a hand on an arm. "You're not old, but there's nothing wrong with accepting help at any age."

"Accepting help?! That sounds like I'm nearly dead." He banged shut the coffeemaker lid. "Everybody thinks I'm good for nothing but trouble. And old."

My heart felt like a puppy that had been admonished for chewing up a slipper. The sheriff grimaced, waiting.

Grandpa grabbed his ceramic cup and I thought he might throw it at the sheriff.

I relieved him of the cup. "Who is 'everybody' who says you're old?"

"Al and all the guys at Erik's bar. My card group has become like a 'babysit the old guys' club, too."

"It sounds like you lost money at cards recently."

"Hmmpf." He began fussing with straightening a shelf filled with fishing bobbers, reels, and fishing line.

"Al and everybody in that group are around your age."

Grandpa turned to me with hiked fuzzy eyebrows. "Yes, but they're always bragging about this hobby or that. I don't want to be relegated to building birdhouses."

The sheriff stood in the middle of the shop waiting with arms crossed. After a sheepish grimace, I went back to Grandpa.

The coffee had dripped through its filter, so I filled Grandpa's cup and took it to him. "Now you're dissing Dillon. His birdhouses are a work of art. His birdhouses that look like Santa's North Pole chalet are selling out constantly at the Christmas shop in Ephraim." It was a shoreline village just five minutes north of us. "Dillon could use your help."

Grandpa slurped his coffee while I offered a cup to the sheriff.

Jordy put down his ticket pad on my register counter next to the pan of cooling peanut butter fudge.

The front door banged open then. In a rush of cold air and swirls of snow Mercy stomped into the middle of the shop. She was a stout woman encased in a blaze-orange coverall and matching stocking cap. "Where the heck is my snowplow?"

Grandpa plopped his cup on his register counter, grabbed his coat and then ran for the back hallway. The back door slammed.

The sheriff sighed but didn't go after Grandpa. He was staring at Mercy, as if waiting to hear more.

Mercy pulled off her stocking cap, leaving behind a matted mop of blond curls. "What the heck was he thinking stealing my snowplow?!"

I shoved a cup of hot coffee at her along with a piece of fudge, hoping to keep her from chasing after Grandpa. "How could he do that, Mercy? Weren't you inside the snowplow cab?"

She stuffed the peanut butter fudge in her mouth, then slurped coffee. "I've been plowing since three a.m. and with a lot of coffee. I got around this neighborhood a bit later and had to get out of the cab to find a toilet. We women can't just find a tree, you know. I was on Duck Marsh Street and saw Dillon's lights on. So I hopped out, knocked on the door. He let me use his toilet. I came back outside after doing my business and the snowplow was gone!"

Sheriff Tollefson shifted his weight. "The snowplow appears to be okay. It's parked on the other end of Main Street, past Erik's bar and in the lot by the beach. Here are the keys." He took the key out of his front chest pocket and handed it to Mercy.

I said, "Okay. All solved. Everything is just fine."

The sheriff said, "Not quite."

He walked back to my counter, put down his coffee next to the fudge, ripped the ticket off the notebook, and then handed it to me. "Somebody has to dig out the car your grandfather buried with snow on the other end of town, across from Erik's. I'll want to take a look later to see if there's any damage that Gil has to pay for."

Mercy said, "I'll dig out the car for a price."

After my pointed sigh at her, I said to Jordy, "I'll grab Dillon and snow shovels and we'll rectify it. I'll call you once we've uncovered it. You can inspect it."

Jordy handed me the ticket, which made me gasp. I said, "Certainly my grandpa shouldn't have to pay this much?"

Mercy interjected, "Snowplows are expensive to replace. He stole it, and who knows what damage he may have done to the engine or the blade or the tires. And if he changed my radio station, he's in for more trouble. Gilsen can't get off with just a slap on the wrist this time."

She walked over to my register counter, put down her cup, scooped with her fingers into the middle of the peanut butter fudge pan, and then headed for the door with a smile. "Have a nice day. Thanks, Sheriff."

As soon as the cowbell clanged behind her, I waved the ticket at Jordy. "This is an insane amount."

"Gilsen can choose to contest it before a judge." Jordy enjoyed his coffee, looking around, as if stalling for some reason.

"What is it, Jordy?"

His next breath expanded his uniformed chest. "I'd give anything to sit here and drink coffee and munch on whatever you have in that kitchen. I smell cinnamon. Speculoos?"

I nodded. "Fresh-baked."

"Yum. You make the best Belgian speculoos. Sweet with light spice."

A crooked smile bloomed, punctuated by a twinkle in his eyes. We'd known each other since our childhood, and it was well-known that Jordy wouldn't mind spending more time with me, but mostly he was harmless. I stepped behind my register counter. "Would you like to take fudge back to your office? No charge, of course." I picked up a white bag, ready to fill it.

"Sounds like a bribe." He winked at me.

I turned to filling the bag. "It'll be a variety pack of fudge for your whole crew."

"Thanks." As I bustled about, he added, "You and Dillon set a date yet?"

"None of your business."

"I thought with Pauline's wedding coming up that you'd get in the mood."

"None of your business." I handed him the sack with a smile.

A glint lurked in his dark eyes. "Thanks. A perfect way to start my day." He grabbed up the ticket for Grandpa. "I'll catch up with your grandpa."

"I wish you wouldn't."

He winked. "Bye, Ava."

Around eight o'clock Dillon picked me up in the harbor parking lot in his construction pickup truck with its blade on the front. He had cleared the area. Pleasant smoky perfume from village fireplace chimneys softened the razor-sharp effect of the icy air.

After Dillon turned left onto Main Street we spotted Pauline trudging up the middle amid the serpentine path left behind by Grandpa's snowplow escapade. She carried a backpack--likely filled with the dreaded lace for my maid-of-honor torture. With snowflakes glistening on her cheeks and eyelashes, Pauline climbed into the back.

I updated her about Grandpa while Dillon wove north on Main Street.

She said, "Was Gil nipping at hot toddies when he did this mischief?"

A "hot toddy" was a hot winter drink laced with whiskey, bourbon or brandy.

I said, "You know how he is in winter before ice fishing starts."

Dillon offered, "Bored as a bobcat with no rabbits to chase. He just keeps tracking and sniffing for trouble."

We laughed as we headed toward the edge of the downtown.

Our downtown was short--only five blocks. Shops opened at ten o'clock. Giant, plastic snowflakes and red-striped candy canes hung from canopies sagging with snow. At the inn's end of the street, the bookstore's windows sported holiday picture books and the mercantile's windows displayed toys, holiday hats and gloves, and ornaments. At the other end of the street was the Troubled Trout, a historic stucco-and-pine log building, popular bar and restaurant.

There were no cars on the street save the one Grandpa had buried with snow up over the windows on the driver's side. The dark gray sedan sat across from the Troubled Trout.

Dillon had shovels, so I cleared the back bumper while he took the driver's side. Pauline used a windshield scraper to work on the back window.

Dillon startled us by calling out, "Ava! Pauline! Come here!"

We slogged through the snow. Dillon knocked on the foggy driver's window. "Hey! Hey, Mister!"

A man sat in the car, head tipped with chin resting on his chest.

"Is he asleep?" I asked, stomach queasy already.

Pauline mewled. "I don't think so."

Dillon said, "Neither do I."

He pulled the door latch. The door popped opened.

We gasped.

A black knife handle stuck out from the man's belly. Copious amounts of blood had spilled onto tan slacks.

A second look at the man's face startled me. "I know him. And this won't be good for Grandpa."

Chapter 3

Christmastime Crime

A shiver rippled through me but not from the chilled air.

Snow wafted into the interior of the gray sedan. Fluffy flakes settled on the dead man's shoulders and blood pool darkening his lap. White and red. Christmas colors.

I backed away.

Pauline muttered amid audible chattering teeth, "Who is he? This is horrible."

With visions of Grandpa getting into bigger trouble than just the snowplow mishap, I replied, "Usher Westergaard, the tax assessor the village hired a few weeks ago. Grandpa is going to be in so much trouble."

Usher had slumped in the driver's seat, no seatbelt on. He wore a black stocking cap and cherry red sweater, the latter darker around the knife. The victim's coat lay in the passenger seat.

Pauline backed away. "Ava, don't you dare get involved."

"Why would I get involved?"

"Just now you mentioned Grandpa. Why? Dillon, don't you let her get involved."

Dillon stood on the other side of the open car door, phone in hand. "I've called 911."

Dillon stepped away, perusing the messy street.

I scrutinized the scene, too. Surely we'd erased the murderer's footprints in the snow with our activity to unbury the sedan. Of course Grandpa's errant plowing had probably done the murderer a favor, too.

I joined Pauline in the middle of the snowy street.

Her dark eyes had opened wide. "I've never met this guy. He never assessed our house."

"Only a matter of time. He was making the rounds. Taxes were going up for everybody."

"Mom won't like that. She pinches every penny. You said something a moment ago about this not being good for your grandfather." Pauline gasped for breath. "What about my wedding a week from Saturday? Don't you dare get involved and miss my wedding!"

"Your wedding isn't for ten days."

Warning steam spewed out of my BFF's nostrils. She stamped a boot, crunching snow. "You and your grandfather cannot be mixed up in anything. Do you read me loud and clear?" She swiped at her teary eyes with her mittens. "Gil is supposed to be Saint Nicholas in Monday's parade and then next Saturday he has a date to walk me down the aisle with your father! Now he's going to be in jail!"

I wrapped an arm around her shoulders. "Slow down, friend. All I meant by my comment about Grandpa being in trouble was that he'd probably end up answering questions for the sheriff."

"Because he stole a plow and killed a man!"

"Pauline, stop." My hug came with the fierce girlfriend love Pauline needed.

Dillon closed the car door, then grabbed his snow shovel and backed away. "Is there any possibility of your grandfather being involved with this?"

Pauline groaned.

Snow peppered my face in a sudden gust. "Grandpa had a big argument with Usher in the fudge shop a week ago about our assessment."

Dark concern lined Dillon's forehead.

I explained, "Our old building changed a lot since Grandpa fixed it up for my return from California." That was almost two years ago. "He had the new shower and restroom installed last winter, and added a new cooler in the fishing equipment sales area for beer and worms. Everything new means higher taxes."

Pauline said, "But you still haven't updated the kitchen plumbing. Remember last July when I lost my engagement ring in that old rusted trap in the drain under the sink? Dillon had to come with a sledge hammer and wrench to take that apart. The assessment can't be that high for just a shower and new toilet."

Pauline could be bitter about the silliest things, such as a lost engagement ring.

I said, "The assessment will go up because we haven't been assessed for ten years. Our village is behind how buyers value property in Door County."

"So paradise is punished because people from the coasts and Chicago buy condos or want homes here and drive up prices?"

"I guess." I wanted to comment on her penchant for popping consonants for her kindergarten kids, but held back. We were all in a rotten mood. "Grandpa said higher taxes might wipe out the gains over the past year in the sales of fishing equipment. He can't sell enough rods and reels and minnows in our tiny shop to cover the taxes. The fudge shop area might have to carry him, but I'm not sure fudge sales even at Christmas can cover any big increase in taxes."

"Your shop isn't in a bad way, is it? You're not going to have to sell or move, are you?"

"No. At least, not yet."

"What?! Yet? Like you might move?" Pauline blinked several times.

"I don't know." The taxation and valuation business worried me because Grandpa seemed concerned. "Selling would be a defeat for Grandpa. An embarrassment. He has his pride." A vision of him scouring the newspaper lately came to me. Was he studying real estate sales? That had to be it.

Pauline stamped her booted feet against the cold as she hugged herself. "It's going to be embarrassing for Fishers' Harbor if the village's Saint Nicholas goes to jail, not to mention that one of the most precious people in my life won't be able to walk me down the aisle."

"Don't be silly. Grandpa didn't kill anybody."

"Are you sure? His temper is famous." She sighed. "Sorry. Of course Grandpa Gil is innocent. It's just that your grandpa has always been close to me, too. He's like my grandpa, too."

"I know." I touched Pauline's shoulder to reassure her.

Pauline's mother had only returned to Door County last spring after a long absence living out East for years. Pauline's family had split up and split our county long ago.

Her family's fissure had ripened Pauline into an uber-organized, responsible woman who wanted to leave her poverty and any hint of bad blood behind. A superb teacher, she excelled at making and following lists. Since meeting John she'd begun wearing nicer, more expensive clothes, though she'd always been addicted to big purses in bright colors. She carried a big red these days. A purse organizer would make the perfect Christmas gift for her.

Pauline pulled a tissue from a pocket, dabbed her eyes, then blew her nose. "I'm freezing my tush off out here."

"Go sit in Dillon's truck. I want to look around."

"Oh no you don't." Pauline pushed her long dark hair off her shoulders then pulled down her stocking cap until it reached her eyebrows. "You promised me on our vacation in Belgium that you'd change. You're engaged to Dillon now. Stop playing detective with the sheriff."

Snowflakes hit my eyelashes. I glanced toward Dillon, who stood several yards away seemingly surveying the snow.

I stuffed my ponytail inside my own stocking cap and pulled it down over my ears, which were feeling frostbitten. "I'm not 'playing'. I have to protect Grandpa and anybody else I care about, including you. I promised you and Dillon on our trip that I would spend more time doing things I loved to do with you and Dillon. I happen to love doing this."

"Do you know how you sound? It's as if you merely added sugar to a recipe and you think all is well because of that."

"I did add sugar to my life. Dillon is sweet. And so are you." I smiled, though the smile felt bent. "You walked into that one, Pauline."

She shrugged. "Okay, I did. But Belgium was supposed to be a watershed for you. You crossed the famous kissing bridge in Bruges and into a new life committed to Dillon and something different for yourself, different from being hooked on helping the sheriff."

The trip to Belgium had been a gift from my grandfather because he wanted to reward Dillon and me for changing and embracing change.

Dillon had proved himself a hard worker and a man who deeply cared about my welfare. Dillon had left his parents' real estate firm to become his own man, building things for others and me with a strong arm and hammer instead of a pen on contracts. He'd committed to staying in Fishers' Harbor when his parents moved to Texas.

Dillon had asked Grandpa--and not just my dad--for my hand in marriage. That hadn't happened twelve years ago when Dillon and I had eloped. College kids do stupid things sometimes, right? We divorced within a month. I took a job in California where I sold fudge and candies to TV crews in order to pay the rent. When Grandma suffered a broken leg, I came home to help her. Grandpa set me up in his fishing tackle shop to sell fudge.

I dove into proving my worthiness to my grandparents. Grandpa saw how hard I'd worked and so he paid for the trip to Belgium. The trip changed me. It made me slow down, smell the flowers--and Belgium has famous flower gardens to do just that. The leisure unsettled me, to be honest. How does a woman slow down after being driven for a couple of decades?

Dillon had gotten down on bended knee on the sunny day in October in Belgium on the kissing bridge. Applause echoed off the stone, historic buildings that lined Bruges's famous canal. A different light glinted in Dillon's eyes. Sparkles--like sugar crystals--were sweet promises of good things to come. What would those good things be? I felt lost. Pauline had a plan for her life. I had nothing.

Grandpa's escapades often led me astray--something I had to change. I couldn't keep dragging Dillon and Pauline into my troubles.

Distant purring of more snow blowers filtered through the air now. More store owners would soon be navigating Main Street.

We stood straight across from the Troubled Trout bar and restaurant. I struck off in the building's direction. The tax assessor must have come from there. I needed quick reassurance that Grandpa wasn't involved in the death.

Pauline scrambled next to me. "Stop, Ava! Let's get in Dillon's truck and wait for the sheriff."

As I shuffled through snow nearer the Troubled Trout, it was easy to see somebody had come out the front door or at least stood there for a time in the snow. Other tracks led across the slim terrace between the sidewalk and street, though flakes had obscured the footprints.

Pauline grabbed my left arm. "Those tracks mean nothing. Erik probably came out to look at the snow or collect his newspaper. Leave this to the sheriff."

Her voice became babble in my head. A trail caught my attention. Somebody had shuffled in the sidewalk snow heading in the direction of the other end of Main Street, toward my inn to the south. I set off following alongside the tracks and not in them in a hopeless attempt to preserve any evidence like a bootprint. The breezes and occasion swirl of snow were already obliterating patches of the trail.

Pauline trudged next to me on the street side. "What are we doing?"

"This could be the killer's escape route."

"Ava, we might be tracking one of the owners of a business or somebody who lives upstairs in the apartments. You know those people and they aren't killers. They might have come downstairs to buy coffee from Erik."

"Maybe."

"Jane lives upstairs. With her neighbors, trusted people. Let's go back to the truck and get the lace and head to your grandmother's house. My nose feels frozen and you're giving me a headache."

My nose was cold, too, but I was compelled to follow the trail.

The snowy prints stopped at the Klubertanz Market, an old-fashioned mercantile store that carried groceries and anything vacationers needed in a pinch. The front stoop had been shoveled. The accessible door was in the rear, in the same parking lot I shared on the harbor.

Pauline said, "We know the Klubertanz family. Good people, not killers."

Verona Klubertanz had been a pupil in Pauline's kindergarten class last year. Verona's father Travis ran the mercantile. His mother was Verona's grandmother, Dotty Klubertanz, a woman in her sixties who frequented my candy shop with other local retired women to kindly check on me. They also brought sewn items to sell on consignment.

"Yeah," I mused as I stared at the dark windows. It didn't appear to be open. "Dotty's handmade aprons with their glitter and my fairy tale logos sell out instantly. Definitely not a murderous family."

"Great. You agree. Now let's get back to the truck."

I pulled on the heavy front door's brass handle but it was locked.

Pauline said, "I hear a siren."

We headed back toward to the crime scene.

The siren of a local ambulance grew louder as the sheriff's vehicle barreled past us after visiting Grandpa on Duck Marsh Street. I would have loved to have been a mouse--or an elf--and witnessed the conversation between Grandpa and Sheriff Tollefson.

Pauline and I upped our pace as we left the sidewalk and slogged through the street.

The sheriff hopped from his vehicle with its whirling blue and red lights to inspect the car. He started taking photos.

I journeyed past the scene a few yards to check the sidewalk on the passenger side of the car. None of us had disturbed the sidewalk while shoveling out the car. Shadowy imprints in the snow lay in both directions. Were two people responsible for killing Usher Westergaard? Had the people split up and run?

I mentioned the possibilities to Pauline. She huffed, "Or are these merely tracks from people walking dogs? Or jogging through the snow? People pass by my mom's house in all kinds of weather and time of day."

Pauline climbed into Dillon's truck, slamming the door.

To my right, which was to the south and toward the intersection by the inn five blocks away, the tracks continued on this sidewalk. To the left or north, where the ambulance had come from, probably from the fire station in Sister Bay--the next community beyond Ephraim--the tracks continued until my eyesight lost the distinction in the gray light and shadows under trees.

If Grandpa had driven the snowplow to the beach parking lot beyond the edge of downtown, had he seen the killer? What had he told the sheriff?

I hiked back to the sheriff. The Emergency Medical Technicians (EMTs) were lifting the dead man from the car. Blood had dripped onto the snow in the street, leaving a red splotch.

Chapter 4

Thanks, Sheriff

Dillon was talking with Sheriff Jordy Tollefson near the car.

The ambulance motored on its way to Sturgeon Bay's hospital morgue.

Sunlight strained to push back the winter morning. Snow and sparkling ice limned rooftops and tree branches of the tall oaks on the hillsides.

The sheriff wore his aviators now. A stocking cap with the Door County Justice Department logo covered his head and ears. A gloved hand held a small notebook. "Dillon tells me you know the victim."

"He came into the shop a week ago to do our assessment."

"A week ago exactly? Thursday?"

I nodded.

Jordy withdrew a pen from a pocket inside his jacket. He scribbled a note, then tucked away pen and pad. "Anybody else in the shop at the time?"

My stomach flipped. "Me and Grandpa, of course. Usher came in right after lunch at one o'clock. We had an appointment."

"Anybody else there?"

"A handful of customers came and went."

"What was the exchange like with you and your grandfather?"

Sweat popped onto the back of my neck. "There was a discussion."

Jordy lifted off his glasses, his look piercing me. "Was the discussion amiable?"

"Sheriff, I don't like what you're implying."

Dillon put an arm around my shoulders. "Listen, Sheriff, it's cold out here and we're in shock. I've already told you how we found the assessor in the car. That's all we know."

Ordinarily I was the kind of woman who didn't like a man speaking for her, but this time I wanted to kiss Dillon for stepping in.

Jordy donned his aviator sunglasses against the glare of morning sun glinting off white snow. "Thanks, Dillon, for going over everything with me." He indicated the car. "I'm sorry you both had to witness something like this."

I said, "Thanks, Sheriff."

As he walked to his vehicle parked in the street, I remembered something. "Sheriff, wait."

He turned around. "Yeah?"

"There are fresh footprints up and down the sidewalks and outside the Troubled Trout."

"I'm on it. Thanks. What would I do without you?"

Sarcasm dripped around his words, a resounding brush-off of me.

Dillon steered me away from the crime scene with an arm locked around my shoulders. We walked toward his truck. He said, "Let's get you back to my cabin and I'll light a fire and make hot cocoa. My plowing jobs can wait a half hour."

"I can't. Pauline's waiting for me in your truck with a backpack filled with scary lace."

He chuckled as we walked, our heavy lugged winter shoes squeaking in the snow. "I'm looking forward to seeing you in something other than jeans and boots."

"You are not."

"Really, I am." His grin warmed the air around us.

"You're trying to change the subject and keep me from thinking about what's happened here on Main Street. I hope Erik's okay. What if the killer got inside the Troubled Trout and is holding Erik hostage?"

Dillon laughed. "Didn't you just say there were tracks all over the sidewalks? That person is long gone. Leave it to the sheriff. Let's think good thoughts. I've never seen you dressed in frilly stuff, except last summer for Fontana Coppens' wedding. You were beautiful. You will be lovely in lace."

"Give me a sweatshirt and blue jeans any day of the week."

"I can't lose. I also like the way you fill out a pair of jeans."

I gave him a playful punch in his stomach area. He opened the door of the truck and I slid into the seat.

Dillon turned the truck around just as Mercy Fogg was bringing the plow into position to finish Main Street cleanup. The sheriff flagged her down to make her wait while he went over the street looking for clues in the snow. My mind went to the blood in the snow, how the man's blood would be pushed into oblivion, as if the man never existed. It chilled me.

Dillon carefully maneuvered in the street according to the sheriff's wishes, then Jordy went into the Troubled Trout. What would the sheriff find for evidence inside there? Why hadn't I tried the door myself and peeked inside? Was there a possibility Erik or his cook had done it?

Dillon dropped us off at my grandparents' place, calling to us through his truck window, "Don't worry about the mailbox or the walk. I'll get to those later."

"Thanks!" I said.

Dillon dropped the blade on the front of his truck. He proceeded to push snow off Duck Marsh Street. In between carpentry work, he hired out to clear driveways, which, in a Wisconsin winter brought in a good amount of cash. Door County received an average of forty-eight inches of snow every year, very little compared to other areas of the state and country.

I tried to shake off what had happened as Pauline and I navigated the snowy walk to Grandma's door. Christmas was special here, with a special history. On the other side of Door County--what we called the lake side-- a special memorial freighter loaded with Christmas trees would take off soon and navigate down to Chicago in honor of those who lost their lives in a storm many decades ago. Door County and other nearby counties used to be the origin of not only Christmas trees for Chicago, but also wood shingles and lumber that helped build and rebuild the city after the 1871 fire. The timber for those shingles was felled and processed by Scandinavian, Icelandic, and Belgian immigrants, including my own ancestors.

Pauline and I stamped our feet outside my grandparents' front porch, then proceeded through the glassed-in porch and onward into the living room where we shucked off our boots. We set them on a rug next to the front door.

"Hello!" I called. "Grandma, Pauline and I are here!"

The place smelled of pancakes and bacon and maple syrup, and cooked apples with cinnamon, and coffee and of course, snickerdoodles and speculoos.

A low fire crackled in their living-room fireplace. Pauline ditched the backpack on the sofa. We veered into the kitchen.

Grandma greeted us with a smile. "What have you girls been up to this morning?"

Of course she knew everything. The sheriff had been here earlier, after all. She was alone pulling a one-inch high waffle out of the Belgian waffle maker. The golden, steaming waffle joined a couple of others on the table along with a stack of pancakes.

Grandma Sophie's white-as-snow hair floated in waves about her face and shoulders from a side part. She wore black jeans and a red cowl-necked sweater that set off the rosiness in her cheeks. Her eyes seemed shiny as Lake Michigan agates.

Pauline and I gave her a hug.

She said, "You just missed your grandpa. He's at the shop." She stepped to the table to pour coffee in front of two place settings. "I can't bear to tell you how much the ticket is for stealing a snowplow."

Since I'd already seen it, I said, "You can use it to get a mighty big Christmas gift out of Grandpa this year. He owes you an apology."

She chuckled. "I told your grandfather he has to behave. He's going to play Saint Nicholas in Monday's parade, for heaven's sake. Your grandfather says we can't afford to pay that ticket. He'll contest it, the ol' trouble-making buzzard."

Pauline and I smiled at that. She sat.

I sank my butt into the chair opposite Pauline. Cooling snickerdoodles covered half the table. Ravenous, I snatched one. "We'll scrounge up the money somehow."

"You, my dear granddaughter, will not bail out your grandfather this time."

Pauline said, "Keep repeating that. Ava doesn't hear things until they're said forty times."

With a shrug and chewing on the cookie, I focused on the hot coffee mug that warmed my hands. I hoped we could skip the other trouble--the murder we'd happened upon. Instinct, though--and respect--told me Grandma needed to know about the tax assessor because of Grandpa's arguing with the man a week ago.

I glanced across at Pauline, hoping for courage. She hid behind her coffee mug.

I slid a fat waffle onto my plate. While dousing it with locally made, fragrant maple syrup, I said, "Can I take waffles with me? I have a couple of guests who might pop in early and I can freeze these and warm them up in the microwave."

"Of course, Ava." With a mug of coffee in hand, Grandma settled in a chair at the table between Pauline and myself. Her facial expression clouded. "The sheriff wanted to conduct a breath test on your grandpa, but Gil refused, of course. Your grandfather doesn't drink hardly at all and certainly not in the morning."

She sipped coffee, then reached over to pat Pauline's nearest hand. "Honey, don't worry. Gil and Peter will both be walking you down the aisle as planned."

Distress flickered across Pauline's face, wrinkling her brow. Mine wrinkled, too. Grandpa had argued with the dead man last week. Most of the town probably knew about the disagreement. Grandpa would have crowed about it at his weekend card game with the guys and with every person he met.

I put down my fork. "Grandma, there's something else that happened this morning you need to know about before somebody else tells you."

After I related what had transpired within the last hour, Grandma rose off her chair with mug in hand. She walked to the counter where she set down the mug with a big THUNK, then faced us. "Well."

Grandma grabbed a dish towel, working it about her hands. "Gil was out with the plow at approximately the same time somebody murdered Usher. Is that the size of things?"

I nodded.

Pauline fingered her mug.

Grandma took a deep breath. "We aren't going to borrow trouble. The sheriff might solve this within the hour and it won't involve any of us."

She took a step away from the counter, hung the towel over the stove door handle, then turned to pour more coffee in her mug. She came back to the table, but remained standing. "The best thing we can do is get on with the task at hand--finishing that lovely maid-of-honor dress."

Grandma fluffed her beautiful white cloud of hair, then regally left the room.

Pauline and I exchanged a look.

Pauline said, "I love your grandmother."

"Me, too." I took my phone out of the pocket of my jeans.

"Your grandmother is right. Stay out of this."

"Can't I call my grandfather?"

"Why? To remind him that he plowed snow over the top of a car, burying a dead man? Stay out of it. Too many times you've sacrificed the people around you in your preposterous passion for perpetrators."

A smile felt good. "I knew it! You were teaching your kindergarten students about the 'P' letter this week."

"Yes. And next week is Q, for 'quiet' and 'quit'--things you need to be and do. You're always trying to show Jordy you're as smart as he is. Why? What is it about him you can't shake?"

She mimicked Grandma by fluffing her long, dark hair, then marched from the kitchen.

I rose from my chair, trying to muster the élan shown by Grandma and Pauline.

Outside the kitchen sink window snow flurries eddied about as the breeze blew them from branches. I thought about Usher sitting in his car, impaled, watching the snow fall on his windshield as he closed his eyes for the last time. Death amid beauty. For what reason? Pauline was wrong about me being in competition with the sheriff. I hated the unfairness of murder. I hated bad things in life. I lived with memories of how Pauline's drunken father treated her when she was a girl--the slaps, the thrown bottles. Righting wrongs felt good. A murder always hurt somebody else besides the victim. I just couldn't walk away.

I headed to the living room where Pauline slumped on the sofa along with tears sliding down her cheeks. She held her phone.

After sliding in next to her, I peered at the phone. "What's going on?"

"My sister is still missing." Pauline showed me her mother's texted message. "We haven't been able to locate Lucie. And my mother's giving up. She's giving up!"

For two months, Pauline had been trying to get in touch with her sister who was in South America. At least we thought she was there because months ago a short email from her said she was thinking of helping people in Peru. The text message from Pauline's mom said: My heart can't look anymore.

After I took the phone and showed Grandma, she sat down on the other side of Pauline and patted Pauline's knee. "Dearest, your mother is not giving up. None of us are. We're going to find your sister. Tell me what you've done so far to try and connect with her."

From her red purse, Pauline withdrew a notebook, flipping it open to show us a list of calls, emails, texts, and more that she'd undertaken. The list went on for pages.

Chapter 5

Wedding Blues

G randma rose from the sofa. She grabbed pillows and tossed them aside. "Girls, the best way to handle any problem is to get busy. We have a maid-of-honor dress to finish."

I stacked pillows on the floor while Grandma and Pauline laid out packages of lace on the sofa.

Grandma said, "Pauline, your sister is just off the grid, as the saying goes. Isn't she doing some project with indigenous people?"

Pauline nodded.

"Then we mustn't worry so much. Maybe she's in some deep valley in Peru and there's no cell service."

Pauline's sister Lucie Mertens had graduated college in the East not long ago with a master's degree in social work and sociology. She'd traveled the world for her theses projects. Lucie hadn't been back in Fishers' Harbor since her high school graduation.

I said, "We have to assume she got your messages about the wedding."

"Agreed," Grandma said. "Pauline, the best thing we can do for your sister is get everything ready for the wedding. Agreed?"

Pauline swabbed her tears with a tissue. "You're right. It's just... What if...something happened...?"

I threw my arms around Pauline. "Stop that thought. We've had a horrible morning and you're borrowing trouble because of what we saw out on the street. Grandma's right. Let's think about Christmas right now and your holiday wedding."

Grandma Sophie's living room was already a cozy nest for Christmas. Red and green decorations festooned doorways and framed pictures. A chocolate Advent calendar hung on one wall, a few days opened and the sweet treats eaten. She had no stockings hanging from the mantle, nor a decorated Christmas tree because in Belgian holiday tradition, those activities were saved for Christmas Eve when we decorated together with my parents and Pauline and anybody else who happened by. Sometimes the cottage burst with thirty or forty people leaning against counters and walls and sharing eggnog and fruitcake, smoked salmon, pickled herring, oyster stew, and of course red Door County cherries atop pies and tarts. A whole table tucked in some corner would be devoted to cheese. Wisconsin produced over six hundred types of cheeses--the most in the country. Every holiday season I made chocolate cheese, which tasted like fudge.

Grandma clasped my face between her work-roughened hands. "This is about you now. We have a beautiful, magical ruby-red dress to finish that you are going to wear to this girl's wedding."

Pauline crowed, "Ava Mathilde Oosterling in a dress!"

"Pauline--!"

Pauline popped open her backpack now sitting on the sofa. More white lace bounced out. All of this had been purchased in the Bruges lace shops.

Grandma handled the lace with reverence, her face angelic, and a smile in appreciation of the artistry of handmade lace. When she asked me to try on the heavy velveteen Victorian dress, I did not complain. One does not refuse an angel's command.

So there I stood in the living room, shoulders to toes draped in heavy, confining fabric. I said, "I feel like a mouse caught in a tall bucket."

Grandma laughed. "A Christmas mouse! I believe I read you a book about such a mouse when you were little. Your grandfather loves the little elves."

"I wish he'd quit expecting me to put milk and cookies out for them. Actually, it's been fudge. I can't believe I make fudge to feed mice or whatever else is out there."

Grandma pinned lace here and there on the dress. "Won't you be surprised when elves show up to help you in a time of trouble. The elves talk to the Belgian skritek, too. I'd make friends if I were you."

Skritek were gnomes of course--bigger beings than elves but still short beings.

"But who is leaving the gifts, Grandma?"

She shrugged, taking a pin out of her mouth. "You're sure it's not Dillon?"

"He says it's not and I believe him."

Pauline asked Grandma, "Do you still have the storybook about the skritek and elves? Maybe there's some clue to this in that children's book."

Grandma said, "I gave the book to Ava over a year ago along with a bunch of books when she and her grandfather bought the inn."

I said, "I should go up to the inn now and look around the bookshelves." I started taking off the dress.

Both Grandma and Pauline grabbed me, one on each arm.

Grandma said, "Nothing doing. You can take lessons from this dressmaking for your own wedding--whenever that is." She winked.

"We'll set a date when we're ready, Grandma. Dillon and I promised to take our time getting used to an engagement. It's all new to us."

Pauline said, "You might try getting used to wearing an engagement ring. Where is it this time?"

"At the shop. I can't wear it while I'm making fudge."

"An excuse. You simply don't know how to be engaged."

"Pauline, being 'engaged' is not a talent one acquires or a job. There are no rules for how I'm supposed to act."

"That's an understatement. You've never followed any rule since we were in first grade."

Grandma laughed so hard her loose white hair flew about in the air around her head.

Then she perused me in the dress. Lace hung off me like drooping snowmelt. "Pauline, we need more lace. Hand me that other package, please."

Lace got sized, cut, pinned, unpinned while I stood in the middle of the living room. The fire crackled along with our laughter. At least this activity had taken Pauline's mind off her missing sister and I let go of thinking about Grandpa's plow covering up a dead man in a car.

Finally, Grandma said, "Pauline, did you bring the shoes?"

Pauline hurried to her backpack and withdrew red, lace-up shoes that made my feet hurt just looking at them.

Grandma clapped. "So cute! Put them on, Ava. Now I can finish hemming."

I groaned. "Nobody's going to see under this skirt. Can't I just wear my work shoes?"

"Steel-toed work boots?! Hah!" Grandma left the room mumbling about getting the ironing board and iron.

I gathered up folds of the dress's skirt to find my phone.

Pauline gave me the evil eye. "No more detective work. This isn't the 'Murder' Christmas time of year. It's 'Merry' Christmas."

Grandma trundled back, setting up the ironing board and saying something about adjusting the mutton sleeves and lace.

Grandma clucked on about our autumn trip and buying the lace. She regaled us with a recap about being invited inside the king's Royal Castle or residence because we were related a couple of generations back. The castle's official name was the Palace of Laeken, situated three miles north of Brussels' center. The palace and its royal greenhouses and gardens were usually closed to the public. Grandma swooned over the beauty of it all and how she had felt so at home.

And then...

Just like that she started crying in front of Pauline and me.

Grandma plopped down on the sofa.

After shoving the lace and dress and shoes aside on the floor, I sat next to Grandma. "What's wrong?"

Pauline settled on the other side of Grandma. "Sophie, how can we help?"

Grandma came up for air. "I'm so sorry. I thought I could ignore everything about this morning, the things going on with Gil. Ever since our trip to Belgium, he's been acting different."

I asked, "Like what? How? I mean, besides stealing the snowplow."

"It's as if he's bored. With me. Our life." She flashed us a soulful look. "Gilsen and I are dull, don't you think?"

"Not at all, Grandma!"

Pauline found a tissue and handed it to Grandma. "Sophie, you're a loving, kind, and talented and smart woman. You're certainly not dull. Ava's dress for my wedding is amazing, not to mention my wedding dress."

Grandma's fingers toyed with the tissue, shredding a corner. "Gil has been talking about...moving."

I almost popped off the sofa. "You can't move. Why would Grandpa want to move? Where?"

"I don't know. But he asked the other day where we'd move to if we moved!"

I hugged her. "Let's finish this dress." Volunteering about killed me. "You aren't moving, Grandma. I'll find out what's going on with Grandpa."

She nodded. "Thank you. Maybe all Gil needs is more cherry juice every day."

Pauline laughed. "Why?"

"Haven't you heard? All the professional football players drink cherry juice now all season because it reduces inflammation in the body and helps muscles recover from injuries. It might even help a little with sleeping better."

I offered, "So more cherry juice might help Grandpa feel more cheery?"

We laughed together and Pauline and I hugged Grandma in a "Grandma sandwich".

For two hours, I made sure nothing more was said about Grandpa, the stolen plow, the murder, or the idea of moving. We talked chocolate cheese and fudge recipes for the wedding day, and about mice turning into elves, and the elf costumes for the ring bearers.

After the dress session, at nearly the noon hour, I called the shop.

Grandpa said we'd had only a few customers--winter tourists coming in for cocoa and fudge after trying out snowshoes in nearby parks.

I hiked up Duck Marsh Street with a sack of Grandma's fluffy vanilla Belgian waffles to put in the inn's freezer. Pauline stayed behind with Grandma, wanting pointers about sewing with lace. The idea gave me shivers. As I walked along, sunlight beaming between maple and oak branches and onto snow made me squint.

Main Street had been cleared partially by now. Huge piles of snow sat here and there on the slim terraces and street, taking up parking spaces. Some snow would surely end up used in the snow-sculpting contest. Mercy and Al would load excess snow on trucks and haul it to the countryside before the weekend festivities.

A couple of blocks away from me I spotted Al talking to Greta Truelson, our newspaper delivery woman. I wondered if the two of them had started the day at their usual four o'clock or if the snowfall had delayed them, too. Had they seen anything unusual or anybody else? Had they witnessed the murder? I was dying to ask but didn't have the time at the moment.

I turned to the right and ascended the hill.

As I stepped onto the inn's verandah, Lucky Harbor galloped up to snuffle into my gloved hands in search of treats. He sniffed at the waffle bag.

"Oh no you don't," I said.

Lucky Harbor wore a red plastic tube about three inches long on his collar. Dillon and I used the dog and tube for sending hand-written messages to each other. It was a romantic thing Dillon started last summer. The exercise and training also kept Lucky Harbor out of trouble. As with Grandpa or myself, if the active dog didn't have enough to do he'd find mischief to get into.

At the front door I put the waffle bag down next to the door. I unhooked the red tube and opened it. The note read: "Please come to my cabin when free. Something important to discuss. I'll be plowing until around five o'clock. Dinner at my place? Love you. Dillon."

Something important to discuss? I smiled at the mystery.

I said to our shared dog, "Lucky Harbor, you're staying with me for the moment. Dillon's busy today."

He wagged his tail and then barked.

I tossed the dog some gold fish crackers, his special treat. Once I opened the door, he flew in, shaking snow on the entryway hall's massive blue rug. The melting droplets twinkled under the chandelier lights above us.

While the dog rolled about on the rug in happiness, I checked phone messages in the dining room reception nook. I returned a call to guests to assure them we were plowed out, but waiting until tomorrow afternoon to travel would be best.

After storing the waffles in the kitchen freezer, my thoughts went back to the mystery of the gifts and the childhood storybook that seemed missing.

My dining room and parlor shelves contained a couple of books about the nisse or "nissen"--the gnome popular in Scandinavian holiday lore, but that wasn't the same as the Christmas elf--disguised as a mouse. I suspected some guests had taken books home with them, and I didn't mind that. Books were meant to be shared. I had no book about the Belgian skritek, which wouldn't do in a county famous for its Belgian heritage. My guests loved to hear about the rich history here. I would have to contact the local Belgian Heritage Center to see if they had any such books. The Center was in the lower half of our county; a trip there on a good day was about forty-five minutes but the rural roads to the Heritage Center--which was near my parents' farm--would be slippery for a couple of days.

I made a mental note to ask Jane if she could order the book that I now felt desperate to acquire. How could I have lost my Christmas mouse book?

My guests delighted in the tales from picture books.

The nisse or nissen hid in barns and watched over the animals. Elves--or holiday mice--on the other hand, lived in fields, woodlands, and even homes, but were scared of cats for an obvious reason.

Other traditions included leaving speculoo cookies in the shoes left out by children on Saint Nicholas Eve for the Belgian skriteks.

Other traditions from my childhood included my father leaving treats in the barn where he said animals talked to each other and with the skritek on Christmas Eve. As a child, on Christmas morning I raced to the warm, fragrant straw-filled barn at the early morning milking time with my father to see if skritek or elves had been about. Sure enough, the cinnamon-rich speculoos were gone, the plate clean. Dad always pointed out, "Look how content the cows are, thanks to the nisse, the skritek, and elves."

Some believed nisse, Belgian skritek, and other gnomes could be tricksters, more so than elves. If they didn't like you, or wanted to teach you a lesson for any reason, they could cause havoc. I didn't think, though, that they were capable of sticking a knife in anybody. Or, were they?

Chapter 6

Guilty Face

Grandpa had the shop under control that afternoon so I stayed at the inn experimenting with fudge. Or, to put it another way: I didn't want to deal with his troubles. I mean, seriously? Stealing a plow? Plowing in a dead man? And grumbling to Grandma about moving?

Everything shook me. Add on Pauline's missing sister and I felt untethered. I built small holiday trees out of mint fudge. By slicing triangles, the shape came about easily. I'd also made Red Riding Hood Fairytale Fudge at the inn. Guests would like the red holiday color and the rich velvet-cake flavor.

I hiked down the hill around three o'clock that Thursday. The sun glowed pink from the southwest. Trees and buildings cast elongated, gray mimics of themselves across the sidewalks and street.

I took my time meandering toward the shop. Dotty Klubertanz had called earlier and said she'd be stopping by with baby quilts to sell. She offered to stick around to handle the cash register if Grandpa took off--

or got arrested. By now the whole village and probably most of Door County knew about the morning.

Pauline had texted me about meeting John to talk about filming the wedding parade, something I was glad to avoid by going to the shop.

Her fiancé John Schultz produced a public television series about Wisconsin's small towns and cultural happenings. To my dismay, he planned an entire episode around their wedding. That included the Belgian wedding tradition of a parade with the entire community participating to wish the couple well. Dillon and I were required to be in the parade.

When we were in Belgium we witnessed a wedding parade. Grandma said she remembered being a little girl witnessing a wedding in Namur, Wisconsin--named for Namur, Belgium. They had tossed dandelion blossoms as the newlyweds' horse-drawn carriage went by.

As soon as we returned from our trip, Pauline announced on social media she'd be honored to have all of Fishers' Harbor in attendance at the wedding, its reception at the school gymnasium, and the parade down Main Street. I suggested kids might throw snowballs at us. Pauline didn't find that funny.

Dillon and I--being best man and maid-of-honor--were to ride behind in a carriage as well. I preferred the inside of Dillon's heavy-duty construction pickup truck with its blazing heater. Luckily, John was having trouble finding horses and a carriage. A local riding stable and a winery that gave sleigh rides was booked all the way through Christmas.

Main Street was relatively calm at the moment in the late afternoon.

My heart wanted this murder solved by Monday--for the Saint Nicholas parade. Grandpa was scheduled to play Saint Nick, or Santa Claus. His costume always mixed the two.

As I walked, I sized up the distance of the five blocks from Erik's bar to the Klubertanz Market. The tracks I'd seen early this morning on the sidewalk between the bar and market still intrigued me. Had Travis Klubertanz murdered the tax assessor? Was Travis that upset about his taxes? Was the mercantile in a bad way financially? Bad enough for Travis to have murdered and then run to his establishment, figuring those tracks would soon be obscured by townspeople?

I also thought about the tracks on the other side of the street going in both directions past the sedan. Who had been there? What had they seen? Where had the killer gone after doing the deed? Had a vehicle been waiting for the perpetrator on some side street? Or a little way north of the parking lot near the beach area? If so, had Mercy or Grandpa seen the vehicle while driving the snowplow? Were they too involved in watching the plow blade to notice?

I passed The Wise Owl bookstore. Its big window and glass door showed Jane Goodland busy with a customer. Jane lived upstairs and dated a former beau of mine, Sam Peterson. Had Jane heard or seen anything from her view of the street? I'd talk with her later.

Shoppers hustled along in the crisp, cold air, some with very young children out of school toddling alongside. Holiday window displays caused some to pause, but not for long in the crackling-cold December air. I gave a quick look in windows. I had no idea what to get Grandma Sophie and Grandpa Gil. They had everything they needed or wanted.

My feet pulled me back to the Klubertanz Market.

The buttery aroma from a popcorn machine popping off in a corner embraced me. The wood floor creaked. Old buildings talked back and I enjoyed the conversation.

A mother and children headed for an aisle filled with jams, cookies, and fruitcakes. I headed to the front counter, removing my stocking hat and gloves.

Travis Klubertanz was re-loading his sack carousel with paper sacks decorated in holiday red-and-white candy-cane stripes.

"Travis, happy holidays!"

"The same to you, Ava. How are things at Oosterlings'?" Travis was in his early forties, tall, muscular, with brown hair secured in a short ponytail today. He wore a blue shirt with the market's name on the pocket.

"We're doing well enough," I replied. "We could be better. I have high hopes for the snow sculpting festival."

"Is the new Fudge-of-the-Month Club doing well?"

"Sales are building. Cody always has good ideas." Cody Fjelstad was going on twenty and in college. I'd hired him almost two years ago when he was finishing high school.

"That young man loves working with you and Gil."

My face warmed with a blush, but I also felt the heat of not knowing how to broach the subject of the dead man in the car. "Thanks. I worry that Cody will graduate from college and move away for a real job. Then what will I do? Grandpa's good with engines and covered in oil half the time. There's no way I can put him to work making fudge."

Travis laughed. "That reminds me. I need to stock up on your fudge for this weekend. We always get a good crowd in here during holiday activities and I've also got relatives in town for Monday's parade. Your grandfather will make a good Saint Nick."

Sweat slicked my palms. After looking around to make sure customers weren't about to approach, I said in a low voice, "I suppose you heard about this morning."

He leaned my way. "Word gets around fast. The sheriff called me this morning asking a lot of questions." Then Travis peered straight at me. "Are you here because you heard I'm a suspect?"

"No." He was a suspect? "I saw tracks from Erik's bar to your shop, about the time of the murder perhaps."

Travis's mouth flinched. Guilt about something played on his face.

I continued. "I tried your front door this morning, but you hadn't opened yet. There weren't any lights on. Were you in here? Were those your tracks from the bar to the front door?"

His face paled. "The tracks weren't mine. I told the sheriff that. It could've been somebody coming from Erik's."

"Why Erik's place?"

He looked at me with surprise. "Sometimes Erik lets people in early for a free drink or leftover dessert from the night before while he's cleaning, but I didn't stop there this morning."

Travis finished putting sacks on the carousel hooks.

I didn't know about Erik's generosity in the mornings. I was a little perturbed I hadn't been told or invited to join them for a morning repast. "If you hadn't gone to Erik's or been outside, then who did you let into your market this morning? The tracks clearly stopped right at your door. They didn't move on up the street to the bookstore or Duck Marsh Street."

He looked about, then leaned toward me. "Greta."

"Our newspaper delivery woman? Greta Truelson?"

His face reddened. He turned to straighten coupons littering the cash register area.

"Travis, are you protecting Greta? Did she...you know?"

"No." He gasped. "She didn't kill anybody. And we're not having an affair. She was cold. She knocked on the door. I've let her in a lot on cold mornings to warm up before she continues delivering her papers. You'd think more people would get electronic delivery."

"My grandfather insists on paper. Greta didn't see anything this morning?"

"I knew nothing about the murder until the sheriff called. Greta only talked about her husband. I heard way too much about Logan. I encouraged her to patch up things before Christmas."

"But there were no lights on. You sat in the dark?"

"No." He grew redder. "I don't want everybody catching us together at four or five in the morning so I keep the lights off when I let her in. I take her downstairs to the basement. I keep a coffeepot down there so I'm fueled for when I do inventory or pack things to bring up for stocking shelves. We had coffee. That's all. She talked about Logan, nothing else."

"Did you tell the sheriff about this visit? Maybe Greta saw something significant and doesn't know it."

He shook his head. "It didn't seem relevant or prudent to mention Greta's visit. Greta and I certainly didn't kill that man."

While I felt embarrassed now about learning this personal business, one more item bothered me. "Travis, there weren't any other tracks near your door. Pauline and I were on the sidewalk later than five o'clock or so. Where did Greta go after talking to you?"

"She left by the back door. She goes to your shop next on her route then circles back to Duck Marsh Street and then up the hill to your inn and then back to finish Main Street on the other side."

The image of the tracks in the snow on the sidewalk by the dead man's car came to mind. Had Greta passed that way? Had she seen anything?

The woman customer and her children came to the counter then. I bid Travis goodbye.

An orange sunset frayed the horizon after four o'clock when I walked into my shop via the front door. The cowbell clanked. Grandpa, alone, was reading the newspaper from his perch behind his counter.

"Hi, Grandpa." I gave him a hug, then took off my parka, stocking hat, and gloves.

"Hey, there." He seemed absorbed in the newspaper.

"Cody come by?" I hung up my gear in the back hallway and came back.

"Nope."

"He's probably still on EMT duty because of the snowstorm. As long as he shows up tomorrow, that'll be good. It's the start of our big weekend in Fishers' Harbor."

"Oh yeah. Hill 17 over at Peninsula will be crowded."

Grandpa referred to Peninsula State Park's golf course. The steep, long hill on Hole Number 17 was considered the best for miles around for sledding, tubing, and tobogganing.

"Well, I hope nobody gets hurt on Hill 17 because I'll need Cody here all weekend."

I must have heaved a sigh because Grandpa asked, "What's wrong, dear granddaughter?"

"Just tired. I'm going to look at inventory, place a couple of orders for supplies and set out things for tomorrow morning. And then I'm due at Dillon's at five for an early dinner."

"What're you having?"

"I don't know. I just talked with Travis Klubertanz."

"Oh? Does he know who killed the assessor?"

"No. Did the sheriff contact you again?"

"Yup. I told him to get lost. Again."

I groaned as I inventoried the glass shelves. I only had a few pieces of a dozen flavors of fudge still there. I was glad I'd taken the time to make several small-batch pans in my industrial kitchen at the inn. "We had to have been there within a nanosecond of the murder. Did you notice anything while in the plow?"

"I was having fun just trying to control that darn machine so I wasn't really gawping at scenery." Grandpa shrugged as he turned the page of the newspaper.

I cast my eyes to my inventory sheet. "Did you know Erik offers free drinks during early mornings?"

Grandpa kept perusing the newspaper.

After a pointed sigh, I said, "Does Grandma know you go over there for morning handouts? And drinks?"

"It's not like I go there a lot."

"Which means Grandma doesn't know about this. Don't worry, I won't tell."

"I certainly wasn't mixed up in that murder this morning but I was at Erik's place last night enjoying a steak. I sleep like a baby after a good steak."

"I believe you, Gilpa. It's just all so strange, isn't it?"

What was he circling in the newspaper? He turned another page, the paper crackling.

After finishing fudge inventory, I put on my parka and stocking hat. "Thanks for locking up, Grandpa. You'll remember to put out the milk and cookies for the elves and gnomes?"

"Will do, honey. Those little imps still leaving you presents?" He didn't look up from the newspaper laid out across his register counter.

I hesitated telling him about the gold leaf. "Yeah, always trinkets about nature."

Was Grandpa circling real estate ads? Him leaving Fishers' Harbor panicked me. The shop without Grandpa would be like ice cream without chocolate syrup. We were a sweet fusion.

I said "Good night."

He waved without looking back. "Toodle-oo, honey."

Concerned, I headed out the back door. Deep snow in the yard made it a tough go to reach the shoveled sidewalk. I needed to freshen up before meeting Dillon at his cabin. I wondered about the secret he wanted to tell me. Mysteries swirled about worse than snowflakes blown by the ill-tempered winds coming off the bay.

Chapter 7

Christmas Child

After hiking to the inn to freshen up, I checked the Oosterlings' Internet sites for online orders. We had a few. I asked Dillon if we could postpone our dinner slightly so I could make a couple of small fudge batches. They'd need to set before being ready to sell tomorrow.

While I stirred sugar and cream with the melting Belgian chocolate the inn creaked in the wind. The old wood in the walls and framing around the antique window glass made me think about the harsh life of my ancestors in the 1800s. The musing took me to Pauline's family. Where was Lucie? Was she in some kind of trouble?

I called my attorney and friend Parker Balousek. He'd look into how to find a missing person.

I changed into a cream-colored Scandinavian cable-knit sweater I'd bought in a Sister Bay. I left my dark brown, shoulder-length hair loose. Ordinarily I didn't take the time to worry about my looks, but Dillon's invitation indicated he had something important to discuss.

At his cabin door, Dillon swept me up in his arms as Lucky Harbor raced outside. Dillon kissed me on the lips while closing the door with a gentle kick.

"You're cold," he said, helping me take off my coat. "Sit by the fire. I'll get you hot cocoa. Or, I could just keep kissing you and maybe that would warm you up?"

The gleam in his eyes tickled me, but worry crept in. "Charm will get you everything usually, but I know you have something important to talk about."

While hanging up my coat on a nearby hook, he said, "That's why I love you. I can't get a thing past you. How about you set the table while I dish up dinner?"

To my right was the tiny kitchen where the redolence of Italian sauce and bubbly cheeses charmed a smile from me. The fireplace to my left crackled, smelling of oak wood.

"Lasagna?" I asked.

My tall, dark-haired cowboy in his red-and-black checked flannel shirt was taking a big pan out of the oven. "One of your favorites."

"With three cheeses?"

"I went for a five-cheese lasagna." He laughed.

"You're making me nervous. What is it you want to discuss that warrants five cheeses?" I headed to the cupboard for the plates. "You found out something about Usher? They arrested the killer?"

"Nothing like that. I have something different to discuss, important. But right now, could you let the dog back in?"

Lucky Harbor galloped in with snowballs hanging off his red-brown fur. He shook, plastering me with snow before he leaped onto the blanket on the sofa. He circled a couple of times, then plopped down facing the fireplace. His heavy sigh signaled satisfaction.

Dillon chuckled. "I guess we won't huddle under that blanket by the fire after dinner."

We made pleasant clinks with plates and stemware in a choreographed assemblage of dinner at the small table with two chairs. Steam rose from the lasagna on our plates as well as from the broccoli that accented the Italian food.

Dillon poured sparkling water into wine glasses. Once he sat down, he held up his glass for a toast. "To us."

After we sipped, I dove into the lasagna. The cheeses and rich tomato sauce created a tsunami of pleasure.

Finally, I said, "This is delicious. And different from the last time you made it."

"Found this recipe in a cookbook in the house I'm restoring."

It was a six-bedroom house near Sister Bay on a plateau overlooking the village and marina. A Chicago couple bought the place last summer because the nearby village of Ephraim had an airstrip for small planes. The couple planned to commute from Chicago.

Dillon said, "I'm gutting the kitchen and expanding that with a giant island I swear will seat twelve people. Knocked down a wall today, which meant moving a full bookcase of cookbooks within the pantry. A cookbook fell open to this recipe."

Then his face grew serious. He put down his fork.

"What's wrong, Dillon?"

"I know this has been a hellish day, but I need a big favor."

"What do you need me to do? Grandpa could help, too?"

Dillon chuckled. "No, I definitely don't want Gil's help. One of us would likely get hurt." He moved broccoli around his plate. "There's been a squatter in the house."

"Don't tell me you're finding leftover beer cans or drug paraphernalia."

"No. Just a woman. Actually more than a woman. She has a baby with her." He dove into a forkful of lasagna again.

I couldn't eat. "How old is this baby?"

"Maybe weeks. It's tiny."

"Did you call the authorities?"

"That's just it. I was going to, but she begged me not to."

"Why?"

"She refused to say. She's scared for some reason." He twirled his fork in the food on his plate. "I was hoping you could find out. You have a nose for investigation."

"Dillon, you don't like me investigating anything. Social service agencies should be contacted. You can call Sam Peterson."

"I was hoping you could take in the woman and child. At least for now. An emergency kind of thing."

I sat back in the chair. "Take them in?"

Hope crept across his face and settled into a twinkle in his dark eyes. "Yeah. You know. A mother and child looking for a room at the inn. Sort of a Christmas thing I've heard."

"And you're going to tell me her name is Mary and her only transportation is a donkey."

Dillon chuckled, his shoulders relaxing a bit. "Her name is Ellany Jakobsson. I didn't ask the name of her child. I was too shocked at finding her in the house. She can't stay. I have to cut the electricity tomorrow and drain pipes to replace some and also add a bathroom, so there's not going to be plumbing or heat for a few days."

I smiled. "I'm proud of you, Dillon. Of course she can stay at the inn."

Dillon rose and then came around to lay a kiss on my lips. "This is why I love you. You have a generous heart."

Within minutes Dillon and I were on our way to fetch the woman and her baby.

Stars abounded, their light brighter than normal it seemed, as if guiding the way.

Chapter 8

Tiny Tree

Dillon had dropped us off at the inn at seven-thirty that Thursday night. Under the sparkling lights of the foyer chandelier, Ellany Jacobsson's loose hair glistened like a golden river all the way to her waist. She had a freckled face and fear feathering around her eyes. Slightly shorter than myself, she wore a simple turtleneck red sweater over skinny black jeans and brown knee-length leather boots.

She carried no purse or bag, nothing except a baby boy in her arms named Henry Olaf Jakobsson.

"What do you need for Henry? Are you breastfeeding?"

She nodded. "But I don't think I have much milk. He cries a lot when he's not sleeping."

Fortunately I had a couple of friends with babies. "We'll figure it out. You can take the biggest room upstairs. It's at the end of the hall to the right. It has the biggest bathroom and a view of both the bay and the back yard, during the day that is."

She appeared pained. "I'll need diapers."

"Oh. Of course. I have an emergency stash for little ones visiting. Just like you, I guess." I smiled.

Ellany smiled back.

"You're sure you don't want me to call the Red Cross or somebody to help you find a place? Our local church ladies can bring you things, too."

She backed off two steps. "Please don't do that. They'll just put me in a motel somewhere where I'm not welcome and I'll be moved around again."

"You've moved around a lot?"

Her answer was to look about. "This is a nice place. I like the color blue, too."

"Thanks. Would you like some fudge?" I sounded inane.

Ellany giggled. "I haven't eaten since yesterday. That house didn't have much. They emptied the cupboards."

"I know. Dillon's re-designing the kitchen."

"I couldn't sneak food anyway. I was hiding from him."

"Because you were afraid he'd get mad and call authorities and send you back somewhere." My voice had become a mere whisper.

She nodded. "Fudge sounds really good."

We went to the kitchen where we settled across from each other at the island. While holding tiny Henry Olaf. She ate two large pieces of Cinderella fudge and a bowl of cornflakes in which I put a scoop of ice cream on top for extra calcium and nourishment.

She said, "Ice cream in cornflakes! I like you."

"I also make ice-cream omelets for breakfast."

"I know what I'm eating tomorrow morning." Her smile charmed me.

"I also have waffles I can fix. Did you want me to call somebody for you?"

The hand with her spoon stopped mid-air. Her face darkened. She set down the spoon.

What had gone wrong in her life? I said, "You know what? Let's get a good night's sleep. We can talk in the morning. I think the mercantile down the street is open until eight. If I hurry I could probably find a couple of sweatshirts and underclothes for you."

"Thanks. That would be lovely of you."

At the Klubertanz Market I bought the necessities for mother and baby, and couldn't resist the baby sleeper outfit with the slogan that said: "Door County Makes This Baby Giggle."

Upstairs at the inn, Ellany had made a baby bed out of a drawer in the dresser. She'd put the drawer atop the desk that sat against the wall. A blanket folded a couple of times created a solid and safe mattress for the little one. Little Henry Olaf was fast asleep.

I told Ellany, "I'll get you extra hand towels for your shoulders. My friend Fontana has a baby girl that spits up a lot."

Ellany sat down onto the bed, glancing over at Henry asleep in the drawer. "Thank you."

"In the morning, we'll go shopping for anything else you might need."

"Thank you, Ava. I appreciate this."

After bidding good night I went downstairs to my own apartment, which was below Ellany's room. I kept thinking of that needy little one above me in the dresser drawer.

When I got Pauline on the phone, the first thing I said was, "I have a baby."

"What?! You're having a baby? This is wonderful news!"

"Pauline, no. I already have a baby."

"You're not making sense. Are you drinking?"

"No. Dillon's and I found a baby." None of this was coming out right.

"How do you 'find' a baby? Babies don't just appear. You do know how they are made, don't you? Elves do not bring babies at Christmastime."

"Please, Pauline, I'm serious." I told her the story of my evening. "What am I going to do? She doesn't want to talk. And she needs everything for the baby. She came with nothing."

"Fontana will know what to do. Her little Happy Valentine is the happiest child around. Fontana can bring a boatload of things Happy has already outgrown. Maybe she's got formula on hand, too. I'll call her and we'll be there in the morning first thing. And remember Laura's twins have outgrown everything and she might have extra baby clothes, too, and baby blankets. I'll text her. I've got a list started already."

"Pauline, you're a wonder."

"Girlfriend, it's what we women do. We help each other."

I went to bed confounded. The day had begun with a gold leaf at my back door and then finding a dead man, and then news that Grandpa wanted to move. The day ended with a baby arriving. Nothing else had better happen tomorrow. Enough was enough, as Grandma might say.

Instead of heading to the shop by five o'clock on Friday morning, I called Grandpa to let him know I'd be late. I didn't tell him about my visitors, knowing he'd tell everybody in town.

Outside my front door I found another box. After bringing it inside, I ripped off the wrapping. Pine scent burst at me when I lifted the box cover to find a soap carving of a tiny Christmas tree. It made me smile. I put the box and gift on the shelf in the dining room.

By five-thirty Ellany surprised me by settling in at the dining room table with a sleeping babe in arms. She mumbled about leaving because she assumed I'd have guests for the weekend.

"There's always room at the inn," I told her as I served Grandma's waffles with cherries and whipped vanilla cream on top. "Our sofa folds out in the parlor, and I have a couch in my own apartment, too."

I turned up the radio in the dining room so she'd hear the wicked weathercast. I wanted to convince Ellany to stay. Some back roads still needed plowing. The communication tower that had been damaged by ice and snow was still being repaired. Internet reception was spotty, the radio report said. Unfortunately, newscasts also related Usher Westergaard's murder.

Ellany stopped eating her waffle. "A murderer on the loose? Right here?"

"Whoever did it is likely long gone. And most murders are very personal, not random."

Wide-eyed and pale, she said, "I can't stay here."

The doorbell rang. I lurched. Nobody rang the bell at six o'clock in the morning. It was still dark outside.

At the front door, I flipped on the outside light, thinking maybe the newspaper carrier wanted my attention for some reason or that Pauline had come over early.

Neither woman stood there. Instead, a zealous journalist who had covered a murder I'd been associated with at this very inn in the past, stood there. I groaned. Jeremy Stone's office was in Madison, the state capital--a good three-and-a-half hour drive away.

I opened the door a crack. Icy air hit my forehead. "Jeremy, what are you doing here?"

He held onto the handle of a suitcase. A backpack hung off one shoulder. Frost lined the nostrils of his big hooked nose and eyebrows. "I'm looking for a comfortable place to stay while I cover the weekend events, including the Saint Nicholas festivities on Monday. I also heard about some Belgian wedding parade the following Saturday."

He pulled out his phone and scrolled through a screen. He showed me the news headline. "And I heard there's a murder. Again you're part of the story."

A shiver riddled me. "There's no room at the inn, Jeremy."

"How un-Christmas-like of you. Maybe this piece of information will persuade you. I was actually here in town on Wednesday, staying at a local motel on the edge of town. Then, early yesterday morning I jogged through the snow past that sedan on Main Street. Want to know who and what I saw and heard? I haven't even reported it to the sheriff. You'll be the first to know."

Darn. I had to let him in.

Chapter 9

Stone Cold

U nder the chandelier's sparkling crystals Jeremy Stone's nose sniffed the air. "Smells like waffles and cocoa."

I invited him to sit at the dining room table. Ellany had disappeared. It was well past six in the morning now. I hoped she hadn't left by the back door. The thought of her in this weather worried me. Then I heard a baby's cry upstairs. Relief relaxed my shoulders.

Jeremy pulled a waffle onto a plate and lavished it with maple syrup.

After pouring him cocoa in one of the expensive antique china cups I'd laid out for Ellany and other expected guests today, I sat across from him. "So? What did you hear and see on Main Street yesterday morning?"

He finished enjoying a bite of waffle. "Damn but these are good."

"My grandmother made them. Give her credit in the expose about me you're going to write this time."

"Hey, I thought we'd made peace after I was able to locate that Mertens woman involved in some heavy illegal stuff."

He'd found Pauline's evasive mother Coletta months ago by following a trail of stories about a gang of thieves and extortionists on the East Coast.

"Jeremy, I let you into the inn. Were you there yesterday morning on the street? What did you see?"

A gleam sparkled in his eyes. "Your journalism degree is showing."

"No, my sense of responsibility to this village and the people living here is alive and well. It's called being a good citizen and friend."

He nodded before sipping the cocoa. "You run a quaint inn. I win awards. It's how we motor, Ava. I earned a big prize for my last story about you folks here in Door County. That's why I'm back."

"To sensationalize our lives."

"No." He rubbed his nose. "You have to believe me. This trip is a follow-up feature because I care about two or more sides to any story. I came here to report on cultural traditions at the holiday time. I get mail asking about Fishers' Harbor. I aim to reveal a softer side about the people and community."

"And finding a murder tossed into the mix again is an unexpected bonus."

He swallowed a bite of waffle. "I have to do my job, make a living just like you. I report stories when and where I see them and I don't lie or leave out facts. Democracy is built on freedom of speech and sharing cultural information." He worked another piece of waffle onto his fork. "Don't you try to be the best you can be at making fudge and making people happy?"

"Of course."

"A good journalist doesn't ignore a good story."

He stuffed the waffle piece into his mouth, chewing with gusto.

I sank against my chair back. "You're only doing your job, but maybe focus more on the Saint Nicholas event on Monday and my grandpa as the kindly saint or Santa Claus, and the downtown decorations and the friendliness, and the snow sculpting contest, and of course the great fudge. Maybe only tuck the murder in as a tiny sidebar."

"A tiny sidebar? Give it maybe one inch of space?"

"A half inch."

"As many inches as it needs, Ava."

I knew he'd find out everything soon anyway, so I told him my role in what had occurred yesterday morning. Maybe he'd have insights.

Jeremy finished his waffle. "So you were there within moments of the murder."

"And you had jogged by? When?"

"I had jogged by that darn car twice. Or, at least I'd tried to jog. That snow was deep. I didn't expect it to be. I love this cold weather, though. It's invigorating."

"So the tracks in the snow on the sidewalk by the car were yours?"

"Yes, but in only one direction at first. I came from the south, breaking through the snow, but then after the car there were tracks heading north."

"So, you covered up a set of tracks--"

"No, that's not what I said."

"Sorry, go slower." I got up and grabbed a pocket-sized notebook and pen from the reception counter in the corner of the room.

After I sat down, Jeremy continued. "From my motel on the edge of town I jogged down the middle of the street at first because that had one lane plowed. By the time I came to the downtown, the snowplow had disappeared."

"That's when Mercy probably turned onto Duck Marsh Street."

He nodded. "The woman who drives school buses, road graders, limousines."

"That's her."

"It was quiet on Main Street but I took to the sidewalk thinking the plow would be coming back. I passed the car but didn't bother looking to see if anybody was in it."

I whipped my head up from making notes. "You must have been there moments before the man got in his car."

"Could be. I was huffing and puffing, thinking what a mistake I'd made trying to jog yesterday morning."

Different timing by Jeremy or any of us could have saved Usher.

"You jogged on?"

Jeremy nodded. "I followed the tracks to the north quite a ways, then I turned around, coming back toward your way. That's when the snowplow burst out of Duck Marsh Street all crazy-like. It seemed out of control so I leaped onto a snowy lawn between a couple of businesses. I shielded myself behind evergreen bushes to avoid getting plastered with snow."

Jeremy drained his cocoa cup and then lowered it to the saucer with a clink. "As I was coming out of the bushes, I saw the door to the bar open and the owner peeked out, looking in both directions, then he went back in. I jogged back through my tracks on the sidewalk."

"You saw nobody besides the owner?"

"Just Erik Gustafson. I met him in the past."

"He's also the village president."

I couldn't imagine Erik killing anyone. Why had he poked out his head? Had he seen or heard something suspicious? Who else had been in the bar yesterday morning?

After I poured us more cocoa, Jeremy said, "Those tracks going north from the car turned off after a couple of blocks and it seemed they headed over to one of your beach areas where there are maybe five parking spaces. The plow had been through and there were vehicle tracks crisscrossing the snow ridges left by the plow's blade."

"Vehicle tracks made by the killer driving away perhaps. Likely somebody with a four-wheel drive vehicle because of this weather." I sighed. "Just about everybody around here has four-wheel or all-wheel drive."

"Your only ace-in-the-hole is if somebody actually saw a vehicle leaving Main Street at around five or six or so in the morning."

"When it was dark and most people weren't up yet." I wondered about the people inside the bar yesterday morning. Their vehicles were likely parked on a side street, which people did when it snowed so the plow could have an easy time cleaning Main Street. I rose. "Are you going to call the sheriff and tell him all this?"

"Not at this point. I suspect the sheriff has talked with Erik Gustafson at the bar already."

I nodded. "That was the first thing he did."

"Do you know what Erik saw?"

"I haven't talked with him."

A sense of competition surged within me. I wanted to question Erik before Jeremy made him clam up. To keep my enemy close, I offered Jeremy a room at the inn and suggested he settle in now.

Then I packaged fudge and trekked to the Troubled Trout at the other end of downtown.

Chapter 10

A Motive

S even-thirty in the morning was still quiet in the downtown. A few shovels scraped against concrete stoops and sidewalks. Some owners tossed ice-melt crystals across stoops and walkways.

On my way to Erik's bar I called Grandpa. Cody had shown up at the shop. Maybe Cody could figure out why Grandpa wanted to move. This felt personal somehow, as if he were tired of sharing the shop. Did he want to move to give me more shop space? Did he think it was time for "me" to become a "couple" with Dillon? Did Grandpa feel like what he would term the "fifth wheel"? Usually I could talk to Grandpa about anything, but my mind was such a jumble over this that I kept mulling over my approach and putting it off.

Once inside the Troubled Trout, waiting for my eyes to adjust to the darkness after the stark whiteness of outdoors, I spotted Piers Molinsky, the chef, behind the bar. We'd met in the past during a cooking contest I had sponsored.

"Hi, Piers. Is Erik around?"

Piers was grabbing a plastic bin of dirty plates and glasses that sat on the bar, obviously full from clearing tables late last night. Another bin of silverware waited to be handled, too. He set the dishware bin down on the interior bar counter and then opened the dishwasher. He proceeded to load glasses onto the top rack.

"Hey there, Ava. The sheriff already talked to me. I don't know a thing."

"I'd love to know what Erik told the sheriff."

"Not much, from what I heard. I was in back, in the kitchen when it all came down."

"Sounds serious."

"You mean like Erik threatening Usher with that steak knife?"

I gulped, shocked. "So it was a knife from here?"

"The sheriff seemed to think so."

"Does Sheriff Tollefson believe Erik killed Usher? Erik threatened a customer?"

Piers turned toward me, bracing himself with both arms on the bar top. "Erik didn't kill anybody but he would have reason to. I heard him yell at Usher a couple of days ago, and then they had words last night here in the restaurant. Usher's appraisal of this place will take our taxes sky high. Erik might have to close, he says. And I'll be out of the best job I've had in years. I was saving up, you know, to start my own bakery."

I didn't know. "Starring your famous muffins?"

He nodded.

"Was the assessment really that high?"

"Oh, yeah. Same for a lot of folks along this stretch of downtown. Didn't you think your own assessment was mighty high?"

Now my face felt hot with the knowledge at the obvious motive many people had for killing the tax assessor. "Grandpa met with the assessor last week. I haven't looked at the papers yet. I just know Grandpa was mad about it being high."

"Well, you're sittin' on prime land on the harbor with your fudge shop. All around you it's ripe for a bunch of those condos our former village president wanted. Mercy Fogg is finally going to get her way, it seems. She probably paid off Usher just to get the ball rolling."

I stood in shock. "I'd still like to talk with Erik. Is he around?"

"In the back. Stocking the kitchen refrigerator. This is Friday. We're expecting a big crowd for the fish fry. With the murder right outside our door, I'm sure we'll be slammed despite the roads." He nodded toward a chalkboard nearby on the wall. "I'm making several specials, including seared salmon with baby reds. And, of course, brandy old-fashions at half price."

I headed around the bar and toward the door to the kitchen. "I'll be sure to tell customers at my shop. Thanks, Piers."

When I went through the swinging door to the kitchen, Erik took one look at me then slumped onto a stool. His short brown hair appeared whipped by the wind outside. He looked far older than his twenty years.

"Erik, I know you didn't kill Westergaard."

"Thanks."

The soft steamy air pressed softness onto my cheeks. I smelled chickens roasting, obviously for a lunch special, maybe soup or a booyah. I dropped my fudge bag on a nearby counter, then took off my coat.

Erik worried his hands in front of him. "When Westergaard came in for a drink last night with his wife we got into it. I told him he was going to ruin our town and my business."

"That sounds reasonable to say, though it's not exactly polite dinner talk. You were upset at your assessment. Piers told me."

"I was really stupid. I said that Usher wasn't going to kill my business. I said I'd rather see him dead first."

That shook me. "Did you pick up his steak knife when you said that? Piers told me that, too."

"I might have. But I had on plastic gloves. My fingerprints won't be on the knife." The young man appeared about to cry.

"But of course you didn't kill him."

"I dreamt that I did, damn it all. How could this be happening?"

"My grandmother always says not to borrow trouble. Somebody murdered Usher, but it wasn't you. A dream means nothing. Did you tell all this to the sheriff?"

"I had to. What's the point of lying? I'm going to jail, aren't I?"

"No. If you're arrested, it'd be a mistake." I leaned on the counter next to me. "Did you have a men's breakfast club this morning?"

He shrugged. "No. With the snow, nobody came in and that was okay."

"What about yesterday, when Usher...?"

"Yeah, several people were here, all planning the weekend schedule for the festivities."

"Who was here?"

"Businesspeople and the snow sculptors. Didn't get their names. The sculptors were from out of town. And Mercy stopped by. Nobody can miss her, she's always so loud. She got coffee and left fast though."

"Was she avoiding eye contact? Did she look guilty?"

"She always looks shifty to me and always in a hurry."

"She was on plow duty, heading my way."

"I gave the sheriff what names I knew for people here yesterday morning. But I didn't see anything happen. I was busy doing prep work for the day."

"What else did you tell the sheriff?"

"That I was in the kitchen setting out pots and pans when I thought I heard somebody come in the door after Mercy. I heard voices and assumed it was from the people meeting. But by the time I went out to the front, nobody was there. I figured they'd all left. I found my newspaper right inside the door and I looked out and saw nobody. I went back to work here in the kitchen."

"That's it?"

Erik shifted off the chair in the other direction from me. He reached for a pot but I could tell it was business meant to distract himself and maybe me.

"What didn't you tell the sheriff?"

After heaving his shoulders, he faced me. "I believe Usher was in my establishment all Wednesday night. I know this sounds crazy, but I think the man hid and slept here. It made me wonder if he had been waiting to surprise me and kill me yesterday morning."

Chapter 11

Sparkly Things

When I came through the front door of Oosterlings' fishing-and-fudge shop after eight o'clock, Cody was stirring in one of the copper vats. The redolence of sugar and raspberries hung in the moist air.

"Hey, Miss Oosterling! I'm making Rapunzel Raspberry Fairy Tale Fudge."

Cody rarely called me by my first name. I'd given up long ago trying to persuade him. Formality and routines in his life had a calming effect. It was a personality trait I didn't possess.

"I've brought a couple of pans of fudge I made at the inn last night."

"Cinderella Pink Fairy Tale Fudge?"

"Yup."

"Good. I bet we'll get a lot of customers today, this being Friday after a big storm."

"Let's hope they don't stay home by their fireplaces."

"Nah. The snowmobile trails are going to be busy. Hot chocolate and fudge after a cold ride is good stuff."

Grandpa drew my attention as he fumbled with folding today's newspaper. He sat on his usual stool.

"Hi, Gilpa. What's in the paper?"

"Not much." He stuffed the newspaper into the open shelf under his counter. "Everybody's got a big Christmas sale."

"Maybe you should advertise a few fishing-gear gifts. It might increase sales."

Grandpa huffed, then grabbed a box of lures on the floor. He took the box to a sales area, then used his penknife to open it. "Still three weeks until Christmas. And this weekend festival should help us a lot."

As I unpacked and shelved the glitter-topped Cinderella fudge into the display pans, I tried to sound casual but needed information. "You never said much about our tax assessment. I heard from Erik about his high assessment. What was ours?"

"A ridiculous number. You'd think this shop was a castle made of gold."

Cody yelled over, "Edible gold glitter maybe for sprinkling on our fudge and candies."

I helped myself to Grandpa's aromatic chocolate-laced coffee near his register. The coffee's steam caressed my face, still chilled after the five-block walk from Erik's place.

While Grandpa began pulling new lures and fishing reels from the box, I said, "Where did you put the report from the tax assessor? I'd love to see it."

"Tossed it away in the recycle bin in the kitchen." With hands full, Grandpa headed down a fishing equipment aisle.

After setting my cup aside on a register counter, I hurried to the kitchen.

The new assessment made me moan. Erik and Grandpa were right--this seemed ridiculous. If every business saw this type of tax increase, the whole town might shut down. Even my rising online sales for fudge lighthouses and the new "Fudge-of-the-Month Club" wouldn't generate enough to make my time worthwhile.

After putting the report down on the kitchen counter, I felt sure Grandpa's wanting to move had to do with the new tax assessment. I was curious as to what Grandpa had been circling, though.

Yesterday's newspaper hadn't been put in the paper recycling bin. Grandpa might still have it out at his counter with today's paper. I hurried into the shop. Sure enough, yesterday's newspaper was still stuffed under Grandpa's counter.

I took my bag off my counter, then secretly pulled the folded newspapers out of the shelf and into the bag.

I hurried to the kitchen. With quickness I unfolded yesterday's paper--already marred by brownish oil spots along one edge. Grandpa had a way of attracting oil, as if it spoke to his soul. In winter, he missed working on boat engines.

In the real estate sales section Grandpa had circled a handful of properties in Door County. Most were small homes, but a couple were condos on the lake side versus our bay side. That didn't sit well. I'd miss seeing Grandpa every day, and Grandma as well. Grandma was right to be disturbed. If they moved, Grandma might have to leave the downtown decorating committee. Her Belgian heritage came out when she helped choose and plant the flowers in the spring along our street terraces. She'd also headed the committee to choose the green-and-red holiday garlands and lighted snowflakes decorating Main Street.

Grandpa's thought of moving aside, the Main Street assessments amounted to a very good motive by anybody for murdering Westergaard.

I sat for a moment in the kitchen. Maybe the sheriff already had a suspect. Whose fingerprints had the sheriff found on the handle of the knife stuck in Usher's belly? But a smart killer would have worn gloves. I sighed.

Erik had also said Usher had been with his wife at dinner. I didn't know the woman. Had the two of them had a big fight? They must have. Why else might Usher have slept overnight in the restaurant, which Erik had implied? Had Usher's wife returned in the morning and killed him?

Or was it a business owner who happened to come in for the men's "breakfast club" and an argument ensued? I hadn't thought to ask Erik if Usher and his wife were dining with anybody else. Maybe a feuding relative or a stranger had put the knife in Usher's stomach.

Maybe the murder had nothing to do with anybody in Fishers' Harbor.

I pulled the pad of paper out of my pocket and added items to the list I was building. Pauline would be proud of me for this list-making.

Out in the shop with my bag in hand, I spotted Grandpa loading beers and sodas into his shop refrigerator. I sneaked his newspapers back into the shelf below his register.

Cody was pouring hot raspberry fudge onto the marble table at the window.

I was about to go back to the kitchen to get the ingredients for Golden Goose Fairy Tale Fudge--a blueberry flavor--when the shop door opened with a clang of the cowbell. In walked Bethany Bjorklund, Cody's former girlfriend.

"Bethany! Happy holidays! So good to see you. I heard you were helping with Pauline's kindergarten students."

"Just a couple of hours a day now and then. It's a blast."

Cody had told me he broke up with Bethany because he wanted to focus on his studies. He'd also added EMT and volunteer firefighter training because his plan was to be a forest ranger and he'd need those skills. He also needed dating skills.

Cody grew up with a mild form of Asperger's and he suffered from OCD, Obsessive-Compulsive Disorder. He liked things clean and orderly. He also liked shiny, sparkly things; Christmastime was his favorite time of year. He loved working with wrapping paper and crinkly cellophane and ribbons. With medications and help from Sam, he was doing well. What would happen if we lost the shop, though, because of the ridiculously high tax assessment? What if Cody no longer could come to what he considered a safe haven--this fudge shop?

Troubling thoughts swirled in my head as I gave Bethany a hug. Her blue eyes twinkled. Her blond hair was cut in a short, avant-garde style befitting a college freshman. "College going well?"

She said, "I have to hand in a final paper next week for one class yet."

"Cody's done with his exams. Aren't you, Cody?"

He kept loafing the fudge at the window area, the scraping sticking with their rhythm. "Yeah, Miss Oosterling."

Bethany shared a private wince.

I said, "How can I help you? Maybe we can enjoy coffee together and chat? Don't say anything bad about Grandpa, though. He's hiding over there by the beer."

Grandpa called out, "I heard that! Bethany, you want a beer for breakfast?"

"No, Mister Oosterling. I'll stick with brandy on my cornflakes," she said, joking.

Grandpa chortled. Cody coughed from his corner, likely trying to hide a chuckle.

I headed behind the glass cases. "What can I get for you, Bethany?"

"Mom is stocking up for Monday's parade and celebration." The young woman leaned with her hands on the glass case. "We have aunts and uncles coming and several of my cousins."

"Gosh, maybe you want to buy the whole case?"

"Pretty much." She laughed. "I knew I'd have to get here early before the late morning rush or I'd be out of luck. My mother says your fudge is the best she ever tasted."

From across the shop Cody said, "It is the best."

We couldn't see him for the store shelves. Bethany smiled. So did I.

I said loud enough for Cody to hear, "It's the best fudge because I have the best helper."

Bethany whispered, "He's doing okay? I mean, with school and all?"

I nodded.

"Is he, well..."

I whispered back, "Dating? No."

He'd tried to date a girl last summer, but that hadn't worked out.

Bethany's soulful eyes revealed how much she still cared about Cody. It made my heart ache because once Cody made up his mind about something--such as a "no-dating Bethany policy," he never reversed course.

I packaged the fudge and sent Bethany on her way.

Cody and I spent the next hour making several flavors of Fairy Tale fudge and Fisherman's Tall Tale fudge in the copper kettles. I told him about my experimental fudge flavor made with holiday fruits and that it needed a name. He said he'd think on it.

At almost noon I realized my weekend guests would be arriving at any moment. I was also expecting my girlfriends to drop by with things for Ellany and her baby. I wondered how Ellany and Jeremy had gotten along. Had he scared her off?

I bundled up in a sudden panic and left the shop in Cody's capable hands.

Chapter 12

Girlfriend Wisdom

To my relief, the Blue Heron Inn bubbled with chatter when I arrived. Ellany and my dearest girlfriends were seated around the dining room table.

My bakery friend, Laura Brecht, had brought her special cheesy garlic bread. It'd been warmed in the oven, as well as cinnamon rolls. The inn smelled heavenly.

A bowl of grapes and other fruits nestled among several cheeses on the table. Coffee cups and glasses of orange juice sat next to plates. I enjoyed the fact that my friends could feel so at home at my inn. The feeling couldn't be bottled and sold.

Laura--our friend we always called a cheerleader because of her short, petite stature--sat at the end of the table near the foyer. Her twin babies were over a year old now, Spencer Paul and Clara Ava. They crawled about on the big blue rug with soft toys as I greeted everybody.

Pauline sat at the far end of the table near the kitchen door.

Ellany sat to Pauline's right with a sleeping Henry in her arms.

Our red-headed friend Fontana Coppens sat next to Ellany. Fontana held her baby born last spring, Happy Valentine. Happy was fast asleep, too.

I hung my coat over the back of a chair and sat opposite Ellany. I reached for bread and cheese. "Sorry I'm late. What did I miss?"

Pauline said, "We unloaded bags of clothes and supplies upstairs already. Henry Olaf and Ellany aren't wanting for a thing."

Ellany nodded. A tear trickled off the corner of one eye. She swiped at it. "Thank you. I'm feeling so grateful. And stupid."

"Stupid? Why?" we chorused.

"Running away from my husband. It sounds so stupid when I say it."

Pauline said, "Depends on the husband."

That received chuckles.

Pauline went on to mention her own growing-up years with a father who drank too much and yelled at everybody. "Thankfully, I lived mostly over at Ava's house through much of grade school and high school. I saw my mother age prematurely, and then she and my sister left for good. Some husbands aren't worth sticking around for."

I got up and grabbed a box of tissues which I set next to Ellany. I suspected the rest of us might need them, too.

Ellany took a deep breath as she looked down at sleeping Henry. "It's been nothing like that. My husband is from good people. It's all...really stupid."

Fontana said, "What's stupid? We're here to help."

When Ellany's face crumpled, I reached across the table. "Ellany, whatever you say won't go beyond this room." Then I recalled I had a guest already. "Did Jeremy leave?"

Pauline gasped. "Jeremy Stone is staying here?"

I nodded. "He promised to behave and write something nice."

"Okay. I guess he did find my mother."

I pressed my question again to Ellany. "Did the reporter leave?"

"He's a reporter?" Fear registered in her eyes.

"He is, but if he's not here right now, our discussion will stay a secret."

"He left about the time you did this morning."

"Good," I said. "Now tell us what's going on with your husband."

Ellany looked down at her little one. "Henry looks just like his dad. The hint of the hairline is just like Brendan's."

We women sat transfixed by the obvious love Ellany had for Henry. And her husband, I would bet.

Fontana asked, "How old are you?"

"Nineteen," Ellany said. "Just turned."

"And so you got pregnant while in high school?" Fontana asked.

Ellany winced. "Stuff happens."

Fontana nodded toward her own sleeping baby. "Indeed it does. This one was conceived in the back of a car with two of us who should've known better."

Ellany gasped. "Really? You feel guilty, too, about getting pregnant?"

Fontana shook her head, but did it with a gracious smile. "Not at all. This child's father was murdered before Happy was born."

All of us remained still and silent for a moment, sorry about the professor's passing. Fontana had been fortunate to fall in love again soon, and it was to a farmer in the southern part of the county, near my own parents' farm.

Laura said, "Ellany, we don't always plan these things. I wanted to wait until my husband was out of the service, but the twins came along when they did and it was just me with them for a while until he came home. Then..." She paused with a pained look. "My husband suffered from Post Traumatic Stress Syndrome. It took him a while to pull himself together and feel healthy enough to get a job."

I said, "He works with other veterans now in our county, and he's filling in as a kindergarten teacher for a couple of weeks for Pauline."

Everybody paused to say nice things about Brecht Rousseau.

I said to Ellany, "What does your husband do?"

She winced. "Nothing. We just got out of high school. He says he doesn't want to do anything. He just wants us to live with his mother. He says we can live off her. That made me so mad at him."

The four of us other women shared a look.

I offered, "So, you don't want to live with his mother? Or is your leaving really about teaching your husband a lesson?"

Ellany shook her head, then shrugged. "His mother is okay, but if we live there, then Brendan won't do anything to get a job. He doesn't want to go to college or anything."

Pauline said, "Not everybody needs college. Does he have skills he'd like to learn?"

Ellany shrugged. "He's good looking. I guess he could be a model."

The four of us friends chuckled. I said, "That's a start."

Fontana said, "Modeling pays well. I did a fair amount of that myself as a teenager."

I said, "She was the prettiest girl in school and she never let us forget it."

"I'm also older than you, Ava, and wiser."

"Hah."

Pauline said, "Probably true. We all know more than Ava. She gets into trouble and then we rescue her. She was in her wedding dress and ready to marry another guy, but then she eloped, then divorced the guy within a month, and now she's engaged to the same guy eleven years later.

If you want advice about romance and marriage, talk to the rest of us, not Ava."

Everybody laughed, including Ellany.

I didn't mind the jab at my romantic history. "All true, Ellany. Dillon used to work for his parents, but last summer he decided he wanted to run his own construction company. I did a few other things, too, before I ended up as an innkeeper and confectioner. My grandfather and grandmother helped me out and gave me a place to stay when I returned to Fishers' Harbor. Then I moved to this inn. What do you want to do next? It doesn't mean you have to choose something that will last forever and ever. Maybe that's what you tell Brendan."

The young woman peered down at her baby. "Can I stay here for now? I feel so stupid, though. I'm sorry."

Laura gave the table a gentle slap. "No more of that talk. You're not stupid."

"Not at all," chorused Fontana and Pauline.

I said, "You were smart enough to get inside that empty house Dillon is fixing in this cold weather. And now you can stay here for a few days if need be. But we should call somebody to let them know you're okay."

She grimaced, but nodded.

Chatter ensued about babies, Victorian fashions, wedding traditions in Belgium versus here, and other topics I hadn't previously cared much about. We were drunk on our friendship. Ellany and her baby had brought all of us together in a new way.

Chapter 13

The Dress

Have you ever heard of "flounced pagoda sleeves"? Pauline insisted my Victorian-styled maid-of-honor dress should have them. After the lunch with my girlfriends and Ellany, Pauline had called Grandma to see if the extra Belgian lace Pauline had brought yesterday was cut and ready for its "flouncing".

As we walked down the hill to Grandma's house, I had two calls to make--the first one to my sometimes-friend Sheriff Jordy Tollefson. I didn't want an Amber Alert going out for Elleny and her baby.

"But, Jordy, she's adamant about not talking with her husband or mother-in-law or anybody at the moment. Can you just let them know she and the baby are okay and somebody will be in touch soon?"

He agreed. "A mother and child at the inn? You sure know how to get in the Christmas spirit, Ava."

Jordy could sometimes make me smile, like now. "Thanks for the help. She's just a mixed-up kid."

"Staying with a mixed-up woman."

I stopped smiling and gave him a growl. I then called the shop.

Cody and Grandpa assured me they were handling everything just fine. Grandpa said Dotty Klubertanz and Lois Forbes had stopped by with beautiful handmade winter scarves. The women were entertaining customers with stories about my bad luck with murders and scoundrels. Cody said somebody suggested a new fudge flavor called "Felonious Fudge".

On the phone yet as we walked in the chilly day, I said to Grandpa, "Did Dotty say anything new about the murder?"

"Nope. Why would she?"

I was fishing for information. Not wishing to worry him, I hadn't told Grandpa about my visit with Dotty's son Travis at the Klubertanz Mercantile yesterday.

"Grandpa, you know how it is with Dotty and Lois. They know things that are important before the sheriff does."

He laughed on the other end of the line. "Honey, I have a line of customers staring at me, fortunately."

"Okay. Bye, Grandpa. Thanks!"

As I walked through the cold, I noticed a call had come in from the sheriff.

Pauline grabbed my hand. "Don't call Jordy back. He can handle whatever it is on his own."

I growled at her as we opened Grandma's door and then stamped our boots.

Grandma had my maid-of-honor dress over one arm. It still looked like a big curtain to me. The wide, bell-shaped sleeves of the red Victorian dress had a "flounce", which was a frilly layer of lace sewn around the arm as an accent.

Pauline appeared near tears. "Isn't this beautiful, Ava? To think you'll be wearing this at my wedding only a week from tomorrow."

"Yeah, to think."

Grandma tapped my nose with an index finger. "Now don't be such a spoil sport. You will look like a princess in this dress."

She turned to Pauline, holding up the dress sleeve with the one flounce. "What do you think? Two lace flounces? Three?"

"Let's go for four. The Belgian lace looks like beautiful snowflakes against the red background. The more lace the better, right?"

Grandma's eyes twinkled. "You only get married once." She puckered immediately, giving me a wide-eyed look. "Well, some of us. Some of us plan to marry the same man twice."

Pauline doubled over with laughter.

Grandma asked me, "When might you set a date?"

I said, "We were thinking April Fool's Day."

Grandma whooped with laughter, then sat on the sofa.

Pauline took the dress from Grandma and held it up in front of me. "Dillon is going to take one look at you and want a wedding the very next day."

Grandma asked me, "Did Dillon's top hat arrive yet?"

I plopped next to Grandma. "I don't know. Does he really need one? It's going to be cold. Maybe his stocking cap will do?"

Pauline scoffed. "Stop it." Pauline was helping lay out the lace on the sofa arm. "Clothes and hair are very important. I'll check with John. He said his top hat and frock coat had arrived, but the frock coat seemed a bit long. Maybe he got Dillon's order instead of his own." Pauline gasped. "What if John's clothes don't arrive on time?"

Grandma offered, "Don't worry. I can take up the frock coat if needed and we can find something else for Dillon if we must. Keep in mind the Peninsula Players Theatre uses costumes."

Pauline clapped a couple of times. "Thank you. My mother isn't good at sewing or any of this wedding stuff really, and John's parents are still in Hawaii."

I said, "Where I'd rather be at the moment."

Grandma paused in sizing lace for a flounce. "Maybe that's all Gilsen needs--a vacation in a warm place for a couple of months."

Pauline interjected, "But he loves ice fishing here in January and February. Our harbor gets so busy. We get tourists coming to look at the ice shoves." Blocks of ice as big as cars were shoved by the winds from the north and west, piling up sometimes across the docks.

I added, "He gets people interested in coming back for summer fishing in his boat."

"A boat he doesn't have," Grandma said.

We paused for a moment's reflection. His boat had been ruined last summer in a stormy escapade on Lake Michigan.

I said, "You don't suppose that's what's bothering him? Maybe he thinks he should give up being a fishing guide? He's loved his boats but he always has bad luck with them."

Grandma went wide-eyed. "Oh, honey. Maybe he wants to take up fly fishing and move near streams instead of the bay."

I almost slipped and revealed what I'd seen circled in the newspaper at the shop--homes that weren't near any water.

Pauline said, "Maybe he's just feeling old, down a little."

Grandma said, "When I mention going south for a month in the winter or even a week, he insists that only old people are snowbirds. He says he'll be too hot in Florida."

I said, "I could work on him a little for you."

"But I like staying here. I like being here for all my meetings with the girls and my committees." Grandma's friends where in their sixties through nineties but always called themselves "girls".

I offered, "You could use online video meetings to stay in touch."

"We can't hug or linger with gossip. And we can't smell the last of the coffee burning in the pot in the church basement during our meetings."

Pauline and I laughed.

Pauline said, "A true Belgian. We hug a lot and need our coffee. With cream. And Ava sure loves gossip."

"I call it collecting information. Journalism."

Pauline rolled her eyes. "You're not a reporter. That's Stone." She directed herself at Grandma. "Did you know that guy is staying at the inn?"

Grandma gasped. She put down the scissors to skewer me. "He's never good news."

I reminded them both he'd found Pauline's mother Coletta in the past.

Pauline slumped into a chair opposite us. "He may have found my mother but Stone is here for a big story, Ava. He loved reporting on the disasters last summer--and at a wedding I was coordinating for the first time! The stories about that awful event ruined any chances I had of building a business for summers when I'm not teaching."

I felt compelled to defend my guest. "Jeremy does good research, and he's not so bad if you know how to control him."

"He's out of control. I wouldn't put it past him to have had a hand in the murder of that tax assessor. Didn't you tell me that reporter said he was out jogging past that car? Was that a lie? He doesn't strike me as the type to go jogging in deep snow."

My stomach did a flip-flop. She made sense. "I'll have a talk with Jeremy." I rose from the sofa. "I really need to go."

Pauline got off the chair. "I'm going with you."

Grandma said, "Please do. Keep her out of trouble."

The moment I was outside in the brisk winter air I called the sheriff.

Jordy came on the line. "Ava, I wondered if we might meet soon, today in fact."

"Why?"

"We've matched the fingerprints on the steak knife to someone."

"Erik Gustafson? Jeremy Stone?"

"No." After an audible intake of breath, he said, "Your grandfather."

Chapter 14

Fingerprint Folly

Jordy agreed to meet me at the inn before going to the shop to confront Gilpa about his fingerprints on the murder weapon.

Pauline insisted on being with me. She got a big hug from me.

The sheriff arrived around three o'clock that afternoon. During the time it took him to drive up from the Justice Center in Sturgeon Bay, my guests had arrived. Magnus Olson was a cultural and art history professor from the university in Green Bay. Fontana's aunt, Skylark Neubauer, worked with Habitat for Humanity and resided in New Orleans. Both had stayed with me for Fontana's July wedding and it appeared romance had blossomed.

Magnus had promised to return for holiday celebrations with two college students majoring in cultural arts. They planned to offer art carts on the street for children this weekend and through Monday's holiday parade. With gusto, Magnus introduced his twenty-something college "nisse" or Christmas elves: Nova Cervantes, with dark sepia-colored hair down to her waist; and Dax Llewellyn, a fresh-faced guy with a shaggy mop of hair the color of an antique brass lamp in my parlor.

After pointing them to their rooms, Pauline and I rushed to the kitchen to wait for the sheriff. I put together a pot of rich coffee.

Pauline and I sat opposite each other on the white marble island. I took out paper and pen from a drawer and set them in front of me. Soon, Jordy knocked on the back door.

He removed his boots and set them aside on the mat next to the door. Jordy was the same height as Pauline's six feet but he always seemed taller. He retained the muscular build he'd had since college twenty years ago when he'd made it onto the Green Bay Packers football team practice squad. "I'm sorry about this, Ava."

I took his coat and hung it in the nearby closet.

"There's no way Grandpa would murder anybody."

Jordy slung himself into the seat at the end of the island, setting his hat in front of him. The part in his hair was as crisp as his demeanor.

With shaky hands I managed to bring him a mug of coffee without spilling any. I filled a mug for myself and Pauline, then offered cinnamon buns made by friend Laura Rousseau at her Sister Bay bakery.

Nobody took a bite of the aromatic pastry, but Jordy sipped his coffee. "The fingerprints are conclusive, Ava."

A deep breath kept me from snapping at him. "Are fingerprints enough for an arrest?"

"Not always. That's why I'm here. Your grandpa's been in so much trouble over the years that I'm bound to consider his history."

"There's no way he'd kill anybody."

Pauline nodded at Jordy with vigorous head bobs.

"And I hope that's true, of course." Jordy fingered the cinnamon bun.

I asked, "Are there other prints on the knife? There must be."

He shook his head.

Tapping my fingertips on my cup, I said, "The true killer had to be wearing gloves. It's cold outside. The killer must have taken the knife off Grandpa's table the night before, saved it, then killed Usher Westergard yesterday morning."

Pauline nodded again. "Somebody intentionally wanted to put the blame for murder on Ava's grandfather."

Mercy Fogg came to mind. "That's it, Jordy. Somebody is framing my grandfather."

"For what?" Jordy asked. "If I can find other suspects, other motives, I can follow those leads and maybe clear your grandfather. Can you give me something?"

"I can," Pauline said, raising a hand. "A week from tomorrow Gil is walking me down the aisle. Please don't ruin the most important day of my life by arresting him."

Jordy slurped at his coffee, then sat back, glancing at me. "Do you know when he was at the Troubled Trout? Time exactly? Start and finish? That could help me."

I had no idea what time for certain that Grandpa had been at the Troubled Trout. "He'll have to tell you."

"He doesn't always like to talk to me. Did he mention anything to you?"

"He was playing cards with the guys on Wednesday night. They always go out for steaks afterward. He usually eats dinner around five or six, but this would've been after cards, so maybe eight o'clock. Have you asked Erik who he saw at his tables that night? Or at the bar?"

"Erik confirmed seeing your grandfather. Erik says he sold twenty steak dinners on special that night, plus a few take-out dinners people picked up at the bar."

"So," I began, thinking hard on that, "there are at least twenty suspects because they were given steak knives. My grandfather touched or picked up a knife to use, all logical. If the killer were careful they wore gloves. The killer picked up Grandpa's knife when the killer came in for takeout. Nobody would notice gloves in this weather of course. The other theory is this: Anybody eating at Erik's could have exchanged their knife for Grandpa's when he wasn't looking."

Jordy finished swallowing a bite of cinnamon bun. "Gil was with his buddies, though. Seems to me somebody would've noticed another customer reaching over to swipe or exchange knives. And Erik recalls your grandfather having words with Westergaard. At the restaurant."

That surprising information caused me to swallow against a dry throat.

"Erik told me several people had words with Usher. Have you talked with Usher's wife? Erik said she was with her husband on Wednesday night. Maybe she recalls someone threatening her husband."

"She says she doesn't know who would do such a thing. I didn't speak of your grandfather or of anybody with her. I can't tip my hand in this investigation."

Pauline piped up. "But did Usher's wife suggest a scenario?"

Pauline usually hated it when I tried to help Jordy but in this case she wanted Grandpa walking her down the aisle.

Jordy drained his coffee cup. "I have to go. I just wanted to know if you knew of anything that would point to another perpetrator." He'd ignored Pauline's question.

In desperation, I said to Jordy, "You haven't said much about the guys who there at the Troubled Trout yesterday very early in the morning. I think they were there by five o'clock. It was a special meeting about the Main Street festivities. Every one of those people must be a suspect."

"And please do not poke around and ask them questions."

"What if I do?"

Jordy pushed off the stool, rising to his full six feet. "You don't know what you're doing, Ava. I have the questions that need to be asked. Stick to making fudge."

Pauline gasped, staring wide-eyed at me.

I kept my slow simmer hidden behind a smile. "Maybe the people know me and would rather talk to me than you. And I need to ask questions because Grandpa is unfairly implicated."

"Then go ahead and ask this key question for me: Would murder be a reason to go crazy and steal a snowplow?"

Jordy's rhetorical question froze my tongue.

The sheriff found his coat from the closet, slipped on his boots, and then left, closing the door so quietly it was as if the world had ended and that was the last whisper of life.

Chapter 15

Too Cozy

After the frustrating meeting with the sheriff, Pauline and I stepped onto the inn's verandah. The drab Friday four o'clock light matched my mood. Shadows from bare tree branches and buildings cast lavender images across the snow.

Pauline hunkered into her coat, pulling down a stocking hat to her eyebrows. "The sheriff was just fishing for information. He can't possibly arrest your grandpa."

"I know."

We wandered down my steep driveway, parting ways at Main Street. Pauline was meeting her fiancé, John, and her mother to work on details about the filming of the wedding parade.

As Pauline trotted away from me, I spotted Al Kvalheim digging ice off a gutter grate in front of The Wise Owl bookstore. I recalled seeing Al talking with newspaper delivery woman Greta Truelson yesterday during the excitement over the murder. They knew all the town gossip.

"Al!" I waved, hurrying to him.

Al leaned over the top of the shovel handle. "Ava, if your grandfather's going to start a new profession stealing snowplows, the least he can do is take the blade along the street curb and clean the gutters. You know I can't just toss salt on this stuff. We don't want that in the bay."

"Sorry, Al. I can't control Grandpa."

"Well, somebody has to."

"You played cards with him Wednesday night, right?"

"Yeah." Al slid me a sideways glance.

"And you guys went out for drinks and steaks at Erik's bar and restaurant."

"If you're going to ask about the argument Gil had with Usher, I'm afraid that's true."

I'd heard about that already. "Did you see anybody take his steak knife?"

"Nope." Al resumed punching at dirty ice over the grate. "You mean to tell me your grandfather's prints are on that knife? Gil couldn't kill a fly."

"Somebody had to have taken his knife, though. The sheriff said his prints are on it."

"Like I said, I didn't see anybody swiping knives. Your grandpa likes his steak. He hung onto his knife something fierce, cutting the meat and chowing down like usual."

Shadows on the street were growing longer, the air becoming frosty as a freezer. "Did Greta say anything to you? I saw the two of you talking yesterday."

"Greta Truelson?"

I nodded. Al liked to drag things out, which was frustrating me.

He leaned over his shovel again. "Not a thing."

"What did you talk about with her?"

"The taxes! Westergaard had no business writing up those high assessments. Greta and I agreed downtown could become a ghost town. Your inn wouldn't have guests if this harbor area had no amenities. If owners of the mercantile, the book store, coffee shop, clothing shops, the spa across the street, and the Troubled Trout bar moved out to avoid higher taxes, Fishers' Harbor would die. And if the tax base disappears, my job gets cut, and I'm in my sixties."

"We can object to assessments. The government has to provide a time for objections."

"True. But rarely does an assessment get changed downward much at all, Ava."

His words made me happy because the reasoning pointed to somebody other than Grandpa murdering Usher. I felt sorry for the sheriff; the suspect pool might be very large.

I asked Al, "Did you and Greta talk about who might have killed Usher?"

"That didn't take long. We concluded it could be just about anybody. I was surprised he wasn't tossed in the lake. Heck, even one of those snow sculptor people got into a hot argument with Usher's wife Hailey on Wednesday night."

"Who was the sculptor?"

"Stella Zanderson."

"I don't know her."

"I heard her say she lives up on Washington Island. Couldn't pay me enough to be there in winter, and sometimes with no way to get back to the mainland if a ferry isn't running or the ice got too thick but not thick enough for cars to run on it."

"What was she arguing about with Hailey?"

Al took a deep breath, then looked about the street as if to make sure the two women weren't around. "Hailey said something about not tagging around with Usher anymore. It seems Stella asked Usher to introduce her to some of the business people he knew."

"Why?"

"Beats me. She's an artist. Probably needs more sales. Maybe she wanted to paint things for business people."

"Maybe Usher's wife thought Stella was getting too cozy with Usher?"

"Usher blushed mighty big when Stella stopped at his table with Hailey sitting there."

"Did you tell the sheriff all this?"

"Nope. People having affairs isn't my business."

"What about Mercy?" I'd once spied Mercy and Al kissing behind a building, and another time sharing a cigarette after both said they'd given up smoking. Al's words right now might not be worth more than spit.

Al scoffed and went back to poking at the ice. "Mercy told me she wanted to run over Westergaard with her plow or school bus. But I know she'd never do such a thing for real."

He was likely right. Mercy wanted a clean record so she could run again for village president. She would, however, be glad to help someone else do her dirty work.

I said, "The murder works in Mercy's favor because it weakens Erik's re-election hopes. He and the village board approved of Usher and might be called responsible for higher taxes."

"Mercy might have mentioned that, last time I saw her."

"Shouldn't she be happy about higher assessments? The trouble works in her favor."

Al stopped to shake his head at me. "Heck, she got a low assessment. That's what she's mad about. Usher Westergaard downgraded her house to something akin to a cattle shed."

"Why?"

"I don't rightly know. She just said the man was nuts."

"Do you happen to know where Hailey Westergaard lives? I have Usher's business address on the tax assessment form he gave us, but I don't know a home address."

"Yeah, no more telephone books makes things hard to find people anymore. I wish they'd bring back telephone books. We used to keep ours in a drawer by the refrigerator--"

"Al, do you know their address?"

"You aimin' to visit her?"

Until this moment, I hadn't planned anything. "I was the person who saw her husband maybe finish his last breath. She may appreciate a visit."

"Or not, if you're nosin' around again like some detective."

I ignored that.

He pointed with a thumb behind him, toward the north end of the street. "Their house is a yellow one on 42, close to Ephraim. It's where I turn the snowplow around when I'm drivin'. Usher worked out of his home. Your address for him is good."

I almost turned to leave, but was compelled to ask, "Were you at yesterday's early-morning meeting at the Troubled Trout?"

Al's cold, red cheeks paled. "I was, but what does that matter?"

"It's likely somebody ran after Usher and stabbed him just before my grandfather drove by with the snowplow. Did you see my grandfather earlier?"

Unease wrinkled Al's brow. "Somebody said Gil was there. But I didn't see him. Maybe he was in the john."

"So he never came out of the restroom? How long were you in the bar?"

"Nursed a hot toddy for a half hour. After Westergaard left I never saw Gil. Probably left out the back door."

This news gutted me. Grandpa wasn't seen at the same time Usher was stabbed. "Did you tell the sheriff this?"

"No way."

"Thank goodness." I flung my arms around the stout man.

The holiday lights on cottages, houses, and businesses--including the trees lit along the harbor piers--kept darkness at bay in the late afternoon. From the front of Oosterlings' Live Bait, Bobbers, Belgian Fudge & Beer, the world appeared cheery.

Customers hailed me with "Merry Christmas!" The floor creaked continuously from feet moving in and out of the aisles. The air smelled of sugar and vanilla.

Cody yelled from a copper vat as I reached the front, "Hey, Miss Oosterling, your boarders came by and we experimented with your new fudge recipe."

I whipped on a pink, bibbed apron with a "Cinderella Pink Fudge" motif. I put my hair up in a loose bun in back, donned a hair net, then headed over to the copper kettles.

"Who helped make fudge?"

Cody laughed. "That professor and Fontana's aunt."

"Magnus Olsen and Skylark Neubauer."

"Yeah. And the professor brought along students." Cody focused his gaze down into the vat in a way that tipped me off.

"Oh, you mean Dax and, and..." I pretended to forget her name.

"Nova," Cody said, a blush overwhelming his freckles.

"She's cute."

Cody shrugged. "When she stirred the fudge, she did it faster than I do."

"What's wrong with that?"

"It's just not how I do it." He shrugged again.

"But she helped make the fudge anyway?"

A shoulder lifted again. "It's on the marble table cooling. We're thinking up a name."

"Do you know what kind of fudge you want to make next?"

Customers had wandered over along with several children.

Cody said, "How about Rudolph-the-Red-Nosed-Reindeer Fudge?"

The children yelled, "Yeah!"

I said to the crowd, "It's peanut butter fudge with a few secret ingredients added, Rudolph's favorite. The peanut butter gives him protein and energy to fly high in the sky."

A boy of about five wearing a Green Bay Packer stocking cap said, "We make peanut butter cookies for Santa at our house."

"Good choice," I replied. "Do you want to help stir?"

"Yeah!"

Several children raised their hands, jumping up and down, yelling, "Me, too! Me, too!"

Time passed swiftly. I regaled the children with tales of the mischief that nisse or elves get into, but said elves also liked to help others and be rewarded with fudge.

Every child got to taste-test the Rudolph fudge. They giggled over the idea of eating "reindeer poop"--raisins. Each child also received a small bell on a red ribbon. "If you tinkle that on Christmas Eve, the nisse will hear it and tell Santa to be extra good to you."

My young customers and their parents left in a buoyant mood, chattering like sparrows picking up popcorn on a street. The cowbells clanked happily in the children's wake.

Exhausted and emotionally spent by the day, I shut off the lights at seven o'clock, put on my coat, and then stepped out the back door--only to be knocked to the snowy ground.

Chapter 16

Moonlight Menace

I face-planted in the cold snow.

"I'm sorry!" Jeremy yelled, his body across mine.

I'd landed alongside the narrow path shoveled behind the shop. Jeremy grabbed my shoulders from behind and helped me to my feet. I spit out snow and his name. "What the heck is wrong with you?"

He brushed snow off the front of my coat.

I pushed his hands away. "Don't touch me."

"It was an accident. I didn't see you coming out until the last minute and I tried to step back but stepped on something next to the door and slid on the slick ice. A little kitty litter out here wouldn't hurt. What did I step on?"

"Never mind." I swiped at snow icing my eyebrows and forehead.

He bent over near the door. "Cookies?"

"For the elves and skritek. Grandpa believes in them."

Jeremy grunted. "I didn't come to argue or talk about skritek. I have news."

113

"Jeremy, just go away."

"But I'm staying at your inn."

He made me growl. "What's the news?"

"About Usher Westergaard." The moonlight reflecting off the snowy landscape rendered his face a ghoulish blue.

"What did you find out?" Curiosity anchored me in place despite the icy air coming off the lake. I hugged myself, stamping my feet.

"Westergaard and his wife were discussing a separation or divorce."

"How'd you find that out?"

"I ran into your newspaper carrier at the mercantile and asked her what she knew about yesterday morning. She heard the couple wasn't getting along. It seems Hailey was receiving marriage counseling from the priest at Saint Ann's. Alone. Usher probably didn't want a divorce."

"How does Greta know that? Isn't such counseling private? Hailey told her?"

"No. Greta said Hailey was part of a church cleaning committee. They gossip while cleaning. Your newspaper lady overheard someone mention this." Jeremy hopped up and down. "I'm cold. Can we go inside?"

"No, I'm locking up." Which I promptly did. "I'm on my way home."

I led him through the snowy trail in the dark. We approached a crooked square of light shed by a window in Dillon's cabin. "This is gossip. Can't trust it." That led my thoughts back to what Al had said about artist Stella Zanderson perhaps having an affair with Usher.

Jeremy said, "You're right. It's definitely something to follow up on. I don't know how besides asking Hailey point-blank if she were having marriage problems."

A chill rattled my already-cold body. Al had told me he witnessed Hailey Westergaard arguing with her husband Wednesday night at the Troubled Trout.

We turned onto Duck Marsh Street's sidewalk, heading left to go past Dillon's cabin, with Jeremy walking at my right shoulder like a gentleman.

"Jeremy, don't you think the sheriff has already asked Hailey about anything wrong between herself and her husband?"

We neared the intersection. Our breath created frost clouds illuminated by the moonlight.

Jeremy said, "I'm sure he had to ask. But any killer worth his or her salt would have practiced a lie. Hailey might have cried in his presence and the sheriff melted."

"No way. Jordy does a good job. Nobody makes him melt. Did you talk to the sheriff about this marriage possibly crumbling?"

"No reason to. The sheriff won't tell me a thing that's not public record. I need to interview Hailey Westergaard, but I doubt she'll talk to a reporter. I need a way to get to her without actually interviewing her myself."

I halted, seething. "You came to find me because you want me to talk with Hailey. You want me to do your work for you. You disgust me." Never mind that I'd already decided to visit the woman. I wanted it to be my idea, not Jeremy's!

The snow crunched under his leather shoes as we started up the driveway. "Just take her some of your fudge and start a conversation."

"You're using me. And admitting it!"

His smile widened until his teeth appeared like pearls.

A hundred reasons not to "go in" with him darted about inside my head like atoms on the loose. I was in the middle of Pauline's wedding plans and the plans for Monday's parade. I also needed to work a full day tomorrow--Saturday--because tourists would descend on the big weekend for the snow sculpture contest and activities in our parks. I had announced on social media that I'd hold a Christmas Elf Fudge demonstration for kids at two o'clock tomorrow.

However, Grandpa was in trouble and acting mysterious lately--simultaneously with me finding Hailey's husband dead. My heart had already decided I should pay Hailey a visit and express my condolences, so I saw no real harm in helping Jeremy.

"I'll visit with Hailey and let you know what I find out. But this was my idea, not yours."

"Sure." Jeremy gave my right shoulder a friendly fist bump.

Saturday morning burst forth with uncommon sounds at the Blue Heron Inn at five in the morning: laughter right outside my apartment door in the parlor, a blender whirring off in the distance, and a baby crying.

A quick look out my frosty window revealed a bright red tiny gift box at the back door. Starlight still shone on the hoar frost lining branches of the maple trees, blue spruce, and cedars at the edges of the backyard. There were no gnomes or elves, no mice.

After donning jeans, a long-sleeved white shirt, a cable-knit red sweater, and heavy socks, I ventured outside my door. Magnus and Skylark looked like pretzels on the rug--their yoga routines.

Skylark had pulled her long, wavy red hair tied into a loose ponytail atop her head. Curly strands cascaded to her ears. She appeared younger than sixty-some years. Her multi-colored leotard revealed rounded curves and cleavage, which the professor seemed to be using as a focal point as he moved through his routine.

Magnus was taller than me by a couple of inches, a willowy thin man, with graying curly-brown hair, brown eyes, and dark-rimmed eyeglasses. He wore a Green Bay Packer sweatshirt and black exercise pants.

Skylark stopped giggling when she noticed me. "Sorry. Did we wake you, Ava?"

I edged alongside the front of the nearest sofa. "This is my normal time to rise, but aren't you two up a bit early?"

Skylark bent into a new position. "Magnus challenged me last night. He said, 'early to rise gets worms'." Giggles hit her again.

Magnus moved into a cross-legged position, peering up through his eyeglasses. "No, the sayings are 'Early to bed, early to rise, keeps a man healthy, wealthy, and wise', and 'The early bird gets the worm'."

Skylark huffed at him then peered up at me. "See how ridiculous he is? If I exercise with this professor I get worms for my reward."

Magnus collapsed with guffaws.

I said, "Instead of worms, would you like fudge-filled muffins, waffles, orange juice, fruit, and the makings for ice-cream omelets?"

Skylark said, "With chocolate-cherry coffee? I still remember that from our visit in July."

"I'll put on a pot." I paused to ask, "Who's in my kitchen using the blender this early?"

"Mister...Stone." Skylark ground out the name as she leaned over outstretched legs.

"I take it you don't like him much."

"Don't trust him any further than I can throw the man. He's a snoop and uses people for his own gain. I can't forgive him for that mess last summer in which Pauline's poor mother Coletta got her name dragged through police reports. All because of Stone."

"He did find her out East and was responsible for reuniting Pauline and Coletta. We have to give him that. Coletta will be by later, by the way. She still works as the inn's maid when I have a full house."

Magnus asked, "Can I be of help with this awful mess concerning your grandfather and that poor man's death?"

Last summer Magnus had helped when a murder case interrupted my life. I sank into the nearby blue loveseat. "Oh, Magnus, thank you for offering, but I doubt there's much you can do."

Skylark unbent from an impossible position. "We could go out and about today and just listen for gossip and report back."

The professor said, "We can call it 'research' if we have a research question to follow."

Before this got out of hand, I said, "Don't you have things to do with your two students who are sleeping yet upstairs?"

"That's it!" He rose to his feet, stretching, looking down on me. "Nova and Dax can go with us. We have to check in with the bookstore and other places where we'll be setting up our art tables for kids on Monday. I'll instruct Nova and Dax to listen around town. Active listening is a lost skill in society at times, and it's crucial for the marriage of art and community growth."

While rising to her feet, Skylark said, "Brilliant, Magnus. When I work with Habitat for Humanity, we always ask about the local culture and the dreams of the homeowner."

"Dreams and art--two ingredients for community growth," the professor crowed. "Oh, and we are to meet up with the snow sculptors today sometime, too."

I said, "I heard that Stella Zanderson is from Washington Island. Do you know the others?"

"Sadly, because of the storm we couldn't get here in time for the early-bird meeting at the Troubled Trout on Thursday. But it's a good thing we weren't there."

"Are you saying the artists were scheduled to be there, too?" I sat back on the sofa. "It wasn't just a casual thing for them?"

Magnus nodded. "Reece Allard--one of the artists--emailed me about the horrible morning. He said he slipped away before the sheriff showed up to question everybody."

"That's a little suspicious. Why wouldn't he stay to help with the investigation?"

"Reece's email said Usher and the owner of the mercantile got into some argument. Reece didn't want to implicate anybody, I guess."

"The owner is Travis Klubertanz."

"I remember him. Big guy. There's more. The email said Travis went outside, but then Usher took a swing at Reece. They ended up knocking glasses onto the floor. The owner threatened to bar Reece and Usher from the establishment. I guess both men left at that point."

I realized Erik hadn't told me everything about that morning. Why not? Was he protecting somebody? Was he guilty? I filed that away. Why was Reece Allard mad at Usher? Probably about the taxes. Or was something else amiss?

"Do you happen to know where Reece lives? Or where is studio is located?"

"Oh, yes," the professor said, stretching into a new pose. "He's east of this village, out on Highway F. He's a painter whose sunsets are beyond compare, but I gather nobody buys them at a price that will pay the rent."

I said, "The rumor is none of us will be able to afford to stay because of the new taxes."

From upstairs, the baby cried more loudly, making us pause.

Magnus tapped Skylark on the shoulder. "Let's head into the kitchen and hatch our strategies. And maybe we should look into whether Mister Westergaard was properly licensed by the State. Perhaps his assessments reflected his ineptitude."

This felt like the beginning of another disaster. Magnus had hatched pretty weird stuff last July to help me and he'd ended up in jail.

My two enthusiastic amateur-detective guests were walking through the dining room by the time I rose from the parlor sofa.

As I stepped into the foyer, young Nova descended the stairs with baby Henry in one arm. Nova's long brown hair was plaited in a braid that hung over one shoulder. She wore LL Bean hiking shoes and black leggings under a long, bulky-knit cream-colored turtleneck sweater.

"You're up already, Nova?" It was maybe around five o'clock.

"Henry was crying and I was awake anyway. So I knocked on Ellany's door to ask if I might help."

"That was very sweet of you."

"Ellany was crying, too." The girl peered at me with questioning eyes.

"I'm afraid I don't know much about her except there seemed to be some argument at home about she and her new husband living with his mother and the husband not doing much right now. Dillon found her as a squatter in a vacant house."

Nova switched the sleeping baby to her other arm.

I said, "Why don't you sit in the parlor where it's comfortable. If you need to get relief for your arms, lay him beside you on the sofa. He seems to like you."

Nova smiled down at Henry, a cherub inside his swaddling. Then she looked at me. "Who's Dillon?"

"Dillon Rivers. My..." The hesitation plagued me again. "Fiancé," I said, "new fiancé. I'm still not used to saying that."

As she walked away from me and into the parlor, Nova said, "I get it. Crushed on a guy myself, then had to crash the whole thing two weeks into college this last fall."

"Oh. But then you met that good-looking Dax?"

She sat on the blue sofa, then laid the baby next to her. "Dax? No. He's just a student I'm stuck with for this project. Professor Olsen pairs off students because we're supposed to learn to work together. It's part of our grade. No, I've given up on dating."

I grabbed a pillow and walked over to her. "Is this like going on a diet? It lasts a month and you're back to eating sugar again?" I tucked the pillow in front of the baby.

She giggled while patting the pillow. "No. For real. No more boyfriends until I graduate."

"That's a long time, about three-and-a-half years from now."

"Graduation is my priority. Ellany seems to be about my age and she didn't look very happy this morning. She looked tired, scared, and confused. If getting married and having a kid is that hard and scary, I sure can wait. It's hard enough just doing my course work."

Nova had a good sense of herself. I hoped Ellany would also find a way to figure out her life. Knowing one's self was hard. Didn't I know it!

I realized I wanted to skip dealing with Jeremy, who was in my kitchen early for some reason. It was best to get to the shop and begin my day.

I was almost out the door when I also realized I'd forgotten "the ring". I trotted past a curious Nova to my apartment to retrieve the precious jewelry. After slipping it on my left ring finger, it made me pause and think how devastated I'd be if Dillon were suddenly gone.

My heart bled for Hailey Westergaard.

Or should I be sadder for Stella Zanderson? Had she been crushing on Usher?

Was either woman jealous enough or angry enough to kill Usher so the other couldn't have him?

The world outside my front door at five-thirty on the cold winter's day made me pause on the verandah. The hush of winter snowfalls usually soothed me. Instead, a brittleness crackled in the air, almost a warning, like that a crow's incessant cawing.

Remembering the mystery box, I circled around the inn to the back. I stuffed the box in a pocket, then set off amid the snow squeaking under my boots.

I spied our newspaper carrier in the distance on Main Street. "Greta! Wait up! I want to ask you about something!"

What had she witnessed, if anything, on Thursday morning? Hadn't she, after all, opened the door of the bar-and-restaurant to leave the newspaper? She'd heard and seen something.

Chapter 17

Diamond Promises

Frost nipped the fake-fur trim around the hood of Greta's parka. She stamped her feet to keep warm in the freezing, dark morning. We met in front of the Klubertanz market. Greta wore her newspaper satchel with its strap crossing her front.

"Greta," I said, unsure how to broach my subject matter. "How are you?"

"Cold." Her blue eyes blinked above fog forming on the lower half of her eyeglasses.

I suspected she'd been about to duck into the market where Travis waited with hot coffee in his basement storage area. "Yeah, but it's going to be perfect for the snow sculptors and skiers, not to mention the holiday parade on Monday."

Greta perked up with a huge smile. "I'm taking photos for the Herald."

"I didn't know you were a photographer."

"I wasn't until now. I begged for a chance. This assignment is huge. I can let the world know how wonderful it is to live in Fishers' Harbor. Some people might scoff at 'quaintness', but not me!"

She was smiling so broadly that I thought she might melt the snow around us. I broke into a big grin. "This new gig is exciting for you and for the rest of us. Anything you can do to bring in more tourists and shoppers is fine with me."

"My photo credit should go wide beyond just our newspaper."

She referred to our daily, the Harbor Herald.

"That's great." I took a fortifying breath. "Are you as shook up as I am about what happened Thursday morning? I mean, right out here on our street of all places."

She hunched her shoulders in an obvious shiver, nodding. "I'm traumatized. Somehow I was only minutes behind the murder of that man. It could've been me left for dead."

"So you didn't see anybody?"

"No. I've heard there were tracks on the sidewalk heading out of town." She pointed behind her using a thumb over one shoulder.

"Yeah. You must have heard that from Jeremy Stone. He told me he was jogging early on Thursday morning and went past the car. It sounds like he may have gone past the crime scene around the time it happened. He ended up hiding in some bushes before my grandfather took the plow up the street."

Greta looked at me bug-eyed. "How do you know so much?"

"Jeremy's staying at the inn. We've had discussions. He said he jogged back north up the street and saw tracks going to where maybe somebody had parked a vehicle in the lot past Erik's restaurant. You didn't look that way or see anybody?"

"No. I was minding my own business and in a rush to ..." She flinched.

"To get inside here where it's warm." I indicated the market's door next to us. When she hesitated again, I said, "Travis told me there's nothing going on between you two."

Greta's shoulders relaxed. "It's just that by the time I walk a good five blocks from the Troubled Trout in this weather I'm freezing. Nobody else is open at five in the morning. Travis leaves his door open for deliveries."

"For you." I regretted saying the words. "Sorry. That didn't sound right. I spoke with Travis recently. He mentioned you and Logan..." I ended with a one-shoulder shrug.

Her mouth flinched. "Just a bump in the road. Listen, I need to go."

"Did Travis mention getting into some fight the morning Usher died?"

"Huh? What?" Greta appeared genuinely surprised. And intrigued.

"Probably had words about the taxes. I heard that Travis left before the fight got involved, but it seems one of the snow sculptors got into the battle, too."

"How horrible."

"Yeah. It's cold out here and I have to get to my shop." My toes were filling frosty. "If you give me my newspaper you won't have to cross the parking lot behind the buildings and waste more time in the cold. Go inside and get warm!"

"Thanks." She handed me a newspaper.

I hesitated to leave. "The sheriff questioned me. You, too?"

She nodded. "I told him the truth. I didn't see anything."

"Even inside Erik's front door when you left the newspaper? Were there men in there having Bloody Mary drinks and eating eggs and bacon? I heard about the breakfast club."

Greta blinked several times. I couldn't tell if she'd seen men or was just confused. "Gosh. I don't recall noticing any group. When I open Erik's door to toss the newspaper inside I'm in a hurry. Maybe I should take notes. I hadn't planned on writing for the newspaper, but..."

"Erik told me he thought he heard voices near the front door at one point."

"I usually holler 'hello'." She stamped her feet. "Aren't you freezing?"

"Yeah. Sorry." I waved the rolled-up newspaper in my hand. "Thanks. Good luck with the photos."

Greta beamed. "Thanks. I'm really excited."

I paused next door at the bookstore, pretending to look in the window. Greta slipped inside Travis's store. I chided myself, though, for being a snoop. Why should I care if Greta and Travis were having an affair? And then again, maybe they were both telling the truth. They were merely sharing coffee in this cold weather.

The thought of a coffee cup's heat in my hands set me off at a fast trot toward my shop and Grandpa's strong, chocolate-infused brew.

As I hustled through the cold, I thought about Greta's pride in taking photos of our weekend events. The snow sculpture blocks would appear along Main Street. The sound of laughter and joy would echo about.

Beneath the blanket of snow Fishers' Harbor was a special place. People cared about each other, had good hearts, enjoyed frolicking in winter, and were kind and welcoming to strangers. Something in my psyche about it, though, was niggling me. After Dillon and I married, would we just stay the same? Stay in place here? Dillon had lived in Las Vegas for a while, and I'd been in Los Angeles for ten years. Would we get the bug to go adventuring again? Sometimes I tired of all the work required of me with the shop and the inn, and even the responsibility of watching over Grandpa. Greta was so vibrant because of taking on her new gig. I could easily be jealous of her feeling so alive because of the change in her life.

I liked living in a quaint place, though. Greta would photograph the meaning of "quaint". We didn't apologize for liking quaint here. There'd be ice skating and pond hockey on Kangaroo Lake. There'd be cross-country skiing, and wreath-making at the nature center, and Christmas story hours for kids at the Kress Pavilion in Egg Harbor. Older adults would be doing creative arts at the retreat centers called The Clearing and Write On, Door County. Later in the season, for New Year's Eve, our big event happened in Sister Bay with the "Cherry Drop". It was like the crystal ball dropping in Times Square in New York City except we used a three-hundred-pound lighted cherry. I sold my cherry-vanilla Cinderella Pink Fairy Tale fudge at the event.

As much as I found reporter Jeremy Stone insufferable, I also felt pride that my village intrigued him enough to lure him back repeatedly.

Through their photos and chats with townspeople this weekend, Jeremy and Greta could possibly solve the evil lurking in our midst. Journalists did that sort of thing routinely.

I thought again about the tracks that led to the possible vehicle parked a few blocks away from the crime scene. The killer could be a stranger to the village who merely drove away. If a stranger, the killer still had to have known Westergaard. He had been targeted. There was an intimacy in following somebody to his car at five or so in the morning and plunging a knife into his belly.

Why his belly? Was there significance to that? Why not his heart? Or neck? Or face? I was sure the sheriff must be asking the same questions.

The killer had to be somebody close to Westergaard because the choice of time and place seemed significant. Did Westergaard's wife have a lover and he--or she--murdered our village assessor? What about Travis, the mercantile owner? He left the Troubled Trout moments before Usher was stabbed, a possible fact the sheriff didn't yet know if nobody mentioned it to him.

Chills rippled over me by the time I went through the shop's back door.

Then I smiled.

The mouth-watering, sugar-coated air always buoyed me--like a hug. This was home to my heart and soul. No way was I going to lose this shop to some ridiculous assessment hike. I'd fight it. My shop lived with sweetness and cheer, its interior rinsed in rainbow colors, and it sported handmade gifts from the town's ladies. The colorful fishing equipment, too, made memories for kids and their parents out on the Door County waterways and Lake Michigan. I'd do anything to save this shop. Though I wouldn't kill a tax assessor.

Oosterlings' was now famous enough for my fudge--with lots of Belgian chocolate--chocolate being a universal symbol of love.

My mind gravitated toward a love triangle being the motive for murder. I vowed to visit Hailey Westergaard today. Curiosity was killing me.

As I hung my coat and sweater over hooks in the back hallway I heard metallic clink-clank, clink-clank.

With newspaper in hand, I went to the front. I laid down the newspaper on my clean counter and then threw on a Cinderella Pink Fairy Tale Fudge bib apron over my white shirt and blue jeans.

Grandpa had several coffee cans sitting on his register counter. He filched through one can filled with screws.

"Morning, Grandpa. You're like a kid getting all dirty just as soon as you're turned loose."

"Bah. This is only a little oil and rust. The iron is good for you."

Grandpa wore a black-and-white checked flannel shirt and denim jeans that sagged a bit in the butt. The clothing wouldn't stay clean long. His gray hair already stood in stiff peaks from greasy hands running through it.

A half-empty cup of coffee sat next to the coffee cans. I breezed by him, picking up the cup to re-fill for him. After setting down his cup next to him, I returned to fill a cup for myself. The chocolate-cherry brew warmed me all the way to my toes.

I asked, "What are you doing?"

"Al called. Said the guy with the sleigh for Monday brought the thing to the village's garage okay yesterday, but Al says it's in poor shape."

"So Saint Nicholas is going to fix it?"

"He sure is. That's me. Al says it's got a few rusted screws I can replace around the decorative framework. The wheel hubs need paint, too."

"So this is the same fiberglass float built around the old VW Beetle you used last year?"

"We're repairing the big fiberglass sack built out of that back seat for toys and candy."

"How so?" I loved these quiet moments with Grandpa. I sometimes resented when my work had to begin, even if my day was about making candy.

"I got one of the shipyards down in Sturgeon Bay to repair all the plastic and fiberglass cracks. They're making the sack a little bigger. That big fake sack is going to be strong enough to practically hold you and me and a good six other skinny people."

"But of course it's going to be stuffed with bags filled with balloons and candy to toss out for the kids. I heard the church ladies are making up the bags."

"You bet. Five hundred of those bags."

"Seems like our Saint Nicholas celebration gets bigger every year. I'll be sure Greta knows you're working on the sleigh at the town garage. She's taking photos for the first time for media usage. She's pretty excited."

"Tell that snoopy Stone fella to come by, too. Maybe he and Greta can scare up business for us with their free publicity. We can't pay a lawyer to fight our new assessment."

He plunked six screws the size of his fingers onto the counter. I grimaced at the probable oily spots that would remain. Cody was forever cleaning Grandpa's counter with grease-dissolving detergent. I thought about telling him to use the newspaper, but then thought better of it. I hadn't read the paper yet.

As I headed to my side of the shop, I asked, "Have you tried on your outfit yet?"

"Your grandma is taking care of the Saint Nicholas outfit. She complained about the sleeves being too long. She says I have to look 'kingly' more than 'saintly'. She says I'll never be a saint. Hah!"

Laughing, I picked up my checklist to go over the contents of the glass cases. "You should see Grandma fussing over that costume I'm supposed to wear in Pauline's wedding. Sheesh. I swear that dress looks like some curtain stolen from a museum."

He rattled coffee tins. "Wait until she makes your wedding dress."

I dropped my pen and pad on the floor with a clunk.

Grandpa laughed. "What's a matter?"

"The mention of a dress. I embarrassed everybody the last time I wore one."

"Well, heck, last time you didn't even get inside the church before you ran off, so nobody saw the white dress. How's Sam doing these days anyway?"

Leaving Sam Peterson behind outside the church and taking off with Dillon happened twelve years ago. A different "me" had done that. An immature one. I peeked at my engagement diamond. And smiled.

"I don't see Sam much, but he's forgiven me. He and Jane seem pretty tight these days."

Grandpa walked to me with a grin. He touched the tip of my nose with one finger. "Life hands us all kinds of adventures. Go with the flow and keep grinning. None of what you did so long ago was a mistake. It was only a learning experience, a turning point. We all have them. Did your mom ever tell you how she met your dad? He gave her a bloody nose."

"What?!" I shook my head, eager to hear this. I put my pen and pad aside.

Grandpa wiped at his hands on a rag while he leaned back against his counter. "Your mother went to a kermiss the fall they met." A "kermiss" is the term Belgians use for their fall harvest festival; it's a traditional word straight out of Belgium. "It was on a farm and there was a dance.

131

Peter opened the big barn door too fast and hit your mother smack in the face. She literally fell for him."

"Why didn't she tell me about this?"

Grandpa shrugged, eyes twinkling. "If she'd told you this when you were a kid, it'd be all over school and eventually embarrass your father."

"So she kept it from me and my big mouth." I smiled. "Out of love."

"Some things stay between a husband and wife." Grandpa nodded, staring at the rag in his hands. "Honey, that's what love does--it puts aside and ignores things that aren't worth poetry. Time marches on. Nobody cares now about a dozen years ago."

I wrapped my arms around him, squeezing tight. He smelled of toast and bacon from his breakfast, and of a little bit of oil and grease--all of it comforting. "Thanks, Grandpa. Dillon and I are going to work out. And we're going to make sure you don't end up arrested for something you didn't do."

Grandpa waved my words off as he returned to his bolts and screws. "Gossip making the rounds already is that Erik's chef killed Usher."

"Piers Molinsky? Why?" I tried to recall my conversation with Piers. Nothing of significance came to mind except he thought Usher had stayed overnight in the restaurant. "Piers is a good person. He wants to open up a muffin bakery. We could use one on Main Street."

"If rents around here go sky high, then entrepreneurs like him can't get a start. People are saying that when he found Usher sleeping in the restaurant in the morning, Piers grabbed a knife off the table and chased him down."

That shocked me. "I thought I was the only one he told about Usher possibly sleeping in the restaurant."

Grandpa shrugged, laying aside a screw.

"Because Piers is a chef or cook, he wears plastic gloves. Thus, no fingerprints from him on the knife that people think you used because of your prints. That's what they're saying?"

"That's the size of it."

Wow. Piers a killer?

I paced to the front door and noticed the pan for the elves outside, empty. It reminded me that I'd picked up a small box again from the inn's back door and had left it in my coat pocket.

Outdoors now held sunrise's blush. The fish clock overhead said it was past bass, or six. "I need to make fudge to clear my head. There's no way Piers would've of killed that man."

"He was a murder suspect in this town a while back."

"He was cleared, Grandpa."

I brought in the empty pan, then headed toward the back when Grandpa said, "You've got a spot of grease on your nose from my fingers nipping at your nose."

Somehow being sullied felt like a metaphor for Fishers' Harbor.

After retrieving the gift box from my coat pocket, I went into the kitchen where I sat at the table. This box held a small, painted egg--a colorful rendition of a stained-glass window pattern. A ribbon glued on made it an ornament ready for the holiday tree.

Who was doing this? I wanted to thank them. And WHY were they gifting me? Had I done something in the past few months that warranted these gifts? I couldn't think of a thing.

About three hours later, just as I was about to unlock the front door at nine o'clock--or "perch", Lucky Harbor bounded up with a pal-- Queenie, Mercy's golden retriever.

Mercy did not like it when Queenie ran away. In the past Mercy had accused Lucky Harbor--and me--of encouraging the forays. Queenie was expecting puppies in the spring, so I knew Mercy would be upset if I lingered even one minute in returning her dog.

Grandpa said he'd cover for me.

With dread I grabbed leashes, threw on my coat, and took the dogs out the back door.

Chapter 18

Fogg Trouble

I arrived at Mercy's home on her back street in my second-hand, battle-gray SUV with the hissing, bad defroster fogging up my windshield. Mercy loved to drive and appreciated good vehicles, just as I did. Oh how I wished I had pulled up in a sleek, shiny new racecar to make her jealous. Alas, she met me at my piece-of-junk's door.

I rolled down the window.

She said, "You just missed that journalist staying with you. He thinks I killed Westergaard." Her plump face was red. "Did you concoct that theory to throw the suspicion off your grandfather? I can sue you for defamation of character!"

Hmm. That didn't seem friendly. I mulled over what to do.

Mercy stomped, crunching the snow. She wore a reflective yellow vest over a parka that made her look bigger than her normal muscular self.

"Well?" She flipped back the parka hood. Frizzy blond curls stood up from static electricity.

She hated silence, so I didn't say a word. Competitiveness is a fault of mine, but her rudeness wasn't nice. To spite her, I got out and then opened the SUV's back door to let both dogs go. They zipped off in the direction opposite of Mercy's house.

Mercy screamed, "What the hell?! Get them back here!"

While driving away over snow-packed back streets I focused on the pleasantness of drumming up fun holiday fudge recipes. Instead of returning to the shop, though, I veered into another route through the back streets until I parked in front of the Mertens' house.

Nobody answered the doorbell. Coletta had to be at the inn already making beds and helping my guests. It was nine-thirty.

Back in the SUV, I called my bestie. "Pauline, where are you?"

"At our house."

"I'm at your house and you're not there."

"I meant the house that John bought!"

After selling a public television series about Wisconsin several months ago John had bought what I called a mansion. It had room for a small studio and office for his production business. Situated just outside the village, the property included a pool, and three-car garage, a stable, and a beautiful pasture with a white board fence.

"So you're doing what now at the house?"

She squealed like one of her kindergarten students. "I have to buy furniture!"

"John has furniture. He has a house here in town. Aren't you just moving that furniture?"

"He's selling everything, starting fresh. Be happy for me."

I laughed. "I am. Of course you need new furniture. That's what I'll get you for a wedding present, furniture that comes in a big box and you have to put it together yourself."

"Don't you dare. All I want from you is your presence at my wedding."

"If I have to wear that heavy velveteen dress, my sacrifice is enough of a gift."

"You're wearing the dress, Ava Mathilde Oosterling. Now, you called me. What's up?"

"I need you to come with me to talk with Hailey. She had every reason to murder her husband."

Silence met me.

I tried again, "Pauline, we owe her a visit. We were the last ones to see her husband alive. We'll just pay our respects."

"Of course not. You love helping the sheriff."

"Pauline, it's not about me helping Jordy."

"Then it must be Stone who put you up to this."

Why are best friends so aggravating at times? "This is about me, Pauline, who I am, what my gut says. I have this really strong feeling Hailey has to know something valuable."

"Oof-duh."

"If you come with me you can tell me all about the new furniture you're buying for that fancy mansion."

"You're jealous?"

"Of course. Now, are you coming with me? You can show me photos of furniture while I try to drive on icy roads and not guffaw at your awful choices."

She laughed. "Phone hug back at you. See you soon."

Before picking up Pauline, I checked in with my guests at the inn.

Ellany was breastfeeding her baby alone at the dining room table. Skylark and Magnus had left with students Dax and Nova to finalize details about their art carts. Jeremy had left, too. I recalled Mercy had said Jeremy accused her of murdering Usher. Mercy had likely made up Jeremy's accusation. A professional reporter wouldn't make accusations, or at least unfounded ones.

For Hailey I put together a basket of baked goods and fudge from the kitchen larder.

As I headed into the foyer with the basket, Pauline's mother Coletta descended the stairs with a bucket filled with cleaning supplies. Her smile warmed my heart. With the upcoming wedding for her daughter, Coletta sparkled like a sassy elf. Her dark pixie haircut seemed particularly cute today in the way it framed her large, dark eyes Pauline had inherited.

She said, "Is it okay if I'm not coming back later today to vacuum? I hate to do this to you, but Erik said that he wasn't allowed to clean the Troubled Trout until the cops went over it, and he needs a cleaning lady this afternoon. The sheriff is letting him open for tonight's usual Saturday dinner specials of prime rib and white fish."

Dillon and I loved those Wisconsin supper club specials. "Of course, Coletta." I hadn't realized the Troubled Trout had been closed. What had the sheriff had found?

Ellany called from the dining room, "I can vacuum after I put Henry down."

I said, "Thank you, Ellany."

With my hand on the front doorknob, I turned back. "Coletta, have you heard anything about Piers being a suspect?"

She nodded. "Stone was blabbing about it over the breakfast table to all your guests. He said something about hunting down all the men who were at the bar on Thursday morning. He evidently questioned Piers and Erik, maybe stopped by the bar this morning?"

"Probably while on his early morning runs."

"He was still in his running outfit at breakfast."

"Did Jeremy say who all was there this morning at the Troubled Trout?"

"Nope."

Piers hadn't said anything to me about the people in the bar on Thursday morning. There was mention of maybe Usher sleeping overnight there, though. Had men been in the back room overflow dining room? It had a door to the back party patio and to the lake inlet and beach. I partied there when Pauline celebrated her engagement last July. Somebody could easily slip out after committing a crime.

What I knew flapped in my brain like laundry items pinned to Grandma's clothesline and coming undone in a storm.

Erik had told me he'd picked up Usher's steak knife on Wednesday night because Usher had been arguing with other customers. Who were they?

Also, Jeremy had seen Erik looking out the front door on Thursday morning. Erik told me he thought he heard a voice and peeked out the door after retrieving his newspaper. Could it be that Erik had been checking to see if anybody saw him chase outside to kill Usher? I didn't believe that, though I had to stay open to possibilities. Did Erik cover for somebody? What about that fight between Usher and the artist, Reece Allard? Did Erik cover for Reece?

Erik said he'd been in the kitchen.

The key seemed to be Usher either sleeping overnight in the Troubled Trout or crashing the breakfast club.

By now, Jeremy had probably visited all the businesses along Main Street asking questions. So, it was foolish of me to follow in his footsteps. I'd pin down Stone later.

Minutes later, I picked up Pauline at the mansion. The small estate sat four miles southeast of Fishers' Harbor, on Sunflower Road.

John's van was parked ahead of my SUV in the semi-circular driveway in front of the stone-and-cedar manse. Pauline didn't have a vehicle yet. I'd give anything for a new vehicle myself. The defroster in my SUV buzzed and whirred, mocking my thoughts, reminding me to give the dashboard a whack with my fist.

Pauline climbed in with glittering eyes.

"You look nice, Pauline."

"Thanks." She settled in, clicking on the belt, and then wrestled with the red purse the size of a pony. Pauline wore a new tailored camel-hair tan coat and brown riding-style boots.

She hadn't had much as a kid. I'd shared clothes with her. Mom and Grandma made clothes for her, too, when she lived with us weeks at a time. When her alcoholic, abusive father abandoned his family and left the state, it was a relief. Pauline's sister Lucie also left the minute she graduated high school. Pauline deserved every new piece of clothing and bauble and makeup she could afford. She loved lipstick and wore a bright red variety today.

I was dressed in my usual white shirt and red sweater, a parka, jeans, and my work shoes that could handle snow and ice. No lipstick. The usual ponytail held back my hair.

We poked along on snowy Sunflower Road. I turned back onto Highway 42. We headed north through Fishers' Harbor.

After leaving the village, Pauline dug around in her purse. She brought out her phone, bringing up a photo she tried to show me.

"I'm driving, Pauline."

"Just take a quick look."

"I see a red sofa."

She lowered the phone. "John and I agreed to get a red sofa. I love red."

"Yeah. My dress for your wedding is red."

"So Christmasy. Red stands for love. Remember, we wanted to get matching red cars."

"That was last summer. A lot has happened since then. And I can't afford a new vehicle." The SUV rattled then, as if objecting to me trading it for something new.

"But, Ava, I'm getting married. You're engaged. Think creatively, with cushy leather, crisp lines, crimson color, and conquest of the country roads."

"Too much alliteration and dollar signs, Pauline." Her kindergarten kids loved her alliteration but right now it irritated me. My bank account was poor and she was mocking me.

"Come on, best friends forever do stuff like buying matching cars."

"No, they don't. Especially if the budget doesn't stretch that far."

"We promised. Let's at least plan for our new vehicles. It'll be fun to make a list."

"Of what?"

"You are being dense. Lists of the types of cars that come in a convertible style, and lists of amenities we must have on our cars, lists of dealerships to visit for test drives. We could even make this a trip to the capital, make a week of it. I'll make a list of things we can do in Madison, like visit the capitol and go next door for a show at the Overture Center. Or, we could just ask Santa to bring us each a new car."

"Santa's sleigh is not big enough for cars."

"Then Santa needs a bigger sleigh because a red car is on my wish list." She laughed. "Maybe your grandfather's big sleigh on Monday can fit a couple of cars in it?"

"Sounds like it's big enough according to him. That reminds me, I need to tell Greta and Jeremy it's at the town garage and they can take photos of it."

"Greta? Our newspaper delivery woman?"

"She's excited. The Herald is letting her submit photos for publication."

"That's nice of them. She's delivered newspapers for something like ten years. I'll text Greta and Jeremy now. You have their numbers?"

"On my phone."

She grabbed my phone from the holder and went to work. "There, texted them." She put the phone back. "Now, more important things. My car has to have a back seat."

I got the feeling she didn't want to talk about our destination and the widow. "Why must it have a back seat? A lot of sporty cars don't have a back seat or not much of one."

She went quiet on me. I glanced over. She was looking out the window, hiding from me.

"Pauline?"

Finally, she withdrew a tissue from her purse.

"What's the matter, Pauline?"

"I want a back seat so my sister can ride with us." She sniffled. "She's not coming to my wedding, I just know it."

"You don't know that."

"We've emailed, texted her number, and nothing. She doesn't want to come back here. The memories are bad. My damn father ruined things. He ruined our family."

Her sadness weighed me down. I wanted to hug her but had to focus on the icy patches on the road. "Pauline, she'll be in touch soon, I'm sure."

"She's not replying because she doesn't want to come back."

"She could be using new addresses for everything. Maybe we're using the wrong email addresses and phone number. We'll keep looking."

Pauline's sigh was noisier than the SUV's defroster. "Will you please stop trying to be so supportive?" She honked into her tissue. "But thanks."

"It's my job."

"You're the best non-sister sister a person can have."

"You're always going to be my sister." I sniffled a bit myself, then for Pauline's sake plastered on a big smile. "So we'll get matching convertibles with a back seat. What else do we put on the list? I'd like glow-in-the-dark and lighted hubcaps."

Pauline laughed. We recovered and avoided the serious topics by working on our convertible list until the road descended into the bay area before the village of Ephraim.

I spotted a yellow house up ahead--the Westergaard residence.

Chapter 19

The List

P auline and I parked in a cleared driveway the length of two vehicles. Snow cleanup had been so perfect that even decorative rocks the size of small melons along the driveway had been purged of snow.

Pauline commented, "I'm neat, but even I wouldn't bother cleaning rocks. A few are missing."

"Whoever plowed shoved a few back into the snow probably."

Small talk came with our nerves. Incongruent with the winter, yellow, plastic roses and daisies in flower boxes lined the porch railing.

With strain on her face, Hailey Westergaard welcomed us into a warm, quiet house. Heat vents pinged from the furnace turning on from somewhere in the basement. Sunlight streaming through a living room window planted a square of light across maple flooring.

Hailey was maybe only a little older than Pauline and me, mid-thirties. Her straight, blond hair in a blunt cut accentuated a heart-shaped face and sharp chin. She wore a pink leotard and black sweatpants and socks. A sheen of sweat reflected light off her forehead.

I handed her the basket of baked goods and fudge. "We're sorry for your loss, Mrs. Westergaard."

"Call me Hailey, please." She peeked under the paper Christmas napkins and plates. "Your famous fudge. Thank you. My...husband liked your fudge." Her forehead wrinkled. "He didn't like your grandfather."

She obviously knew about Gilpa's fingerprints on the knife. "I'm sorry. My grandfather would never harm anyone."

Hailey stood like a statue, staring down at the basket.

An awkward silence engulfed us.

Pauline said, "It's got to be hard being a tax assessor."

Hailey said, "Try being the tax assessor's wife."

She strutted to the open kitchen with a large white island. "Please sit down."

We followed, keeping our coats on to make it easier for a fast getaway.

After setting down the basket and facing us on the other side of the island, she said, "Nobody liked Usher. All he got were complaints. And that's all I heard, too."

I thought she might start crying but she went on. "People didn't say 'hi' to me on the street anymore since he took on the assessor job. It was more like, 'Tell your husband to go back to school so he can learn to add correctly.' Do you know how many exams he had to pass to get his license? Never mind."

"We're very sorry," I said.

Hailey retrieved a pitcher of orange juice from the refrigerator. "Want some?"

"Sure," I said, curious where this conversation might go.

Pauline and I removed our coats and slung them onto the backs of the stools.

Hailey poured the juice and then settled onto her stool. "Thank you for stopping by. You're the first people to bother coming to my door."

She grabbed a tissue from a nearby box. I didn't see any tears though. Hailey said, "My husband was afraid of your grandfather."

That stunned me. "Why?"

"Usher said Gilsen threatened him. Said he'd toss him in the lake if he didn't change the valuation of Oosterlings' bait-and-fudge shop."

"That was just talk."

"Not according to Usher." She sipped her juice, eyes casting about like a rabbit contemplating an escape.

"I apologize for my grandpa. I'm so sorry."

Hailey started shredding the tissue in her hands. "Doesn't matter now, does it? People will say my husband got what he deserved. When I've left everybody will say 'good riddance'."

"No, no we won't."

Pauline asked, "Are you moving away?"

Hailey nodded. "Heading to Miami."

I said, "At this time of year, Florida is a good place."

Pauline added, "A lot of Wisconsin snowbirds winter there."

"Smart," Hailey said. "My husband was from New Orleans, where weather is decent in winter. But he insisted on us moving to Door County after we vacationed here once. I went along with it because it's so darn beautiful in summer and fall, but look how my vote turned out?"

Her gaze dropped to the shredded tissue, then clasped her glass with both hands.

Again, silence crawled through the kitchen like a dangerous animal.

A shiver overwhelmed me and I wished I'd kept my parka on. "What will you do in Miami?"

She offered a weak smile. "Swimsuit modeling. It's tough around here to take photos in winter that sell a bikini. I'm an online influencer."

Pauline asked, "How long have you been in Door County?"

Hailey gave another shoulder-lifting shiver. "Five years. We moved around in rentals while Usher finished his certification with the Wisconsin Department of Revenue. At first, I thought that was a quickie thing, and then we'd leave. But there are five levels of certification for tax assessors and he wanted to earn them all." Her voice had risen.

Pauline said, "I'm a teacher. I know all about licensing. You must have been proud of your husband."

Hailey nodded. "Thanks. But the more he studied every burg in this county, the more he wanted to stay. He raved about the eleven lighthouses, the parks, and the cool cave with the underground river. He'd go on and on."

I said, "People come here from all across the country and from around the world to vacation. Many end up buying property. They also drive up prices on real estate at times, but that's why your husband was needed."

Pauline said, "And he liked his profession."

Pain shrouded Hailey's eyes. "Liked? He was obsessed. He was studying for another license when he died, the CAE, the Certified Assessment Evaluator."

"What's that?" Pauline asked.

"A professional designation from the Association of Assessing Officers." She grabbed another tissue from the nearby box.

I said, "You loved him."

Hailey went quiet. She finished her orange juice. "I just wished things had turned out differently."

"So do we, Hailey." I rose. "We should go. I'm so sorry for your loss."

Pauline said, "Very sorry. He was a good man."

Hailey nodded but didn't otherwise move.

I realized I hadn't gotten what I came for, so I asked, "Do you have any idea who might have ended your husband's life?"

"I told the sheriff the entire county, but he didn't think that was helpful."

Hailey went to her counter where mail sat. She filched about in the pile, withdrew a large piece of notebook paper, then handed it to me. There were eight names on it, including my grandfather's name.

Unease hit my stomach. "What's this?"

"Usher kept a list of people who complained the loudest about their assessments because he suspected they would appear at the meetings or sue him, or..."

Or worse, she probably was going to say. "You gave a copy of this to the sheriff?"

She shook her head. "I only just found it this morning. I've been cleaning drawers."

There were only names on the paper, no notes. I handed it to Pauline and said to Hailey, "How can you be sure this is the list of people he was afraid of?"

"Because we argued about it." She covered her face for a moment. "I feel horrible. I yelled at him that we should have moved away long ago, and now he had people who were wanting to sue him."

My grandfather's name was on the list. "Where did Grandpa and Usher meet to talk about assessments? Here in your house?"

"No. I never let Usher meet property owners here, or others. I knew the meetings could be contentious sometimes. Usher met people, especially women, at the Troubled Trout in Fishers' Harbor."

A corner of her mouth twitched. She took back the piece of paper and turned away.

"You said 'especially women'. What do you mean?"

"At first I was excited about the artists that my husband met across the county. Art is my thing. Bright colors. But I don't think Stella Zanderson was meeting with those men or my husband in the mornings recently just to figure out the snow sculpting logistics for this weekend."

Back on the road, it only took a minute before Pauline said, "Do you believe she did in her husband because he was having an affair?"

Chapter 20

Questionable Value

As I drove us back to Fishers' Harbor I mulled Pauline's question. An affair is a classic reason for murdering a husband. Sometimes things in life are that simple. If you watch a lot of television cop shows.

I concluded "yes" to the "possibility" only of Hailey "offing" her husband. There was no proof and the woman hadn't confessed, though she'd come close to doing that during our visit.

Hailey disliked her husband's job and its grief. She disliked winters that stymied her influencer career. She suspected her husband's affair, but didn't offer proof. A mere meeting with the artist didn't amount to an affair.

My suspicion alone didn't automatically make Hailey a murderer either. Just like Grandpa's fingerprints on a steak knife didn't make him guilty. And yet...

Something about the things Hailey revealed kept knocking at the back of my brain.

Pauline said, "Maybe having everybody in the community complaining about her husband was the last straw. If you can't be proud of your own husband, what is left to love?"

"So the scenario on Thursday morning, perhaps at four or going on five o'clock, would be her waking up to find no husband home, then getting in her vehicle, and knowing he'd be at the meeting, Hailey merely waited for him to get in his car before she stabbed him. She ran like hell to her vehicle parked down the street and left. But when and how did she get the knife without being seen?"

Pauline said, "She swiped your grandfather's knife from the restaurant the night before, being careful to take anything other than her own. She may have switched knives somehow."

I'd already thought about this knife-switch scenario. It was possible. Hailey had become a prime suspect in my mind.

Once back in Fishers' Harbor, at around eleven o'clock, Main Street and our sidewalks were a riot of color, mobbed with shoppers. Every parking space was taken. The company that created bigger snow blocks for the snow carving contest had delivered five of them. White snow boxes stood along the street terraces. Each massive block of packed snow was about six feet tall and six feet in length and depth. By tomorrow and Monday's parade day, local residents would be invited to use garbage tubs to pack their own snow, too, and create whatever they liked. The whole affair had been the idea of Grandma's street beautification committee.

Because the professional snow sculptors were all supposedly at the fateful Thursday morning meeting, I gave the three extra scrutiny: Reece Allard, and a young guy from Sturgeon Bay south of us by the name of Buck Ingersoll, and finally, Stella Zanderson. All smiled while explaining their techniques to passersby.

As Pauline and I puttered along at a snail's pace in the traffic, we spotted Professor Olsen. He appeared to be showing a child how to create some artful thing using pages he ripped from a thick book. Re-using books thrilled him; he said words lived and felt the art themselves.

The professor's college student, Dax, stood on the next block handing out paper holiday bags with art supplies to children and adults. I didn't see Nova.

Near the end of the street and close to Travis's market, I turned into the alley to the harbor parking lot. Vehicles filled the place but my reserved spot remained available in front of Oosterlings' Live Bait, Bobbers & Belgian Fudge & Beer.

Pauline marveled at my shop's crowd. We could barely squeeze around customers loading up with fudge and fairy tale fudge-themed items, and fishing gear. Nova Cervantes stood in front of the long glass case, with Cody opposite her behind the case wearing a crooked grin. After Nova pointed, Cody nestled fudge into a white bag.

He spotted me suddenly, turning red enough to cancel out his freckles. "It's the fudge lady! Hi, Miss Oosterling!"

Several echoed "Hi, Miss Oosterling!" and some called out "Happy holidays, Ava!"

Others approached Pauline, thanking her for teaching kindergarten and congratulating her on her upcoming wedding. A couple of past students slung their arms around her legs, cooing, "Miss Mertens, guess what I want for Christmas?"

Their answers varied from "pony" or "puppy" to the latest electronic toys and gadgets.

With the "puppy" request I thought about Lucky Harbor and Queenie. What had become of them this morning? I called Dillon. He said he was on his way back from Sister Bay and would cruise the backstreets until finding the dogs.

The crowd waned a bit over the lunch hour.

John arrived to pick up Pauline. He came into the shop in a hibiscus-flowered tropical shirt over a red turtleneck. He wore a green stocking hat, and tan pants with green socks inside his hiking sandals.

"You like my Christmas spirit, Ava? Red and green?" He spread his arms wide.

I laughed. "John, you look like Santa's head elf."

When I had first met John, I couldn't see him and Pauline as a match. She was tall and he was short. He loved crazy clothes; Pauline went for conservative glamour. I soon admitted opposites can attract. John spread fun wherever he went. Just like Pauline.

His television audience loved his stories about Wisconsin lore as varied as where to find a giant ball of string as big as a car, to giant prehistoric beaver skeletons. The nation's most complete mastodon skeleton had been unearthed in our state, a story John was proud of, too.

Before John left with Pauline, I called to him, "Be sure to come back at two o'clock when kids will be making Christmas Elf Fudge. We're also going to sponsor an elf hunt. Bring the cameras!"

John hooted. "There you go again looking for free advertising! Wouldn't miss it!"

My two friends left to the happy cowbells clanking on the door.

Cody was finishing ringing up Nova's fudge purchase. The giant bag impressed me.

I asked, "Nova, did you just finish all of your Christmas shopping in one bag?"

With a giggle, she shook her head. "Some is for Ellany and some for your maid."

"That's very sweet."

Cody cackled. "Of course it is, Miss Oosterling. It's fudge! Fudge is sweet!"

Customers laughed in the line behind Nova.

After Nova left, Cody trotted over to help Grandpa with a customer. I finished ringing up more sales as the sheriff walked through the door.

Jordy didn't remove his official-insignia stocking cap, but he made a show of taking off his aviator-style sunglasses.

Off to my right, my vision caught Grandpa ducking into hiding behind a shelving unit, abandoning his poor customer--a man with a little boy. Good thing Cody had hustled over.

When the sheriff saw the little boy coming with his dad to the counter, Jordy softened, smiled and knelt down. He held out a hand. "I'm Sheriff Tollefson. What's your name?"

"Cade."

They shook hands.

"Looks like you want some front teeth for Christmas," Jordy said.

"No, sir. I want a drone, a train set, and a kitten. I already got five dollars for my teeth. I'm using the money to buy this new reel." He held out his purchase.

"The fish won't have a chance." Jordy stood and shook hands with the dad.

After the dad and child left, I said, "Let's go back to the kitchen to talk. I have something to tell you."

"I'm looking for your grandfather."

"He's not here at the moment." I dared not blink. My dad said I inherited a liar's prowess from Grandpa. "I'm expecting a crowd later when the kids and parents come back for the elf hunt and fudge making, so we should talk now."

154

He relented.

We soon settled into the two chairs at the small square table in the kitchen. "I found out something about Hailey Westergaard."

Jordy popped off his stocking hat, then set it aside. He unzipped his coat but didn't remove it. "What's this about Mrs. Westergaard?"

"She might be hiding something."

He sat back with surprise raising his eyebrows. "Like what?"

"I don't know yet. When Pauline and I were with her, she was edgy and yet oddly at peace, and she didn't cry. I think she tried to cry. She reached for tissues a couple of times, but nothing much came of it."

"If she's in shock, maybe she wouldn't cry. Not everybody cries when mourning."

"She told us nobody liked her husband, and she didn't like that."

"She said that? She 'didn't like that'?"

I nodded. "She told us about wanting to move to Miami to be a swimsuit model. She wants to leave Door County. Her husband refused evidently."

He took out a notebook and wrote. "Maybe you could talk to your grandfather like you did with Mrs. Westergaard and report back to me."

I gaped at Jordy. "Why?"

"There's something he's not telling me."

This made me nervous because there was something Grandpa wasn't telling me either concerning his wish to move. Egads, he was just like Hailey! Both wanting to escape?

Jordy leaned toward me, eyes potent as an intimidating wolf's. "He was up early in the dark this past Thursday morning and what does he think to do? Steal a snowplow. And he covers up a car with a dead man inside."

The kitchen air seemed hotter suddenly. "Because of Mercy Fogg. He wanted to teach her a lesson about snapping off his mailbox."

Jordy sat back. His leather holster squeaked. "Al Kvalheim tells me your grandfather had stopped by the Troubled Trout before hopping into the driver's seat of that snowplow."

No surprise. I had gathered that had occurred from my own questioning of people. I let Jordy go on.

"When I told Al he could lose his government job here in Fishers' Harbor if he didn't come forth with a little more information, Al saw the light."

Stunned by this usage of pressure tactics by Jordy, I kept silent.

Jordy poked the table while he leaned his face toward me. "Listen, Ava, there were a bunch of people at that bar early in the morning. Real early. It was a real important meeting about the weekend hoopla you got going on now."

Giving in, I withdrew a piece of paper from a pocket and set it on the table. "Here. Yes, my grandfather might have been there."

The eight names included my grandfather's. "Who gave you these names? Erik? Piers?"

"Hailey Westergaard. That's not her handwriting, by the way. That's Pauline's. When we were at Hailey's, she showed us a paper she'd found in a desk drawer. Her husband made a list of people he was afraid might sue him if he changed their real estate valuations too much. I think Hailey believes they were all at the bar on Thursday morning."

Jordy read aloud: "Gilsen Oosterling, Al Kvalheim, Spuds Schlimgen, Boyd Earlywine, and Mercy Fogg, and the artists Stella Zanderson, Reece Allard, and Buck Ingersoll. Plus, I know Erik and Piers were there."

He mulled for a moment, then went on. "What the hell is Mercy worried about with that strange house of hers? She'd have to be glad somebody raised the valuation of that thing."

"Mercy's mad because her house value went down, probably by quite a bit."

"Down? Who the hell doesn't like taxes going down? Huh. Why is she mad about that?"

"The only reason I can think of is she wants to sell and get more money out of it."

Jordy nodded. "Who's Spuds?"

"Been around a while. Erik told me in the past that Spuds stops by for a beer a lot at the Troubled Trout. Spuds mows the grass at area golf courses. He's not likely to have much to do in winter, so he shows up at the breakfast club."

"Breakfast club? Meaning early morning eggs with a beer?"

"So you know about such things."

Jordy grunted. "Common enough. For men, anyway, especially those with early-morning jobs. There's a bar or two in other counties that show porn on the televisions with the eggs and bacon. I don't stand for that here in Door County."

"Thank you for that."

"Who's Boyd Earlywine?"

"When I returned to Fishers' Harbor a couple of years ago, he and his wife were staying at the Blue Heron Inn. I wasn't the innkeeper then. You remember, I'm sure."

"A homicide involving your fudge and diamonds."

"Boyd is a history professor. He researches early Great Lakes shipping and lost treasure in Lake Michigan. I didn't know he owned property here."

"I remember him now. In his forties. Sandy-colored hair. Serious." Jordy stared at the names for a long time. He tapped the paper. "A woman?"

"Stella is one of the snow sculptors. Hailey feels she was having an affair with Usher."

Jordy jotted in his notepad. "Did Hailey think Stella could kill Usher?"

The idea surprised me. "Wouldn't it be the other way around? The wife would kill her husband? Or try to kill the woman having the affair with her husband?"

"We obviously can't ask the husband for his opinion, Ava, so we ask the other questions. It could be Usher had decided to end the affair and Stella couldn't stand that. Or, we also have to wonder if the two women had fallen in love and both decided to get rid of the husband."

That sent me reeling. "Could those women have framed my grandfather with the knife?"

Jordy flinched, as if he hadn't thought about that angle. Then his eyes took on a glint. "There's another angle. Your grandfather killed the man, then those people in that bar rushed the body to the car, then cleaned up the restaurant while your grandfather ran off and stole the snowplow as a cover."

I sprang up, my chair screeching behind me. "That didn't happen."

"Humor me." When I sat again he showed me the list of suspect names. "What do they have in common?"

"They like it here in Door County." I wasn't about to mention Grandpa wanting to move. Too suspicious. "And they thought Usher wasn't being fair and could ruin the town by making people sell and move because of high taxes."

"Even the artist Stella Zanderson who lives on Washington Island?"

"It's still part of the county, Jordy. Westergaard was hired by other villages, I believe. Several people across our county may have plotted together."

Jordy stuck the paper inside an inner jacket pocket. "It's impossible hundreds of people could have plotted a murder together without word getting out or somebody bungling it. Has your grandfather seemed mysterious lately?"

My stomach coiled. "Grandpa had nothing to do with it. How many times do I have to repeat that?"

"I have a knife with his fingerprints on it."

"Maybe my grandfather took the knife away from somebody at the breakfast club."

"Or, when your grandfather climbed into that snowplow and drove it, he was in shock. His alibi is Mercy Fogg knocking over his mailbox and he got mad. Maybe he's blocked out all the other stuff about the knife, as if it's a bad dream. Killing somebody can put a person in a state of shock."

The sheriff rose, making the kitchen seem smaller. The air's sweetness now seemed suffocating, mocking me.

Jordy pulling on his hat over the short-cropped hair with its severe part. "For now, I can't make an arrest. Gil can be Saint Nicholas on Monday, but I'm betting his memory will come back as he's playing a saint and tossing candy where the blood was spilt. Gil knows more than he's telling you, Ava. I'd bet my badge on it."

Chapter 21

Elf Fudge

D illon came through the back door shortly after one o'clock while I was in the shop's kitchen. I rushed into his arms, not even letting him remove his coat.

"I enjoy being popular, Ava Mathilde, but what's going on?"

"The sheriff was here. Jordy is convinced Grandpa is involved in the murder."

Dillon kissed me on the forehead and then the lips, his skin was cold yet the kiss felt refreshing and reassuring. "Ridiculous."

He removed a black stocking hat, leaving his wavy dark hair tousled with a lock caressing his forehead. He slung his coat and hat over the back of the nearby chair, then rolled up the sleeves of his blue-and-black-checked flannel work shirt. "Gil couldn't murder anybody. Maybe Mercy, but that's different."

Dillon's arms enveloped me in warmth. He smelled of wood shavings and paint--better than aftershave and twice as sexy.

He said, "Tell me what else you've found out."

I set to making a small batch of chocolate-and-walnut fudge. It was a favorite around Christmas. "Grandpa told Grandma he wants to move. I found a newspaper that had his circles around a few properties several miles from Fishers' Harbor."

Dillon got a glass from a cupboard then filled it halfway under the faucet. "I'm surprised he's not shopping for boats. Spring fishing season will be here in no time."

"What if he's giving up on this shop? I can't imagine this place without my grandfather's presence." I chopped chocolate off a kilo bar I had ordered from Belgium.

Dillon set aside the glass and then found the canister of sugar for me. "You can handle the shop. Cody helps. Brecht Rousseau would love a second job, unless he decides teaching kindergartners is right for him."

"Dillon, I want Grandpa to stay." I went to the refrigerator for butter.

"Sometimes a move helps a person. Didn't we both move away from each other long ago so we could become better people?"

"We were young, stupid, and needed to find ourselves. Grandpa's in his late seventies, an institution. He simply can't leave me."

"Because you say so?"

I chopped the walnuts, glad to punch something. "Yes. I'm selfish as heck that way."

Dillon relieved me of the big knife. He chopped chocolate from the kilo bars while I updated him about the "breakfast club" and the visit with Hailey and the sheriff. "What if, as the sheriff posed, they're all covering for each other?"

"Could be. There's safety in numbers. Age-old mob trick."

"But if somebody snitches, they die. At least in the movies and on TV."

I grabbed bags of white chocolate chips with the Christmas Elf Fudge in mind. I'd be making it in less than an hour out front. "Maybe I should confront Grandpa, instead of just talking about him with others. Maybe I could get Dad to do it."

Dillon took a long time to respond, looking down at the aromatic chocolate he'd chopped on the counter. "You're a person who won't quit until you get answers to the puzzles in life. I'm scared that if you dig too deep into all of this you might end up... I'm worried about you. Because I love you."

"I love you, too. I'll be careful, Dillon, really I will."

We scraped the chocolate shards into a bowl. I set it into the microwave. "Tell me about Lucky Harbor and Mercy's dog. Where'd you find them?"

"When I got home, Lucky Harbor was sitting on the front porch of my cabin with Queenie. Mercy Fogg's dog is now in my cabin."

"And you haven't told Mercy?"

"I called her. She said she'd called the cops about you losing her dog, and she was going to call the cops about me kidnapping her dog."

"Thanks for the levity. Mercy is a trip. Bad as Grandpa."

"She wants to be your best friend."

I guffawed. "How can you possibly conclude that?"

"She thinks irritating people is how you engage people, like a little brat of a boy or girl who did that in grade school. The kid wants attention, needs a friend."

"I don't know what you've been smoking but I'd say Mercy needs to go to obedience school. Like those two dogs."

My handsome fiancé graced me with another kiss. "I gotta go. Mercy should be wheeling onto Duck Marsh Street any second to pick up her dog."

"Good luck!" I started loading my arms with butter, sugar, and other fudge ingredients for out front in the shop. "And thanks again. I needed to get back to what's important in my life."

"Like making the best Christmas Elf Fudge in the country!"

"World!" I corrected him.

"World!" Dillon called out as he pulled on his coat and headed for the back door.

I kept the Christmas Elf Fudge recipe simple so children could make it easily, as if they were elves helping Santa and Mrs. Claus.

By two o'clock that Saturday afternoon the shop was crowded. Many had rosy cheeks from ice skating or taking sleigh rides across fields with handsome Belgian draft horses or Percherons. Families chattered about making wreaths at the Ridges Sanctuary at Baileys Harbor. Still others had come up from Sturgeon Bay where they'd seen the Festival of Trees display as well as the new lighthouse at the Maritime Museum. Some children in hockey uniforms were heading later to Kangaroo Lake in the middle of our county for a pond hockey game.

Grandpa had stuck around for the pleasant holiday noise. He loved watching the delight in the eyes of the children becoming little bakers, or elves.

My mother, Florine, also stopped by. She'd driven up from the farm in southern Door County to bring fresh cream and her award-winning cheeses, including her chocolate cheese. She made her delicacy using a sharp white cheddar cheese from my parents' organic dairy, cocoa powder and dark chocolate shavings, confectioner sugar, and vanilla flavoring.

"Mom, thanks." I gave her a quick hug. "Did you bring enough? This chocolate cheese will sell out in a minute."

With pride and a smile, she fussed with her shoulder-length hair, making a statement. "Well, if I'm that popular, I'll just have to come by more often."

"With cheese, please."

"Not for my personality?" she kidded. "I sparkle like this shop." She sniffed the air. "No need to wear perfume. I'll just walk through the air here."

Sweet vanilla and chocolate notes floated about.

When I headed for my presentation station, Lois Forbes and Dotty Klubertanz took me aside near the mitten section. They repurposed old sweaters into mittens and stocking hats, favoring pink, red, and white colors to match the fairy-tale fudges Cinderella, Rapunzel, and Snow White.

Dotty wore a pink knitted hat over her short, white hair. "Honey, we have to talk with you." White eyebrows lifted, indicating seriousness. Dotty was the father of Travis, who owned the mercantile, so I had to pause.

Lois, with no hat over her red-dyed hair and a lot of makeup, said, "It's concerning the other morning. That morning."

Dread created ice in my middle. I whispered, "Could we talk later? I have to give a show for the kids."

Dotty grimaced. "Of course. Give me a call when you're free."

For this fudge demonstration, I didn't use the copper kettles. This was a simple recipe and small batch that used only the hot plate, which was set up next to the marble table at the window. I wanted to demonstrate how easy fudge was for parents and grandparents to make at home with their own little ones.

The children helped pour the bag of white chocolate chips into one pan. Each child helping wore an elf hat made by Dotty and Lois.

Once those chips were melted and stirred by the child elves, then I had them mix in the vanilla frosting. Three elves stirred and stirred, taking turns.

Next, the elves and I separated that mixture into three bowls. Each stirred in food coloring. We created bowls of red, green, and left one white.

"Do you like the colors?" I asked.

"Yes!" they chorused.

"These are the colors of the outfits Santa's elves wear."

Now three other newly dubbed elves used big spoons to drop piles of their colored sugary mixture into a small, square pan. One elf accidently hit his own forehead with a green-colored frosting spoon. The crowd clapped and cheered. Fortunately the child giggled, too.

Once the globs of sweet confection were in the pan, another elf got the honor of taking a safe knife and running it through the globs in any pattern he or she liked. In that way, the fudge would end up with a pleasant pattern of mixed colors when cut to eat.

This batch went into the refrigerator in the kitchen to set for an hour. Because elves are impatient, I always had a batch pre-made to offer for taste-testing. The elves helped me pass out the Christmas Elf Fudge to the crowd.

For their help, I gave each of my elves a package of glitter play dough to take home and a large square of pre-packaged Christmas Elf Fudge I'd made yesterday.

One little boy asked, "But what about the fudge we made?"

Several expectant faces looked up at me.

"Would it be okay if I gave your fudge to Rudolph and his reindeer pals?"

That got screams of affirmations and shout-outs for Donner and Blitzen.

A girl elf asked, "But how do you get it to Rudolph? Isn't he at the North Pole?"

"Well of course," I said. "But just think about his big nose! That nose can smell this fudge all the way from the North Pole. I'll set out the fudge tonight and you can bet it'll be gone in the morning because Rudolph flew here and took it back to the North Pole for Santa and Mrs. Claus."

The girl went wide-eyed. "Really?"

"Really. Now, did you forget it's time for the elf hunt?"

The kids hopped up and down, clapping, and chattering. I explained there were little elf statues in the windows of the shops on Main Street. The goal was to make a list of the stores with elves, note the color of the hats, and then stop at an art cart to color their own pre-drawn elf where the child could collect a prize. All of the colored elf pictures would be hung at a local retirement village facility.

As they left chattering with their parents, I smiled. Fudge had magic involved. There was no denying it.

After three o'clock that Saturday afternoon, the shop emptied out. Cody left. Grandpa was clearing his counter.

"Grandpa, on Wednesday night, when you were at the Troubled Trout with your card buddies for steaks, what really went on?"

He paused, then let nickels clink into the cash tray. "I don't want to talk about it."

"I do because you're in a heap of trouble."

"Bah." He went back to flipping coins into their proper slots.

I came over to stand in front of him. "Usher was there with his wife. Did you see anybody else talk to Usher? Specifically Stella?"

Now Grandpa peered at me, eyebrows hiked. "That snow sculptor artist? She was there. I believe all of the artists were there at their own table."

"Did you meet them?"

"Heck, no. My friends and I were too busy chowing down. And those snow sculptors were busy anyway being interviewed."

That surprised me. "Did you know who the reporter was?"

"Sure thing. It was our newspaper delivery lady."

"Greta got a job for this weekend with the newspaper."

"I saw her out on Main Street snapping photos today."

"What did you see on Thursday morning?"

Grandpa's face paled. "I drove the snowplow and didn't see much." He withdrew a bank sack from under the counter. "I need to make a trip to deposit all this cash, then I'm off to the town garage to see how the sleigh is coming along."

With that, he grabbed his bag, his newspaper, and went for his coat. Soon after, the back door banged shut.

Tremors ran up my arms. Grandpa knew a lot about Thursday morning but wanted it buried. What if...he...?

Cody came into the shop with Nova to taste the chocolate cheese-and-fudge combo. With a sack of the goodies in hand, Nova hurried off saying she had to get back to her booth.

Cody stayed. After a couple of customers entered, I whispered to Cody by the register, "Did you or Nova hear anything about the murder today? Any gossip?"

He shook his head.

"Maybe Nova heard something? You could make conversation with her." I was still reeling from Dotty and Lois stopping me earlier and wanting to talk. I needed to call them.

Cody wrinkled his nose at me. "Talking about murder is not how a man gets a girlfriend, Miss Oosterling."

"Sorry. It came out wrong."

"No, you meant it. Nova and the professor were pretty busy. Did you know he makes little Christmas trees out of books?"

After my shrug, Cody added, "They're cool. He folds back the pages like a tree, and then he spray paints them all kinds of colors."

"I bet he's had a lot of children involved."

"And parents, too, looking for stuff that'll keep kids busy during the two-week school break coming up."

I was about to go back to the kitchen to clean up when Cody said, "Mister Kvalheim seemed pretty frustrated with people asking him about the location of the murder."

"The poor man. How awful being asked to be the tour guide for a murder on our Main Street."

"He didn't like Miss Truelson snapping pictures of him." Cody chuckled. "Mister Kvalheim didn't much like it when she called him a 'witness'."

I took off my fancy shop apron and set it aside on the counter. "A witness? To the murder? She said that in public?"

This time his face turned red, his green eyes looking down--actions he did when scared or feeling pressured. "Maybe she was trying to be a good journalist so she could impress the editor?"

"Likely. But tell me about Al. What did Al say after she called him a 'witness'?"

"Al fake-laughed. He said loudly he had to go see if the sleigh was ready for Saint Nicholas and Monday's parade. He charged through the crowd."

"And what did Greta do?"

"She followed him."

"To the town garage?" I looked at the clock. My grandfather was headed there now.

Cody shrugged. "Don't know."

A chill came over me. If Grandpa, Greta, and Al were at the town garage, was that a meeting of those who'd been inside the Troubled Trout on Thursday morning? Would Spuds Schlimgen, Boyd Earlywine, and Mercy Fogg and others show up? What about Erik Gustafson and his chef Piers Molinsky?

And had Dotty Klubertanz and Lois Forbes heard something on the street, too, about Thursday morning? Dotty was Travis's mother. Had he mentioned something to Dotty about that morning he hadn't revealed to me? Was that why Dotty wanted to talk to me?

The scent of danger muddled the air. "Do you mind taking over the shop for a bit?"

"You're thinkin' of goin' to that town garage to confront those people, aren't you?"

"Not exactly."

"So you're not goin' but you're thinkin' of sneakin' around it, though, to see if you can hear what they're saying. Sneakin' and goin' are two different things, aren't they?"

"You're what Grandma calls a smarty pants." I gathered up aprons to take to the kitchen.

He laughed. "Don't get into trouble, Miss Oosterling."

"Never do."

He scoffed.

In seconds I was on the phone with Pauline. "I need your help."

Chapter 22

The Sleigh

Pauline blew into the phone. "We're not going out to the town garage to snoop. Call the sheriff."

"I talked with him this morning. He said Al told him Grandpa was at the Troubled Trout before he stole the snowplow. Grandpa won't talk about it."

"He's a murder suspect and he wants to spare his granddaughter."

"Old news. Now listen up. I found out Al is going to the town garage and my grandfather's there. Grandpa Gil might be in danger. Remember that list we got from Hailey?"

"So?"

"I believe the people on that list are going to be there. What if they think my grandfather ratted on somebody?"

"I thought you left your penchant for storytelling back in Los Angeles."

"I did, but what about instinct? Intuition?"

"Wild animals use instinct to run the other way."

"My instinct says Grandpa shouldn't be at the town garage. Please, Pauline, we can say you're checking it out before you, Brecht, and Bethany take students to see the big sleigh."

"You want me to lie."

"Of course."

Ten minutes later Pauline and I drove the mile or so south to the outskirts of Fishers' Harbor. I parked many yards back from the township garage on the road's gravel shoulder. Grandpa's SUV sat in the garage parking lot.

The building was a steel box style but with cedar siding and rock accents on the lower half of the office area, which faced us. On the other side of the front entrance two massive overhead doors featured rows of windows.

Pauline said, "See the school bus? Mercy drives it to keep the battery up in cold weather. Let's turn around."

I flashed her a look of admonishment. "We can't leave Grandpa."

"Of course not, showing up is a big tipoff the sheriff might have sent you to spy."

"That's ridiculous."

"No, it's not. You've been undercover for him in the past."

She was right.

Pauline added, "And I have to meet John soon at our new house. I think he's planning another surprise."

"Besides buying that mansion for you? And furniture?" I checked my jealousy. "John loves you."

Pauline rolled her window down an inch. "Are you going in? I'll wait here."

"If we go in right away, they'll just stop talking."

"Your grandfather is not in danger here. There are too many witnesses." Pauline shuffled about in her purse.

"What are you doing?"

"Finding lipstick."

"You don't need lipstick to go into that building with...possible murderers."

"Lipstick helps me think. If I'm focusing on putting on lipstick and sorting glittery stickers in my purse, I can think. And if I don't think, then you do stupid stuff. Last summer you almost got us both shot and drowned. And a year ago we were almost burned alive."

"That's all in the past, Pauline."

"Not so distant past that I don't recall the trauma. Here." She held out a lipstick tube.

"No, thanks."

"Put on the damn lipstick. It'll make you feel strong, smart, sexier than you really are. I guarantee you."

"Hmm. I should be offended, but..."

A moment later with lips feeling moist and soft as flower petals, I perused the scene. We could probably sneak up to a side door or under a window and listen in through a crack. Pauline was right; barging in might cause trouble for Grandpa.

I drove the SUV to a stop on this side of the school bus, out of sight of anybody looking out a garage window.

We then duck-walked around vehicles until we came to a building side door. We couldn't hear a thing.

I whispered, "Around back they have another set of the big overhead doors with more windows. Those aren't as insulated. We'll be able to hear what they're saying."

Pauline rolled her eyes. We duck-walked through more snow, staying under windows.

When we got to the first set of massive overhead doors I realized we were still at the end where the road salt was stored. The people and sleigh were at the far end of the garage.

Pauline whispered, "Let's go home. My legs and knees are killing me."

"I can hear arguing."

Ignoring Pauline, I crawled on all fours over snowy gravel beneath the windows. With my jeans on, the gravel didn't poke too badly.

Three-fourths of the way across the area of the second overhead door, the voices became clear. I signaled for Pauline to approach.

Inside, Al said, "Gil, if you take the fall for us and go to jail, that'll take the pressure off us."

Grandpa said, "There's no guarantee I'd be out in time for the parade. Darn it all, but it's my turn as Saint Nicholas and I'm not going to miss this. I'm not so young, you know."

Then Al said, "You're too stubborn to die. You'll live to be a hundred."

Mercy said something I couldn't make out, then continued, "Listen, if the sheriff finds out we're here now he's going to put us all in jail and shake us down for the truth. And the truth is, one of us could be a murderer."

Grumbles and gasps were audible.

Pauline and I exchanged a look of panic.

It shocked me that Mercy was here after the rampage she'd created concerning my grandfather stealing the snowplow. Unless that was all manufactured as a cover. Had Mercy and Grandpa worked together to create an alibi? For each other? Or for whom?

Another woman's voice said, "Don't we already know who did it?" It was Greta.

Grandpa said, "Maybe one of us is guilty, but I think we have to look to others who aren't here. We need proof."

"Erik or Piers must have proof," Greta said. "I can't believe they don't have cameras in that place."

Al said, "Only over the cash registers. Standard stuff."

The gravelly voice of Spuds Schlimgen explained about how the golf courses had cameras outside their buildings. "They helped catch teenagers who ruined some greens."

Greta offered, "Maybe there are cameras somewhere else across Main Street in some tree that would have caught Hailey."

Hailey? The group believed Hailey murdered her husband? Pauline and I exchanged a glance.

Another man's voice asked, "We need to do a little research." That voice belonged to history professor Boyd Earlywine. "Maybe some homeowners across the street such as the new manager of the Glass Slipper Spa have cameras somewhere and haven't thought to check them."

I whispered to Pauline, "It seems everybody that may have been present on Thursday morning are here except the snow sculpture artists, and Erik and Piers."

"They're all back in town busy with the tourists."

My phone buzzed in my parka's inside pocket. It was Jeremy texting, telling me he stood at the other end of the building behind us.

Pauline and I crawled back across the rocky driveway.

He said, "What the hell are you doing?"

"Shhh," I replied, brushing off my jeans. "What are you doing here?"

"I came to take photos of Santa's sleigh."

"No. You got suspicious and came out here, just like we did. What have you found out?"

He raised an eyebrow. "Can't keep anything from you, Miss Ava Oosterling. Is that lipstick you're wearing? Nice change."

"You should try it."

He laughed.

I said, "Cough up what you know."

Jeremy led us back toward the parking lot. "Erik Gustafson is in a lot of debt with the Troubled Trout."

"Not news," I said. "He could be a suspect."

The three of us stamped our feet and were rubbing gloves to keep warm.

Jeremy continued, "I went to the county clerk's office and asked for everything known on Fishers' Harbor assessment records. Tax records are public documents. The clerk offered that there had been a title search on the restaurant."

"Those are done when somebody buys or sells property. Erik's selling?"

"Not to my knowledge. But here's the kicker. The title search was asked for by Usher."

I asked, "Was he going to buy the Troubled Trout?"

Jeremy nodded. "Could be he was about to put in an offer on it."

"But that would be a conflict of interest."

Jeremy shook his head. "No. A certified professional assessor does his job assessing property, and then that job is done. Nobody and no law exists that can stop him from later on offering to buy anything he has assessed in a professional way."

I looked at Pauline. "Hailey didn't say anything about this."

Pauline shrugged. "Maybe she didn't know."

"Or maybe she did know and that's why she killed Usher. She wants to move to Florida. Having a husband buying a restaurant here would mean he's entrenched."

Pauline blew frosty breath into the air. "I'm freezing."

Jeremy nodded. "Let's go inside. I came out here to take photos of the sleigh."

Pauline whined, but the three of us went through the front door. We let Jeremy talk up his fib about how he asked me to come along so he could get details about the sleigh and our Christmas-time traditions.

Grandpa scowled at me.

Mercy hurried out.

The men suddenly talked about sleigh repairs, a bit too loudly.

Jeremy began snapping photos, taking charge in a way that only professional newspaper photographers seem to do at events.

A couple of the men hopped into the huge, green Styrofoam-and-plaster replica of Santa's big toy bag. Grandpa posed in the front seat, in front of the toy bag.

Greta tagged along beside Jeremy, mimicking his photo-taking with her own camera.

Her presence here intrigued me. "Greta, do you attend the breakfast club meetings, too?"

She shook her head. "I've known about the club, but it's a guy thing. Besides, I have to get papers delivered early. Your grandpa would be calling me up if his paper wasn't there by five a.m. outside your shop's front door." She laughed.

I chuckled with agreement. "Did you hear anything about Erik Gustafson maybe wanting to sell the Troubled Trout?"

A cloud passed over her face. "Not outright, but he was troubled by a slump in business. His cook, Piers, growled once about not wanting to go looking for a new job or place to start over. Travis has talked about selling, too. I'm surprised you aren't worried about your place making it. If the harbor area gets re-zoned for condos finally, you'll be taxed for that value."

"You probably know Mercy tried to get it re-zoned when she was village president. Grandpa's been extra worried lately." I held back telling her he'd been thinking of moving. "We're in-between fishing seasons at the moment and that always means a bit of a slowdown for Grandpa's sales."

The words came off my tongue like sand.

I said to Greta, "I guess we all hope for good sales for the Saint Nicholas parade day and for lots of candy in the shoes kids put out for Tuesday morning on Saint Nicholas Day."

"Thanks for reminding me. I need to find a family with kids and take photos of their shoes with candy in them. I took photos of your grandpa. He's sure excited about being in Monday's parade."

Grandpa was still posing for Jeremy.

Greta held up her camera. "Jeremy sure knows how to get good people shots."

"Maybe Jeremy will let you tag along tomorrow and Monday. I bet you'll get photos for the local paper you wouldn't otherwise get."

Greta nodded. "You're right. I need to be bold and just ask."

I congratulated Grandpa on the good-looking sleigh and gave him a hug before Pauline and I ventured outside. Several others were leaving, too.

Dark at almost five o'clock, stars twinkled in the ebony winter sky. I looked off in the distance hoping to see Northern Lights dancing across the sky, but alas, nothing.

Once in my vehicle, Pauline said, "I know it when a group of my kindergartners are hiding something together. The happy, chatty mood inside that shed didn't fool me."

"Me neither. But we got something from Greta. She said Piers is upset about the possibility of Erik selling. Maybe it's true that Usher gave Erik an offer for the place, but I still can't see Erik murdering the man."

When I started the engine, it groaned, mimicking my feeling. I drove onward.

Pauline took off her gloves and then blew on her hands. "Maybe Piers didn't want Usher for a boss."

"So Jeremy might be right. Piers is a solid suspect." We were almost to the village limits. Lights from windows dotted snowy lawns and driveways.

I kept thinking of Grandpa in the middle of all this. He had been searching the newspaper listings for home sales. He'd lied about being at the Troubled Trout in the early morning hours before stealing the snowplow. Now he'd met with this breakfast club cabal. The little bit of discussion I heard seemed to indicate they were covering for each other. Or not. Were they all just scared? And trying to talk it out to reassure themselves of the truth?

I rubbed my lips together, feeling the soft emulsion of the rose-colored lipstick still there.

Pauline asked, "You're too quiet. What's up?"

"Your lipstick just helped me come up with a new plan."

"Oh, no. Just drop me off at Mom's. Your plans usually backfire. I'm meeting John."

Pauline texted, punching her phone so hard I thought she'd break it.

Chapter 23

Christmas Carols

Befor I walked in the front door of the Blue Heron Inn the noisy chatter and laughter within held me suspended for a time on the cold verandah.

This was Saturday night, and I was tired.

I turned from the front door and its light overhead to peer into the darkness. Main Street's secrets lurked in the gloom at the bottom of the hill.

Snowflakes whirly-gigged down like a lace curtain. The air held a clean, sharp scent, a wintery perfume. Every arrangement of crystals was different, every snowflake on the tongue a pleasant surprise--like every batch of fudge with its sugar crystals. Unlike Hailey Westergaard, I enjoyed winter and had an affinity for it. When in California, I missed winter terribly and couldn't wait for the holiday trips home. This feeling of bliss in Wisconsin was why the murder case tortured me so much. It was a stain on wonderful winter and the community I loved.

Indoors, to my surprise Dillon sat among the parlor crowd--and with little Henry on his lap. And Dillon was singing! In a festive, but gentle tone.

In all the years I'd known him, I'd never heard him sing much and certainly not like this. When he'd suffered through his college boozing days, songs were boisterous fight songs for the Badger team or Packers. Now, his sweet, whispery tone filled the room with the lyrics for Rudolph, The Red-Nosed Reindeer.

The guests clapped along--including Jeremy. He stood opposite me and next to the open staircase overlooking the parlor. Other guests sat about on the blue velveteen furniture. Dax and Nova were cross-legged on the floor, swaying to the holiday tune.

Baby Henry's mother, Ellany, enjoyed the loveseat across from Dillon, wedged between a singing Skylark Neubauer and Professor Magnus Olsen. Skylark had an arm around Ellany while the professor clapped.

Dillon winked at me. The action caused a tremor in my psyche. How could this man be in love with me--a mess? What did I bring to our relationship? Trouble. We were so mismatched.

While I always seemed to be in the middle of a mess, Dillon helped with practical things such as finding me a vehicle, building the backyard gazebo, and adding the screened porch outside the parlor last year. And he made the best lasagna in all of the county.

In this moment I realized what was special about Dillon: He knew what was most important and how to put things in the right order. I had no sense of order. I was miserable with lists, though Pauline kept trying to teach me to use them. Opposites might attract, but could Dillon and I last this time?

How does a person build a relationship? Is it like building a gazebo? One nail and board at a time? But which board comes first? Ach!

The future scared me. Would I lose something about our friendship after Pauline married? Was I only imagining deeper feelings for Dillon because I was afraid of loneliness again? I had been so lonely in California and way too stubborn to admit it for too long.

Jeremy stepped close as the song ended. "Dillon brought leftover lasagna he's heating in the oven. I got here just in time, it seems. You, too."

"I guess so." The Christmas-card tableau made me smile because I did indeed love having guests and pleasing them. "I'll bring out more of Mom's prize-winning chocolate cheese to go with the wine everybody's having."

After I turned to head through the dining room, Jeremy's footfalls whispered behind me. He joined me in the kitchen. I said, "There's something I need to discuss with you. A favor I need, actually."

He sniffed the air. "It won't spoil my dinner, will it?"

"No. What I need from you might make quite a story in the end."

Later that Saturday night, once everybody dined on Dillon's lasagna and retired to the parlor or upstairs to bed, I stayed in the kitchen to call Dotty Klubertanz.

"I'm so sorry for this late call, Dotty, but a lot of things came up since I saw you this afternoon." It was now nine o'clock. I hoped she wasn't already in bed.

"Dear, that's fine. Your life is full and you run two businesses. Maybe what I had to say wasn't important anyway."

"That's never true, Dotty. Please tell me anyway."

"Okay. I'll be quick. My son said he saw somebody on Thursday morning running down the street."

"Around the time the murder had to happen?"

"Right after, Travis thinks. My son stopped by my house yesterday and mentioned he might have seen somebody going north up the street. He said he couldn't tell who it was."

Travis hadn't mentioned this to me, but I wondered if he knew the person and lied to his mother. The person could've been Jeremy Stone out for his jog.

I asked of Dotty, "Had the street been plowed yet?" I wanted to figure out exactly when my grandfather and Mercy had traveled amid the fateful morning.

"He didn't say and I didn't ask. Sorry."

"That's okay."

"Travis got to his shop around sometime before five or so, he said, and he unlocked his front door and then went out real quick with his shovel to scoop snow away. He said the figure was trotting. He said the individual looked like they wore a dark running suit."

"Was the figure short? Tall? Skinny? Portly?"

My mind drifted to Hailey or Jeremy.

"Travis couldn't tell because by then the figure was off in the dark."

"Thanks for telling me this, Dotty. At least I know that couldn't have been my grandfather. You wouldn't catch him dead in a jogging suit." I suggested Dotty call the sheriff.

After I hung up, I needed to think this through. There was no way Jeremy had killed Westergaard. Hailey had to have killed her husband. But I had no proof. Everything was supposition and circumstantial.

I left the kitchen, needing time to think. Guests had all gone upstairs now. Once in my tiny apartment I used a half hour to embroider another letter on Pauline's wedding handkerchief. I was only at the "U" in her name.

A Belgian wedding tradition called for the bride's name on the handkerchief she carried down the aisle. Typically the maid of honor or somebody close to the bride embroidered the handkerchief. I was mostly "thumbs" when it came to embroidery. When Grandma taught me a few weeks back for this purpose, she had to look away after I'd stabbed myself several times.

The Belgian tradition said that after the wedding this handkerchief would be framed and hung in Pauline's house. The first-born girl of the household would inherit the handkerchief and her name would be added to it, and so on it would go, down the line. Sadly, the Mertens had been a broken family and such traditions hadn't been formed. Yet. My heart expanded with pride and love for my friend as I fussed with the threads and needle.

A framed handkerchief with "Florine"--my mother's name--hung in my parents' farmhouse. That handkerchief also held the name of her mother--my deceased grandmother, and my great-grandmother, and a great-great-grandmother who had lived in Belgium. Did my mother look at those names and wonder when she or somebody like Pauline might begin embroidering my name?

The threads in front of me were crimson--Pauline's favorite color.

As I stitched the flowery "U," tears welled up. I was glad for Pauline, but would I also lose a little of her in this deal? She would spend more time with her husband John. Could BFF really stand for Best Friend Forever? Or would it become Best Friend Forgotten?

Did other women feel this way when a best friend got married?

Disgusted with myself, I put the embroidery away and then fell into bed.

On Sunday morning boundless energy showed up, as if I'd settled down for a long winter's nap as the Christmas poem said.

Maybe embroidering agreed with me.

Maybe last evening's melodious notes by Dillon and the vision of him holding little Henry had changed something in my chromosomes.

After setting out breakfast items for guests, I slung on my coat and headed out the front door at a little after five, not thinking to look for the usual secret gift but stumbling into it along with the newspaper. With a sigh, I tossed the newspaper inside and then stuffed the package in a pocket and set off down the hill.

A bitter breeze created a clicking cacophony amid the maple and oak tree branches overhead. Snow swirled about me, stinging my cheeks.

As soon as I opened the back door of the shop I recognized something amiss.

Why was it so frigid? The lights were on.

"Gilpa?" I called out.

"Help!" his gravelly tone beckoned.

Chapter 24

Dangerous Surprises

Without shedding my coat I trotted to the front. "Gilpa!"

He sat on the dark wood floor amid a glacier of broken glass. Blood stained his hands. "Stand back, honey."

The big picture window on his side of the shop had been shattered. A winter blast whooshed in from over the tall snowbanks outdoors lining the harbor parking lot.

My heart raced. "What happened? Are you cut badly?"

"Not sure, honey."

He still had his coat on, which probably protected his backside from the sharp edges of the ancient windowpane scattered about. I didn't know where or how to step in all of the broken glass surrounding him. "Don't move, Gilpa. I'll get towels for your hands and a broom."

After grabbing "Cinderella Pink" terry hand towels nearby that we normally sold to customers, I tossed them to Grandpa. He wound them around his hands.

"How did the window break? Did you fall into it?" I fetched the broom and dustpan in the hallway and came back.

"I came through the back door just like you and felt the cold wind and then saw the broken window but rushed too fast and slipped on the glass like it was an ice pond and found myself ass over teakettle in this mess."

Within a minute I'd shoved aside giant shards containing the shop's lettering. Grandpa put his bandaged hands on the floor and attempted to heave himself up.

A wind gust puffed snow into the shop around us. Light-weight packages of fishing flies on a nearby shelf took flight over the tops of other shelves.

As he tried to push off from the floor Grandpa plunked back down in the glass with a grunt.

Now panicked, I said, "Grandpa, stop. You're not steady. I'm calling 911."

"No need for foolishness." He gave himself another shove to all fours.

I took one arm, helping him up. His heavy denim jeans and work boots had been good protection from the razor-sharp glass edges.

I spotted an unusual dark lump next to a tray of sinkers behind us. A rock.

"Grandpa, we have to call the sheriff's office." Grandpa's hands had bled through the pink towels. "I'm also calling 911. You must have glass in your hands."

"No need to call anybody, Ava honey."

"Sorry." I hit 911 on my phone, and also called the sheriff's office.

Next, I phoned Dillon. Already on the road to his work site, he said he was turning around and would see us in ten minutes.

I helped Grandpa to the stool behind his register counter. "Don't move, please."

"I'm fine. I'll go home and get fixed up."

"No way are you going to make Grandma clean your bleeding wounds. You might have glass buried deep in your hands that could affect your nerves or a blood vessel or tendon."

"We need to worry about that busted window."

"The 'we' will be me and Dillon. He's finding something to cover the window."

While waiting for help, I took phone pictures of the damage. Snow and perhaps glass fragments had carried across the shop to land in the copper kettles. Wind had scattered many items. Fairy-Tale Fudge doll-house-sized china figurines of fudge-loving fairies for girls had broken, pieces scattered across the floor in one aisle.

Snow also dusted the white marble table by the other window.

The destruction made me fume. Who would bust our window? And why?

To my surprise, snow sculptors Reece Allard and Buck Ingersoll knocked on the front door. We hadn't had a chance to unlock it. Grandpa's fish clock over the door said it was now minutes before the bass, or six o'clock. I rushed to let in the artists.

Buck handed me our newspaper that had been left outside the door.

"Thanks. Did you guys see who did this?"

Buck shook his head. "Nope, but we heard the glass shatter. Sound carries a long way over snow." Buck sported a shaved, round face and brown hair sticking out from under a Green Bay Packer stocking hat.

Reece offered, "We were behind the businesses down the way, filling the trash barrels with snow. Getting ready to haul them to Main Street later. Maybe we can help clean up?"

"No," I said, "better not. I called the sheriff. This is vandalism." I pointed to the rock.

Reece, in his fifties, with a salt-and-pepper beard and a ponytail sticking out from under a red stocking hat, puffed out his disgust. "You better ask Travis about this."

"Why Travis?"

Reece hesitated, as did Buck.

I asked, "What's going on? What about Travis?"

Buck pulled off his stocking cap to run fingers through a mop of hair. "There was trouble with Travis at the bar the morning Usher died."

"You were there?"

He nodded, confirming what I pretty much already knew, then glanced toward Reece.

Reece said, "I was there, too, but we didn't have anything to do with the man being killed, I swear it."

Buck said, "Usher and Travis were arguing, coming at each other. Usher took a swing at Reece."

"That true?" I asked.

Reece nodded. "I pushed Travis and Usher apart, and Usher swung at me. We wrestled on the floor and broke some glasses. Erik was upset and told me and Usher never to come back."

I realized Erik knew much more than he'd been willing to tell me. "What was the arguing about? The tax assessments?"

Reece said, "Yeah, for sure. I'm just an artist. He thought my studio and land should be assessed like some big gallery you'd find in Chicago. He is, was an idiot."

"He had credentials," I said. "He knew what he was doing." They didn't respond to that. "How did Usher end up dead?"

"Don't know," Buck offered. "I helped him to his car after the fight with Travis and Reece. And he was alive, I swear."

"Did Usher call anybody during all of the arguing inside the bar?"

Grandpa sat at his counter listening. His silence was unlike him.

Buck said, "You mean like the cops? No. Certainly not his wife."

"Why do you say it that way, 'certainly not' his wife?"

Buck winced. "Usher was hanging around with Stella Zanderson."

"The other snow sculptor." This seemed to confirm what Hailey Westergaard had hinted at during my visit to her house. But was that true? "Were they appearing as a couple at this breakfast?"

"No," Buck said, flinching. "I didn't see her inside the joint at all, but we were supposed to all meet there to discuss stuff for this weekend. I don't know where she was."

Reece said, "She might have been out back of the restaurant, looking at the trash barrels Erik had promised for the snow sculpting collection." His face darkened. "I feel really bad. I can't believe I didn't offer to drive Usher home after wrestling him to the floor. If I'd done that, the man wouldn't be dead."

Reece appeared genuine, but could I trust these two guys? Were they covering up a murder? A chill rattled down my back that wasn't from the freezing air.

If Stella Zanderson had been outside the restaurant Thursday morning looking at snow barrels, she might have heard or seen something related to the murder. The man could have yelped or called out as the killer plunged the knife into him. Had Stella heard it? Seen the deed? Or done it? But what would have been her motive? Especially if she loved Usher? I went back to the possible relationship between Stella and Hailey. My brain was exploding with scenarios.

I turned to Grandpa. "What do you know about any of this, Grandpa?"

"I was plowing the street. That's what I told the sheriff."

After Buck and Reece exchanged a glance, I gave Grandpa a stern look.

He wiggled his mouth, ruminating. "I believe I did haul ass through the bar briefly to use the restroom, but I didn't witness any of this stuff they're talking about. Then everybody seemed to be gone when I finished my business." He kept his gaze averted.

I was having a horrible time believing my own grandfather, whom I'd always trusted.

Cody arrived then with another rescue squad volunteer, a woman I didn't know. They inspected Grandpa's hands. Cody wielded a magnifying glass.

Dillon rushed through the back door soon after, giving me a kiss. "Are you all right?"

"Yeah. But not Grandpa."

Dillon nodded toward Reece and Buck, then took a peek at the EMTs and Grandpa. "Gil, did you see anybody?"

"Do you think I'd still be here if I saw somebody? I'd be after them to wring their scrawny neck."

My phone pinged. "The sheriff says he'll be here in about ten minutes. He's doing business on Main Street."

Grandpa jerked his hands from the EMTs and then trotted for the back door.

Reece and Buck hustled out the front door.

Dillon and I exchanged a quizzical look.

Chapter 25

Icy Threats

Cody said, "Your gramps needs a doctor's attention for that glass in his hands, Miss Oosterling. We got most of it, but he could still have slivers." Cody popped off his stocking hat. His red hair fluttered up in the breeze coming through the broken window. "He's not himself lately, for sure."

Cody hugged me briefly then backed off.

Any hug was hard for Cody, so his action spoke volumes, making me more worried about Grandpa. "Thanks, Cody." I gave the shop a purposeful glance. "Are you free today to come back and help clean up? I've got to get this in shape pronto. This is a big weekend in town."

"Sure, Miss Oosterling. I'll be back." Cody and the woman EMT left.

I called Grandma to make sure Grandpa had gotten home okay. He had. She was flushing his cut hand under the kitchen faucet.

Within ten minutes Dillon brought in boards and heavy clear plastic to cover the window.

I turned up the electric baseboard heaters. "Can you can replace the window today? I hate for kids and tourists to see a boarded-up shop. That's just not Christmas cheery."

With hammer in hand, Dillon shook his head. "Not likely, but I'll see if one of the glaziers I work with can come through for you. The thing is, that window casing is rotten and needs replacing before you try to set in new glass. Looks like it's been here since the 1800s."

"That's how old this building is. It's always needing repairs."

"What if you got Professor Olsen and Dax and Nova to create a holiday mural on the plywood? Maybe give art supplies out to the kids."

"Of course!" I kissed his stubbly cheek. "A Christmas art window. You're brilliant."

He flung both arms around me, hugging hard. Then he glanced at the rock sitting on the shelf. "This violence worries me. Honey, somebody doesn't like you poking around about Usher's death."

I snuggled deeper into his arms. "Let's pretend it's Grandpa's naughty skritek."

"The Christmas tricksters? Hardly."

We went to work cleaning. The sealed glass case had protected those treats within, so I'd have something for sale this morning but it would likely be depleted by noon.

Dillon said while mopping a section of floor, "I've got to get to my construction site. Maybe call your church ladies?"

"Brilliant idea. I'll message them."

Jordy pulled to a stop then in the parking lot with Deputy Maria Vasquez. Each shook their head at the mess.

Jordy said, "Ava, it's only six-thirty in the morning. You're starting my day awfully early."

"Somebody wanted to end my day or Grandpa's, it seems. Grandpa got cut up. He's at home getting doctored by Grandma." I pointed out the rock.

Jordy nodded. "Blast it all. Why do people do dumb stuff like this? He get hit?"

"No. That was here before he walked in."

"Are you sure? Somebody might have seen him in the shop and aimed for him. Or, he might have set this up to get him off the hook for killing Westergaard. Make it look like somebody else is a murderer."

The air went out of me. "You can't be serious?!"

Dillon stepped next to me. "That's a stretch, Sheriff."

Jordy's answer was to walk around the place.

Maria took photos while Jordy came back to ask about the condition of the window.

Dillon said, "I boarded up the window to keep the snow and cold out."

Jordy grimaced. "We'll try to figure out the trajectory of the rock or at what level it was thrown from. It might tell us the height of the person or from how far away the rock was thrown. But I doubt it." He made notes on a pad. "Anybody in town hate fudge?"

He smiled but I didn't appreciate the joke.

I said, "I can't think of anybody who'd want to ruin our shop."

Actually, I could. Mercy delighted in the thought of razing our building for condos. I also thought of the people Pauline and I had seen at the town garage. Could our presence there have frightened one of them?

And what about Hailey? Did she hire somebody to toss the rock? Or throw it herself? She was athletic.

My mind circled next to Reece and Buck. Why had they showed up this morning? They ostensibly showed up to check on my welfare after hearing the window break, but was that a cover for one of them tossing the rock?

The sheriff asked of me, "Have you been out asking questions of anybody about that death on Thursday morning? Maybe you pissed off somebody?"

He was reading my mind, which irritated me. "I'm a business woman, part of the Main Street chamber. And my grandfather's prints were on that knife, so yes, I've been asking questions."

His eyes grew hawk-like. "Who did you talk to about the crime?"

I gave him the names of my guests, Usher's wife, Travis Klubertanz, Greta Truelson, Erik Gustafson, Piers Molinsky, Buck Ingersoll, Reece Allard, Jeremy Stone, and Dotty Klubertanz. I mentioned the spying at the town garage with Pauline Mertens.

Dillon said, "Whoa! You were spying?"

The sheriff huffed. "Telling Dotty means the whole county is in on every detail, you realize."

"We can solve things faster that way."

"We? There's no 'we'. You're not an officer. You might have warned the murderer you're onto them. That rock was certainly a warning for you."

"You think the rock was meant for me?"

"It could be somebody wants to keep you busy fixing stuff so you'll stop playing detective, and maybe let them slip quietly from the county."

I shook my head. "The damage here seems to mean the killer is still in the county. That's an important detail, don't you think?"

The sheriff burst out with, "Ava, your life is in danger!"

Dillon caught me as I stepped back from the blast. He said to the sheriff, "I've been telling her that. Keep at her for me. She needs to stay out of this."

Dillon excused himself to head off to his construction job.

Jordy stomped about the shop making notes.

Maria bagged the rock as the sunrise filtered through the windows in the double doors. She took the rock to the sheriff's vehicle outside. She returned with the pan for the elves and asked about the pan. When I told her about leaving treats for elves or skritek, she said she'd have to take it, in case the perpetrator had touched it. They'd look for fingerprints.

Jordy asked me to sign the damage report. "Ava," he said in a quiet voice, "I didn't mean to upset Dillon, and I'm sorry I yelled at you, but somebody is messing with you."

"To set up my grandfather to take the fall and go to prison."

"Nobody goes to prison here if he'd just tell the truth. Usher Westergaard had a knife plunged into his belly. I don't want to find you in that condition. It would kill me."

He seared me with potent eyes. He appeared to be struggling, wanting to say a lot more.

The pause made me think about the conversation with Reece and Buck. "Was there any glass anywhere on Usher when he was taken to the morgue?"

"Why?"

I told Jordy about the fight Reece and Buck reported minutes ago. "If Usher landed on the floor amid glasses breaking, it's possible and probable there'd be evidence of his sweater being on the floor, maybe picking up pieces of glass."

Jordy sighed. "I shouldn't be telling you this because the autopsy report isn't cleared for public consumption yet, but we found no glass on him. The sweater was clean."

This set me back a step. "Clean? Not even dirt from the floor?"

"That's right. Clean." Jordy added, "As far as I can tell, everybody at the Troubled Trout on Thursday is now covering for the others. I'll talk to Reece and Buck."

"You haven't talked with them yet?"

He blew a gusty breath out. "I didn't know they were there. Nobody coughed up their names until you did just now."

"Talk with the third sculptor, Stella Zanderson, too." I repeated what Buck and Reece had related about the possible affair with Usher, and about her not being inside the restaurant when the murder occurred. "That means she might have been outdoors, with the knife."

I let Jordy think on that, then added, "She's likely downtown now. Buck and Reece are getting snow ready for sculpting. I assume she's doing the same."

He was about to leave but I asked, "You've looked at all the security camera footage around downtown?"

Jordy said, "The few working cameras were covered with snow. Maria and I found a trail camera in a tree but the wind shook the tree so badly it looks like somebody shaking a glass of milk. We canvassed a couple of houses but Main Street was out of reach of doorbell cameras or all that we saw was the backside of the businesses."

"Did Dotty Klubertanz call you?"

He nodded, then waited for me to say more.

I said, "Dotty told me that Travis saw a figure jogging away from the scene. That was likely Jeremy Stone, though I can't swear by it. He said he was out jogging but a lot of people around here jog in winter and in early mornings."

Jordy nodded, ruminating for a moment it appeared. Then he pivoted, going out the door, setting off extended clanks from the cowbells.

After collapsing into a chair alone in the shop, I called Pauline.

She whispered, "Do you know what time it is?"

"Yeah, it's going on seven and time for you to roll out and let John sleep in."

She huffed in my ear.

I regaled her with my morning tale.

She said, "Ava Mathilde, lay low. I don't need a dead maid of honor."

"Pauline, we're close to getting Grandpa cleared. I've got a bunch of new information to go over with you. I need you to stop by as soon as you can."

Pauline said, "To do what? Get in line for a rock to be thrown at me? Your grandfather might've been killed. You, too. Things happen in threes."

"Nobody harmed me."

"This is scaring me, Ava. Count me out."

"You can't do this. You're my best friend and that's a forever thing."

"I want to be alive to get married in a week. John would not like to find his bride-to-be left for dead somewhere. He can't marry a corpse." Her voice had risen.

"You must have gotten out of bed and gone into the bathroom with your phone or otherwise you wouldn't have shouted at me."

"I'm actually heading to the kitchen. And it's a long way from the bedroom in this house so that means John can't hear me."

"So you stayed at your new mansion overnight with John. Was a new bedroom set delivered yesterday? Was that the surprise John had for you--a new dresser for the mansion?"

"It's not a mansion. It's just a big house. You sound jealous. Which is not like my best friend. You're afraid for your grandfather, aren't you? He didn't kill anybody. We know that."

I heaved a big sigh. "I'm sorry. You're right. It's just that when Grandpa isn't himself it seems to rub off on me. When he's confused, life makes no sense for me."

"Because you love him. So do I." Pauline made noise in the background that sounded like filling a coffeepot. "Wait until I show you the surprise."

Her words reminded me that I still had the small, mysterious gift box in my coat pocket. "I received another box. We can open it together."

"I'll be there within an hour." Pauline clicked off.

Chapter 26

Stocking Disappointment

While waiting for Pauline, I looked about the shop and in the back rooms for the old Christmas elf book I'd had as a child. My search yielded nothing but a couple of Grandma's cookbooks on a shelf in the storage area that I'd forgotten to return to her.

Honking drew me to the front of the shop. The look of the boarded-up window deflated me again. I couldn't see out, so the persistent noise made me hustle to the front door.

Pauline sat in a racy-looking, cherry-red convertible with its top down. I was shocked. Against the white snow under the brilliant morning sun the sleek car appeared to float on a cloud.

Pauline motioned for me to join her.

I grabbed coat, stocking hat, and gloves and then headed out.

Pauline said, "I'll take you for a ride. Do you like it?"

Did I? Excitement bloomed at the imagined thrill of us sailing through the famous snake-like road in upper Door County that drew tourists and their cameras.

Once I was seated, Pauline put the top back up. The interior enveloped me in the sweet tangy smell and comfort of buttery, new leather. Shiny dashboard displays dazzled, and so did the silence. There was no engine noise.

"All electric?" I asked.

Pauline grinned. "Quiet as a cat creeping across snowy country."

"Great work with those consonants. You must miss your students."

"I do." She backed out of the parking spot, the car only whispering.

"A short ride, Pauline. The shop is a mess. You clearly saw the broken window." I told her about my morning.

"I'll go down Main Street and turn around. Just enough to make you jealous."

She headed out of the harbor lot, and the trim automobile continued its mere tick-tock utterances, punctuated by Pauline's giggles.

I said, "So this was John's surprise?"

"Yes, no, and sort of. You and I talked about getting matching red convertibles not long ago and John remembered me mentioning that. He encouraged me to just do it, to buy it. He said his business will cover the payments if I ever need some help. He offered to cover the insurance, too, if I want."

A twinge of some elusive emotion pinched me again. Was something shifting in my relationship with Pauline? It felt like she'd grown ten years beyond me suddenly.

"So, did John get a new show contract or inherit something?"

"New contract." Pauline glanced at me with perfect red lipstick, a happy face with dark eyes wide with childlike exuberance. "Remember how he sold the Wisconsin cultural series last summer?"

"Sure."

"The national public broadcasting head honchos sold the rights to some streaming service. They came back to John for anything else he wanted to produce."

"Wow." The heated seats warmed my butt and back in a pleasant way while we tooled through Fishers' Harbor. "This is the same John who wears tropical shirts and sandals with socks in winter."

"Isn't he amazing?"

"I'm happy for you, Pauline."

Peevishness hit me. That elusive emotion I was trying to understand was disappointment. Pauline and I had agreed months ago to get matching convertibles someday together. As in TOGETHER. Her "someday" came without us sharing the experience of shopping for our vehicles. She'd violated an invisible friendship contract.

Stuffing the pity party in a pretend pocket, I said, "You're the happiest I've ever seen you and for that I'm really glad because you deserve it."

She executed a turnaround outside the village limits. "Thanks. I love this car and the house, but... There's all the other stuff in my life. I've never had it easy. Every time something good happened for me, then it was followed by something bad. My drunken father leaves us, then your family came to our rescue, but then my mother ended up leaving too."

"But she's back. We got her back, Pauline."

"After a lot of years of estrangement. She's back, and now I'm due for that 'something bad' that comes."

"What's really bothering you?"

"My sister is not back and she's out of touch."

"I'll find her."

"Just like that you'll snap your fingers and she'll be back?"

"Sooner or later, she'll show up."

"My whole family has this ability to disappear under the radar. Lucie won't be back anytime soon."

Her sad tone made my heart cry out. "You don't think you deserve everything. Is that it? You have John, a new life, this car, and yet you feel guilty. Is that it? Is that why you're so sure your sister won't show at the wedding?"

The car slowed through a quiet Sunday morning Main Street. "Yeah." Pauline barely choked out the word.

"Pauline, you had a rough upbringing. That history is your history and will never go away, but there are dozens of kindergarten kids you've taught since getting out of college and they were lucky to have you. You changed the lives of many. Your background helped you understand some of those kids when they were going through rough times. Right?"

She nodded, then swiped at a tear streaking down her face as she drove on.

"Please be happy. Even if your sister doesn't show up, you still have an entire town behind you. And John seriously loves you and wants you as a partner for life. He's a goofball sort of guy, but that's what you need. He's going to wear that goofy Victorian men's getup for the wedding. That's true love. Enjoy it."

She laughed. "Thanks. I think he hates that suit but he hasn't said that. You hate that red dress."

"Maybe it just makes me think too much about you leaving me behind in the dust."

"We'll always be friends."

"Things will change, though. You'll be doing lots of things with John."

"And you'll be doing lots of things with Dillon."

Dillon and I couldn't afford a new red convertible or a house much less a big one like John's new purchase. Dillon struggled with his new construction firm. I had a mortgage on the inn. My vehicle was a gray SUV over ten years old that Dillon had found for sale on a bulletin board in the Piggly Wiggly in Sister Bay. It ran on four tires held together with rust.

As Pauline pulled up in front of the plywood window, a realization hit me. "Pauline, the rock is the key to catching the murderer."

"The rock somebody threw through the window? The sheriff took the rock with him. It's not likely he'll get fingerprints."

"We don't need them. I think the rock can get the murderer to confess. Can you come to the inn after lunch? Cody will handle the shop. I want to check on Ellany. Somehow I need to fix this rift between her and her husband about living with his mother or whoever else might be in that house."

"What about the rock? You're leaping ahead on me. Slow down."

With my hand on the door, I said, "I need your help. Are you in?"

She turned off the silent car with a click of a button. "What do you need me to do?"

I withdrew the box from my pocket. "Help me figure out who's leaving these gifts."

The box revealed a tiny reddish-brown dog figurine whittled from what looked like maple wood. A likeness of Lucky Harbor perhaps.

Pauline exchanged a look with me. "There must be a message in all these gifts. Maybe line them up and see what letter each word starts with. There could be a secret sentence."

"I haven't thought about that."

"It's the type of game I play with my students."

"Hmm, so I just need to de-code the gifts."

Pauline nodded. She was my best friend for a reason.

Chapter 27

Grandpa's Secret

O n normal winter Sundays the shop didn't open until eleven, but today we were opening sooner because of the festivities in town. Prior to opening, Mom was vacuuming the shop. She had made the trip up from our farm near Brussels with chocolate cheese to replenish my stock.

Pauline had left after hearing her kindergarten students would be at the bookstore. Professor Olsen, Dax, and Nova were helping store owner Jane conduct an art lesson about how holidays were celebrated around the world. Our local business chamber had donated money for books so each child would receive a new book before they left. I mused to myself that I should go and see if the Christmas mouse book was handed out.

While Mom's vacuum roared in a corner, I cleaned Grandpa's register counter. The morning's newspaper was tucked in the shelf. This being Sunday the paper was extra big including real estate and sales sections. Grandpa had taken the paper home. Grandma had returned it, apologizing because she thought maybe Grandpa had gotten a spot of blood on it here and there from his hand that had been cut in our window mishap.

In the real estate section a tiny spot looked reddish like blood, but it also looked like his usual mix of rust and oil he got on everything. I was more interested in Grandpa's hunt for a new home. Sure enough, Grandpa had circled properties, including condos in the canal zone in Sturgeon Bay. He knew the city well because of its long history of shipbuilding and boat repair.

I walked the page to my mother.

She clicked off the vacuum cleaner. "What's up, honey?"

"This." I pointed to circled items. "What is Grandpa up to with all this talk of moving?"

She tucked dark strands of hair behind her ears. "I heard your father on the phone with Gil the other day talking about condo versus house and so on. You know I don't take your grandfather too seriously."

"Grandpa and Grandma wouldn't really leave Fishers' Harbor, would they?"

"They are in their seventies, Ava. Maybe they'd like a change of pace, especially in winter. We've never had so much snow this year that maybe a condo in a warm place makes sense suddenly. Maybe some place more south than just Sturgeon Bay. Maybe Tampa Bay."

"But Dillon shovels their walk and cleans out the driveway all the time."

"Maybe they want to free him up. For you."

I felt dumb. I'd never thought about that. "For me? If they love me they can't move."

"Why not?"

The ticklish feeling of tears lurked around my eyeballs. "Because I...I...need Grandpa. And Grandma. They help with everything."

"Including your heart?" Mom gave me a quick hug. "Oh, honey, you're almost thirty-three. You can handle things on your own. Don't you think it's time to take over a bit more?"

"So you believe Grandpa is serious?"

"Let's leave that between your dad and his parents. Sometimes your grandfather gets wild hairs, as your grandmother always calls it. And remember Gil is bored, which happens every year at this time because there's a lull in the fishing business."

My spirit brightened. "That's what it is--a wild hair. And he's going to be Santa Claus tomorrow! That will cheer him up."

My mother nodded, and then rolled the vacuum cleaner to another shop aisle as Bethany bounded into the shop to help, surprising me.

I said over Mom's vacuum vroom-vroom, "How nice to see you."

The willowy blonde took in the damage, her head flipping a ponytail back and forth. "What happened?"

I explained it in brief. "Can I help you with something?"

"I saw the professor at the bookstore and he told me about the plan for letting kids paint the plywood. I'm here to protect the shop from the kids."

We chuckled together.

"You're probably right." I had to add, "Are you okay with being here while Cody's here? He's coming any minute."

Bethany shrugged. "We're cool."

Cody entered minutes later, but when he noticed Bethany coming from the back with paintbrushes from our supply room, Cody rushed to the copper kettles.

Over the vacuuming, Cody yelled, "What's the recipe for the new fudge? Does it have a name yet?"

Oh, darn. I knew I'd forgotten something. I'd wanted to get ideas from my guests.

Cody said, "I'm making Rudolph-the-Red-Nosed Reindeer Fudge and Christmas Elf Fudge."

After Cody disappeared into the back of the shop, Bethany laughed. She took over my register. "You better get to candy-making, Miss Oosterling. Cody's going to bother you about that new fudge flavor until you're sick of hearing about it."

"I know," I said. Then I whispered, "I think Cody still likes you."

Her cheeks grew rosier. "He told me last summer he didn't want to date."

I remembered his announcement but still had hope.

Bethany continued. "He's into his studies for being a forest ranger. He likes bears and snowmobiles and studying trees better than dating at the moment. And I understand, what with his OCD and ADHD that he's keeping under control. He doesn't need one more distraction. I want him to like himself first."

I gave Bethany a hug. "He respects you giving him space to deal with college and other stuff. He still likes you, even if it's not as a girlfriend right now."

"I know." She giggled. "But he sure did run and hide when I walked in."

We exchanged a shrug and then I headed out the back door.

While walking along the snow-packed path, I called the sheriff.

"What now, Oosterling?"

"Happy holidays to you, too, Sheriff."

"I'm on my way to clear a slide-off accident near Jacksonport." It was on the opposite side of the county, the "lake side" versus our "bay side".

"Why are you calling me again? Is the other window broken? Shouldn't you be in church atoning for your sins?"

I ignored that. "I need to see the rock again."

"What rock?"

"Stop teasing. The rock that went through my window."

"It doesn't have fingerprints on it if that's your brilliant idea of a clue."

"Don't hang up on me! I have an idea. I believe the rock may take us to Usher Westergaard's killer."

"I'm listening, Ava."

We made our plan to meet. He'd have to return to the Justice Center in Sturgeon Bay to retrieve the rock from the evidence area. That gave me a couple of hours to talk with Ellany about getting back together with her husband.

Things were looking up. I would solve the murder case today, get Ellany's family back together, and tomorrow Grandpa would play Santa Claus in the town's parade and be in the perfect mood for me to tell him to forget about his foolish decision to move away because of me.

I smiled to myself thinking Pauline would be proud of my list.

Chapter 28

Party Favors

Coming from the fudge shop late that Sunday morning, I was on the sidewalk by Dillon's cabin when Lucky Harbor came bounding to me. He wore the message tube.

After tossing the dog gold fish crackers from the ever-present bag in my coat, I retrieved the message: I'm at the inn with a surprise.

So, maybe Dillon hadn't gone to his construction site after all.

My inn's small parking lot held vehicles I recognized, including Pauline's new red car. The abundance of visitors--all good friends--warmed me amid the cold winter's day.

As I came through the front door, the delicious aroma of chicken baking in the kitchen told me Dillon was cooking. He loved a big, seasoned hen. He often shared his cooking with my grandparents, which softened Grandpa Gil toward Dillon, though Grandpa never admitted it.

The kitchen was crowded with friends Fontana and her husband Jonas, Pauline and John, Laura and husband Brecht, and finally, Grandma and Grandpa, and my guest Ellany. Three babies wiggled about on the floor beyond the cooking area in various bassinets or on blankets with toys. They were being watched by John, Brecht, and Jonas. Ellany's swaddled baby Henry slumbered in a bassinet sitting atop the island and watched by Grandpa.

Joy sparkled in the air.

Ellany was tossing salad fixings into a giant crockery bowl while Grandma hand mashed boiled potatoes in a stainless steel pan.

Fontana had a loaf of steaming, homemade pumpernickel bread under control, slicing it and letting loose a wonderful aroma.

Pauline wielded a knife over a four-layer chocolate cake somebody had made--likely Grandma.

I stood in awe of the grand kitchen cacophony. "You're all like Christmas elves."

Dillon shut the oven door with a pleasant bang, then gave me a quick kiss. "I decided we needed a party and gave everybody a call for Sunday dinner."

Grandpa said, "Traditional dinner--at noon. The other one is supper."

John said from the floor, "I don't care what you call it as long as you call me."

Jonas got off the floor to grab a baby bottle that had been warming in the microwave. He stole a kiss from his wife, Fontana. "Just wait until these young ones get to be teenagers. Do you think any of us will have a chance at the food?"

Grandma said, "The food bills maybe, but not the food."

Again laughter erupted amid the clink of utensils and clang of pans and bowls. Snowflakes fluttered past the windows. Bodies bumped into each other in a friendly rhythm with giggles and laughs abundant.

Food and fixings soon festooned the island. Henry was wide awake, his gaze roaming about while one tiny hand clasped Grandpa's index finger of his uninjured hand.

Ellany took in the kitchen clatter and laughter--what Grandma called a hubbub.

When I turned to help Dillon with buttering the chicken for its final browning in the oven, he winked. I suspected Dillon had created this homey party to make Ellany realize how important it would be to go home to her husband and family at Christmastime.

I said aloud so others could hear, "Dillon, maybe Ellany can bring the chicken out of the oven with Fontana's help while you and I set the dining room table."

It was a ruse to get us alone. Once in the dining room, with the swinging door coming to a close, I kissed Dillon.

He chuckled. "What's that for?"

"You look handsome in an apron, and I know what you're up to."

"And what is that?"

We set the china from a sideboard in place on the table covered with a Belgian lace tablecloth.

"You invited our friends--namely friends who are either married or about to be married--so that Ellany can see what she's missing by not patching things up with her husband."

Dillon set a cup in place on a saucer with a tiny clink. "I can never fool you, Ava."

"And you're brilliant. I hope it works. She said she doesn't want to live with his mother. She wants a place of her own with her husband and new baby. But if she has no money, no job..."

"Give her time. Maybe she'll see today that having built-in babysitters is okay." He came around the table and took me in his arms. He smelled like the kitchen, yummy.

The dining room door burst open then, with Pauline and John leading the parade of people and food, everybody talking at once as the table overflowed.

Ellany settled at her chair between my grandparents with Henry in her arms. The other little ones were moved to the parlor floor's cushiony rug with their toys. They'd been fed before I'd arrived so they were succumbing to napping.

After the meal and Grandma's delicious chocolate cake, my grandparents left, as did Brecht and Laura with their twins.

Fontana and Jonas cleared the table, taking care with the antique dishes. They were now hauled to the kitchen because of the space used on the dining room shelving for the mysterious gifts on display. Nobody had said a word about them, to my dismay.

When everybody left in the inn was in the kitchen, I pulled Pauline into the dining room. "We're meeting the sheriff in half an hour."

"No 'we' are not." She was looking down her nose at me, as she liked to do.

"Don't do that. You're barely two inches taller than I am. And I need you."

"What is it that you've gotten us into now?"

"I asked the sheriff to bring the rock that went through my shop window."

"So now you're a geologist?"

"No. Well, sort of. Where the rock comes from might tell us a lot about the murder obviously. It could solve the case." I grinned.

"Where are we going to meet the sheriff with the rock?"

When I told her, she gasped so loudly I thought she might bring everybody from the kitchen.

I insisted on driving my gray SUV to our meeting with the sheriff. It somehow didn't feel right showing up in a shiny new red convertible to accuse somebody of murder.

It was two o'clock now on Sunday afternoon. I checked in with the shop before we left. Cody had to shout above the customers and the Christmas music. Lois and Dotty were helping and Grandpa had just walked in. I wasn't needed. For a flicker of a second I wondered what was wrong in my life. The shop didn't need me? I didn't need it? Why was I obsessing over all of these potential changes in my life?

Within about ten minutes we parked on the street in front of the Westergaard house.

Sheriff Tollefson pulled in behind us.

The low sun from the west made the house's yellow exterior gleam. Frigid air hit us once we alighted from our vehicles. Pauline pulled her wool scarf up over her chin.

The sheriff carried the rock in one gloved hand. "Now what, Ava?"

I squinted to see if Hailey were watching out the windows, but I didn't spot her. I took the rock from Jordy. "Follow me."

Nerves jumped in my stomach. What if I were wrong? I wasn't. The rock fit into place in an open spot shaped just like it within the lineup of stones along the driveway.

Jordy stood next to me. "Okay, it fits. Now what?"

"Sheriff, Hailey Westergaard took one of her decorative rocks and threw it through my window."

"Why?"

"Maybe to warn me to stay out of her business?"

"I'm frankly surprised more people haven't done that previously."

Pauline smirked but I ignored her.

I said, "She gave me a warning because she killed her husband and she believes I know it."

"So you think a mere rock is all it takes for me to arrest somebody? Anybody could have stolen her rock to frame her."

I had to admit to myself I hadn't thought this through. Haste makes waste, the expression goes. "Hailey might know who took the rock. She's probably had visitors." I turned to Pauline. "She acted weird when we were here, didn't she?"

"She was edgy, more interested in moving to Florida."

Jordy sighed. "Of course she acted weird and edgy. She lost her husband, and you two were among the last to see him possibly take a last breath. She's also got people in mind that she believes had something to do with the murder, including your grandfather. He knows more than he's telling."

Jordy walked up the short sidewalk, then onto the front porch. He hit the doorbell button. Nobody answered. He hit the doorbell again.

The silence made me edgy.

When Jordy descended the step off the porch, I asked, "What if she left for Florida?"

"Do you happen to know her phone number?"

"No." I tried the business phone for Usher but there was no answer. Jordy told me to try it again after he went back to the front window and listened. I hit the number again.

Jordy came back shaking his head. "It's ringing inside, a landline. Nobody answered. She's out on errands."

"Or gone for good."

He shook his head at me, then plucked the rock from the ground and took it with him.

After he drove off, I said to Pauline, "The killer was here and stole that rock. Hailey is gone. She has to be the prime suspect."

"Maybe not, Ava. Didn't you find it interesting the sheriff didn't have her phone number handy? Any sheriff worth his salt would be able to pull that up on his phone or from a notebook in his pocket if he's got a murder case on his hands and knows his suspects."

Pauline's words made me pause. "For some reason he didn't want to confront Hailey." I stamped my feet in the cold. "I'm still confused about that list of names. Maybe she really was trying to get our help."

A sudden breeze peppered our faces with snowflakes.

Pauline headed to the vehicle. "It's possible Hailey actually loved her husband and is as confused about all this, maybe even naming artist Stella Zanderson as a way to vent sorrow and rage at her husband's death."

"Stella was allegedly out back during the fighting in the bar. I haven't talked with Stella."

Pauline scooped up snow and threw a soft snowball at me. It hit me on the forehead, kersploosh.

"Ow! Pauline! Why did you do that?"

"To wake you up. Stop poking your nose in amateur detective business because it always turns out badly for you and for me." She was shouting at me as we got into the vehicle.

"We can't forget Mercy."

"You think Mercy would throw a rock at Gil?" Pauline asked.

We were buckling up. "Oh, yeah. She's nuts."

"Not like you at all."

I ignored Pauline's wry words. "Mercy is athletic. She could have leaped off that plow, killed the man, and then hopped back on to drive onward through the snow."

I started the engine, which grumbled. I had to use a credit card to swipe at the thin layer of frost on the inside of the window as we waited for warm air.

To her credit, Pauline didn't say a word about my crappy vehicle. I'd always been the one teasing her about driving an old car, and now I was the one driving a hunk of junk.

Chapter 29

Snow Sculptors

Main Street vibrated with life that afternoon. I had to drive at a walking pace.

A new set of snow sculptures took shape along the street's terraces. They depicted cartoon characters, space ships, and dinosaurs. Children ran everywhere with garden tools, buckets, and spray cans. Screams of delight echoed back from buildings.

Greta snapped photos on one block, and Jeremy worked the next block, both photographers darting in and about the moving crowd.

After dropping off Pauline at her mother's house, I parked at the inn, then trotted down the hill to join the party.

I caught up with Jeremy. "I need to talk with you. Somewhere private."

We settled for a walk in the cold along the harbor, since I needed to get back to work. I called Cody to tell him I'd be there within minutes.

After huddling deeper into my parka and facing away from the bitter breeze off the bay, I told Jeremy about the rock at Hailey's place.

Jeremy agreed with the sheriff. He pointed at the plywood shop window. "Somebody may have decided to set up Mrs. Westergaard and let her get the blame."

"Yeah, I thought of that, too." I hadn't, really, but I wanted anything he could give me.

"Do you think the rock was actually meant to, well, you know...? Kill your grandfather?"

I shivered and not from the cold. "Everybody knows he drove the snowplow. Somebody has to be running scared, thinking he saw them kill Usher."

"It would take a strong arm to throw a rock hard enough to go through that window to kill Gilsen. And the person had to be accurate."

"The rock could have been meant for Grandpa. The rock thrower thought they saw him in the shop's shadows and threw the rock. Grandpa arrived maybe only a moment later and slipped on the glass and cut himself." I recalled other conversations. "It seems Grandpa knows something about the breakfast club that has agitated him, something he's not told anybody yet. He's not been himself. He only told the sheriff he got mad at Mercy and drove the snowplow erratically on Thursday morning."

"Maybe he drove erratically because he was trying to run down the killer."

"No, he'd have said something about that. Whoever did the deed waited until Mercy headed toward Duck Marsh Street, which meant my grandfather had probably hiked back to his house by then."

The afternoon sun from the west hit Jeremy's face, making him squint. "What if the killer or an accomplice went to Hailey's house, got the rock, and came back here to harm your grandfather and blame it on Hailey Westergaard."

A new idea popped into my head. "That stolen rock points to somebody who knew the Westergaard place well, such as a friend or somebody who shoveled their walk and had seen the decorative rocks. Business owners didn't do business at their house, so that could mean many or most of them are innocent."

"Find out who clears the driveway for the Westergaards and you might find the killer." He backed away from me a step. "I need to get back to work before the sun gets too low."

"Sure. Thanks, Jeremy."

I called the sheriff before entering the shop and gave him the tip about investigating the snow-removal service the Westergaards may have hired.

The sheriff revealed he had tracked down Hailey. She'd been trying on swimming suits at a women's store in Egg Harbor. Hailey said she hadn't noticed the rock missing in her front yard's flowerbed edging.

The Main Street crowd continued to swell Sunday afternoon as social media got the word out about the fun and awe-inspiring snow sculpting.

I walked among the crowd as a barker offering fudge samples. "Free fudge samples! Fudge for your elves!"

Dillon had made my small, pink wood tray with the straps. Cody glued on glitter. I wore one of the shop's fancy pink Cinderella-motif aprons over my winter coat. Cody had gifted me with a sequined pink stocking cap made by Ruby. He'd said, "That hat is first-rate advertising, Miss Oosterling. Social media will love you. You'll see. Go get 'em!"

Squeezing through the crowd I called out, "Oosterlings' Live Bait, Bobbers & Belgian Fudge & Beer is just around the corner, a sweet retreat. Buy Rudolph-the-Red-Nosed-Reindeer Fudge and Christmas Elf Fudge, both on special today! Get your free sample of fudge here!"

Greta materialized out of the crowd to snap several shots. "You are so cute, Ava. These photos online might help me secure a permanent new job with the paper."

I handed her a piece of wrapped pink, sparkly cherry-vanilla fudge. "I'd hate it if you stopped delivering newspapers, Greta. You're always on time, which Grandpa loves, as you know. He reads the paper at five o'clock every day in the shop with his coffee."

"Except for last Thursday. I'm so sorry about all this mess, but I'm keeping my ears perked. Maybe I can find something to report that'll please the editor."

"Not to mention my grandfather who's in the middle of the mess."

She noshed on the fudge. "Sounds like he was literally in the mess. I wanted to take a photo of your plywood window but didn't. Out of respect for you and Gil."

"Thanks. Jeremy Stone will post a half-dozen photos anyway."

"Yeah, he's everywhere, except in the trees. If only there had been cameras in those trees last Thursday."

I wondered aloud, "Is it possible there are cameras somewhere the sheriff hasn't thought about or that owners forgot about?"

"I've walked this street for several years and know it inside and out. No hidden cameras. It's not like we're a big city snooping on everybody." She downed the last bite of the fudge.

I leaned in closer. "Have you heard anybody talking about the murder?"

"Professor Earlywine and Jeremy were exchanging information. They mentioned Usher stayed overnight at the bar. He'd been left there by his wife after an argument on Wednesday night."

"So she couldn't have done it."

"But she could, Professor Earlywine said. She drives a four-wheel drive truck and could have driven through the snow to Fishers' Harbor that morning."

"Greta, did you ever see Boyd Earlywine at the Troubled Trout over the past months in the early morning when you deliver the paper?"

"Sure."

"Boyd is a newer property owner here. Did you ever hear him get upset with Usher?"

"No, but that artist Buck Ingersoll got upset. Buck mentioned to me weeks back that Usher was headed for trouble by encouraging Stella Zanderson's attention."

"This thing about an affair keeps coming up."

"Buck said he saw Usher and Stella show up at the wreath-making workshop over at the nature center, and he'd seen them at other places. They didn't sit together, but they'd just show up and enjoy talking. I'd classify it as flirting, being together without the wife finding out."

"Do you know if Buck and Reece ever engaged in fights, things like that?"

Greta leaned in. "The worst of the bunch was your grandfather. Gil told Usher that if taxes went up on old buildings, history would be taken down board by board."

I sighed.

"If it helps, I agree with your grandfather about history being destroyed. I'd never want your shop sold or harmed. It dates back to the 1800s when my Scandinavian ancestors came over with yours to tame this peninsula. Our ancestors endured disease outbreaks and the Great Fire of 1871 that killed hundreds. Our people felled trees, farmed, and fished. You and I come from hardy stock. Your grandfather's going to be fine. We've got a good sheriff. He'll catch whoever murdered Usher and then Fishers' Harbor will be back to a quiet Christmas holiday season."

"You should write an article about county history. Your enthusiasm makes me smile."

"A great idea!" Greta excused herself to take photos of children posing on the back of the snow dinosaur.

Chapter 30

Holiday Hope

S unday evening brought a much-earned quiet time at the Blue Heron Inn. It gave me an opening to nudge Ellany about leaving.

I assured her she could stay through Wednesday if she must, but then the rooms had been rented for guests arriving for Pauline's Saturday wedding.

I was embroidering Pauline's handkerchief in the parlor after dinner at six o'clock. Ellany and baby Henry sat across from me on the loveseat. We were alone, the place quiet as a Christmas elf or mouse. Jeremy was pursuing interviews. Skylark and Magnus had gone out to dinner at the famous Swedish restaurant in Sister Bay. Dillon was on phone calls with construction workers coming tomorrow. Pauline was of course with John.

The clock ticked in the dining room as I wove needle and thread through the big "N" in Pauline's name.

Ellany finished breastfeeding Henry. He'd slipped off to sleep in her arms.

I stilled my hands for a moment. "He sure is a good baby."

"Yeah. He never cries much." Ellany rubbed his chubby cheeks with a fingertip.

"I'm glad he's happy." I kept my gaze cast down. "Are you happy, Ellany?"

A moment of silence ensued. "I want to be."

"What do your parents think of you staying here?"

"I didn't tell them either."

"So nobody knows where you are?" This time I gave her a bug-eyed stare for the sake of effect. She didn't know that I'd asked the sheriff to contact her husband and parents.

She shrugged, but pain wrinkled her forehead.

"What about your husband?"

"Brendan works a little now and then and is out a lot so I don't think he has time to think about me and Henry."

This was a new wrinkle in her story. "From what you said before, I thought maybe he was at his mother's place mostly and didn't have a job. So, did you fudge?"

Ellany hesitated, her gaze flickering to one side and back before she nodded. "He does part-time stuff. He's got nothing steady. I wish he'd try harder."

"So, have you been living with both of his parents and not just his mother?"

Ellany cast her gaze to the side again. "His dad works in insurance. He's in and out a lot but he works from home, too. His mom works from home."

"You wouldn't want to stay with his parents alone while your husband is out working? Is that the issue?"

She rubbed Henry's head with its wispy hair. "They're okay. I don't want to stay with anybody."

"You're staying with me."

"You let me be me. You don't order me around."

I nodded, though the nod was more to keep her talking and not to agree with the unknown definition of "ordering around". I asked, "What is your ideal situation?"

"Like lunch today. Everybody in your kitchen laughing and helping and being friends."

Dillon's wonderful idea to have the gathering make her homesick seemed to have worked. "Do you have friends?"

"They're in college or busy now."

"Maybe you need to invite them for a meal at Brendan's place over the Christmas break."

"I don't see why."

Boy, she was a tough cookie. "Brendan's parents might like showing off their grandchild."

She looked down at Henry. "I suppose."

"You can't hide out forever. I tried that once in my life and it just never works out."

"What did you do?"

I told her in brief about my past mistakes. I reached for new thread on the table next to my chair. "All I did by running away and hiding out from those who loved me was to stall getting on with my life. I didn't become who I could really be until I came home and faced the truth."

"What's your truth?"

"My truth is that I belong here with my family."

She gazed at me, hard-like, then said, "But you're just like me in a way. You seem scattered."

"Scattered?"

"Too busy to catch up with yourself."

"I--" She was right. I had been thinking a lot lately about my life changing. My best friend was about to get married and was going to move to a new chapter. I felt myself wanting something different for my life, but I couldn't identify it quite yet. My new chapter was a blank page yet. And that bugged me. "It's true that I'm busy, I guess. I always thought busy would be good, though, and keep me out of trouble."

I tried a laugh at my own words, but it came out half-hearted. Ellany recognized that and we both fell into silence. I fixated on my embroidery.

After a few moments of us listening to the clock ticking from the dining room, Ellany said, "I don't know what I am. I don't know my truth."

I put down the embroidery again. "What do you mean?"

"You know about your ancestors, and you have a family that really loves you. You know what you are to a certain extent--a person people care about. You know bunches of stuff about your Belgian ancestors and the history of this county. I don't know much of anything except the name of Jakobsson came from a Scandinavian background."

"Probably. Likely not Norwegian. They spell it with an 'E' instead of an 'O' usually in the 'son' part. Maybe you should pursue your background and that of your husband's, connect to your genealogy. After all, Henry will love hearing about it from you very soon. The years will fly by." I sounded like my mother and grandmother, the way I was doling out this advice.

Henry started fussing.

Ellany said, "Tomorrow is the parade. I want to see your grandfather in the big sleigh. Maybe I can catch candy for Henry. He can't eat it, of course, but maybe we could begin a tradition of coming here every year for Saint Nicholas Day celebrations. I'd like Henry to get to know your grandfather more. He's very nice."

"Thank you, Ellany."

She got up with the baby in her arms. "Good night."

"You'll think about going back to your parents-in-law's place?"

"I suppose I have to." She shrugged. "I have ideas for some poems and I want to write them down before I forget them."

"Okay. See you tomorrow."

After she went up the creaky staircase, I couldn't concentrate. I kept remembering her saying, "I don't know what I am."

With a burst of energy, I put aside the embroidery, picked up my phone from the table next to me, and then hit a number I knew would have answers for Ellany.

Monday morning dawned with sparkling sunshine. Another box appeared at my back door. It contained a tiny frame about the size of the palm of my hand. Inside was a sketch of the gazebo in my back yard, right down to the details depicting the ducks and ducklings Dillon had carved around the roof's eaves. The gifts were getting more personal. And lovelier. Dillon denied involvement, though.

I had asked guests to leave a pair of shoes outside their doors before going to bed so that I could give them an early taste of Saint Nicholas Day. I left small gifts including a deck of cards sporting depictions of my fairy tale fudge line. Local shops and restaurants also offered me coupons to drop in the shoes. Magnus and Skylark had immediately set to playing a wicked game of Euchre against Ellany and Jeremy in the parlor at seven in the morning. Jeremy had already been out for his run and showered.

The game ended when Jeremy left to take photos of the preparations going on for the big day, including witnessing the magical sleigh coming out of the town garage. He grabbed a banana-chocolate chip muffin on his way out the door.

The weather forecast predicted a perfect, sunny, winter-wonderland day with temperatures a notch above the freezing.

At the breakfast table I noticed Ellany still didn't wear her wedding band. She was in good spirits, though. The plan and surprise I'd put in place last night would come to fruition at noon, a long way off. I might be doing exactly the wrong thing for her and her husband and in-laws, but I had to take a chance. Christmastime was for families.

Students Dax and Nova came downstairs later, appreciative of their shoe surprise. They wore elf hats and expressed excitement about meeting with children again. The artwork the children created depicting Christmas nisse and Christmas around the world would be placed in store windows. School children were always let out for the big parade day.

Dillon was already helping Spuds and Al set up traffic direction signs. Cody was at the shop early today.

While I finished cleaning up after breakfast, Lucky Harbor scratched on the kitchen door. I let him in. He shook snow all over the towels I'd laid down in preparation for him.

At nine o'clock I took the dog with me down the hill to check on Grandpa and Grandma.

Grandpa growled about the heaviness of the Saint Nicholas costume. He stood in the living room with Grandma buttoning the regal red coat with its green satin placket and white fur trim.

Lucky Harbor barked at him.

I laughed. "He doesn't recognize you, Grandpa. Grandma knows how to make a great costume."

Grandma wrestled with buttons on Grandpa's front. "Thank you, Ava. I certainly got no compliments from this man."

Grandpa growled.

The dog barked again, hopping up and down. Grandpa wriggled from Grandma to pet the dog. "And I don't even have my wig and fake beard on yet. Patience, you curly mutt."

Grandma said, "Stand up, Gil. I've got two more buttons to button."

Several knocks on the front door silenced us.

Grandma said, "Who could that be?"

I went to the front window. There on the glassed-in porch stood Mercy. She wore black-tie attire. Her yellow curls looked freshly dyed and trimmed into a fluffy bubble. Beyond, out on the street sat a limousine, vapor from its tailpipe curling into the air.

I turned to Grandpa. "Did you hire a limo?"

"No. What the...?" Once he saw Mercy, he added, "Don't answer the door. She wants to drive me out in the countryside somewhere where she'll roll me and take this costume, leaving me for dead."

"Grandpa, you're being a drama queen. It's time you and Mercy buried the hatchet."

Grandma said, "Amen."

Grandpa said, "Let me get my hatchet. I'll show Mercy some mercy."

"Grandpa, puh-lease. It'll be nice to ride in a limo out to the town garage. The limo is warmer and nicer than my SUV that doesn't get warm for five miles."

Grandma patted Grandpa's back. "Gil, let that crazy woman drive you out there. It can't hurt to be nice." She kissed him, probably not so much out of love but to prevent another retort.

I opened the front door. "Hi, Mercy."

She growled. "Sure took you long enough. It's cold out. Think you can get rid of me by ignoring me?"

"I've tried that in the past and it doesn't work."

Grandpa yelled, "She's like a bad penny! Can't get rid of it either!"

Mercy snapped, "Certainly not like you got rid of that tax assessor."

I wailed, "Stop! Both of you, please."

"Hummph," Grandpa said.

I turned to Mercy. "Maybe we'll pass on the limo. We didn't order your service."

"It's not my idea, believe you me. The young village president coughed up dough and said he wanted to treat your grandpa right, seeing as how, well, you know."

Erik obviously felt bad that Grandpa was the Number One suspect in the murder based on the fingerprints on the murder weapon--one of Erik's steak knives. Who had pilfered that knife? Was I staring at her? I shook off the thoughts.

Grandma and I got Grandpa into the limousine. The passenger compartment sported hot coffee and several Swedish holiday pastry treats. Grandpa reached for one while his other hand slid shut the curtained window between passenger and driver.

As they drove off, Grandma muttered, "What is that woman up to?"

Chapter 31

Saint Nicholas

Local residents and tourists packed Main Street by ten o'clock. Pauline, Grandma, Mom, Dad, and I stood near the north end of the route at the fated Troubled Trout.

John's crew hurried about videotaping. Dillon chatted up acquaintances who appeared to have interest in hiring his construction services.

Several horses clopped by with riders decked out in holiday colors.

Our high school drum-and-bugle corps marched by banging and blaring out a Christmas tune. Several floats--pickup trucks, really-- followed sponsored by local businesses. Owners and their llamas from a ranch on Washington Island off the tip of Door County went by dressed in crimson regalia with tassels.

Then came goats pulling carts holding small holiday trees. Friends Jonas and Fontana walked alongside. Pauline and I jumped up and down, calling out, "You look beautiful, Fontana!" She and her husband wore green elf costumes, which made Fontana's red hair look like a flame flickering in the breeze.

Clowns and jugglers strolled by while we stamped our feet to keep warm.

Finally, Saint Nicholas--Grandpa--was coming up Main Street. He tossed candy toward kids who screamed with delight and scrambled to pick up the treats. Next to Grandpa, Spuds Schlimgen in a pointy green elf hat drove the motorized sleigh.

Grandpa called out to the crowd, "Come get your Christmas cheer! Children, children, your treats are near!"

I didn't see Jeremy but Greta moved in and out of the crowd--which maybe had swelled to about fifteen hundred or more on our short main drag. Greta smiled as she snapped photos of everything around her. It made me giggle just watching her. I hoped she got a permanent job with the newspaper. Christmastime was for wishes to come true.

When the parade finished a block past where we stood near the Troubled Trout, Spuds Schlimgen halted the Saint Nicholas vehicle in the spot marked "Reserved".

Dad and Dillon helped Grandpa in his cumbersome costume from the sleigh.

We were all congratulating Grandpa on a job well done when Spuds hollered, "Criminy, what's this?!"

He stood on the sleigh vehicle's seat with one hand holding up a white bed sheet while the other hand pointed to the bottom of the giant candy sack.

We rushed over. Dillon asked, "What's wrong, Spuds?"

His pointer arm began to shake. "Santa brought us an unusual gift--a body."

Dillon leaped aboard. "It's Jeremy Stone."

Jeremy lay scrunched in an awful curl at the bottom of the sculpture sack. He wore a coat, but no cap or hat. His camera and equipment were nowhere in sight.

Dillon called 911.

A wide-eyed Grandpa ripped off his fancy Saint Nick hat. "Let's get him out of there."

Dillon slung a leg over the rim of Santa's candy sack, climbing in gingerly, letting one foot at a time slide down next to Jeremy. Dad joined him. With help from John and Spuds as well, the men lifted out Jeremy.

Grandpa shed his bulky costume coat and offered it. "Wrap him in this."

With Jeremy trussed in the satin and gold-trimmed costume, the men hauled him to the nearest door--that of the Troubled Trout.

Customers scattered.

Erik charged at us. "What's going on? He's not dead, is he?"

Piers hauled up short next to us, still carrying a tray of beer glasses. "Not another dead man!"

I said, "He's not dead."

The men laid Jeremy on the floor only feet from dining tables and customers milling about in the bar area.

Pauline and I shut the door.

Dillon was checking Jeremy's pulse. "Still with us." Dillon checked Jeremy's head and neck. "There's blood. It's clotted, old."

"Or frozen," said Spuds.

Grandpa grunted. "He had to be in that sack well over an hour, since the time we picked up the float from the garage."

I asked, "You didn't see anything suspicious?"

"No. The candy was in the sack on the float when Mercy dropped me off. Spuds was already there."

Everybody looked at Spuds.

He held up his hands. "The candy was in the sack when I got there. I got in behind the wheel and we drove right to town in the rig and joined the tail-end of the parade like every year. Smooth as silk."

Greta rushed in, bug-eyed and breathless. "Everybody outside is talking about the Madison reporter being found dead."

"He's alive," I said. "We're waiting for the rescue squad."

Greta hopped back and forth on her feet, hunched into her coat. "Should I be taking photos of the sleigh? I don't know what to do. This is my first day as a reporter and this happens." Her teeth clattered loud enough for me to hear.

I said, "Take photos of the sleigh from every angle before people ruin evidence. The sheriff may need your photos."

Greta took a deep breath. "Thank you. I hope he's okay. I looked up to Stone."

Erik had rushed away and come back with a bar rag, handing it to Dillon. "I ran warm water in it. This might feel good to him."

Dillon applied the warmth to Jeremy's forehead, which elicited a small grunt. Many of us gave a sigh of relief.

A siren wailed outside. Greta hurried out.

Pauline and John held onto each other as they looked on.

The Emergency Medical Technicians were Nancy and Ronny Jenks, long-time volunteers. Dillon helped Nancy and Ronny exchange Grandpa's costume coat for a warming blanket. They loaded Jeremy on a stretcher and hurried outside to the waiting ambulance.

Grandpa climbed out of his costume pants and handed them to Mom. He wore denim jeans underneath.

Outside, we watched the emergency vehicle drive away.

Sheriff Tollefson pulled his SUV to a stop next to Grandpa's float. When Jordy got out, he said, "The Oosterlings and trouble. Imagine that. Dispatch said some guy was knocked out cold and left for dead in Gilsen's float."

I said, "Jeremy is lucky we found him. Actually, Spuds Schlimgen did. Stuffed at the bottom of the candy sack."

"Not exactly what children expect to have in their stockings at the holidays."

It didn't take the sheriff long to assess things. Snow flurries spewed from a cloud scuttling across the sun.

The sheriff walked up to Grandpa. "I'd like to talk to you more but in my office, where it's warm and private."

Grandpa said, "I had nothing to do with this."

The sheriff nodded. "I understand, but you're involved. We can talk about this out here in the cold in front of half of Fishers' Harbor, or you can meet me at the Justice Center."

Grandpa's face glowed red and it wasn't just from the cold. Then, pivoting, Grandpa took off on a run, weaving through the crowd.

My father hurried after him calling, "Dad? Dad, wait!"

Greta snapped a photo of the sheriff.

Jordy--to my surprise--wasn't chasing after Grandpa. Jordy threw himself into unfurling yellow crime scene tape, making onlookers back off.

I crowded him next to the sleigh. "Jordy, I want you to arrest my grandfather."

Pauline punched me in the arm. "Are you nuts?"

The sheriff looked about. Several people had phone video on. "I don't need your help."

"Pretend that you do. I have an idea."

Pauline groaned. "Oh, no."

Grandma and Mom hurried away, running to catch up with Grandpa and Dad.

I said to Jordy, "Here's my idea. Make a great show of arresting my grandpa."

"He bites," Jordy said. "The last time I tried to arrest him he bit me. I'll wait for backup."

I sighed. "You're wearing gloves so it won't be that bad. Arrest him and haul him into your vehicle in handcuffs. In front of people. Once he's inside, tell him this was all my idea and he's part of a plan to catch the murderer and the person who attempted to take out Jeremy Stone. My thought is this--I can use this to plant seeds around Fishers' Harbor. Feeling safe, the real perpetrator might spill information about what happened to Stone and Westergaard."

Jordy sighed. "Sounds like a bad television cop show. I recall you wrote for television a short time and you weren't that good."

The comment was a snowball in my face. "I was good, but...never mind."

The sheriff took his own photos of the vehicle. Then Jordy gave full attention to the crowded sidewalk up and down Main Street.

Grandpa and Dad were hemmed in by admirers several yards away, near Stella Zanderson spray painting a dog made of snow. Professor Olson and Skylark appeared to be talking with Grandpa.

Jordy strolled around the sleigh again. He looked over at me. "I'll try your idea."

Pauline groaned.

I blinked in surprise.

Jordy ripped handcuffs from a pocket and then set off toward Grandpa.

Pauline yelled, "Ava, what have you done? And to your own grandfather!"

Chapter 32

Skritek Strike

s the sheriff cuffed him, Grandpa ranted, "I'm innocent, you bonehead! Help me, somebody! Ava, where are you? Help! Tell this sheriff he's got it all wrong!"

My heart rate likely registered off the Richter scale for earthquakes.

Several instances of "Oh my gosh!" erupted from the crowd as I trotted forward with Pauline tailing me.

She said, "I see some of my students. Thank goodness your grandpa removed his costume. Those little ones would be traumatized witnessing Santa being arrested."

We dodged people taking photos or muttering. I had to make this plan look good, so I yelled, "Sheriff, stop! You can't do this to my grandfather!"

Jordy stuffed Grandpa into the sheriff's vehicle. My grandfather quieted, as if Jordy told him the plan. Grandpa then yelled complaints, turning red as a Christmas berry.

The sheriff barreled past us to talk with Spuds Schlimgen. Spuds threw his arms about.

With it being lunchtime, the crowd began dispersing for food and shopping.

Grandma and Mom were hugging each other, not aware of the plan the sheriff and I had hatched. I texted Grandma and Mom. They didn't break into a smile--acting, I hoped.

The sheriff hurried back. "Spuds says Mercy Fogg drove your grandfather to the garage where the float was assembled." The sheriff used a loud voice, as if wanting others to hear.

I nodded. "Yes, she picked up Grandpa at the house. Erik hired Mercy to do that."

"So, your grandfather and Mercy were together out at the garage, the same time as Jeremy Stone? And with Spuds, a friend of your grandfather's." His pinched eyebrows said this was no game but a real accusation.

A chill rippled through me. "Sheriff, there's no way my grandfather would collude with Mercy and Spuds to harm that reporter."

"But they were out there." Jordy gave me a laser-like look.

"I...I...guess they were. Of course. But somebody had to be out there before them to stuff Jeremy down into the bottom of the sleigh."

Pauline muttered, "And fill it with maybe a thousand candy bags."

Jordy pulled into his full height. "I suppose you want me to think elves did this."

"That's a possibility, Jordy. We have gnomes around here, too."

"Gnomes?"

"You know. Nisse is what they're called by the Danes and Norwegians, or nissen by the local Swedes, and we Belgians call them skritek. They live in oak trees."

"Aren't these all the same as elves?"

"No. Gnomes like the skritek are small faeries, a foot tall, so they'd be able to work together to heft Jeremy into the sleigh. Elves on the other hand are rather chubby and very short."

Pauline said, "Disguised as mice sometimes. They can spin gold from grain. I know. These are tales my kindergarteners thrive on."

The sheriff heaved a giant sigh but continued taking notes on his small pad. "It would be helpful if you could find your elves or skritek so that I could interview them."

"Well," I said, holding back a smirk, "if I happen across any in the woods, I'll let you know. Do you carry handcuffs small enough for skritek wrists?"

The sheriff shrugged me off, clicked his pen, and then stuffed his notepad into an inside parka pocket. "Thanks. I'll have a quick chat with Erik. And don't touch the vehicles." He indicated the one holding Grandpa and the sleigh float.

Jordy headed inside the Troubled Trout.

Pauline batted me on head. Her eyes blazed. "What are you doing? Your grandfather is arrested five days before my wedding because of you. Why did you want him arrested?"

She took a step away, but I grabbed her purse handle and pulled her back. "You have to help me, Pauline. Grandpa's in trouble every which way I look at this. And it scares me."

Pauline threw her arms around me. "Okay. It's about Grandpa. You had Gil arrested so the guilty party thinks it's all over and tips his hand?"

"Or her hand. I'm just lucky the sheriff and Grandpa went along with it on the spur of the moment. Murderers make mistakes and get too confident. This could draw out the perpetrator."

We said goodbye to Dillon and John. Dillon left to work on the house in Sister Bay. John had to get home for an online meeting with television comrades. I imagined his parade story would need finessing. Public TV wouldn't feature holiday cheer with an attempted murder.

Several yards away Greta talked with Spuds. Had Spuds murdered Usher and had Jeremy confronted Spuds about it at the town garage? Spuds had motive. The golf course would suffer a high tax assessment and Spuds could lose his job, which was his whole life. A chill wrenched my body over the possibility of Grandpa's old buddy being guilty. I could also see why Grandpa would keep it a secret and want to move out of town. He didn't want to routinely see Spuds.

Pauline and I headed down the crowded sidewalk in the direction of the Blue Heron Inn five blocks away.

Greta caught up with us, puffing. "What do you think is going on?"

"The sheriff believes my grandfather is guilty." A lie, and I ached to reveal this to an old friend like Greta, but an enthusiastic reporter could ruin the plan to lure out the perpetrator. "I have to prove his innocence."

"How are you going to do that?"

Lying, I said, "Jeremy must have stumbled onto something about Usher and asked too many questions of the wrong person."

The three of us women poked along, squeezing through the crowd. The smell of buttery popcorn floated in the chilly air.

Greta said, "Do you have any clues? That poor Jeremy. I was hoping he'd mentor me. What about Usher's wife? What do you think about her?"

Pauline said, "Hailey's likely upset about her husband's portrayal in the media."

I said, "Mad at Jeremy maybe. She's in shape. Could have lifted him into the float. Do you know Hailey?"

"No. Should I interview her?" Greta gave a pained look, then consulted her phone. "I'm getting texts from the newspaper for a report. They heard about the arrest of your grandfather already. What should I do?"

"Talk to people in the crowd, Greta. Please don't ask my parents and grandmother anything. They're devastated by my grandfather being hauled off in front of a bunch of people."

"Of course not! Being a journalist is hard. And this is only my first day being a reporter!" Greta shuffled off into the crowd, tapping a person on the shoulder.

Pauline and I headed toward a clothing shop featuring ugly but popular Christmas sweaters. We paused at the window. Staring at red and green sweaters with dizzying holiday patterns and sequins seemed an appropriate match with the chaos around me.

Pauline said, "Do you think Greta will find out anything from Hailey?"

"Nothing more than we did. Hailey wants to go to Florida. You have to focus on wedding preparations. What's left to do?"

She heaved a loud sigh that sent fog into the air. "I don't have the horses and carriage yet for the wedding parade."

"You have your new convertible. Ride on that. I'll drive."

She laughed. "No way. You'd speed and we'd end up in a snowbank. I want horses and a carriage. It's a Victorian wedding, after all." Then she groaned. "There's so much to do. Your dress isn't done, and John's hat isn't here yet, and Saint Ann's people said I'm fifty people over the maximum the church can hold."

"Fifty over?"

"A lot of those are my past kindergarteners. They're like my own children. Somehow I have to get them inside that church."

"Will they fit in the choir loft?"

"It's already stuffed with the county's ecumenical women's council singing the songs." Pauline brushed snow off her sleeves. "Everything is about numbers in life, isn't it?"

She sparked a new thought. "Numbers. Of course. This had to happen between around eight o'clock this morning after Jeremy left my inn and the time Grandpa and Mercy would have arrived at the garage, shortly before ten o'clock and the start of the parade."

"A two-hour window at most for an attempted murder?"

"Yes. Somebody was free for a couple of hours. That would be difficult for any of the business people because they were getting their establishments ready for the crowds."

Pauline said, "True, but many have extra employees at this time of year. They might have ducked out for a, well..."

"For a little murder."

We walked onward. I mentioned my suspicions that Grandpa could be thinking Spuds Schlimgen might be the murderer. She thought that horrifying but plausible.

A few steps later, when the crowd thinned, Pauline said, "You mentioned Mercy said Erik rented the limousine to take your grandfather out there. Do you think this was a setup to blame your grandfather or Mercy for the murder, if a murder had been committed? Why would Erik hire a limo for your grandfather?"

A confusing yet somewhat comforting thought emerged. "What if Erik was trying to make sure my grandfather didn't go out to that garage alone this morning?"

"You mean Erik thought Gilpa was in danger?"

"I believe that's the case, Pauline. Erik isn't a murderer but any restaurant owner worth his salt sees and hears things that he doesn't dare talk about or he'd lose his clientele."

"But him using Mercy as a bodyguard makes no sense either. Erik knows Mercy and Grandpa hate each other." She gasped.

"What?"

"Ava, what if Erik and Spuds are keeping an eye on Mercy because Erik knows or suspects she murdered Usher?" She juggled her purse from one shoulder to the other. "Your grandfather would never have gone with Mercy Fogg in that limo unless he had a good reason--such as trying to get her to confess to the murder."

Pauline's theory hit me. "You could be right! Oh my gosh."

Pauline began strutting faster, as she often did when thinking hard. It came from her old college basketball days. Excitement meant energy that had to be spent. "I'm no good at this, not like you. I don't like Erik endangering your grandfather by having him ride with a murderer."

"Pauline, slow down." She was bumping into strangers who raised eyebrows at her.

I pulled her to the street where we could walk in private. I said, "It's clear Mercy and Grandpa didn't harm Stone. But somebody from the breakfast drinking club might have gone out there knowing Grandpa would be there." My next thought was tough to voice. "They intended to kill Grandpa, but found Jeremy ahead of everybody, alone, and then felt they had to do away with him. Maybe Stone accused the party of murdering Westergaard. When the limousine showed up with two people, the murderer knew they couldn't go through with trying to kill two more people, and so they ran. We have to go out there again and look around, Pauline."

"No, we don't. Do I have to hit you with my purse to knock sense into you? The sheriff can go out there."

"An hour from now after he drives down to Sturgeon Bay. With snow falling, any possible evidence will be covered up."

Pauline stopped us with a hand on my shoulder. She flicked her gaze ahead. "Mercy's coming right for us. And she's not smiling."

Chapter 33

Mercy's Secrets

Mercy still wore her tuxedo, now speckled with snowflakes. Pink furry earmuffs with a furry headband arched over her blond curls.

Luckily I spied Professor Earlywine not too far behind her. "Professor Earlywine!"

Mercy huffed. "What's going on, Ooster Booster? Somebody said you killed the reporter. After your grandfather killed Westergaard. The Oosterlings are racking up bodies."

I wasn't about to clue her in on the shaky plan I had with the sheriff involving Grandpa's fake arrest. After all, Mercy could be Usher's murderer. The best way to fool Mercy was to tell her the truth because she assumed I lied all the time. "It's true my grandfather has been arrested for attempted murder of Jeremy Stone and possibly for the murder of Westergaard. I planned it all behind the scenes to save our town. Are you happy now?"

Mercy shrugged, blinking in confusion.

Professor Boyd Earlywine caught up with us.

"Professor," I said, struggling for a way to shed Mercy, "have you been to Mercy Fogg's house? You remember Mercy, right?"

Boyd was forty-ish, a sandy-haired boy-next-door guy who wore the latest men's fashions. Today he wore an expensive, red down coat worthy of a trek in any of the winter hiking trails found in our state parks.

Boyd shrugged. "Hello, Mercy. Long time no see."

"What brings you back to town? The smell of murder? Be careful. It happens to people staying at the inn, it seems, and eating the local fudge."

"Mercy!" I shouted. "Stop that." She was referring to the professor's stay when the famous actress died with my fudge in her throat--but the fudge wasn't at fault. "He's not staying with me. He owns property in the county now." I turned to the professor. "You're researching local cultural history, correct?"

He nodded.

"Have you been inside Mercy's house?"

"No."

"Well then, you've missed beautiful handicrafts reminiscent of pioneer days."

"Oh?"

Mercy interjected, "I'm a folk artist. I paint stuff."

"Like what?" he asked.

"Chairs, chests of drawers, trunks."

I added, "And walls and ceilings. Her house is phenomenal."

Pauline's eyebrows shot up at my lie.

Boyd's brows rose as well. "Is there historical significance in your folk art, Mercy?"

At that moment, Greta joined us. "What's this I hear about folk art?" She hefted her camera. "I need color, the editor says. We do better on Facebook with color and unusual things."

I said, "Great timing, Greta. Visiting Mercy's home would be worth your time. Yours, too, Professor."

Mercy said with a smile, "Please come to dinner, Boyd. You and I can chat and I can show you what I do well."

Mercy meant that as a double-entendre. The head-tilt and extra blinking gave her away.

Boyd said, "Why don't we all go to the house now." Boyd was married, so this invitation was asking us to be his bodyguards. "I'll take phone pics so I can follow up later."

Mercy's smile reached her ears. "Really? That's great!"

Greta said, "This is working out well for me, too."

Pauline said, "Ava and I need to head to her shop."

Mercy said, "No, you don't. I was just there not ten minutes ago and Cody and that old girlfriend of his were handling things just fine. Your fudge is doing famously well, too, Ooster. Can't you give me a chance to shine? You need to come along to relate the story about John being in my bed."

Pauline groaned about her fiancé being involved in a mishap in which Mercy had rescued him after he'd been knocked out.

The professor gave me a pained expression that said, You're coming because I don't want to be alone with this woman. Evidently he didn't believe Greta alone was enough protection.

Pauline and I relented. After all, this would be just a half hour of my time and I might find out if Mercy murdered one man and attempted to murder another.

Mercy's house was an old bi-level, painted brown with white trim, with a centered white door. A two-car garage sat to the right.

Indoors, Mercy's golden retriever Queenie poked a wet-but-warm nose into our hands. The place smelled of sauerkraut and bacon, potent.

A rainbow explosion of colors assaulted our eyesight. I'd been here in the past, so I wasn't too shocked, but I felt like pulling on dark eyeglasses.

Professor Earlywine, on the other hand, stood perusing the living room area with mouth agape and wide eyes.

Greta clicked away with the professional camera. "This place is crazy wonderful!"

Hand-painted landscapes, flowers, depictions of ducks and deer, red fox, and rabbits in every color of the rainbow covered everything. Pink bunnies, blue deer, polka-dotted ducks, plaid flowers--everything was off-kilter from its natural norm.

Wood furniture in several styles bore hand-painted designs with dots and stripes and animal circuses and rainbow depictions of roses, sunflowers, and tulips.

There were also Native American motifs on objects including pillows.

Colors and patterns collided or clashed at every turn.

The professor wandered into the middle of the living room. "This almost hurts my eyes--and I find it exquisite!"

Mercy pumped a fist into the air. "How much do you think it added to the value of my home?"

Boyd said, "Folk art has its aficionados. But I believe this art may devalue your home."

Mercy ripped off her bow tie and tossed it to a red-striped couch on one side of the room. "Devalue? That's what that tax assessor said. How can you call my art 'exquisite' and then tell me it lowers my house value?"

Boyd appealed to Pauline and me with a pained look.

I did my best to control my voice. "Why do you care if the value of your house goes down? Your taxes will go down. Isn't that what you want? Like everybody else?"

Greta said, "Yeah. You won't have to move. That's what people are upset about around Fishers' Harbor--that Westergaard would ruin our town. High taxes mean people go out of business and move. Pretty soon there's nobody left to buy stuff from each other. But you can stay and enjoy your folk art life while the rest of us have to fight back."

Mercy tossed off her tuxedo jacket, sending it sailing by us to a stuffed chair with an ugly orange-and-olive-colored afghan covering it. "I need to sell my house."

"Why?" I asked.

"I need the money." She marched about the living room, as if confused. "Are you happy to know I'm broke?"

Her admission shocked me. She was a proud woman who didn't like others thinking less of her or pitying her. Maybe she was trying to impress the professor standing in front of her.

Pauline cleared her throat. Greta was biting her lower lip. The professor appeared to have turned to stone.

"Mercy," I began, eyeing the front door for our escape, "I'm sorry you're going through a bad time--"

"No, you're not. Heck, look at you with the inn, and owning that rundown building you call a candy shop on the harbor that people think is so quaint, and your grandparents owning a house on Duck Marsh Street, and your boyfriend renting the cabin across the street. And you're cozying up to young Cody who inherited the rental cabins from Lloyd Mueller. Heck, you're taking over my town."

"Your town? Mercy, you have to get over not being village president. Move on."

"You mean you want me to move out of town, don't you? To end up homeless?" She batted the air, then flopped onto the sofa.

Queenie came to her, panting, sitting and then placing her head on Mercy's knees. Mercy reached out to stroke Queenie's head. The scene tugged at my heart, despite the way Mercy continued to vex me.

The professor snapped more photos with his phone while shuffling toward the front door with an obvious escape in mind.

Greta resumed photographing objects around the room.

I said to Mercy, "Nobody wants you to move out of town. You've been here all your life and you know its history. You're a treasure."

Pauline cleared her throat again, signaling I was laying it on a bit thick.

I pressed on. "You're confusing me, Mercy. You love Fishers' Harbor, and yet you want to sell your house. Is this really about your father?" Her father, in his nineties, wasn't doing well health-wise and was in a care facility for veterans in our county.

Tears shimmered in Mercy's eyes. I'd guessed correctly.

She rose, swiping back the tears as Queenie leaped onto the warm spot on the sofa left behind. "Never mind. It's none of your business. You're all like that Reece Allard fellow, worried he has to sell his studio but he's going to get big bucks for it, unlike me. And Erik? Well, he and the rest of them threatened the assessor and wished he'd disappear."

"They did?" I asked, incredulous by her outburst. "When?"

"Every time I saw them on the street or at the bar."

"What about the morning Westergaard was found dead?"

Mercy huffed, shaking her mop of curls. "I was in my snowplow."

"Not the entire time. I have it on good authority you were inside the bar at one point. What did you witness?"

She did a double-take at me. Her face flushed. "I saw Travis Klubertanz get up from the floor, along with Westergaard. They appeared to have been fighting. Erik looked a bit rough himself but he found hot coffee and filled my thermos and then I left."

"Did anybody follow you out onto the street?"

"You mean like Usher and somebody chasing him with a knife? I got in the plow and drove down the street. By then I had to pee like crazy, and you know the rest."

"Did you see my grandfather at the bar?"

"No, but somebody yelled something like, 'Get back here, Gil, where ya goin'?' I assumed he was heading out the back door. He doesn't like me in case you don't know."

She appealed to the professor near the front door. "Can you show those pictures to anybody who might think the way this place is painted is something special? That my art is worth something? You must know people at the university in Green Bay."

"I, I, don't know," he said.

"You're lying."

I hurried over. "I'm sure he can share the photos with somebody at the university."

Boyd nodded, though I guessed he had no intention of sharing any of this.

Mercy smiled again as if she'd never had an outburst. "This house is an art installation, a museum of art. And if the word gets out, the price will go up and somebody will want to buy this unique house. I'll let them have all the furnishings, too, for a modest price."

Greta joined us at the front door. "I could come back sometime and go through the rest of the house for you." She hefted her camera to make her point.

"Why not now?" Mercy asked.

Greta said, "It's past noon and lunch hour. I have to get the parade and snow sculpture photos uploaded to the newspaper now."

Mercy gave a curt nod. "Okay. We'll make a date later."

We said our goodbyes, then began the long walk across the village residential area to where Boyd had left his car near Main Street.

Greta trotted ahead, in a hurry to get someplace warm and upload photos to the editor.

The cold wind bit at the rest of us.

Pauline said, "Mercy is nuts."

"Always has been," I said.

Boyd muttered, "I have to say she's not much nuttier than some of the art professors I've met on some campuses."

Pauline's long stride kept us puffing along. "She scares me. Somebody that emotional seems desperate enough to murder. She admitted to going inside the restaurant. She might have grabbed a knife and then came out and did him in. Have you thought of that, Ava?"

"Of course. Then she came to Duck Marsh Street and used Dillon's cabin to wash up so there was no evidence on her. Boyd, what do you think?"

"She's got potential."

"As an artist or a murderer?"

"Both. I don't know what to make of her."

A few yards went by before I spoke again. "Boyd, something's been gnawing at me about the breakfast club." He didn't respond, so I went on. "My grandfather did something or said something Thursday morning at the Troubled Trout that upset himself and others. He won't talk about it. And nobody wants to either. What's going on?"

Boyd halted on the sidewalk. A flock of chattering English sparrows flew past. "It has to do with what was not said. You see, your grandfather excused himself."

"Did he hide out in the men's restroom? That's been mentioned."

"A couple of us went into the can during the arguing and there was no Gilsen. We did our business and came back to our drinks and then Gilsen walks in the front door."

My breath caught. "You mean he went out the back door and then circled around?"

Boyd paled. "Uh, yes. It seemed odd."

"So this is what's been making him nervous. He..."

Pauline said, "He witnessed the murder?"

Boyd shrugged. "I don't know. He took off fast."

My brain felt as if ice floes had crashed. "Do the others believe Grandpa had something to do with Usher's murder?"

Boyd nodded.

I took out my phone.

Pauline asked, "Who are you calling?"

"Parker Balousek." Our family attorney. I hadn't heard from him since calling him days ago. Now I wondered if Parker had hesitated returning my call for a good reason--Grandpa had retained Parker last Thursday morning. Had Grandpa killed Usher, used the snowplow to fashion a cover-up, and then harmed nosey Jeremy with Spuds' help?

I didn't believe the scenario for one second. Somebody wanted Grandpa to take the fall. But who?

Chapter 34

Dandy Double-Cross

After excusing myself with Boyd and Pauline, I hurried to Oosterlings' Live Bait, Bobbers & Belgian Fudge & Beer. Deep thinking required making fudge.

I mixed up a batch of Saint Mary of the Snow's Divinity Fudge. It sold well in winter because it looked like snowdrifts. I colored some batches red and green for the holiday, but also pink, blue, and purple. Children loved the colors.

One child had wanted to know why I didn't color some yellow for "yellow snow".

His mother put a hand over his mouth and told him, "That wasn't nice." She doubled her fudge order as a way to apologize. I gave her six free pieces.

Attorney Parker Balousek called back finally. He'd met with Grandpa and Dad at the Justice Center. Things didn't look good for Grandpa.

"Hold on! The sheriff and I agreed to the fake arrest as a way to draw out the murderer."

Silence on the other end of the phone call dug into me like claws.

Parker said, "I'm afraid the sheriff arrested him for real."

"No!" Jordy had betrayed me? Played me for a fool?

"Yes, Ava. This is real."

I wondered if a witness had come forward to reveal Grandpa went out the restaurant's back door and come in the front door at the time of Westergaard's death. I now understood why Grandpa had been acting so strangely lately.

As the probable last of my candy shop customers left late that afternoon, the weight of the day pressed on me. My arms felt like lead while cleaning the copper kettles.

Cody called out from where he was re-stocking the beer cooler on the other side of the store, "Miss Oosterling, buck up! We had good sales today, even in the fishing tackle department. Christmas gift buying and stocking-stuffer sales are heating up."

"Thanks, Ranger. And the front art window looks nice." Spray-painted holiday designs and stapled tinfoil decorations covered the broken window's plywood and plastic inside and out. I took heart in the community support. "Did the professor and Dax and Nova help with that?"

"Just Dax and Nova, and Bethany. The four of us had a blast with the little kids."

I dried the kettles with paper towels.

Cody came over, handing me more towels. "Is your grandpa going to stay out of prison?"

That gave me a chuckle. "Grandpa didn't kill anybody, so he's not going anywhere."

"He hates being cooped up. I bet they're having a hard time with him. So who killed that tax man? And tried to do in that journalist?"

"I wish I knew." We finished cleaning the kettles. I then tackled the front of the display case to clean the glass of fingerprints and kids' nose prints, a daily chore.

Cody said, "You know what I do when I don't know something?" He was emptying Grandpa's coffeepot of its spent grounds.

"What?"

"I write down everything about it I know. It makes me start remembering things, and if there are still holes in what I know, I go out in the woods and take a walk. By the time I'm done with the walk, my head is filled with new, smart stuff."

I paused. "So you're suggesting I get out in the snowy woods tonight?"

"It's supposed to be clear tonight, no wind, a full moon. Nature has a way of giving us answers, Miss Oosterling. Talk to the man in the moon. Maybe he'll give you answers and tell you who murdered that tax guy and tried to do the same to Jeremy." His laughter filled the shop.

"Ranger, talking to the moon isn't going to solve a murder and I doubt the sheriff or local courts would find the moon a credible expert to rely on."

Cody hoisted the empty coffeepot. "How do you know? You tell people that chocolate has good things for the body and brain. Try my idea. When I go into the woods and talk to the trees and owls and animals and the moon and stars, something settles down inside of me and

I can think straight. It helps my condition. Then I go home and in my dreams I get all the ideas I need for my next paper or exam. You have to believe that trees and the moon talk, though."

A big smile split his face. "It's Christmas, Miss Oosterling. If you don't believe in the man in the moon, then talk to gnomes in the woods. You always tell children in our shop the gnomes you call skritek and the elves are protectors of animals. Humans are animals. Those skritek and elves are looking out for you and Grandpa. Take milk with you when you go out tonight into the woods. You said they like milk."

Cody darted back to the kitchen with the coffeepot. He likely felt embarrassed. He'd never lectured me before. It told me how deeply he cared about my welfare and family.

In that moment, it made sense to go for a nighttime hike in the woods. I trusted Cody's wisdom and I needed answers.

Chapter 35

Midnight Madness

D illon was thrilled to take a nighttime hike in the woods. "Do you realize how much time we don't get to spend alone together?"

His words cratered me for a second. Being present, ready, and serving others filled my life. Constant guests, Grandpa and Grandma, Pauline, and Cody, and of course customers kept my attention, which I gladly gave. Where was Dillon in that mix? It shamed me to realize we were often those proverbial ships passing in the night.

When Dillon arrived at the inn, I leaped into his arms. We stood on the front open verandah. My warm cheek nestled next to his cold one.

He said, "Hey, honey, what's this lovin' for?"

"We need to forget this day. Erase it from our minds for a while. Are you game?"

His kiss lifted me off my feet. "Can't wait to get to the park. I need to check out the park's sledding hill anyway before Saturday, make sure there are no downed trees on it."

Pauline's fiancé John wanted a unique activity for wedding guests-- sledding and tobogganing down one of the steepest, longest hills in Door County--Peninsula State Park's golf course Hill 16.

Dillon drove his construction truck. The hot air blasting at my legs and face felt good at seven o'clock this dark Monday evening with below-freezing temperatures. As we drove along, snowflakes swirled across the truck's hood like flocks of white birds creating murmurations.

Peninsula State Park was mere minutes away. It had one of the prettiest and better-preserved lighthouses in the country with living quarters. The park also sported a beautiful new lookout tower that could accommodate wheelchairs. Its wood walkway threaded through treetops to deliver observers to the lookout platform. I couldn't wait to get closer to the sky.

My backpack included cheese, fudge, crackers, a thermos of hot cocoa, insulated mugs, and a small notepad and pen. I smiled at the prospect of meeting up with Cody's gnomes or seeing the man in the moon shining down. Maybe I'd see messages written on moonbeams. Fanciful thoughts, but I surely needed answers in my life.

We were soon well inside the park now, driving on the Shore Road past the golf course and coming to the Minnehaha Trail. We parked in the small lot next to Nicolet Beach and Nicolet Bay. This shallow bay was frozen, though further out it was not.

Moonlight sparkled on everything.

We planned to snowshoe from the Minnehaha Trail to the Eagle Trail to the east. If we weren't too tired, we could make it to the lookout tower and view the bay and lights of Ephraim.

As we strapped on snowshoes in the parking lot, Dillon said, "I can't believe the wedding time is here already. No escaping now for John."

"He better not try to escape. Pauline is over the moon. Speaking of which..."

The white orb smiled down. Trees around us lassoed the breeze and left a hush. The woodland silence and moonlight bathed me, refreshed me already and I'd barely taken a step.

After our hike, we'd circle around in the truck to check Hill 16 on our way out of the park. Dillon had strong floodlights he could plug into his truck.

We had adjustable poles with snow baskets on the ends to help push against snow. From boots to knees we wore gaiters to keep dry. It appeared others had opened the Minnehaha Trail earlier today. Dillon said we'd probably meet deep snow on the Eagle Trail because beginners tended not to enter the uneven, rocky terrain overlooking dangerous cliffs overlooking the bay.

As we started out, the perfume of pines on the frosty air feathered around us.

While my backpack contained provisions, Dillon's held emergency fare: headlamp and batteries, knife, matches, extra socks, and a high-tech sleeping bag to use for warmth if we rested and needed to add a layer against the below-freezing air.

We trudged along, not talking. Our snowshoes whoosh-whooshed in our slow cadence.

After maybe fifty yards, Dillon held up hand to halt us. The moon hung above like a large, white porcelain plate. As the breeze paused, utter silence seeped about us again.

Dillon whispered, "Isn't this great?"

I whispered back, "It's wonderful." The chilly air, though, made me add, "I hope Jeremy's okay. He'd almost frozen to death before we found him." A shiver shook me. "I keep going back to Mercy. Her desperation about her house and money situation spell guilty."

"Mercy may believe Jeremy makes Fishers' Harbor look bad with his reports of trouble and she believes nobody will buy her creative house as a result."

We went ahead a few steps.

Dillon said, "What about all those guys at the restaurant? Each seems to have a very different version of what happened. Too bad Jeremy wasn't there, but you said our newspaper delivery woman was there. What's her take on things?"

"Not much. She says she poked her head in but hurried off to visit Travis Klubertanz and he corroborated that. He was at the restaurant but rushed away after the fight with Usher."

"Could Usher have discovered Greta and Travis having an affair, and then Greta or Travis killed him to keep him quiet? Though, those two are solid people."

"Right. They're entrenched here." I sighed, feeling the exertion. My breath hung in a cloud illuminated by the moonlight. "Hailey seems like the guilty one, if it wasn't Mercy."

As we stood side by side, Dillon's eyes soaked up the moonlight's reflection on the snow. "We came out here to forget all that, remember?" He planted a cold kiss on my cheek.

Darn the man. He was right.

We trekked on. Our snowshoes whispered a step at a time, only occasionally snapping a twig underfoot. Moonglow created webs of shadows among the bare branches around us. I breathed in the scent of nature, clean and fresh as linens that had hung on a clothesline.

We entered virgin snow. Earlier trekkers had turned back. Excitement for the unknown caught fire inside of me. The sense of discovery lured me, step upon snowshoe step. Thoughts ebbed to Grandpa, sitting in jail. Parker said the sheriff had arrested him for real. Maddening.

I must have growled out loud, then sighed heavily.

Dillon asked, "A happy sigh?"

"Cody said the moon would talk to me. He said there'd be gnomes."

"What's the moon saying?"

"I'm still working on the translation."

Dillon chuckled. "He looks happy. He'll probably tell us some silly joke."

We walked on and I felt lighter of spirit.

Minutes later, the hoot of an owl invited a pause. He sat in an oak tree amid brown leaves too stubborn to fall in autumn or winter.

"Elves live in oak trees," I said. "If we look at the base we might see a door."

"Too much snow," Dillon said. "Besides, wouldn't it be rude to start digging around a stranger's house?"

I laughed. "Yes. Somebody took that stone from Hailey's house and threw it through my shop window. That was rude. Not an elf thing."

"A kid maybe. The person had to be fast. They ran off before Gil could catch a glimpse."

"Maybe Hailey who's physically fit. It was her rock."

"Let the sheriff solve the murder. Your job is to relax."

After the owl took wing for a silent glide through the forest, disappearing into the shadows, Dillon kissed me on the lips. "You're beautiful under the moonlight."

"Only under the moonlight?"

"Oh, so that's how you roll? I have to get poetic? You're the essence of beauty and nothing on Earth, heck, the universe, no, the solar system, can compare with you. See the moon up there? He told me he agrees. Cody's right. The man up there talks."

I gave him a playful punch on one shoulder before we moved on.

After another half hour's walk, we were close to the cliffs. We decided to pause and warm up with the cocoa. A small opening with a log invited us to park our derrieres.

Dillon put his arms around my shoulders. "There's just the two of us in the world right now. I like that."

"So do I. Thanks for coming out here with me. I have to admit I haven't taken the time for many walks since coming home from California."

He kissed my forehead. "I'm glad you came home."

"I'm glad you came looking for your lost dog that day in spring."

I poured hot cocoa into the insulated mugs. Dillon unzipped the sleeping bag to act like a blanket over our legs. The fudge, cheese, and crackers sat on top of our backpacks at our feet.

Dillon settled an arm around my shoulders, bringing me deeper into his warm sphere.

I considered the man in the moon. "What's he saying now?"

Dillon's mirthful chuckle answered. "That we were meant to be together."

I kissed him on the cheek. "Do you wonder what's ahead for us?"

"If Cody says the moon has answers, we should ask the moon what our future holds."

I pondered that while sipping warm cocoa. "Cody's going to make a great forest ranger." I reached down for a piece of dark chocolate fudge and cheddar cheese, a delicious combination. "I believe Bethany wants to get back together with Cody."

"Stay out of their love life."

"I will."

"Promise? You realize that poor kid needs a life of his own. He thinks of himself as your babysitter and you're exhausting him."

Dillon was right. Cody watched out for me and nobody had a better employee. "Do you think I rely on him too much?"

Dillon said, "Cody considers you a sister. He'd do anything for a sister."

"When I first met him he insisted I act more like his mother, which he didn't like from me. He said I didn't trust him and I babied him, and, well, he was right."

"See? You can change. You went from being a mother to a sister."

I stuffed my mouth with another bite of cheese and fudge.

Dillon said, "You went from being my friend, and now my fiancée. When do you think you'll be ready to be my wife?"

I almost choked on the fudge. "You mean, be your wife again. We can wait a while. We already know how that felt."

He poured us more cocoa. Fragrant steam fluttered into the air. A breeze ruffled pine boughs nearby, whistling. "No, Ava, we don't know how it felt at all. We eloped. The chapel in Las Vegas was the size of one of the historic Belgian roadside chapels we have in our county. They have enough room for a priest and two people to kneel. I want a big wedding this time, something with a couple hundred people--no, let's go for a thousand--in the church."

I stared at him, shocked. "Pauline and John's wedding is putting you in the mood. It's like a hangover. You'll get over it."

He laughed, the sound deadened by the snow and trees around us. "I want a parade. You'll see. We'll ride in a carriage this Saturday for Pauline and John, and you'll love it."

"Pauline can't find horses that aren't already booked at wineries for sleigh rides."

"Forget horses for us. Our wedding can be in summer, on the beach behind Erik's bar. People could motor up in boats to watch us exchange our vows. Then your grandpa could take us and the wedding party out for a ride on the bay."

Tears erupted from me.

"Hey, my little moonbeam, what's the matter?"

"Grandpa. He always has boat trouble. I think he believes he's jinxed and therefore he has to move away from the water."

"How about we get a boat and get married on it and live on it."

"You're very in the mood for marriage. Why?"

Dillon pulled the sleeping bag up around us. "Finding Ellany and her baby in that house in Sister Bay made me think about what I wanted in life, no, what I needed."

A jolt went through me. "Now you want a baby? You were the one who said we should take things slowly."

He laughed. "I meant finding Ellany and her child during Christmas season made me feel for her because she was alone and lonely. That husband of hers is wasting precious time not being with that sweet child and the woman he loves. She's the one who ran away, but her husband is the foolish one."

"They're mere kids, Dillon. We can forgive them both."

Dillon planted a kiss on my cheek. "That's why I love you. You're sweet."

Kissing him back I inhaled the pleasant sensation of fudge and hot cocoa. "I did something that I hope will bring Ellany and Brendan and their whole family together again soon."

"What's that?"

"I asked Dotty and Lois to find Brendan's parents and explain the situation. The women's group knows everybody in the county. Dotty and Lois know how to make things happen. With their help we can get the family back together by Christmas. If there are circumstances such as them needing help with heating bills this winter, or with groceries if her husband's out of job, we women of the county will help."

Dillon kissed my forehead. "For once I'm in total agreement about your interference in somebody else's life."

"If only Dotty and Lois could solve a murder and get grandpa out of trouble."

"You scare me when you get so involved in such business."

"What will I do if Grandpa retires from our shop?"

"Honey, it's inevitable that your grandparents may want to retire. And you can handle the shop."

"No, Dillon." I pushed the sleeping bag off my chest. "That's Grandpa's shop. He's the heart of it."

Dillon leaned down and began packing our leftovers into my backpack. "Honey, maybe he wants an excuse not to be there every day so you can shine even more, become the true boss of the shop. He knows he causes trouble. If he moves away, it takes the heat off you."

Dillon's words unsettled me. Although Dillon didn't mean to say it was my fault Grandpa was being pushed to move away, I still felt it.

As Dillon rose a loud CRACK! echoed through the woods. He fell forward.

"Dillon!"

Another CRACK! and something smacked my shoulder and sent me flying backward.

Chapter 36

Out Cold

I woke shivering and staring up into the face of the man in the moon.

Pain in my back prevented movement. My right side lay lodged next to the log.

"Dillon?" Only a squeak came out.

My backpack sat over a yard away in the snow and out of reach. Fudge and cheese appeared scattered about. Something--was it an animal?--skittered about in shimmering shapes. What animal wore quaint peasant-style coats? Gnomes? Elves? I was hallucinating.

Harsh hammering pulsated in my head. I must have hit the log when I fell.

A chittering noise--was it actual chattering?--laced the frigid air. They were there again.

About a foot tall, chubby, dressed in winter gear trimmed in bright yellows and reds, and wearing fur-like hats, the beings appeared to be collecting the fudge and cheese.

Yup, I was hallucinating. And freezing.

My right arm was wedged up against the log. When I moved, pain seared my shoulder and back. The left arm felt heavy, immovable. Did I have frostbite? When I groaned, the little beings--Belgian skritek?--rushed over to stare at me.

Quite disconcerting, this headache of mine.

I turned my face toward the log, inches away. If I could focus, my next move was to find my phone and call for help.

"Dillon?"

No answer. As I stared at the log, clarity began to appear in the moonlight. A dark shadow in the log's bark made me wonder if it were my blood.

I wriggled away in the snow, groaning at the stabbing pains. The elves or mice kept bustling about, scavenging for fudge and cheese.

"Dillon!"

After forcing myself up, and feeling the full impact of the icy-cold night air, I spotted Dillon behind me. He lay prone on his stomach, face down in the snow. Dangerous.

The moon went behind clouds. Shadows crossed over us. Skritek-- maybe eight short, one-foot-high men and women--pulled the sleeping bag up and around Dillon. Relief at the help trickled like hot liquid through me. I didn't care if I was hallucinating.

Their coats were adorned with button plackets in intricate-appearing patterns sporting the colors of the Belgian flag--red, yellow, and black. Grandma and Grandpa had long ago explained the meaning of the colors. Red was for the red lion representing Hainut, Limburg, and Luxembourg. The yellow stripe was for the yellow lion of the Brabant province. My memory recalled real history--the young nun who saw visions in the woods here had been from Brabant, like some of my ancestors. Did elves and gnomes also cross the ocean in the 1800s? There was a third stripe on the flag and these gnomes also had black accenting the red and yellow embroidery on the clothing pockets and button plackets. Black stood for the black lion of the Namur and Flanders provinces of Belgium. A lion was strong.

I shook my woozy head, hoping for lion-style strength.

"Dillon?"

I unbuckled the snowshoes still strapped to my boots.

Something trickled down my right arm and into my glove. I inspected under the glove. Blood. I had been shot. Fear crackled through me. Was somebody watching me now? Somebody besides those elves and gnomes in my imagination? I certainly hadn't imagined this blood.

I scrabbled about for my phone inside a coat pocket. It was broken. My fall against the log must have crushed it.

After tossing the broken phone aside, I felt weak and had to crawl in snow to get to Dillon. Dizziness struck, bowling me over.

The moon had reappeared, moved from its position. It still smiled. I mumbled, "So happy that you're amused by my condition."

Cody had said the man up in the sky would have answers for whatever questions I had. I whispered up at the moon, "Can you dial 911?"

I remembered seeing Dillon face down in the snow only moments ago. Now he was face up, the sleeping bag blanketing him. How? I recalled the skritek gnomes. Could they be real?

"Dillon?" I touched his face. "Wake up."

He didn't.

Chills accelerated like cold atoms darting faster and faster inside of me. Blood got in my eyes. Damn! I swiped at it.

I slipped off my gloves to fumble inside Dillon's coat for his phone.

My arms felt heavy.

Why couldn't I find his phone? What was wrong with me? Why was I so dizzy?

Hypothermia is taking over, you fool. You might die.

I willed myself to think thoughts to keep me awake. I loved my parents, Grandma and Grandpa, Pauline and John, and I thought about how much Pauline was looking forward to the wedding and her darn need to find horses to take us in the wedding parade this coming Saturday. I had to live. To find horses for Pauline. I couldn't disappoint the people in my life. I still had to finish the handkerchief she'd carry down the aisle.

I yelled, "Don't you die on me! Dillon, wake up!"

Hypothermia takes about two hours before a person can die. The moon had moved. How much time had passed? An hour? More?

I sat back against the log to gather strength, closing my eyes against the pain all over my body, especially in my shoulders and head.

A shuffling and squeaking drew my attention again. Elves rushed away from me. Had they pushed the backpacks near me? Had they pulled out the thermos? I didn't remember doing either task.

I sat up more to reach for the thermos only to discover something in my lap--Dillon's phone. How did it get here? Its screen glowed.

To my shock, chattering emanated from the phone. The voice on the other end said, "Hello? Are you in trouble? This is the Door County 911 dispatch center. Hello?"

I woke in warmth. Mom and Dad hovered over me to my left. To my right stood Pauline.

Grandma's voice came out of the fog. "Little Ava honey is awake finally."

I was in the hospital. A clock across from me said it was two o'clock, probably two in the morning. Darkness huddled outside a window.

Mom said, "Thank goodness you're alive." She eased a hip onto the bed and then touched my left cheek with her work-roughened hand that felt perfect to me.

Dad said, "Honey, you're lucky. You could have..." He choked.

Tears bubbled into my eyes. The echo of a rifle shot returned to me.

I steeped myself in their loving faces for a moment. Grandma stood at the foot of the bed, her white hair giving her an angel's halo and glow. "Ava, my child, we'll get whoever did this."

"Thanks, Grandma. I'm not sure what happened."

Pauline said, "John and I found you. Cody got called for the rescue team and he called me. The team was right behind us. Thank goodness you dialed 911 in time before hypothermia got you both."

"I didn't dial 911. That had to be Dillon."

Pauline shook her head.

Mom said, taking one of my hands in hers, "Thank goodness you'd texted Pauline earlier about going for a walk at Peninsula State Park. The sheriff and all kinds of people showed up looking for you both. Why would you go out there in this weather and alone?"

"I wasn't alone." There were...Belgian skritek? Had they hit the 911 button?

Dad patted my hand from his side of my hospital bed. "Honey, the sheriff is going to be asking you questions in the morning. You're right. You weren't alone. Somebody shot at you and Dillon."

The pain in my shoulder confirmed that as well as the IV connected to one hand.

Pauline said, "I have your stuff. I'll deliver it later this morning to the Blue Heron Inn. No worries, girlfriend."

"Thanks, Pauline."

Mom started crying. She got up and went around the bed and into Dad's arms.

I choked up a little. "Come on, you guys. I'm fine. How's Dillon?"

Everybody looked at each other. Again.

I tried to sit up further but yelped in pain. "Tell me about Dillon. He's alive?"

Dad took my hand again. "Alive but in bad shape, honey. A bullet struck the side of his head from the back, which evidently knocked him out. He's got a concussion. He was in surgery to sew his head back up. And he's going to suffer frostbite on his face. They're not sure..."

"What, Dad?"

"They find it all puzzling. His injuries show that he fell face down into the snow and some nearby brush, though the rescue people found him face up."

"The elves rolled him over."

"Elves?" Dad said.

"Gnomes. I get them mixed up. I think both were there."

Everybody stared wide-eyed. If only Grandpa were here; he believed in such skritek. I was embarrassed, though. Did I believe? What I'd seen had to have been a hallucination from the pain and hypothermia setting in. "I must have rolled him over. My memory's fuzzy."

Dad said, "There are scratches on his eye."

Pauline said, "The doctor said he's going to have to wear a patch for a little while over his right eye. The doctor said he'd have trouble with his balance, so he's supposed to take a break from construction work for a couple of weeks."

The weight of that hit me. Dillon needed work to stay sane. "I need to see him." I fumbled with my loose hand for a button on the bed to raise me up.

Dad said, "Honey, it's two-thirty in the morning. Dillon needs to sleep after surgery. And you've got nasty things going on in your shoulder and shouldn't be moving."

The pain in my right shoulder was enough to make me think I'd fallen off the cliff along the Eagle Trail. "What happened to me?"

Pauline laughed, which I loved to hear. "Hey, girlfriend, you're bionic. A bullet grazed your shoulder blade, but didn't go through. It tore up skin and muscle, though. No basketball hoops for a while. You'll need help stirring fudge ingredients."

I groaned. "And my head?"

Dad said, "You hit your head on a log."

Pauline said, "And the log lost. Your head will be fine."

Grandma giggled.

I asked Pauline, "Am I going to be hideous for your wedding?"

"You're not getting out of wearing that Victorian dress. You can hide your black eyes under a floppy bonnet and Fontana's paste she calls makeup."

Everybody chuckled.

I said, "I wouldn't miss your wedding for the world, Pauline. Whatever hat you want me to wear, I'll wear it."

Mom said, "Famous last words. You haven't seen the bonnet yet."

I turned back to Pauline. "You mean you already have one picked out?"

Grandma answered, "What else is there to do sitting three hours in the waiting room for you to get patched and wake up?" She pulled out her phone. "Here, see what you think. I can make this from the leftover fabric from your maid-of-honor dress."

She showed me a broad-brimmed, red velveteen Victorian bonnet with white lace trim.

I laughed and didn't mind at all that I hurt like heck.

"Where's Grandpa?" I asked.

Dad sighed. "In jail yet, but he'll be out tomorrow, I mean today. Parker Balusek arranged for me to borrow against the farm for the bail. Your grandpa said he wants to talk with you first thing."

"Dad, his being in jail was supposed to be a trick. The sheriff was supposed to only make it look real. You shouldn't be paying bail money."

"Honey, the sheriff has to do his job. It doesn't matter what you want in a case like this. A man was killed. But don't worry about your grandfather."

"Dad, no!" My loud voice hammered me back against the pillow. "OW! Grandpa's in danger."

"It looks like to me that you're the one in danger. Somebody was gunning for you."

Dad took my hand again and patted it. He leaned down to kiss my cheek. He smelled good, like snow, but his expression was of weariness and worry. "Your gramps says you know who killed Westergaard and sent that rock through the window. He says the same person had to be in the woods shooting at you. Is it true, honey? You know who this person is?"

Everybody peered at me in an expectant way that made me tremble.

Chapter 37

Hospital Holiday

I lied to Dad and the rest of them in my hospital room that early Tuesday morning.

Dad asked who might have shot at us. I said, "It could've been somebody mistakenly thinking we were raccoons. People hunt raccoons year-round."

Dad shook his head. He knows a lie from a mile away, but he only sighed.

Everybody was leaving my room. Mom hugged me with ginger care. "Please don't leave the inn again at night and go into the woods like that."

Pauline echoed her. "I want you alive for my wedding, girlfriend."

Grandma added, "Stay out of trouble. The Lord knows we have enough of that with Gil."

Dad chuckled. The last to leave the room, he turned and winked, his way of saying, "I love you, kiddo."

By ten o'clock on Saint Nicholas Day I was released but Dillon remained in intensive care, no visitors allowed. I was told he was progressing well, so it was likely he would be out of ICU soon and possibly discharged later. I'd get a phone call.

When I went to leave finally, I discovered Jeremy had been released at the same time. Both of us sat in wheelchairs at the entrance waiting for Pauline. Jeremy's nose wore a white bandage, making his hooked appendage appear twice its normal size. I chuckled.

He said, "My nose, right? It's big anyway."

"Sorry." I shrugged.

"At least somebody can laugh. I was left for dead in your grandfather's Santa sleigh." Jeremy had a concussion, so he had to take it easy for several days and travel wasn't advised. "Wherever your grandfather is, trouble follows."

"Grandpa didn't hit you over the head. I have suspects in mind. Do you want to hear my theory?"

"No. I just want to pack up and get home to Madison, never to see you again."

The statement panicked me. "You can't. You promised to help me find Pauline's sister."

"I can't help you, Ava. Look at me."

"You have to, Jeremy. You like winning awards. This story will make you look good. Don't you want to look good? You're not always the most pleasant person, you know. I bet you can't even get a date."

Jeremy glared at me. It was a good thing our wheelchairs were a few feet from each other because I could tell he might have pushed me over.

"Listen, Jeremy, what else are you going to do while recovering from your concussion? You can't drive for a few days and nobody wants to get stuck in a car with you for five hours."

"I just want to rest."

I felt bad. "You have to check out tomorrow. I have new guests coming for the wedding."

"Hit me while I'm down, huh?"

"I'll find you a place. The professor can give you a ride to another local establishment when he leaves with his students. Wait. I know somebody who'd love to have a newspaper person in her house--Mercy Fogg!"

Jeremy swore. Bad words. Blue words. Then he chuckled.

I asked, "What's so funny?"

"Me. And you. I want to be mad and leave, but I can't and I don't want to leave."

"You sound mixed up."

"I am. I've gotten to like Fishers' Harbor."

I had hope! "Maybe writing about finding Lucie Mertens will bring you another award."

He took a deep breath. "Okay, Oosterling, I admit there is no way I'll leave town until I figure out who murdered the assessor and who tried to kill you and your boyfriend, and myself. I can continue searching for Lucie Mertens, though there is something odd about a person disappearing like that. People just aren't off the grid for long anywhere in the world these days."

"I told Pauline it has to be extenuating circumstances. Lucie is supposedly in Peru. That's all we've been able to find out."

Jeremy nodded. "I'll keep asking questions. I didn't want to have to do this, but I have some contacts in the Chicago FBI office."

A warm glow flickered to life inside of me. "Thank you, Jeremy. I have another mystery for somebody to solve, if you're game."

"Oh, no. What is it?"

"Do you believe in Christmas elves? Gnomes? I think they're bringing me gifts every morning and I don't know how to catch them."

Jeremy stared at me for a long time, then guffawed, then yelped in pain.

Pauline dropped us off at the Blue Heron Inn an hour later, past eleven that Tuesday. Her mother Coletta was at the inn cleaning rooms. The professor and Skylark were in the kitchen building a chicken casserole and fresh cheesy bread for a late lunch. They reported Dax and Nova were on Main Street mounting children's artwork in shop windows and doors.

Ellany and baby Henry were upstairs for a feeding.

The professor paused his culinary tasks long enough to escort Jeremy up the staircase.

Coletta came to my rescue and taped plastic wrap over the bandage on my right shoulder blade so that I could take a shower. Snowflakes danced past the small bathroom window while I renewed myself. The memory of being cold stuck with me.

While I was dressing, Skylark tapped on my door. She held out a small gift box. "The dog brought this inside this morning before your grandmother took him."

The memory of the elves in the woods lingered. Of course they were hallucinations. The elves couldn't have found the phone and hit 911. Could they? They couldn't be behind these gift boxes. Could they?

The box contained a beaded bracelet; each multi-colored wood bead looked hand-painted.

Skylark lifted the bracelet. "Beautiful. Too small for my big wrists used to slinging a hammer and boards, but if I were your size I'd steal this."

She made me smile. "I haven't been able to guess who's leaving these."

"You have quite the collection in the dining room. Do you want me to add this one?"

I nodded. "Thanks."

"You're sure it's not Dillon?"

"He says it's not him. And besides, he was with me last night and then in the hospital. There's no way he could have done this."

"I suppose, unless he hired elves to help him." Skylark laughed as she left the room.

If only she knew, I thought.

Chapter 38

Holly Jolly

After the exchange with Skylark, I headed out the front door. Lucky Harbor leaped about on the verandah. He'd obviously escaped from my grandparents' control.

Hugging the dog made me feel close to Dillon, as if everything would be all right. "Thanks, Lucky Harbor. Now please don't knock me over. I'm not as steady as usual."

My hurt shoulder stung and my face itched from a slight case of frostbite. The scratch on my forehead pulled, but I hid it under a soft, knitted wool stocking hat in a cheery red color.

I made it to the bottom step with Lucky Harbor when a gray, rusty mini-van chugged up the hill. It slid to a stop on a patch of ice a few yards from me. Christmas music blared.

The driver's side door opened. Pauline popped out. "Need a ride to work?"

Snow flurries flew while "Holly Jolly Christmas" as sung by Burl Ives blared.

"Pauline, why are you driving this piece of junk? Where's your new red convertible with the heater that can melt the Arctic?"

"Get in and I'll tell you."

"I can walk. I'm only going down the hill to the fudge shop."

"It's slippery. Get in, girlfriend. You, too, Lucky Harbor."

We settled inside on ripped seats. An old rug lay at my feet.

Pauline said, "Don't move the rug. There's a hole that goes all the way to China."

"Why are you driving this hunk of junk? It's worse than your old car. What happened to your new convertible?"

She didn't answer until she'd driven us down the hill and onto Main Street. "I gave the red car to my mother. Her Christmas present."

"You loved that car."

The street was white again from a flurry of snow. Lucky Harbor panted over the top of my shoulder, eager to get out and romp.

Pauline said, "I couldn't bring myself to drive around in that fancy car knowing you'd been hurt and probably wouldn't be stirring fudge or lifting the heavy copper kettles, or enjoying much of anything. Mom said she'd help pay off the loan for the convertible. In fact, that made her really happy. She's been getting more waitressing gigs and they pay better than cleaning."

I was speechless. "She's not quitting at the inn, is she?"

"Not that I know of. She loves helping you."

"But you gave the car to her. That's a big gift." The incredulity stayed with me.

"I just could not drive it and feel happy. You and I were supposed to go together sometime and buy our cars together. Remember how we said that last summer?"

I did remember.

She added, "I violated that promise."

With gloved hands gripping the wheel, Pauline drove the old clunker down the street. Shoppers were few today. People took a break after the long weekend of activities. Dax and Nova were behind the window of a shop working on an art display.

"Pauline, you didn't need to do that out of sympathy. That's a nice car. And this is..."

"Gray. Junky. Ready to be run into and smashed and we won't care. I bought it to match what you drive."

"Match?"

"We were supposed to buy the matching red cars together."

She must have read my mind about all this. I felt guilty now. "We don't have to do everything together, you know. You're getting married, moving to a new place. You're doing different things than I am and that's good. I have to adjust. It's on me, Pauline."

"I don't want to get married and have you disappear from my life because you think everything I do is about John. I was just too full of myself, Ava. I bought a red car and went into debt just because I was thinking of myself and maybe trying to impress John and you and heck, the whole world. Don't you see how wrong it was to be so self-obsessed? I don't want to destroy our friendship. I apologize, okay?"

I gulped back the pain pulsating in my right shoulder blade where the rifle shot had torn me up. I wanted to hug her so badly but couldn't.

"Pauline, someday you and I will shop for our matching cars."

She sniffled. "Maybe this coming spring, after all the snow and slush are gone."

"Sounds good."

Pauline made the left turn to go into the harbor parking lot. "I should have been with you last night instead of going out with John. I should be spending time with my maid of honor, with the best friend who's always been like a sister to me."

The word "sister" made me pause. I looked out the passenger window at the snow flurries whipping at the whitecaps on the bay.

I asked, "Any word from your sister?"

"No."

Oh how I was counting on Jeremy to help me get Lucie back here by Saturday.

Pauline stopped in front of the plywood-covered window now decorated with holiday pictures. Each drawing had been encased in a plastic sleeve to protect it from the weather.

Before I opened the mini-van door, I said, "You're really a good friend, Pauline. I just want you to know that. Thank you."

She nodded. I reached over and we did a "pinkie swear" for "friends forever".

Pauline left to meet with the priest at Saint Ann's to go over wedding details.

Once in the shop, I could do very little. I was able to use one arm to straighten shelf items. Lucky Harbor trailed after my every move, as if he'd been ordered to watch over me.

Cody yelled, "Miss Oosterling, I'm in charge today. Take it easy, okay?"

Cody rushed from stirring fudge ingredients to the marble table by the window. The dog left me to tail him. Cody yelled a couple of times, "Lucky Harbor, no! Get away!"

I managed to check kitchen supplies. When I returned to the front, Dotty and Lois greeted me. The dog nosed their apron pockets for treats.

Dotty said, "You're to relax. We have this shop covered."

Lois already hustled about re-stocking holiday items. There were no customers, which made the aisles efficient racetracks for the women. These sixty-year-olds had twice my energy today, which I appreciated.

Dotty reported that Dax and Nova had brought several gift bags for sale designed for little children and teens. "They're activity bags that parents can buy to take home over the school break to keep their little urchins occupied and out of trouble. Nova suggested you add a free piece of fudge to the deal and the bags will sell out."

I said, "Maybe I should try and make a batch of fudge myself. And I've got to come up with the new name yet for the batch I was experimenting with."

Dotty said, "Loaded with all the fruitcake ingredients?"

"That's the one," I said.

Cody called over, "Sounds like Miss Oosterling needs those activity bags to keep her out of trouble. She's not supposed to be stirring stuff today or lifting heavy stuff."

The women laughed. I had to smile and didn't mind being the brunt of their kind kidding.

Coletta stopped by then to make sure I didn't need cleaning help in the shop.

"No, but thanks. My mother will be coming later with a load of creamery products and she always likes to vacuum once she's here."

Cody said, "I like your mom, Miss Oosterling! This place sparkles after she's been here!"

"Thanks, Ranger. I think you insinuated she's better at cleaning than I am, but right now that works for me."

"I know what you can do without having to hurt your shoulder."

"What?"

"Go work on that special Christmas fairy tale fudge flavor. We need it before Saturday. With the wedding in town, we'll get bunches of customers."

"We have Rudolph the Red-Nosed Reindeer Fudge and kids love raisin deer poop."

Dotty and Lois came forward, along with Coletta, surrounding me at the register counter.

Dotty tisked at me. "Grownups need a grown-up fairy tale fudge flavor for Christmas."

"I feel so dry, with no ideas."

Lois said, "Talk to the nissen, the Swedish elves."

Dotty said, "But I like the nisse--those from Norway and Denmark. We mustn't forget those folks."

Coletta said, "We have to have the Belgian skritek fudge. Did you know you can call on those gnomes to heal you?"

Dotty and Lois shook their heads. The women were enjoying this discussion.

Coletta, who looked like a cute gnome with her short, black pixie cut, said, "When they dance, the skritek raise the energy around you. Their whole job is protection. And of course there are the 'Witte Wieven', or spirits of wise women in Belgian folklore. They're medicine healers, herbalists that go back to Year 600 or more."

Cody guffawed. "You could make fudge with special herbs in it. I think that's been done before in fudge and brownies."

He was referring to marijuana.

I laughed. "Well, those wise women fairies weren't protecting me last night out in the woods, but there were skritek--" I stopped, realizing how I sounded.

Cody came over, wide-eyed as the women. "You were in the woods with skritek? Where? I'd love to see them. Talk about a great way to get an 'A' in my forestry class next semester!"

"There's no such thing as real skritek," I said.

Dotty tisked at me again. "So do you believe in guardian angels?"

"Angels are, well, don't they live up in the clouds? Skritek are at ground level."

Lois nodded. "True. So you believe in gnomes like your Belgian skritek?"

"Well, I--"

Lucky Harbor raced to the front door amid sharp barks. The sheriff was coming through the door. "I'd like to speak with you, Ava. Alone, if you please."

Chapter 39

Sheriff's Offer

A few customers entered the shop, many with a "Happy holidays, Sheriff!"

I led Jordy back to the kitchen where we slid into the two chairs at the table. A tingle of anticipation alleviated my headache.

Jordy removed his stocking hat and set it on the table. "Smells good in here."

Cody had opened fresh containers of cinnamon and nutmeg for the gingerbread swirl fudge. Dark molasses and vanilla also effused the air.

I said to Jordy, "Who's trying to frame my grandfather for Usher's murder? Somebody wants me and Stone to leave this case alone, in a serious way."

Jordy shrugged. "I agree with your conclusion."

"Is Mercy Fogg your suspect?"

Jordy shifted back in the chair, which creaked. "Not so far. You know Stella Zanderson?"

"Sure. One of the snow-sculpting artists here this past weekend."

"You know her well?"

"No, just by association with the other artists."

Jordy leaned forward. "She was present outside the Troubled Trout the morning of the murder."

"Outside? Not inside?" A shiver went through me. "She confessed?"

"No. You talked with her?"

"Once." The past few days spun in my head like dancing sugarplum fairies. "She didn't tell me much. Al had mentioned Stella. Said she was at the bar on Wednesday night and got into some disagreement with Hailey, Usher's wife. Hailey thinks Stella was having an affair with her husband. Greta heard that Hailey was going to separate from Usher. When I visited Hailey, she didn't mention that, though."

"Stella Zanderson tells me she's been studying to become a tax assessor, and she had been spending time with Usher for that."

"Only studying and not an affair?"

We paused as Cody's voice and attendant laughter rose and fell out in the shop.

Jordy worried his hands on the table. "There's a high probability Stella killed Usher, then tried to murder Stone because his snooping scared her. Can you recall anything else about Stella?"

I told the sheriff Stella had been playing with kids on the street during the Saint Nicholas Day celebration. "Why would such a person try to pin this on my grandfather?"

"That's what I aim to find out. If you'll help me."

The pounding in my head intensified. "I'm not really up to that. Sorry."

"Sorry about that." Jordy leaned back. "Would it help if I told you the plan was your grandfather's idea? He's out of jail and at home. I dropped him off before coming here."

The world tilted. "My grandfather agreed to work with you?"

"He didn't have a choice, since he's intimately involved with what happened to both Westergaard and Stone." Jordy breathed in audibly. "I believe Gilsen is innocent."

"Thank you."

"I have to go by the law, though. Your grandfather suggested he get out of jail and make it look like he's innocent--which he is--as a way to draw out the murderer."

"My father bailed him out, true?"

"Yes. I want it known I believe Gil is responsible for murder and the harm to Stone."

"What about me and Dillon? Grandpa didn't shoot at us."

"People know that. There's confusion out there. Confusion both dangerous and good for me. The real killer is likely getting nervous. He or she might strike again. They likely won't try to run right now because that will draw suspicion. I've suggested those that met on Thursday morning at Erik's bar meet again to review the events. I've already made a few phone calls."

"Calls they can't refuse. For the post-event analysis. Like a Godfather movie." I shivered. "I don't like this, Jordy. It sounds too dangerous."

"I suggested your grandfather wear a wire and he agreed."

The pounding in my head skyrocketed to a jackhammer's blasts. "No. This is dangerous. Is that legal?"

"Not ordinarily. I had a talk with the District Attorney's office and a judge up the line and it was approved in this case because of the egregious crimes involved." Jordy flashed a grin. "Your grandfather liked the idea."

"Of course. He's been bored out of his mind this winter. But, Sheriff, nothing goes right for my grandfather. This may not go down as well as you expect."

"That's why I want you to be at the Troubled Trout. You and your grandpa have to call this meeting. Nobody can think the sheriff's department has set them up."

"No way."

"It'll make Stella nervous to look at the person she tried to kill in the woods. She could confess right then, so be prepared. Deputy Maria Vasquez will be stationed nearby but out of sight in case Stella tries to make a run for it out the front door. I'll be outside the back door."

"She might be armed, Jordy. If she shot at me in the woods, wouldn't she do it again? Can't she shoot us all?"

Pain seemed to wrinkle Jordy's face. "I don't think she'll be carrying a gun, but you're right--she could be. If she takes off her coat early, she's likely not packing. If she keeps her coat on, be suspicious and hit my number on your phone with some excuse."

My monkey mind thought about the gnomes in the woods. What I needed now was an army of them to protect my family and me.

The sheriff left at a little past one o'clock. I had remembered Dotty and Lois said there'd be a surprise for Ellany. The two church-club women had already left the shop.

Cody yelled over from the window where he packaged fudge. "Take it slow, Miss Oosterling, okay? You look pale."

I waved without words, struck numb with concerns and fear.

The brisk winter air helped revive me. Lucky Harbor scampered about, leaping into snow piles and then greeting me by shaking off snowballs, which meant, "Please come play with me RIGHT NOW, MOM, RIGHT NOW!"

He made me smile. "Not today, Lucky Harbor. Here's some fudge." I tossed him a gold fish cracker.

Minutes later, inside the Blue Heron Inn, a small party seemed to have been held for lunch hour. Jeremy, the professor, and Skylark sat at the table, along with Lois and Dotty. Others stood, including the rest of my houseguests.

Lucky Harbor bounded to a young man of maybe twenty and with a mop of curly dark brown hair who stood near a staircase banister. Beaming, he held baby Henry. Ellany clutched the man's nearest elbow, her eyes bright as stars.

"You must be Brendan," I said, hanging my coat on a hook by the front door.

Dotty piped up with, "That's indeed Brendan Jacobsson. We contacted women's group members in Ellison Bay, and they knew his mother. With a big basket of baked goods, the women marched right over to this young man's house, or I should say parents' house."

Cautious now, I smiled for Brendan. "So, they exchanged baked goods for your presence here?"

He grimaced, then looked at the sleeping baby in his arms. "That's one way of putting it. It sounded like a flock of hens clucking and pretty soon my parents sort of told me to get my butt over here to see my wife and baby." His face crumpled. "I'm pretty messed up, I guess. I'm sorry for all this trouble."

"There's no real trouble, not if you're here with your family." Looking at him holding his son and standing with his wife at his side warmed my heart. "I'd hug you but every inch of me hurts right now."

"Miss Oosterling, it looks like you tried to fight a bear in the woods last night."

A few chuckles came from the table and those standing about.

I said, "I don't believe we have any bears in Door County right now that I know of, but it was something like that. Let's not talk about me. You can call me Ava."

The professor offered me his chair and I sat. Lucky Harbor settled on his butt at the couples' feet, staring up at the bundle of baby.

I asked, "Ellany, does this mean you're going back to stay with your in-laws?"

The faces of the young couple drooped in unison. Ellany said, "No, ma'am. We're looking for a place."

Brendan cut in. "I promised to look. That got the hens to stop clucking around me at my parents' place."

Everybody laughed at his reference to the women's club.

Dotty said, "Young man, you're learning. We hens are going to find you a nesting box otherwise known as a house or apartment. That's what we said we'd do and we keep our promises. Housing certainly is an issue around here what with all the rich people buying up properties and driving up prices, but never under-estimate the power of a group of women."

Lois nodded, addressing me. "His parents' place is pretty small. It's quaint and all, but just one bedroom plus the attic space upstairs."

Ellany said, "Where we were sleeping with the baby. It was cold."

Brendan said, "I grew up there. My dad's on disability. The house is paid off and he doesn't want to move to a bigger house. He says he can't afford it."

I nodded. "Like Dotty just said, let the hens help find a coop for you."

The young couple exchanged a look before Ellany spoke. "We don't have any money to pay rent."

Skylark interrupted from across the table. "I volunteer with Habitat for Humanity. Maybe one of the members knows of a house you can get for a month or so for free. I'll make calls."

Dotty said, "There must be a church member with an extra bedroom or second story available. We'll pass the word and all will be well. This is Christmastime, after all."

Ellany took the baby from her husband. "Thanks, everybody, but we still need a place to stay tonight." She looked at me. "I know your inn is full now for the wedding coming up."

Lucky Harbor came to me, wagging his tail, as if nudging me for a solution. I fed him a cracker. He crawled under the table and lay down amid, "Oof."

I said, "You can have my apartment for tonight and even tomorrow night."

Dotty said, "Where will you sleep?"

Jeremy grunted. "She has a boyfriend who might share, or not. Not sure he likes getting shot at. You still together with Dillon, Ava?"

Lois and Dotty cleared their throats. They stood now behind the intrigued professor at the other end of the table. Dax and Nova raised their eyebrows, too.

The reporter was crossing a line with me, but I let it go. "I'll take the couch in the parlor. It's a hide-a-bed. Ellany, move your things into my apartment. Brendan, can you pack up what you need at your parents' house and let them know where you'll be?"

"You mean move out of my parents' house just like that?" A gleam registered in his eyes.

"Yes. Dotty and Lois and the other women will work with your parents and make sure there are no repercussions."

Brendan and Ellany exchanged shaky smiles.

I reached out to touch the sleeping baby's soft head. "It's Christmastime and maybe you've heard about a family with a new baby that got turned away at the inn long ago. We don't do that here. You're staying until all of your new friends here in this room can help you find a place to stay more long term. And we'll be sure your parents are okay, too."

The professor raised a hand. "Dax and Nova and I will put together a basket of goodies to take to them. May we use your kitchen, Ava? I've bought groceries already to repay you for your hospitality and I believe I can whip up a casserole. And these students of mine are expert at oatmeal-raisin-chocolate chip cookies."

Dax and Nova gave a thumbs up and then headed through the swinging door to the kitchen with the professor on their heels.

Skylark rose from the table, phone in hand. "I'm calling Habitat for Humanity now. There's always somebody who can't move into a newly built house on the date planned." She left for the kitchen.

Everybody but Ellany scattered to their appointed tasks.

Ellany went into the parlor and sat on a blue velveteen chair with her baby. Tears trickled down her face.

I went to her, kneeling in front of her. "What's wrong, Ellany?"

"You're so nice." She sucked in with a tiny snort. "Sorry to cause so much trouble."

"Stop thinking that way, please." I touched her jeans-clad knees as I peered into her watery eyes. There was the smell of milk about the baby in her arms. "This is what 'community' is about. It's what Fishers' Harbor is all about. It's what I'm all about."

"Not just fudge?" She giggled while backhanding tears.

"Not just fudge." I handed her a tissue, which she used to wipe her pale, clear skin. I wished my face looked half as good.

Then, despite my pains, I stood, bent over and gave the young woman a hug.

Chapter 40

Lost Lamb

Pauline arrived at the inn mid-afternoon. Her purse bulged, always a bad sign for me. "You have to help me, Ava." She proceeded to the dining room table with me in tow.

I said, "You've made lists and checked everything off twice. I'm wounded. Don't I get to slide now until Saturday?"

She shuddered visibly with a screwy expression, unloading her purse onto the table. A fat book, small boxes, papers, and ribbons scattered across the landscape of Belgian lace tablecloth.

"What is all this?" I asked, sitting in a chair.

Still standing, Pauline picked up the book. "Of course, you don't recognize a Bible. You have to pick out the reading. And I need your opinion on these decorations I want to add."

"I thought the only thing a maid of honor had to do was look pretty."

"That's in doubt now." Pauline laughed while pulling out a chair to sit.

"Don't worry, I'll wear all the makeup you want to plaster on me."

"Now pay attention. I have three selections I believe you might get through reading without choking up or laughing."

"Why would I laugh?"

"I spent my childhood in church with you giggling about every little word the priest made us mumble."

"That's just it. Father Thomas always mumbled. The 'Holy Spirit' always came out as 'Hol Spit' which sometimes sounded like 'Y'all Spit', like a command to spit."

Eyes narrowed in consternation, Pauline pointed to the Bible. "Shame on you. Pick... out... what... you... want... to... read."

I glared back.

She glared more.

We burst out laughing.

Being with Pauline rejuvenated me. Some. That Tuesday afternoon, I took Lucky Harbor with me to the shop. My mind tracked to the sheriff's plan--be part of a meeting at the Troubled Trout to root out a murderer.

Fear crept with cold fingers around my neck, but excitement also tingled.

Cody and Bethany had everything under control in the shop to my relief. Cheery customers hailed me with "Happy holidays!"

Children ran through the store trying to find all the elf figurines hidden about on the shelves next to items their parents might like to buy for them.

Customers asking with concern about my ruddy face got a simple lie. "I was sledding on Hill 16 and took a header." That lie sent the conversation back to the customers and their children talking about their own adventures on Hill 16 or other Door County winter activities.

After downing painkillers, I helped Cody create six of my recipes for the holidays. We mixed small batches of fudge ranging from eggnog to maple walnut, buttered rum to salted maple, and an orange flavor. I called the latter, Stocking Topper Fudge because when I was little my stocking always had an orange on top as the last item. The orange revealed a trove underneath of hard ribbon candy, wrapped chocolates, and small toys or figurines filling the stocking. I still wondered what had become of my storybook about the Christmas elf. That startled me into memories of the images of elves and gnomes I'd seen while in Peninsula State Park last night. They seemed so...real.

I shook myself. There was no way elves were real--despite what Grandpa and Grandma would say.

I forced myself to muse about a special wedding fudge recipe for Pauline and John. What fudge would best express those two opposite and sweet people?

At five in the afternoon I took a break and called Dillon who was still in the hospital.

"I love you," I began the call. "How are you feeling?"

"Concussion protocol is improving fast but I'm required to stay away from power tools for a week and then lay low for another week."

"I miss you," I said. "Can we come and get you now?"

"Sorry, change of plans. The doc didn't like the way my eyes were tracking. I'll get out by tomorrow sometime if I have a watchdog on me. How's Lucky Harbor?"

"Sitting at the shop door waiting for you. He'd love to go for a ride in your truck."

"Where is my truck?"

"Parked in front of your cabin. Cody and Brecht retrieved it from the park."

"Any word on who tried to put me out of business for good?"

"Not yet." I wasn't about to tell him I'd be up early with Grandpa tomorrow morning at the Troubled Trout trying to get Stella Zanderson to confess to murder and attempted murder. My stomach already churned. "The sheriff is working on it."

"Not with you I hope?"

"Of course...not."

"Ava Mathilde, don't you dare put yourself in harm's way. Think about Pauline and John and their wedding. We have to be there for them."

His concern warmed me. "What fudge flavor should I make for their wedding reception? And what should we call it?"

"You know I'm no good at your fudge stuff. I make a mean lasagna and that's as far as I get in a kitchen."

"Well, lasagna fudge sounds really gross, so put your thinking cap on."

Dillon asked about Jeremy. "Has he found Pauline's sister?"

"Not yet. I guess people can really disappear and go off the grid if they try."

The phone went silent, then Dillon said, "Didn't those girls stay at your farm a lot? Especially when things got rough when their dad was drunk and mean?"

"Sure they stayed. You know that. They practically lived with us they stayed so often. Why?"

"Stop looking for a Lucie Mertens. Try to find Lucie Oosterling. She might be in Belgium for all you know with the other Oosterlings, and not in Peru."

Chapter 41

Glittering Cones

The rest of Tuesday passed in a blur with all my myriad thoughts and duties.

Grandma insisted I shower and nap at her place. Coletta managed the inn. That worked well because her aunt and uncle arrived. Coletta hadn't seen them for twenty years. Pauline had been around ten years old the last time she'd seen them.

Pauline came down the hill to Grandma's house in wide-eyed wonder.

"Ava, they speak French and Walloon! And English, of course." She laughed, hands expressive in the air. We sat at Grandma's kitchen table where the two of us sipped coffee. "They will be the hit of my wedding reception!"

"Walloon is so rare," I said in wonder. Our local Belgian Heritage Center took great pains to preserve traditional language, including videotaping conversations among the older generations. "Do you suppose your new husband might record them?"

With eyes shining like sequins, Pauline tossed her dark hair back with a certain élan to the motion. "I'll ask my husband after the wedding."

"How old are they? They must be my grandparents' age."

"Older. Mid-eighties and young at heart."

"What do they do now?"

"Lead tours around the world." Her eyes burned bright. "And get this--they don't have a house. They live on cruise ships or at resorts where they help manage. They hop from one ship or country to the next and next. Isn't that adventuresome?"

"They have the wanderlust. How's your mother taking this reunion?"

Pauline twisted hair in one hand. "She cried happy tears. Mom is finding her family again. We're all coming back to Fishers' Harbor it seems, except..."

I reached across the table and took Pauline's hands in mine. "Lucie evidently has your family's wanderlust gene. Have faith, my friend."

"Thanks, Ava. You're the best BFF."

We put more cream in our Belgian-style coffee, then enjoyed our "calm before the storm" that we understood stalked us.

Wednesday morning I rose at three-thirty, restless from aches and the shift to sleeping on the parlor sofa bed and riddled with fear about the sheriff's plan involving my grandfather wearing a wire tomorrow morning. Grandpa had a way of messing up best-laid plans.

I'd packed a suitcase of clothes last night prior to handing over my apartment to Ellany and family, so it was easy to slip to the kitchen, wash up, and dress. Grandma had offered her spare room, but I didn't want to disturb the sewing room for the wedding.

I collected another gift box at the back door. The box held a pinecone decorated with glitter and a red ribbon for hanging on a tree. The dining room shelf was getting crowded and there were still a couple of weeks before Christmas. The gifts--a lot like kindergarten art projects--made me think about the professor and his art cart for children. He hadn't come to Fishers' Harbor, though, until this past weekend.

My shoulder was able to let me prepare a plate of blueberry muffins, mix a pitcher of chocolate milk, set the coffee pot to perking, and create a Christmas tree effect on a plate with layers of mint-green fudge pieces. I hoped Pauline's great-aunt and great-uncle might stir early. World travelers, maybe they could give me a clue about Lucie's whereabouts.

My antique yellow-rosebud china plates, coffee cups, and the small Belgian cups designed for sipping thick chocolate festooned the dining room table. Large chunks of chocolate, and cheese were set in the table's middle so each guest could carve what they wanted--very European-style, something that had impressed me during our trip to Belgium.

Coletta would be coming later to tidy rooms. One room was empty yet. John's parents had left a message on the inn's landline saying they were going to be delayed from Hawaii because of storms everywhere. They'd arrive on Friday.

Jeremy had moved to a motel in Ephraim, ostensibly to keep a close eye on Hailey's house. He felt the sheriff's suspicions about Stella Zanderson being guilty of murder might be playing into Hailey's hands. Hailey could leave town--or the country--without anybody caring or noticing.

Begrudgingly I was worried for the intense journalist. I had called his number yesterday.

"Oosterling, I appreciate your concern. I realize you come out a winner either way with me dead or alive."

"Stop that. We haven't always been on good terms, but I'm coming around. You're welcome at the inn for breakfast. What did you find out through your Chicago FBI connection?"

"So far, nothing. But they liked the idea of looking for Lucie under a different last name."

"Kudos to Dillon for thinking of that."

Dillon was released in the afternoon. Mom drove him to Fishers' Harbor since she had to make milk, cheese, and cream deliveries to my shop and other places and passed the hospital in Sturgeon Bay. I took Dillon a basket of goodies, including mac-and-cheese made from Mom's cheeses.

Dillon barely let me put the basket down on his table when he grabbed a fork for a bite of mac-and-cheese. "Maybe I did die after all. This tastes heavenly, honey."

He got a kiss for that.

At the shop, Grandpa stayed busy and unusually quiet. He even let his coffeepot go empty for a while before a customer noticed. I guessed Gilpa was nervous about wearing a wire for the sheriff. I also knew he was worried for me, too, because that's how he rolled.

Laura, Fontana, and Pauline stopped at the shop, thankfully distracting me. They were scouring Wisconsin for horses and carriages with no luck. They put up a "Wanted--Wedding Horses & Carriages" poster.

On Thursday morning my stomach wouldn't settle down. I couldn't eat and fumbled at four o'clock in the morning trying to assemble breakfast items for guests.

Could Grandpa and I get a confession out of somebody? My knees felt weak.

After letting Lucky Harbor out the back door, I collected another gift box, this one with another tiny gold leaf fixed with a loop so it could go onto a necklace or earrings. I now had a matching pair. Who was my secret Santa? I had to be missing a clue, but what was it?

Later, with coat put on carefully over my damaged shoulder, I trekked with Lucky Harbor down the hill. Following Pauline's advice yesterday, I had applied Fontana's homemade makeup Pauline picked up for me. It soothed my frostbitten skin. I had argued yesterday with Pauline that makeup wasn't regulated and I could be putting eye of newt on my face for all I knew.

Pauline said, "It's from her goat's milk, silly."

"What about the lipstick you wear? Tested for toxins?"

"Made by Fontana, too. The stains come from cherries she picked last summer."

"So you have Door County's famous cherries on your lips?"

Pauline had nodded.

Amazed, I had quipped, "The spa on Main Street gives chocolate facials. Maybe I should be selling fudge as a way to exfoliate the skin."

That happy, relaxed conversation was yesterday. At five o'clock this December Thursday morning my nerves felt on fire. The cold air outside felt good. Streetlights shone somber amber circles on the snow along Main Street. Tree limbs crackled in an intermittent breeze.

With my own key, I let the dog into Dillon's cabin but didn't venture inside.

Near the shop, the Christmas tree lights on the trees along the dock twinkled, their bulbs shaking in the wind. A freighter's red and yellow lights glimmered in the far distance.

Inside, Grandpa stood in an aisle stocking hooks with bright orange bobbers in plastic bags. With his silver hair, and the slight stoop of his shoulders, and the weather-worn face, he lacked the look of an undercover spy for a sheriff.

"Grandpa, we could call this off. I don't want you to get hurt."

I hugged him.

He grunted. "Ah, honey, you and Dillon have been hurt, and that rock through the window could've done me in. I want the scoundrel caught."

We were due at the Troubled Trout in only half an hour. Would we truly force a murder confession from Stella Zanderson? Something about this felt "off". Stella had a lot going for her. What could possibly be her motive to kill our tax assessor? Her taking over his job didn't feel like enough motive to me, but the sheriff said people murdered for lesser reasons.

Grandpa went across the creaky floor to make coffee. He hummed, though off-key.

"Grandpa, you're going to behave, right? This is serious stuff we're in now."

He turned to me with a big grin on his ruddy face. "Ava, of course I'll behave. I'm wearing a wire!"

"The sheriff was already here?"

"No. Maria stopped at the house and fixed me up. You don't think I'd let that Tollefson guy feel me up, do you?" He shook like Lucky Harbor did when expelling snow from his coat.

"So you let Maria feel you up." I wanted him to grin.

He obliged. "Your grandma was right there watching."

I couldn't concentrate, so I dusted my counter and register while the cherry-chocolate coffee effused the air. "Grandpa, what really happened last Thursday morning in the bar? Some say there was a scuffle and others say otherwise. What do you know?"

"Like I've told you, I took off for home because I saw Mercy on the plow heading down the street." Grandpa didn't face me.

I grew suspicious. "You know the truth is going to come out. There are things you haven't been telling me. True?"

He poured a cup of coffee and then brought it to me. "Honey, it's embarrassing. Truth is I wasn't much up for all the arguing going on in the bar that morning. I did see Usher go out the front door and I tailed after him briefly to tell him to ignore all the badmouthing about people's tax assessments. He was carrying his coat. His sweater was a mess because they had swabbed the floor with him, and I impulsively brushed him off."

"So that's why the sheriff didn't feel he'd been on the floor in a fight or maybe not at all. Jordy told me the sweater was clean. Because you brushed off any dirt."

"Suppose so. Anyway, I saw the plow coming. I hightailed it back inside but went through to the back because I wanted to take the shortcut home." He cleared his throat.

"And? What don't you want to tell me?"

"Here's when things got embarrassing." He turned even redder, wrinkles deepening across his forehead.

"Tell me, Grandpa. This is serious business."

"I hit that cold air and well, I needed to take a whiz."

A cloud had come over his countenance, confusing me. "So, you peed outside?"

He shrugged his assent, raking his thick, silver hair with one hand, creating a disturbance atop his head. He went over to the coffeepot ledge and then topped off his mug.

I waited, more confused now. "Grandpa, guys do that kind of thing now and then. I get it. But there's more to this story, isn't there?"

Grandpa placed the mug by his register. "Honey, because I took a pee, a man died."

"Grandpa, what the heck do you mean?"

"Because I was so obsessed with being mad at Mercy and racing home to yell at her about my mailbox being shoved over every snowstorm, I missed saving a man's life. I might have seen the killer on the way to do in Westergaard if I'd chosen to turn the opposite way I did in back of the Troubled Trout. Because of my temper, a man died. Because I peed in public, because I was angry at that silly Fogg woman, I totally messed up and caused bunches of people a lot of heartache and caused you all this trouble and almost lost you!"

"Whoa, Grandpa!" I put down my coffee, then hugged him. "There was nothing you could've done. Please realize that. If Stella hadn't killed Usher that morning, she'd have done it another way. Look how bold she was with Jeremy, obviously knocking him over the head in broad daylight out at the town garage."

"She did that?"

"The sheriff thinks so. She was desperate, twisted about things. I'm sure she realized Jeremy was getting close to figuring out she was the culprit."

"I can't believe her gall to follow you and Dillon and harm you in the park." He hugged me back with ginger care. "What I did has taught me a lesson. I'm reforming, I promise. I'm trying harder to do everything right from now on. That's why I signed on with the sheriff."

I couldn't tell him I'd encouraged Sheriff Tollefson to arrest him, to make Grandpa a pawn in the whole deal. Let Grandpa think it was the sheriff's idea.

I swallowed a lump in my throat. "You've always done everything right in my eyes, Grandpa."

Minutes later, not much went right at the "breakfast club" inside the Troubled Trout bar.

Chapter 42

The Trap

M y job, according to the sheriff, was to be present and act upset about being injured by "somebody". I was to ask pointed questions that would lead to Stella confessing.

The Troubled Trout sizzled with animosity among all those present.

Erik said he saw Stella Zanderson race out after Usher, which put Stella on the defense. She still had her coat on, which made my heart race fast. Was she carrying a gun?

Timing is everything in life. She stared straight at me, so I couldn't go for my phone to send a text to Jordy.

Stella answered Erik and said she didn't rush out immediately, but she did go outside.

Tall, strong, sculptor Stella stood in the middle of the bar room now, fuming. She contended she went out to Usher's car after he'd left the bar but she never murdered him. When she got to the car, she said his eyes were closed and she thought he had closed them to be rude and make her go away, so she nudged him. Yes, she was mad; she wanted to intern with him and learn the ropes of tax assessment. And, yes, she wanted to take over his job because he was intent on leaving for Florida with his wife. He wanted to save his marriage, Stella said.

I had to ask, "So you weren't having an affair with him? Everybody thinks so, Stella."

"I thought about it once, but, no." She crossed her arms, defiant. Her eyes looked as if pitchforks could fly out of them.

Another of the snow sculptors, Reece Allard, piped up from his seat at the bar where he had a Bloody Mary drink complete with a celery stalk and crisp bacon strips standing in it. "Buck and I saw you two together at the nature center a couple of times. You looked cozy."

Stella flushed, swiveling her head to consider all of us--Erik, Piers, Reece, Buck, Travis, Grandpa, and myself. "You all really think I killed that man, don't you? What about this man?"

She pointed at Grandpa!

He scrambled off his stool. "I didn't kill anybody and you know it. You tried to kill my granddaughter and her fiancé. I'll never forgive you for that."

To my shock, Stella shoved Grandpa, knocking him back against a table and chairs. He tumbled to the floor.

"Grandpa!" I rushed to him as a chair toppled on top of him.

Others advanced toward Stella.

She shouted, "What is wrong with you all? I did not kill anybody!"

Stella glared at Grandpa as I helped him up with the Erik's aid. "Gil Oosterling," she said, "you were the only one outdoors besides me. You went after Usher. I saw you outside relieving yourself! I was behind this place by then looking over the barrels for collecting snow for my sculptures. But you were out back because you killed a man and were so nervous you had to relieve yourself."

On his feet now, Grandpa strained against me holding him back. "Woman, you're wrong."

Stella said, "And then you tried to kill Stone because you thought he was onto you. You complained Usher and Stone weren't friends to our village. Why aren't you behind bars yet? How the heck could our sheriff let you go!"

Stella rushed out the front door--

Right into the arms of Deputy Vasquez.

Minutes later, Grandpa and I ambled back through snow flurries falling on the harbor parking lot. It was only going on six that morning. The events had unfolded with shocking speed.

Stella had been carrying a gun, which gave the sheriff an excuse to detain her, though an official arrest would have to come later with more evidence collected against her.

It seemed only a matter of time before the case was closed. So, peace would reign again in Fishers' Harbor. Could we get on with the wedding and with Christmas in a couple of weeks after the wedding? No way. I had learned to trust my instincts.

"Grandpa, Stella's innocent."

"I've been thinking that, too. I'll tell Maria when she comes to take the wire off me but I doubt she'll believe me."

Grandpa scooped up the fresh newspaper at our front door and followed me inside.

"Are you feeling okay, Grandpa? Stella gave you a big shove and you hit that table and chair and floor pretty hard."

"I'm made of rubber. I'll bounce back."

"Why don't you just sit at your counter for a while and read the paper. I'll make coffee for us."

"No, nobody but me makes coffee in that pot."

"There's a first time for everything, Grandpa. I'll be careful with your coffeepot."

"Well...okay. But it's all in the grind. Double-grind the grounds."

"Okay."

"Run the water for a while to make sure it runs pure."

"Okay, Grandpa."

"Add some fudge to the pot."

"Fudge?" Off his nod, I said, "You mean to tell me all the times you make coffee you steal some of my fudge to put in it? I thought it was shavings from the kilo bars."

"Not sweet enough."

"Wow. You are sneaky, Grandpa."

"But you liked my coffee, didn't you?"

"I sure did and still do. And so did the customers."

While I ground chocolate-cherry flavored coffee beans in the kitchen, Grandpa spread out the paper in front of him. When I returned to the shop, he again seemed intent on the real estate page. This time, though, he was spreading out various hooks and fishing flies across the newspaper. He had an open pocketknife on the newspaper.

I asked, "What are you doing?"

"I'm thinking of taking up fly-tying and selling my flies over the Internet."

"Sounds like a good winter hobby."

"Ouch. Except when a hook catches the end of a finger."

Blood droplets hit the edges of the newspaper. "Grandpa?"

He'd already found his handkerchief from his back pocket to staunch the blood.

I said, "Maybe run that finger under cold water. You know where the bandages are."

"Yup." He chuckled. "What a day for me, and it's still early in the morning." He stood, but stalled, grinning at me. "It was bunches of fun over there, this morning, don't ya think?"

He made me giggle. "It was exciting stuff to be part of but let's not tell Grandma."

Grandpa waved his assent and then ambled to the shop kitchen.

I was about to collect the fishing flies and fold up the blood-spotted newspaper when a realization landed in my brain that shocked me.

I rushed to the back hallway to the storage room opposite the kitchen to look for our stash of old newspapers. They weren't there.

"Grandpa, where are the newspapers? The recycle box is empty."

"Oh, I hauled those over to one of the trash bins Al had on the street for our holiday festival. Those papers were mostly dirty, it seemed. Oil and stuff on them from my hands. Not good for recycling."

I grabbed my coat and gloves and stocking cap. "I have to run an errand."

"At six-thirty in the morning?"

I didn't answer. No time. An idea had exploded in my head--about who killed Usher and attempted to kill Jeremy and Dillon and myself.

The key was in last week's newspapers. I had to find them before they were destroyed.

As I ran out the front door, slipping on the slick snow that kept falling, I called Pauline on my phone. "I need your help."

Pauline met me at this end of Main Street where five big trash barrels sat. I was digging in one already. Thank goodness Al hadn't hauled the trash away yet.

Pauline asked, "What are you doing? Get out of there. That's gross."

"It's only going to be gross if we don't find the newspapers Grandpa threw away. He said he put them in one of these barrels."

Detritus from the weekend festivities filled the barrels--crumpled napkins, food cartons, discarded and empty paint pots from the children's art projects.

Pauline took the top off a barrel and peered inside, then backed off. "I'm not helping unless you tell me what's going on."

One of Al's shovels sat nearby. I handed it to Pauline. "Dig. Look for last Thursday morning's paper. It'll have red smudges on the edges."

"Red?" She poked about in her barrel. "You don't mean--?"

"Blood. Yes, I hope it's blood."

By the third barrel we found it--last Thursday's paper with my grandfather's smudges on the edges. I held the newspaper by its fold, letting the spotted edges hang free.

Pauline asked, "So, you have the paper with your grandfather's blood on them. Why does this matter?"

In my head, all of the pieces were falling into place. "We have to find Greta. She'll love this story."

I handed Pauline the newspaper so I could place a phone call.

Pauline asked, "Who are you waking up?"

"Nobody. The sheriff was awake earlier when he and Maria detained Stella Zanderson." I messaged Jordy with a few words.

Pauline handed the newspaper back to me as soon as I pocketed my phone. "What's going on? You're practically hyperventilating."

"Pauline, just come with me."

"Where?"

"The Troubled Trout." As we marched down the middle of the street I filled her in on what had transpired that morning. "You know how it is--those men will still be there rehashing all of the excitement over Stella's actions and her impending arrest."

I sensed Greta would be there as well, having discovered Travis not at his mercantile business. She would be getting an earful she could report to her editor. This story just might make her career as a journalist.

Pauline barely kept up with me and she had longer legs. "What's the urgency?

"You'll see. What's about to unfold is what the sheriff wanted to have happen earlier and did not."

"What do you mean? Slow down!"

I couldn't. I was mad. A killer was still on the loose. I'd been played.

Chapter 43

Breakfast Club

The breakfast club members were indeed still at the Troubled Trout at seven-thirty rehashing the earlier excitement. Pauline and I stepped inside.

Greta was taking notes, her newspaper bag plopped onto a nearby table.

"Hello, Greta," I said, breathless from my hurried trek back to the bar. "You've probably got the biggest story of your life."

She beamed. "Yes, thanks to you and your grandfather evidently. Is he okay?"

"Yeah, back at the shop and doing well. Unfortunately, he cut his finger and got blood all over today's newspaper."

"Ah, so you're here looking for an extra one? I always have a couple." She went to the table, withdrew a paper from her bag, then handed it to me.

I refused the copy. "Thanks, but I'm really here to show you an issue of the newspaper from last week."

Pauline looked askance, like a doe ready to bolt back to the safety of a forest.

After I paused to look pointedly at the men in the space, they went silent, staring at me from various stools around the bar, their morning Bloody Mary drinks abandoned.

I took the newspaper I'd retrieved from the trash bin and unfolded it to the real estate pages, then folded it all neatly again so certain edges showed.

"Do you see the smudges on the edges?"

Greta nodded. "Yeah. Your grandfather's mishap?"

"Grandpa sure does have his share of accidents with his oil and cutting his fingers."

Greta winced. "I'm so sorry."

My insides went hot. I felt on fire with my rage building. It took all my might to hold back. "You don't understand. This isn't Gil Oosterling's blood."

I waited. Everybody stared. My heartbeat went double-time. I was taking a big risk with what I was about to say and do.

Greta licked her lips. "Should I be taking notes? What're you getting at?"

Travis made a movement at the bar. "I believe I know, Greta." Travis lifted a steak knife.

Behind the bar Erik muttered, "Oh, no."

I stepped to Travis and then took the knife. I then placed it inside my rolled newspaper, positioning the knife so it stuck out about an inch. "Does this remind you of anything, Greta?"

Pauline muttered, "I need fresh air." She scooted to the door and opened it.

I didn't take my eyes off Greta. "You killed Usher Westergaard."

Everybody in the room gasped, including Greta.

I continued. "You murdered him by using a knife hidden inside a newspaper. You hurried outside after my grandfather had left and gone. You used a newspaper to hide the knife. You stabbed Usher, panicked, hid the knife in our satchel inside a newspaper, but then realized the knife was a big problem. You stuck the knife in Usher a second time, then ran back across the street and up the sidewalk to Travis's business as usual."

"No." Greta blinked several times. "I didn't do anything of the sort."

"By the time you reached the mercantile, the newspaper with the blood lay hidden in your satchel filled with other newspapers. You were so rattled, though, that you mistakenly left the wrong newspaper at my business. Grandpa and I got the newspaper with the blood on the edges. Grandpa is so used to soiling newspapers that he didn't even notice and neither did I. We thought it was oil, or maybe his own blood from a cut."

Pain in my stomach persisted because there was the chance I was wrong about this scenario.

Greta flickered a smile, looking at all the faces. "This is preposterous. Stella killed Usher and tried to blame it on your grandfather."

Pauline groaned. Some of the men swore.

I shook my head at Greta. "I don't believe Stella's guilty."

Greta started reaching for her bag.

"Leave it on the table," I commanded.

She paused. "What motive would I have to kill somebody?"

"Plenty of motive. It's simple." I addressed the men staring at me. "Fishers' Harbor is a beautiful place to live." Then I pinned Greta with a meaningful look. "You didn't want it to change. You didn't want taxes to go up, because businesses might close. If people move away, you lose your newspaper route, and maybe your new job as a reporter, too."

"I love it here, so why would I want to kill somebody for it?"

"Because you love it here. I recalled how we talked on the street a few days ago and how you talked so much about how precious Fishers' Harbor was to you, how you loved it being 'quaint'. You let that love become distorted. And I realized later that the way you talked to me was over the top. You were trying to make sure I wouldn't suspect you because you loved it here so much. Love it? Hah. No.

"You felt you had to protect Fishers' Harbor and only you could do it, and the only way to do it was to kill Usher Westergaard and hope that a different assessor would be installed in the position, one that would keep tax assessments low. In your distorted mind you thought you were being a hero. You became desperate, so you picked up a knife at random from the tub of dirty knives sitting on the bar yet that morning. You were wearing gloves because of course it's winter and cold outside. You walked up to the bar to deliver the newspaper and nobody paid attention. You were invisible. The knife happened to be my grandfather's knife from his steak dinner the night before. All an accident or coincidence that it was his knife. You then rushed out with a rolled up newspaper hiding a knife inside of it, plunged the knife into Usher, mistakenly putting it back inside the newspaper in your panic, and then went on your way."

She grew pale.

I hated the thought of her trying to defend her actions. And so I went on. "Later you realized maybe Grandpa or I would find the blood. We didn't at first. Both of us just assumed it was rust or oil from Grandpa's projects. Then, after I started asking questions around town, you had to stop me. Your newspaper routes include Ephraim, where you got the rock from Hailey's front yard and threw it through my window."

"You're wrong." She looked at everybody.

"No, Greta, I'm not. You felt married to this village. I saw your eagerness at Mercy's house, how you took pictures and loved the moment totally."

"Because I love taking photos."

"Yes, you do. That's why you put Jeremy out of commission. Your photos instead of his of our Saint Nicholas Day celebrations ended up in newspapers across the state. You must be very proud."

Greta's eyes shimmered. "I am. You're so wrong, Ava."

I thought she might cry and confess. Instead, she took a step toward the door.

Travis trotted over to grab her. "Greta, how could you do this?"

"I didn't do anything. You have to believe me. Travis, come on, you love me."

A couple of men cleared their throats. Pauline winced.

Travis shook his head at Greta. "I was merely being kind, letting you warm up in my shop."

Greta turned to the assembled group. "What's wrong with you people? We're better off without Westergaard."

"And what about Stone?" I asked. "You wanted him dead, too. An investigative reporter of his reputation and skill wouldn't take long to bring you down. You feared him, didn't you?"

"Yes. No. Stop! I don't need to listen to this garbage."

She headed toward the back, but beefy, tall Piers stepped from the kitchen, blocking her way.

The sheriff walked through the back door then. "Greta Truelson, you're under arrest for the murder of Usher Westergaard, and there may be other charges concerning the attempted murder of Jeremy Stone, Dillon Rivers, and Ava Oosterling."

Jordy took the newspaper from me and then addressed Greta again. "I suspect we'll find your prints on this and match the blood to Usher Westergaard."

Greta screamed and tried to run for the front door, but she didn't have a chance of escaping.

Hours later I received a phone call from Sheriff Tollefson as I stood in the shop kitchen with Pauline by my side.

Jordy said, "There was one camera at the park near a restroom shelter. The camera had been put up when construction workers were busy with the Peninsula State Park upgrade projects. The company always puts up cameras for insurance purposes, in case somebody wants to steal lumber or other supplies. They'd forgotten the camera. Good thing. The footage showed Greta walking into the restroom around the time you must have arrived at the park. It's circumstantial evidence only, of course, but I wanted you to know I've got enough to hold her in jail until bail is set. I doubt she'll be able to cover the bail in this case."

I breathed a sigh of relief. "Thanks for letting me know, Jordy."

After I got off the phone with the sheriff, I plopped into the kitchen chair across from Pauline. "Life is a series of moments that can change everything."

"What do you mean?" Pauline asked.

"If I hadn't gone out to the park with Dillon at night in order to relax and get wisdom from the man in the moon, as Cody said I should do, we might never have discovered who killed Usher. I came back from that adventure remembering all the blood and then noticed Grandpa's newspapers and, well, here we are. It's all so horrible."

Pauline reached over to lay a hand on one of my arms. "Ava, all that matters is that you and Dillon and everybody are alive. Your grandpa and father will be walking me down the aisle and at least for a day we'll forget what happened over the past several days. You're a hero in everybody's eyes. You're going to outshine the bride. I should be upset." She giggled. "But I'm not."

She warmed my heart. "Any word about the horses and carriage?"

Pauline shook her head. "Fontana's Aunt Skylark told me that brides and grooms walk through the streets of downtown New Orleans after they're married in the church there."

"Oh, no. You want me to walk in that heavy red Victorian dress and big hat down Main Street? I thought maybe I could hide inside of a car or truck."

Pauline's face slumped. "That's not traditional."

"Gotchya! Walking down the street this Saturday will be a breeze after what I've been through in the past week."

"Thanks, Ava. Can you believe how much our lives have changed in the past couple of years since you came home to Fishers' Harbor?"

"Maybe not all for the good? Too many mishaps?"

Smiling broadly, Pauline shook her head. "Fishers' Harbor had become dull. And I was lonely. No mother, no family, no you. And then, you arrived to help your grandparents after your grandmother broke her leg and this little community became a bustling adventure ride better than any theme park could dream up. Without your adventures to videotape and report on, John wouldn't have stayed and we wouldn't have found each other and fallen in love. Thank you, Ava, for being you. I love you, my friend."

"I love you, too, Pauline. Now, don't start crying."

She did anyway while we stood and hugged each other. Truly BFFs.

Chapter 44

Victorian Vows

S aturday's wedding at Saint Ann's Church on the south side of Fishers' Harbor was lovely. My father and grandfather beamed in their old-fashioned suits as they escorted Pauline down the aisle.

My best friend had used an heirloom silver pin to secure the handkerchief I'd embroidered onto the waistband of her lacey Victorian dress. The pin depicted a bouquet of flowers. Coletta said it had belonged to her own mother, and mothers before them.

As is customary for Belgian weddings, Pauline carried only two flowers down the aisle--a rose for her own mother and John's mother. It was symbolic of treating them equally as family.

Carrying Pauline's bridal bouquet, I followed her down the aisle. Dillon and I made up her wedding party.

Her entire class of kindergartners dressed like little elves did a great job of spreading petals down the aisle, with a head elf acting as a ring-bearer.

The church overflowed and resounded with angelic songs. To my surprise, John sang a solo to Pauline. He'd written the song himself. The sweet, poetic refrains and John's full baritone echoed about the nave. The ceremony made me shiver with a new kind of sweet happiness for my friends. Dillon and I shared a smile while listening to John sing.

The sparkle about Pauline seemed heaven-sent, as if stars had been sent down to surround her. I was glad to see her smile even though her sister hadn't shown. There was sadness about that, of course. Jeremy and my attorney friend Parker had tried their best to find Lucie Mertens or even a Lucie Oosterling. Jeremy sat in the back of the church taking in the ceremony.

Dillon had trouble with one eye yet after the trauma earlier in the week, and he was feeling as stiff as I was, but he would heal in time.

My face was getting better, too, which a lot of Fontana's goat's milk makeup helped.

After the church ceremony, we climbed into open convertibles for the ride from the south side of town to the entrance to downtown Fishers' Harbor.

To our surprise, a team of matching, mahogany-colored Belgian draft horses and a double-seater white carriage sat in the street by the Blue Heron Inn.

Pauline gaped, screaming her happiness. "Where did they come from? Who found the horses? It's out of a fairy tale!"

My phone buzzed then. I took it out of the reticule I carried to match my Victorian dress. It was the sheriff. I groaned, but then I saw him maybe half a block away waving at me. The phone text said: "Like the carriage? An Amish couple I know just finished building it. They had the horses, too."

I gave Jordy Tollefson a thumbs-up and a tip of my bonnet brim.

The open carriage came with a driver--Mercy. She wore a tuxedo, looking smug as could be.

Mercy bellowed back at us as we settled in, "All aboard?"

"Yes," John said in the seat behind her. "Onward to the reception!"

We wound through Fishers' Harbor to the K-12 school where the reception was held in the school gymnasium. It held three hundred people around tables. Townspeople came and went all afternoon and into the early evening to congratulate Pauline and John and leave gifts. Fontana and Laura took care of watching over those for the married couple. Last summer's events with thieves stealing from weddings and funerals still stuck in our minds.

A versatile band that included an accordion player and fiddle player entertained with slow dances and zippy polkas. After John, Grandpa got the honor of the first dance with Pauline while John paired with his new mother-in-law.

Then, Pauline's eighty-something great-uncle took her for a spin around the floor that made the whole room clap with extended applause.

For Pauline's wedding fudge, I created a special four-layer dessert treat with the colors of the rainbow and called it "Witte Wieven Fudge". The fudge layers stood for the bond among Pauline, Laura, and Fontana, and myself. We always seemed to heal each other no matter what troubles had descended upon us.

Dillon and I could barely stand by eleven o'clock that Saturday night. I wanted to stay until the very end when Pauline and John would leave. They were going to their new house, and then off on a honeymoon for two weeks. I missed Pauline already.

As we headed out the door after the reception and into the icy air of December, Pauline said, "She didn't come." She meant her lost sister.

"It's not that she didn't come. It's that she's merely detained. When she finally connects with you, think about holding a big party again. Winters can get long around here and we'll welcome the excuse."

Pauline shrugged. Her hair--done up in lovely curls--now drooped, the curls sagging, as if in concert with her sadness.

I hugged her. "Go and enjoy your break in Mexico. I'll see you at Christmas!"

John hollered at her to come along. And she did.

Dillon joined me. We stood side by side watching the car motor away with the clanging tin cans tied to the back. A few others had also waited around to toss popcorn and seeds and petals into the air while yelling, "Congratulations!"

For a long time, Dillon and I just stood there, alone finally, staring after the empty space in the street in front of the school in the frozen night.

Dillon said, "This is a big change in our lives. Think you can handle it?"

I smiled up at his handsome face bathed in moonlight. "Frankly, I feel those witte wieven women at work, weaving something new and spectacular for our future, too."

"Good alliteration all the way through that sentence, Ava. A certain kindergarten teacher would be proud of you."

Chapter 45

Grandpa's Gift

Two weeks later, a special Christmas Eve unfolded.

We were holding our Eve celebration at the inn because I was expecting John and Pauline to come home from their honeymoon. The place would accommodate more people than our traditional Eve at my grandparents' place.

But I started the evening at my grandparents' cottage where Grandma guided me through making gingersnap cookies and cougnou pastry for Christmas morning. The cougnou was a sweetbread. We also made cramique (raisin bread). We labored over a fruitcake and put that in the oven, and chocolate truffles. I made old-fashioned chocolate fudge on the stove, too.

While making the treats, we went back and forth to the living room where Grandpa and my parents decorated the live Christmas tree. Wine, hot toddies, and cocoa were involved.

Gifts were put under the tree, but they would stay there until tomorrow morning when I made ice cream omelets for everybody. For

Grandpa's and Grandma's joint gift, Dillon and I created a handmade wood checkers set. We'd actually started last summer in secret. Dillon showed me how to use his carving tools. Together we carved each round checker. I learned how to carve a flower on one player's set (Grandma's), and a fish on the other set (Grandpa's). My talent for carving was at the crude stage, but Dillon assured me my grandparents would be pleasantly surprised at the effort I'd put in. Dillon said my artistic talents went beyond fudge.

Mom paused in the tree decorating to ask, "What did you finally name that new fudge you created with the big mix of all kinds of sweat treats hidden inside?"

"Because of the follies going on around here the past few weeks, I had no choice," I said. "It's 'Holly Jolly Folly Fudge'."

Dad gave it a thumb's up. "No more follies for you, okay? I'm starting to go gray because of my daughter!"

Too many people in the room concurred with hoots and chuckles.

"I'll try," I said, smiling.

The place was so homey, warm, and fragrant that I didn't want to leave its hug and return to the inn, though I expected a big crowd there.

I soon settled into sober thoughts as I placed baubles on the tree.

Grandpa saw my pensive mood. "What's wrong, honey?" He took me aside in the living room where he'd been putting up fresh garlands around the doorways.

Whispering, I said, "I'm just out of sorts."

"Waiting for Pauline to arrive."

"Yeah." He knew me too well. The holiday just wasn't right without her around. "Maybe I should get up to the inn now."

"You know she'll come here first. We always have the Eve at this house. Stay put, little one."

We finished decorating around the door to the hallway that led to their two bedrooms. I didn't know how to broach the subject, so I just plunged in, "You weren't really planning to leave Fishers' Harbor, were you? Why did you circle those houses in the newspapers a couple of weeks ago?"

He looked about, as if making sure nobody listened. My parents and Grandma had gone to the kitchen after an oven's timer bell sounded. The place smelled of molasses and gingersnap cookies.

Grandpa said, "I wanted to find projects to keep Dillon busy."

"Dillon?"

"Yes, honey. I figured I could invest in small houses one by one, and have Dillon fix them up, and sell them for a small profit. It could make you money enough to buy a house all your own that you liked."

I gave him a big hug. "That's a lovely thought. Thank you, but I think Dillon is doing fine on his own."

Grandpa shook his head. "That man needs my help. He's still struggling to finish that house up in Sister Bay."

"Where he found Ellany. And now she and her husband and baby are living there temporarily. Isn't that great? Dillon asked them to watch over the place."

"Their stay won't be for long. The out-of-state owners will show up come spring. Ellany and her little family can't afford that place. That's why I want to buy little houses and have those rehabilitated for young people like Ellany and Brendan. This county needs more homegrown workers."

Dillon would regret going into business with Grandpa. Those two were like oil and water with most things. "Grandpa, maybe you should stick with fixing boats."

"Hmmph. I thought you believed in me."

"I do." Now I'd hurt his feelings and it pained me. "Hey, it's about time to head up to the inn. Maybe Pauline decided to go there first. You want to walk with me? Dillon's probably taken his lasagna out of the oven by now."

Grandpa and I headed out into the crystal clear night. Stars had spread like sugar across the black winter sky. It reminded me of the Belgian myth of "Woodan on the Wild Hunt" sailing through the sky, which was the precursor for the Christian Sinterklaas or Santa Claus fables.

Lucky Harbor leaped about wagging his tail as we journeyed up the sidewalk and then my driveway.

At the inn's parking lot, we discovered a stranger's car parked among those we recognized. "I'm not expecting anybody new. And that's not Pauline's and John's cars."

Grandpa huffed a bit from the steep driveway walk. "Gee, I wonder who it could be."

He sounded suspicious. I pinned him with a look in the meager glow shed from my verandah's front-door light. "You know who it is, don't you?"

He shrugged. "Christmas gifts come in different forms."

I rushed ahead of him, leaping up the steps, then charging through the front door.

There stood a woman I didn't recognize. Then I did. She had short black hair just like her mother.

"Lucie?"

Lucie Mertens screamed in a joyous way and hugged me under the chandelier's sparkling crystals. "Ava Mathilde Oosterling!"

"Lucie, how are you? Where did you come from? We've been trying to find you."

Dillon and a chuckling Grandpa joined us.

I turned to Grandpa. "You had a hand in this surprise, didn't you?"

Grandpa's eyes shone in the diamond-like lighting under the chandelier. "Maybe a little."

I said to Lucie, "What happened? How did Grandpa find you? Where have you been? You look wonderful, all grown up!"

On a hunch, Grandpa and Grandma had checked with the king in Belgium. Grandma was loosely related to him and he'd visited Fishers' Harbor a year ago, giving me the beautiful professional kitchen range. Grandpa believed Lucie was longing to find her roots, too, and he'd wondered if she'd be in Belgium.

I shook with excitement again. "But we emailed, we looked all over social media. Why couldn't we find you?"

Lucie grimaced. "I apologize. I was teaching a unit on social work at a college in Brussels for two months. I was in Peru before that."

Then she teared up and held up a hand. "And I was avoiding contact. I did get a couple of emails from the consulate. The official said somebody from the United States had asked about my welfare. Then a couple of weeks ago, I heard that a reporter wanted to talk to me. That really scared me. I thought my awful father was looking for me."

"No, it was us," I said. I recognized that Jeremy must have found her, too.

"The thing is, it's been a long time since I've been here. The idea of coming back brought back old memories about my father--"

"He's not around. We've had no contact with him." With another hug, I said, "Your sister will give you a grade of A for being here."

Dillon rushed back from the front door. "They're here!" He meant Pauline and John.

I took Lucie by the hand. "Hide in the kitchen. I'll sit the newlyweds in the parlor and you can come out with the wine. Sound like a plan?"

Lucie giggled. "I love it. I'm so glad your grandfather found me."

"Grandpa Gil and Jeremy Stone seemed to have both been working separate missions to find you."

Lucie smiled again. "When the king got in touch with me about the consulate's message, he mentioned your grandfather had contacted him personally." She laughed bigger now. "A king in your family. This is too much!"

She raced to the kitchen.

A few minutes later, my best friend and her newly found sister must have hugged for an hour without letting go.

It gave me a chance to go on an errand.

I knocked on Mercy's door several times before she answered.

"What's got you in a tizzy, Ooster? And on Christmas Eve?"

"For the last time, my name is Ava."

She growled. Mercy was wearing pajamas. It was late, but not that late. I held out a big wrapped box filling my arms and said, "Listen, I was wondering about something."

"It's cold out here. Want to step inside for your long speech?"

Indoors, the bright colors swirling off her walls and furniture woke me up despite the wine I'd downed this evening.

Mercy plopped onto her sofa with the garish colors. "You brought me a gift?"

I sat across from her on a cushion-less chair she'd painted in yellow and red polka dots. "Yes, no, sort of."

"Ooster, spit it out."

I stepped over to her and put the box in her lap. She quickly opened it, then flinched as she peered back up at me. "How'd you know it was me?"

With my arms flung wide to indicate our surroundings, I said, "Your art. You're good, Mercy. I kept everything from the small boxes you left at my doors. I think you're good enough to sell those at the mercantile."

Her eyes shimmered. "You think so? But these were for you. I liked messin' with you."

I laughed. "And you did mess with me. I couldn't figure it out for a long time."

"Not much to figure out. One time months ago you mumbled something to me about not being a collector, about being weird because you didn't collect anything."

Indeed, she was right. Everybody in my family seemed to have a collection of something--everybody but me. It seemed to me that not collecting something was a flaw in my character, but I still didn't collect anything. Until now. I looked at all the items in the box.

I went to Mercy and did the impossible--I hugged her. "Thanks, Mercy, for playing the gifting game. I guess I have a collection now." A warmth took up residence inside of me that made me feel new, feel loved in a surprising way. "I enjoyed getting the gifts made from nature. Thank you for the fun. But, tell me, how did you get the gifts to my doors without the cameras seeing you?"

Mercy put the box aside, then wiggled out of her seat. She went to a big box near the kitchen filled with dog toys. She took out what looked like a slingshot.

I was confused. "You didn't knock down my cameras, did you?"

She nodded. "A few months ago I spotted those darn things at your place and I got the idea of taking them down. Took me awhile to dream up my plan, but finally I figured it out. I'm pretty good with weapons."

"You're giving me the chills again."

"Oh, suck it up, Ooster. My weapon was this slingshot I used to train Queenie to fetch things when she was a puppy." She waved the slingshot. "This baby sends things several yards. And I'm good at a long distance. It was easy to bring down your cameras, take out the batteries or mess with them any way I wanted. Then I put the cameras back in place."

Heat came to my face as ingrained anger at this woman mounted, but I took a deep breath. I wanted to restart our association. I wanted to grow, change, and do better by this unique woman. "I guess it's all water over the damn now, isn't it?"

"Or snow over the snowdrift." Mercy giggled as she laid aside the slingshot.

She sauntered over to a box on her dining room table where she filched about until she came up with a small book. She handed it to me.

I yelped, "My Christmas elf book? You stole my childhood book?"

"Borrowed. I was thinking about writing a children's book featuring my Queenie and her puppies but just couldn't do it. I'm not a writer. Maybe it's something you should do. Write a book, Ooster, and I'll be first in line for an autographed copy."

I hugged the book that had been given to me so long ago. I couldn't be mad.

"Mercy, why don't you throw on clothes and come to the inn and join our party? It's Christmas Eve, after all, and you shouldn't be alone. Nobody should be alone."

Mercy gave me the oddest look. "I'll come, but this won't mean we have to be friends, will it?"

I laughed bigger this time. "Of course not. Just one night we'll get along. Like gnomes and elves that are seen only on Christmas Eve."

Mercy smiled. Then a teardrop slipped from one eye and ran down her cheek. She gave me a thumb's up. "Thanks, Ava." She hurried away to get dressed.

Later that Christmas Eve, while the inn rocked with carols and laughter, including Mercy's raucous out-of-tune but joyous caroling, I went outside with Lucky Harper and discovered Grandpa sitting on my front steps.

"Hello, Grandpa." I sat next to him. "It's cold out here."

"Feels refreshing to me."

Our coats barely kept us warm, but the stars overhead seemed to dictate we should sit and stare up at them. Lucky Harbor snuffled as usual with his nose plowing through snow in the yard, always on the hunt for a mouse or elf.

"You and Grandma did good, really good, with this surprise about Lucie, Grandpa. You contacted Jeremy Stone, didn't you, and the king of Belgium? Anybody else?"

"Bunches of people. I've had a lot of time on my hands. Contacting the king was just an old man's hunch."

"You're always the brave one to plunge into an adventure."

"Hmmph. You fit the bill, too. Why be boring in life when you can do the opposite?"

"True."

"I liked that new flavor, the Holly Jolly Folly Fudge. We're experts on follies, aren't we?"

"We sure are."

This seemed like a good time to tell him my own secrets. A cold breeze sent tree limbs clicking above us in the yard. "I'm thinking about moving my fudge shop to Main Street, and maybe even selling my half of the inn, Grandpa."

He grunted. "You're leaving the harbor?"

"Remember, the shop building used to be your fishing shack alone. Yours. All yours. The location was always meant to be a temporary place for me, until Grandma got over her broken leg. I came back two years ago to help her, so I've overstayed my welcome in your place. Travis Klubertanz says he wants to sell the mercantile. He's going back to farming. He'll sell on a land contract, which means I'll only have small monthly payments that I can probably make with no problem."

"I see."

"It has a big two-bedroom apartment above it. Dillon said he could fix it up. I could live there."

"Uh huh. I see."

"The inn has turned out to be more work than I imagined--"

"How about your grandma and I help run the inn? We could charge big bucks for people to rent your one-bedroom apartment. My fishing equipment could move to the mercantile, too. It's got a lot more room than that small shop of ours."

I was in shock. "You'd leave the old building on the harbor?"

"It's old, like you just said. Did you see all the rot in the wood around that broken window? That old building could all fall apart soon. It's old. But I'm not old. I'm feeling like it's time for a change, too. You'll need me at the mercantile. That place is a darn sight bigger than our current shop. I could still be at your new fudge shop on Main Street every morning at five o'clock, if that's okay with you."

I gave him a lingering hug. "It's very okay."

We were quiet for a while, listening to the trees crackle, the occasional dog barking across the village, our own breathing, the huff of snow moving about in the breeze.

From inside, Dillon started singing a gentle Christmas carol. Others joined in, the voices uneven yet angelic.

Grandpa grunted. "Change is good, don't you think?"

"I'm glad you agree. I wasn't sure you'd like..."

"I love you, Ava honey. And all your ideas. You've become a very fine woman."

"Thank you. I love you, Gilpa. Merry Christmas."

"Merry Christmas, Ava."

Lucky Harbor galloped back then, shaking snow all over us. We took him inside, and all of us enjoyed the best Christmas ever.

Holly Jolly Folly Fudge

Happy holidays! This fruitcake-inspired fudge is a mix of adventures--just like the folly that goes on in Fishers' Harbor with Grandpa and Ava Oosterling. Each bite is filled with mystery--different colors, fruits, nuts, and varying flavor depth depending on the amount of spices and ingredients hidden within or that you choose when being creative.

This recipe took about 20 minutes to make.

Ingredients:

14 ounces sweetened condensed milk

24 ounces white chocolate chips

1 teaspoon vanilla extract

1/8 teaspoon salt

1 teaspoon cinnamon

¼ teaspoon ground ginger

¼ teaspoon ground nutmeg

1 teaspoon orange zest

1 cup fruitcake mix

¼ cup raisins (or half cup if you love raisins)

½ cup chopped walnuts (or pecans)

For decorating: Sugar sprinkles. Be creative!

Instructions:

1. Line a 9x9 dish with aluminum foil or wax paper. Spray lightly with nonstick baking spray.

2. In a microwave safe bowl, mix the milk and chocolate. Melt at medium heat in one-minute intervals, stirring between each minute. This may take about 10 minutes total.

3. Add the rest of the ingredients and stir immediately.

4. Pour into the baking dish.

5. Optional: sprinkle on your favorite sugar sprinkles.

6. Give the fudge time to cool and harden. The flavorings in this fudge taste yummy, and they intensify slightly by Day 2 and Day 3.

Pour hot cocoa or a hot toddy and share the fudge-love this season!

P.S. Gift a friend with the Fudge Shop Mystery Series.

Here's the order in which they were published, however, you can read the books out of order.

Fudge Shop Mystery Series

First-Degree Fudge (Book 1), Hot Fudge Frame-Up (Book 2), Five-Alarm Fudge (Book 3), Deadly Fudge Divas (Book 4/called Book 1 by new publisher), Undercover Fudge (Book 5/called Book 2 by new publisher), Holly Jolly Fudge Folly/called Book 3 by new publisher).

P.S.S. Short on time to read? Try my Mischief in Moonstone sweet romantic-mystery novella series

When Rudolph Was Kidnapped (1), Misbehavin' in Moonstone (2), Mrs. Claus and The Moonstone Murder (3), When the Dead People Brought a Dish-to-Pass (4), A Moonstone Wedding (5)

...Watch for more to come in this nine-novella series.

You can find ALL our books up on our website at:

http://www.writers-exchange.com

All Christine's Books:

http://www.writers-exchange.com/christine-desmet/

All our mysteries:

https://www.writers-exchange.com/category/genres/mystery-thrillers-suspense/

About the Author

Christine DeSmet is an award-winning fiction writer and professional screenwriter. She is the author of the bestselling *Fudge Shop Mystery Series* and the popular novella series called *Mischief in Moonstone*.

She is a Distinguished Faculty Associate in Writing at University of Wisconsin-Madison where she teaches novel writing and screenwriting and directs the annual summer Write-by-the-Lake Writer's Workshop & Retreat. Through her master classes she has seen many of her adult students become published.

She is also a professional writing coach in the UW-Madison Writers' Institute conference's Pathway to Publication program.

Christine is a member of Mystery Writers of America, Sisters in Crime, Wisconsin Writers Association, Wisconsin Screenwriters Association, and other professional associations.

Christine is active on Facebook and you can also find her at http://www.ChristineDeSmet.com

Christine's author page at Writers Exchange E-Publishing is: http://www.writers-exchange.com/Christine-DeSmet/

If you enjoyed this author's book, then please place a review up at the site of purchase, and any social media sites you frequent!

If you want to read more about books by this author, they are listed on the following pages...

Fudge Shop Mystery Series

Deadly Fudge Divas

A taste of trouble is in the air when a group of well-heeled, fudge-loving women descend on Ava Oosterling's newly acquired and lovingly refurbished bed & breakfast inn for a chocolate lovers' getaway.

When one of the women turns up dead--and Ava's grandfather is a prime suspect--Ava plunges into the thick of a murder case stickier than her candy store's line of Fairy Tale fudge flavors and the chocolate facials the women adore at the local spa.

It's springtime and the start of the tourist season in Fishers' Harbor, Wisconsin. Ava has opened the Blue Heron Inn with the help of handsome construction worker Dillon Rivers. Unfortunately, Dillon's mother--Ava's ex-mother-in-law--is among the secretive divas who become suspects along with Grandpa.

Ava turns for help from her friends but they have troubles, too. One is eager for a wedding proposal to unfold on live television, while another friend is expecting her first baby and asks Ava to assist with the birth.

Everything and everybody Ava loves seems in chaos--her fudge shop, her inn, her family, and her own friendships... Until she uncovers a thirty-year-old secret of the "deadly fudge divas".

Publisher: http://www.writers-exchange.com/Deadly-Fudge-Divas/

Undercover Fudge (new cover coming soon!)

Candy shop owner Ava Oosterling has her hands full when her best friend Pauline Mertens takes a summer job as a wedding coordinator-- with the nuptials and reception scheduled in mere days in the back yard of Ava's Blue Heron Inn overlooking Lake Michigan's bay.

To help out her best friend, Ava is intent on making the table favors-- edible fudge lighthouses patterned after their county's 11 lighthouses.

Unfortunately, trying to finish the luscious ruby chocolate lighthouses becomes elusive. The sheriff informs Ava that a band of thieves storming the country may have targeted this wedding. And that's because there's proof Pauline's mother is associated with the thieves.

When the sheriff asks Ava to go undercover, she finds herself in an emotional quagmire. Pauline's mother only recently returned to Fishers' Harbor after years of estrangement from her daughter. And, Coletta Mertens now works as the housekeeper at Ava's inn. Has Ava's fudge-and-wine hospitality provided a hideout for a criminal?

Unfortunately, "until death do us part" takes a murderous twist involving Ava's Grandpa Gil, the dog Lucky Harbor, and Ava's own beau.

Publisher: http://www.writers-exchange.com/undercover-fudge/

Holly Jolly Fudge Folly

An early, deep snow has gifted Fishers' Harbor, Wisconsin, with a perfect setting for the holiday celebration. Unfortunately removing snow from Main Street for the parade reveals the dead tax assessor with a knife in him--containing Grandpa Gil's fingerprints.

It's clearly a setup and one that keeps Ava and Grandpa Gil under the watchful eyes of Sheriff Tollefson. Who wants Grandpa to miss playing Santa Claus in the Christmas parade and why? Who's being naughty instead of nice?

Grandpa doesn't help his case with talk of leaving town for good--words that chill Ava worse than the weather. She can't imagine life without Grandpa's warm hugs and laughter.

When vandals strike the historic shop and someone leaves Ava and fiancé Dillon Rivers for dead in the snow, Ava wonders if she may need the magical help of Santa's elves to solve the holiday folly.

Publisher: http://www.writers-exchange.com/holly-jolly-fudge-folly/

Mischief in Moonstone Series

This delightful series focuses on the humorous mystery and romantic adventures of the kind folks who live in the environs of a small village nestled on Lake Superior in northern Wisconsin. Along the way in the series, silkie chickens, a giant prehistoric beaver skeleton, a kidnapped reindeer, and other flora and fauna contribute to the amusing mischief and mayhem.

Novella 1: When Rudolf was Kidnapped

When her pet reindeer, Rudolph, is stolen from the live animal holiday display, first-grade teacher Crystal Hagan has a big problem on her hands. Her students fear that Christmas will be canceled. Ironically, the prime suspect is a man who lives in a mansion known as the "North Pole". And to her shock, Peter LeBarron admits to kidnapping Rudolph and he won't give him back without some romantic "negotiations".

Publisher: http://www.writers-exchange.com/When-Rudolph-was-Kidnapped/

Novella 2: Misbehavin' In Moonstone

When the men of Moonstone suddenly seem to be off fishing a lot in the evenings, thus cutting down on her new restaurant's business, chef Kirsten Peplinski becomes suspicious. She discovers a topless touring boat has set up business in Lake Superior, just outside the jurisdiction of Moonstone. She sets out to give a "dressing down" to the boat's owner, but Jonathon VanBrocklin kidnaps her, having "undressing" and marrying her on his mind.

Publisher: http://www.writers-exchange.com/Misbehavin-in-Moonstone/

Novella 3: Mrs. Claus and the Moonstone Murder

On her second day of duty, new county deputy Lily Schuster finds herself smack dab in the middle of Moonstone, Wisconsin, trouble. She arrests archeologist Marcus Linden for trespassing, then finds she needs his help in solving the murder of a pie contest judge. The suspects involve none other than the town's Santa, Henri LeBarron, an eighty-four-year-old man now cavorting with the sexy, mysterious newcomer, Felicity Starr, twenty-seven. But can Lily trust her trespassing prisoner, Marcus, who seems to be willing to exchange kisses for clemency?

Publisher: http://www.writers-exchange.com/Mrs-Claus-and-the-Moonstone-Murder/

Novella 4: When the Dead People Brought a Dish-to-Pass

Three days before Halloween, Alyssa Swain finds a man dead in his car but, once she gets help, the body is gone. When scruffy, tall, dead man John Christopherson shows up alive on her doorstep, he insists she called him to help her get ready for a party. Now the crazy man won't leave her house or her heart. How can she keep him from crossing over into the afterlife at midnight on Halloween?

Publisher: http://www.writers-exchange.com/When-the-Dead-People-Brought-A-Dish-To-Pass/

Novella 5: A Moonstone Wedding

When grocery store owner Margie Mueller's fiancé--chef Tony Farina--sends her a "fertility rug" to stand on at their wedding, she panics. Margie's no spring chicken and she's not about to hatch a big brood for the Farinas. Before she can call off the wedding, the Farina clan invades Moonstone for partying and interference in the wedding preparations. But Margie doesn't mind--behind the scenes she's got a murder to solve. A dead man has shown up wrapped in the fertility rug. And it looks like her fiancé may know more about it than he's letting on.

Publisher: http://www.writers-exchange.com/A-Moonstone-Wedding/

Coming Soon:

Novella 6: The Moonstone Fire

Novella 7: All She Wore Was a Bow

Novella 8: Pest Control

Novella 9: The Big Love & Murder Shilly-Shally in Moonstone

Milton Keynes UK
Ingram Content Group UK Ltd.
UKHW020732271123
433341UK00020B/1676